Jessica

By

Donna Foley Mabry

The situation at his father's firm was getting desperate, and it was up to Zachary Belk to do something. The 1869 Manhattan Thanksgiving Ball was the perfect opportunity. He looked around the ballroom for a likely savior.

One by one, he mentally eliminated the eligible young ladies in attendance. The girls were all from wealthy families. He was most attracted to the beautiful Samantha Rogers, but she had too many siblings who would share in any inheritance.

Edwina Horton, attractive enough, also appealed to him, but he'd heard through the Wall Street grapevine that her father's firm was not doing much better than his own. He finally turned his attentions to Jessica McCarthy, an only child, in her mid-twenties, older than most of the others, completely unattached, thin, but not homely. Her father's company was one of the healthiest in New York. Yes, Jessica McCarthy was the most likely candidate. He put a flirtatious smile on his face and walked across the room to where she sat with a friend.

He made a polite bow. "May I have this dance?"

She blinked in surprise. "Thank you, I'd be delighted."

He grasped her hand and led her to the dance floor where he put one hand on her waist and took her into the steps of a whirling waltz.

PART ONE
Manhattan, New York, 1869

Chapter 1

William McCarthy stood in front of the huge fireplace in his Manhattan mansion with his back to his daughter He drummed his fingers on the mantle. "He's only marrying you for your money," he said.

When she didn't answer him, he turned to look at Jessica and saw the tears on her cheeks. He went to her, wrapped his arm around her shoulders, and kissed her forehead. "I didn't want to hurt your feelings, Jess, but you need to face reality. I know very well what sort of man Zachary Belk is, and I want you to have a better life than you'll find with him as your husband."

Whatever his intentions, she was hurt, but even as Jessica resented hearing the words, she knew without a doubt they were true. She'd expected them, had braced herself for them, and already said them to herself. Still, they cut into her heart. Her father was the person she loved most on earth.

Knowing there was more pain to come before their talk was over, she waited for it the way she'd waited for the next wave of the surf at the beach during childhood summers. Since she was a toddler, she stood in the churning water, letting it wash over her, letting it knock her down, and taking pride in struggling back to her feet to face the next wave.

She didn't have to wait long for him to go on. McCarthy looked out the window at the thick, damp snow falling in clusters. It would soon be covering Manhattan. "I have it on the best of authority that his father has practically run his business to the ground, and his firm is on the verge of bankruptcy. If I weren't wealthy he wouldn't give you a second look. You do have enough sense to know that, don't you?"

In his sixties, with salt and pepper hair, an expanding waist draped by a thick gold watch chain, and a creased forehead, William McCarthy made an impressive looking man. He ran his hand through his usually well-groomed hair in frustration, mussing it.

Jessica sat at her mother's elaborately carved piano, her head bent, running her fingertips gently over the keys but making no sound come from them. She looked at him sadly. "Yes. I know that. Whatever shortcomings I may have in my looks, I'm not stupid."

Jessica was thin, but by no means homely. She dressed in a plain, navy blue dress, almost as if she wanted to downplay what good looks she did possess. When her hair was loose, her chestnut locks curled softly in ringlets around her face, but for some reason only she knew, she usually wore it pulled back tightly. Her eyes were brown, with flecks of gold. She focused them back on the piano keys.

Her puzzled father threw out his hands. "Then why on earth would you even consider marrying Zachary Belk?"

"Because I have no other prospects, because every one of my friends I went to school with are married and have families, and because I can't bear the thought of living out the rest of my life in this house."

"Why wouldn't you want to live here? It's the finest home in Manhattan. Haven't I given you everything you ever wanted?"

"I know how much you love me, Father, but there are some things you can't give me."

"Such as what?"

"Such as a life of my own. I need to do something. I can't simply spend the rest of my days being William McCarthy's unmarried daughter. Do you think I don't hear what people say? I see how they look at me with pity."

"For God's sake, Jess, you're only twenty-five. Stop talking as if you were an old maid."

"I am an old maid. At least, that's what people are saying. Most of my friends were married before they turned twenty. Angela Johnson was married at sixteen and was a mother by the time she was eighteen."

"If you ask my opinion that was entirely inappropriate, almost indecent."

"It wasn't the least bit unusual. Most of the other girls I went to school with didn't wait much longer than that. I'm afraid my shelf life as a prospective bride is about up. If I don't marry Zachary, no one else may ever ask me."

"That's ridiculous. Your mother didn't marry me until she was thirty-four, and she didn't have you until she was forty."

"Yes, and she died when she was forty-five. Everyone says how I look and talk and act exactly like her. What if I turn out to be exactly like her and die as young as she did? If all I have left of my life is twenty years, I want to start living them as soon as possible. I want to have a child and see it raised before I die."

"Let me tell you something. You do look exactly like her, and she was the most beautiful woman I ever saw, so don't go saying your looks are lacking."

"I thought you said he was only marrying me for my money."

"I'm sorry. I didn't mean it that way. It's only that you're so quiet and reserved and he's always gone for the more—more—vivacious type of girl."

"He says he loves me and wants to make a life with me. Once we're married he'll settle down. You've mentioned young men who were sowing their wild oats. Can't he be like that, getting all that sort of thing out of his system?"

McCarthy shook his head and raised a hand in surrender. "Very well, if you've made up your mind to marry him, then go ahead. At least he's from a good family on his mother's side. Harriet Belk is a fine woman. She was one of your mother's closest friends."

McCarthy walked to his daughter and patted her gently on the shoulder. "Do you love him?"

"No. I don't even like him as a friend, but he wants me and no one else does, so I'm going to marry him. I'm hoping that, in time, we will come to love one another.

Once we're a family, raising children and living our lives together, that should come naturally."

"I loved your mother with all my heart, from the first time I saw her until the day she died, and even now, she's the first thing I think about when I wake up in the morning. Aren't you going to miss the love and romance part of life? Girls are supposed to dote on things like that. Can't you wait a few more years?"

"Not when I don't know how many years I have left. Maybe I'll never know what romance and the love of a man are like, but at least I'll have a home of my very own and children. I expect to get all the love I need from them."

"I wanted more than that for you, Jess. I wanted you to have the kind of marriage your mother and I had."

"So did I, but it looks as if that's never going to happen, and I intend to make the best of it. Wait and see. When I bring you your first grandchild, you'll see that I did the right thing. If it's a boy, I'll name him William McCarthy Belk, and you'll spoil him rotten, the same as you've spoiled me. If it's a girl, I'll name her Amanda for mother, and then you'll be absolutely hopeless."

He rubbed his forehead. "I don't suppose there's any point in my trying to make you change your mind. I'm afraid you're going to regret it someday, Jessica. There are so many things in my life I wish I hadn't done, large and small. The older you get, the more regrets you have. You can try to push them aside, but they swarm around you and bite at you like gnats."

He took Jessica's hand and pulled her into his arms. He kissed the top of her head. "You are exactly like your mother, and you're every bit as hard-headed as she sometimes was, too. Very well, my dear, I suppose you're old enough to make up your own mind, but I still expect him to come to me and ask for your hand. He really should have done it before he even spoke seriously to you. It shows disrespect that he didn't."

"I'll have him go through every one of the proper procedures. The gossip in this town is bad enough without adding any more fuel to the fire."

"So, you're determined?"

"Yes, I am."

"He isn't going to make you a very good husband, you know."

"I know he may not. I hope he will, but maybe he'll be better than no husband at all."

"I wouldn't count on it. There are worse things than being an old maid."

"Not in the circles we travel in, Father."

She put her head on his chest, and he rested his chin on top of it. In the big mirror over the mantle, their faces reflected their feelings. His face creased with worry, and hers set in determination.

She had a restless night and spent a good deal of it in prayer, asking that Zachary would live up to her expectations, that he would give up his raucous ways and settle down, that having a wife and a home and eventually a family would make him more like her own father and less like his. She knew she was putting her life in his hands, but she was clinging to the knowledge that it would always be in God's hands as well.

Chapter 2

William McCarthy sat behind the massive desk in his office on Wall Street with his back to a large window that looked out at the stock exchange. He leafed through a stack of papers with a worried frown on his face. Joshua Downing, his secretary, showed Zachary Belk into the office and announced him. "Zachary Belk, sir."

Belk was tall and extremely handsome in a slick way. His wavy hair was a rich, deep auburn color. He wore an obviously expensive morning coat, a brocade vest, and carried a pair of white gloves in one hand and a tall, silk, top hat in the other. His cravat was studded with a large diamond pin.

McCarthy looked at him and pursed his lips in disapproval. "Good morning, Mr. Belk, please have a seat. I understand you would like to speak to me."

"Yes, sir, and please, call me Zachary."

Belk tucked the gloves in the pocket of his waistcoat, arranged the fingers to fall evenly, and then, finally, held out his hand. McCarthy half rose from his chair, shook it briefly, and plopped back down.

Belk sat in the chair in front of the desk. "How are you this morning, Sir?"

"I've been better."

"Stock market giving you a bad time of it?"

"For today. You know how it is. The pendulum swings high and low. Today is a low."

"I was at my father's office, and he had the same look on his face. I'm sure there's nothing to worry about. As you said, high and low. Tomorrow it will all be on the rise again."

"Yes, yes. Now I'll pretend I don't know why you're here, and we can get down to business."

Belk blinked at McCarthy's abruptness. "Yes, Sir. I've come to ask for Jessica's hand."

"It's about time. You should have done that before you spoke to her."

"Yes, Sir, I realize that. I apologize. I suppose I got a little carried away by the moment."

McCarthy scowled at him. "I doubt that. I'm sure it was all a very calculated progression and you were quite aware of how much I dote on her. I'm also sure you knew that once you had her consent it would be very difficult for me to refuse her."

"You make it sound as if you don't think very highly of me."

"I don't. I know all about your skirt-chasing, your drinking, and your gambling. I know that you get your ways directly from your father and, if it weren't for his business partner, his firm would have gone under long ago. The only respectable person in your family is your mother, who should very easily qualify for sainthood someday. It's only because of her that I would even consider allowing Jess to marry a rotter like you."

Belk smirked. "I appreciate your honesty."

"I want you to understand exactly what you're getting by marrying my daughter. First of all, she is a sweet-natured, intelligent young woman with the best education money can buy. She is also more than a little talented. She plays the piano brilliantly, is a gifted needlewoman, artist, and gardener. Our roses are admired by the entire neighborhood."

"Indeed. I am well aware of all her many, many qualities. I'm sure I don't deserve her."

"You certainly don't, but her qualities aren't foremost in your mind this morning, are they?"

"Since we're being blunt, no. What sort of settlement will you be making on us as a wedding gift?"

"I've been thinking that over. I had my attorney in earlier and we've drafted a new will. We were discussing the women's property act of 1848. In the state of New York, women retain sole rights to income or property they own before a marriage, or that they come into by inheritance after the marriage. As I'm sure you know, Jessica is my only heir. I have no nieces or nephews, no cousins, no other relatives who would be able to make a claim on my estate. Jessica wants her own house, and I have made an offer on a suitable home here in Manhattan. It will be my wedding present to her, and her name will be the only one on the deed. I have also opened an account for her at several home furnishing stores so she may equip the house in any manner she wishes and, of course, I expect she will want to take some things from my own home, her mother's piano among them."

Belk listened carefully, his face pinched in obvious displeasure.

McCarthy went on, "For my gift to you as a couple, I will give you a European honeymoon. Jessica took the Grand Tour when she was younger and she loved it. I'm sure she would enjoy returning. I am also giving her a yearly allowance that should cover the operating expenses of the house. For you personally, I am quite aware that for several years you have been filling a token position at your father's firm, in name if in nothing else. I expect that in the future, you will go to work and do your best. I am giving you an annual sum of one dollar from me for each dollar you have earned on your own. So, the more successful you are at the firm, the more money you will get from me. Now, for some men, that would be an immense opportunity. The money you would possibly receive could be wisely invested, and in a few years, you would be quite wealthy in your own right, or you could continue in your slacker ways and get nothing."

Belk's voice choked as he replied. "Blunt indeed."

"As to the inheritance when I die, outside of a few charitable bequests, the bulk of my estate will be held in trust for her. Jess will receive an annual allowance, the amount dependent on how many children she has. As long as you are together, the matching funds proviso for you will continue," McCarthy looked at Belk slyly, pursed his lips, and then went on, "providing I die a natural death."

Belk jumped from his chair. "Sir, you insult me!"

"I'm sure you'll get over it."

Belk sank back to his chair, and McCarthy added, "The will also includes a clause stating that upon Jessica's death, hopefully many decades from now, the entire estate will go to the new art museum. So, it will be in your best interests for her to live a long, long time."

Belk's face turned crimson as he fumed. "I should walk out of this room right now and forget I ever met either one of you."

"Nothing would make me happier, but you know, and I know, that you have no intention of doing any such thing. I'm quite sure you did your research before you asked Jess to marry you. If you could have found another prospect, you would have already done it. You know very well that I am the definition of a self-made man and therefore, no fool. My father came to this country with less than a dollar in his hand. He worked diligently and lived frugally until he owned his own farm. He was wise and strong, and determined. He managed to send me to university and now I own one of the largest firms in New York. I would like to flatter myself that I am also wise and strong and determined, even though I never expect to live up to the standard my father showed me. My one weak spot is my daughter. For some reason I will never understand, she has made up her mind to join her future with yours. All I am doing is protecting her—and myself—in the best way I can. Now, have the two of you discussed a wedding date?

"Jessica told me that she didn't want an elaborate ceremony. I quite agree, so we would like to do it as soon as possible. She thought that Christmas Day would be nice."

McCarthy looked at him appraisingly. "Things at the firm that bad, are they? Very well, I'll leave it to you and Jess to work out the details."

Chapter 3

Jessica made hurried arrangements for a simple ceremony. She had no time for a great deal of shopping and she already owned a suitable wardrobe. She made one trip to Lord & Taylor's on Broadway and spent the better part of the afternoon selecting what she imagined would be appropriate for the wedding and honeymoon.

Most of the day on Christmas Eve, she spent decorating the living room of the McCarthy home. A ceiling-height Christmas tree stood in one corner with elaborately wrapped gifts piled under it. Wide velvet ribbons were twined through the banisters, and evergreen branches were arranged with candles on the mantle and tables.

In the living room, the furniture had been moved, and rows of chairs were arranged with an aisle in the center. The seats were filled with family, friends, and the only extended family Jessica had, her fellow church members from Mariner's Temple Baptist Church, the oldest Baptist church on the island of Manhattan. In her entire life, the only time she had missed a service was when she was away from home or too ill to attend.

The minister performed his favorite ceremony, having Jessica read the book of Ruth, chapter one, "Entreat me not to leave thee, or to return from following after thee: for whither thou goest, I will go, and where thou lodgest, I will lodge: thy people shall be my people, and thy God my God: Where thou diest, will I die, and there will I be buried: the Lord do so to me, and more also, if ought but death part thee and me."

In discussing the vows they would take, Zachary had demurred doing a reading himself. Wedding, funeral, or regular service, Pastor Fox never passed up the opportunity to preach the gospel. After telling his audience that the gift of Jesus's salvation was theirs if they would only accept it, he wanted Zachary to hear the Biblical ideal for marriage, so in closing his brief sermon, he read Ephesians 5:22-33.

"Wives, submit yourselves unto your own husbands, as unto the Lord. For the husband is the head of the wife, even as Christ is the head of the church: and he is the savior of the body. Therefore as the church is subject unto Christ, so let the wives be to their own husbands in everything. Husbands, love your wives, even as Christ also loved the church, and gave himself for it; that He might sanctify and cleanse it with the washing of water by the word, that he might present it to Himself a glorious church, not having spot, or wrinkle, or any such thing; but that it should be holy and without blemish. So ought men to love their wives as their own bodies."

He paused for a moment and stared into Zachary's eyes. "He that loveth his wife loveth himself. For no man ever yet hated his own flesh; but nourisheth and cherisheth it, even as the Lord the church: for we are members of His body, of his flesh, and of his bones. For this cause shall a man leave his father and mother, and shall be joined unto his wife and they two shall be one flesh. This is a great mystery: but I speak concerning Christ and the church. Nevertheless let every one of you in particular so love his wife even as himself; and the wife see that she reverence her husband."

He had them exchange the usual vows, closed his Bible, and said, "I now pronounce you man and wife. You may kiss your bride."

Belk kissed Jessica quickly. As the newly married couple turned to face their audience, Jessica noticed that no one in the room had a happy smile except Belk's father, Thomas, and his mother, Harriet. They all moved in a small social circle, and everyone in the audience was aware of the lifestyle Zachary had chosen. Jessica's father and Belk's parents joined them in a reception line, and one by one, their friends filed by with their congratulations. When the last one passed, Jessica turned to her father. He hugged her tightly. She smiled up at him and whispered in his ear, "I'll be fine, Father. Don't worry about me."

"I know you'll be fine. I know it better than you do. I know because you are so much your mother's daughter, and she was the strongest, bravest woman that ever lived. When things are difficult, and somewhere along the way, life always makes things difficult, remember that heritage."

"I will, I promise."

Chapter 4

Even though their wedding night was a disappointment to Jessica, at least Zachary was kind. The next day, they sailed for Europe and an extended honeymoon on the prize of the Cunard Line, the Servia. That evening, Jessica stood by the porthole of their luxurious cabin and watched the choppy waves flickering in the moonlight. She wore a lacy dressing gown from her quickly assembled trousseau. Belk walked behind her and pushed down one shoulder of the gown. He kissed her on the neck. She stiffened and squeezed her eyes tightly shut, but offered no resistance.

He ran his hands over her body and spoke softly in her ear. "You should learn to relax a little, Jessica. After a while, you may come to enjoy this whole business of being married."

Jessica stared straight ahead. "You certainly seem to enjoy it."

"I suppose it's more natural for a man. Give it time."

He turned her to face him and roughly pulled the gown off. She stood naked in front of him, looking at the floor as he tilted his head to one side and looked over her body. "Let's hope some of that European cuisine puts a little meat on those bones. I was never overly fond of thin women."

After landing at Liverpool, Jessica and Belk spent a few weeks in London, touring Westminster Abbey and the Tower of London. They saw several shows at the Royal

Theatre. In Paris, they visited the Louvre and Versailles and strolled along the West Bank of the Seine. In Rome, they tossed coins into the Fountain of Trevi.

When their honeymoon was drawing to a close, Belk and Jessica were with a tour group in Greece. The leader droned on about the Parthenon. Jessica sighed and looked away.

Belk flicked his thumbnail against his middle finger impatiently. "You look a little bored, my dear."

"Oh, I'm sorry. It isn't that I'm bored. I think I'm a little homesick. It'll be good to be home again. We've been gone so long. I miss--I miss New York."

Belk sneered, "And you miss your Daddy, too. Don't you?"

"Of course I do. I can't help worrying about him. He seemed so distracted for the last few weeks before we left. He's not a young man anymore."

Belk frowned, suddenly concerned. "You had a wire from him a few days ago. Was he still having troubles at the office?"

Jessica shook her head. "He never said anything to me about it, but then, he never was one to talk business at home."

"We set sail for New York in two more days. We'll be home before the end of September, and you can see for yourself. I'm sure everything is fine."

Jessica hoped her husband was right, but there had been something in the tone of her father's voice the day they sailed that she couldn't pinpoint, yet couldn't forget. She was relieved to finally board the Servia again for the voyage home.

The ship slipped into the New York harbor in the middle of the night. As soon as she awoke the next morning, Jessica dressed and hurried to the rail to look for her father. She was sure he would be waiting on the dock. After an hour, Belk joined her.

"We may as well go have some breakfast, Jessica. I'm quite sure your father didn't spend the night here waiting for you."

"I know. Of course you're right. It may be hours before we can disembark." Jessica's eyes searched the crowd for her father one final time, and then she and Belk went to the dining room. After they'd eaten, they returned to the rail.

"Daddy knew when we were landing. I was sure he would come to meet us."

"He's probably tied up at the office. You can never be certain when these ships will come to port. I'm sure he has better things to do than stand around here waiting for us to disembark. If you like, we can go to his office first instead of home."

"Home?" She grasped his arm. "Oh, Zachary, I can't wait to be home, not at Father's house, my house."

"Don't you mean our house?"

"Of course I do. I mean, I know we'll have to stay with Father for a few weeks until I can select our furnishings, but then I will have my house. It's so exciting." She closed her eyes and tilted her face to the sun. "Imagine, my very own home. As soon as we've unpacked, I'm going shopping for furniture and linens and everything. It will be so wonderful."

Belk shook his head. "You women have it so easy. All you have to worry your empty heads about is how you look and what china pattern you're going to select."

The remark stung. Jessica was a little hurt for a moment, and then the anger welling up inside made her feel rebellious. She tossed her head, "Yes. It's quite wonderful, isn't it?"

She looked back at the dock and grabbed his arm, pointing excitedly. "Look, there's Tommy with Father's carriage waiting for us. I knew he wouldn't forget."

Belk looked in the direction she was pointing to see an older man standing next to a fancy carriage. He held the halter of one of the beautiful, matched pair of horses. Belk frowned and puckered his lips. "Your driver is getting a little old. If those horses bolted, I doubt he could control them. Why don't you let him go and replace him with someone younger?"

"Oh, heavens, no. He's been with us as long as I can remember. Father told me they went to grade school together. He would never let Tommy go."

"Your father must have a dozen or more servants. I'm sure he could have sent a younger member of the staff."

"Maybe the others were doing something more urgent than spending the day at the harbor waiting for us."

It seemed to Jessica that it took forever before the gangplank was lowered and they could leave the ship. It was another eternity before they claimed their luggage and the carriage was loaded. The drive home took another hour but, finally, the fancy carriage, filled with luggage and steamer trunks, pulled up in front of the McCarthy home.

Jessica and Belk got out, and Belk made no attempt to help the driver as he began unloading the luggage.

Jessica rushed up the stairs and in the house. The housekeeper, Caroline, was walking through the hallway. A large, pleasant, ordinary looking woman in her late fifties, she'd been widowed by the Mexican-American War while still a young woman. She wore her hair in a bun at the back of her neck, and her daily dress included a large white apron. Jessica grabbed her and hugged her tightly. Caroline's face broke out in a huge grin. "Jess! Or should I say, Mrs. Belk?"

Jessica rolled her eyes. "Hah!"

Caroline grinned at her and held out the edges of her apron, making a little curtsy. "It's so good to have you home. We've all missed you so much. Your father is going to be so happy to see you."

"It's good to be home. I missed all of you, too. Is father still at the office? I was expecting him to meet our ship, but I suppose he had too much work to do."

Caroline looked down and twisted one edge of her apron. "He came home early today. He's in his study."

Jessica hurried down the hall and flung open the door to her father's study. He sat behind a desk, shuffling through some papers. She'd been gone for nine months and was shocked by the changes in him. His hair was now completely white, and he'd lost considerable weight. He looked up at Jessica almost as if he didn't recognize her for a moment, and then recovered himself. He stood quickly and came around the desk to embrace her.

"Oh, my baby. You're home at last. This has been the longest six months of my life. Don't you ever go away from me again."

"I promise. I will never leave Manhattan again as long as I live. Oh, I missed you so."

"Not nearly as much as I missed you."

"Father, are you all right? You've lost so much weight, and your hair is so white."

"Uh, well, uh, --the doctor said that I was not doing my heart any good carrying that big belly around, so he put me on a diet."

With her arms still around him, Jessica looked in his face. "You have bags under your eyes, too. Haven't you been sleeping?"

"No. I've been sitting up nights and counting the days until my little girl came home to me."

"Well, now that I'm back, you have to take better care of yourself." Jessica suddenly realized she'd never known her father to be home so early on a weekday. "It isn't like you to be home at this time of the day. Are things all right at the office?"

He opened his mouth to speak, but hesitated. His face tightened, and his tone changed. "You're a grown-up, married woman now, and I'm not going to lie to you. No, they aren't all right. You haven't been home long enough to hear of it, but the stock market fell tremendously a few days ago. I must say, I saw it coming. I've been worried about it for a while now. They're calling it Black Friday. Some of my friends were ruined speculating on gold. There may even be an investigation, and one or two of them might wind up in prison. It could go all the way up to President Grant before the dust settles."

Jessica stepped back from him. "But not you? You never dealt in gold."

"No, thank God, not me. It's only that these things have repercussions in a lot of fields that have nothing to do with gold, and the value of my holdings has fallen a great deal. I've already cut back some expenses. For one thing, our household staff is smaller. Jasper decided to go seek his fortune in California, and Irene married one of the Buchanan staff. She went to live with him and work for them. I didn't have to let anyone go. I simply didn't replace them. Tommy is doing the grounds keeping for us, and we can do without a maid. Caroline can take care of the house. We still have Cook. Now, don't you worry about a thing. I have some irons in the fire and money in the bank. I've been up and down several times in my life, and I'll be up again in no time. You'll see."

"Well, forget about my house. Zachary and I will live here with you, or we'll get a little flat somewhere."

"It's not as drastic as all that. Your house was already paid for before you were even married. I bought it at a depressed price at an estate sale and have no doubt at all that it was one of the best investments I ever made. When I selected it, I was thinking about the future. It's only two blocks away from here and sits on one side of a five acre plot on Central Park. I've already filed the paperwork to divide the land into two separate sections. This island isn't getting any bigger, and you could eventually sell the vacant half for a small fortune, maybe even a big fortune."

She wrapped her arms around him. "If it would help any, go ahead and sell it now."

He shook his head. "That would be foolish. I'm quite sure this situation is only temporary. I hate to go back on any of the promises I made to you about outfitting your house, but I do have to be careful about expenditures. It would be better for the time being if you could hold down the expenses of your furnishings. I've opened accounts for you at Peter Jones on Sloan Square and at Macy's, so go ahead and buy what you have to have right now. Later on, when things have recovered, you can get yourself the finest furnishings in Manhattan."

Jessica laid her head on his shoulder. "You know, you always said that there was twice as much furniture in this house as you needed. How about I borrow some of it? Whatever you don't have for me to use from here, I'll look for on the used furniture market."

McCarthy smiled at her. "You are your mother's child. Take everything you need. Only leave me my bed and this desk and maybe a chair to sit on."

Jessica laughed. "Oh, Father. I'll leave you more than that. I'll leave the big table in the kitchen. You'll need somewhere to eat, won't you?"

"Not if you need it more than I, my love."

"I have every confidence that there's plenty of furniture for both of us."

"Don't forget the attic. It's as big as a warehouse. Every time your mother bought something new, she had us carry the old things up there. It's crammed full of furniture and linens and her clothing."

"I'm so glad you mentioned it. It must be a treasure house."

"At least."

"Zachary wants to go say hello to his parents, and then we're going to look at the house. I want to think out the floor plan and see where things will fit. Daddy, is it all right if I take mother's piano with me?"

"That would be fine with me. It's what she would have wanted. I still remember her teaching you to play. You were almost a baby when she started you. Your feet didn't reach the pedals for years. You always had a gift for it, you know. You couldn't even read a book, but you could read the music from the little primers she bought for you before your fourth birthday. Not that you needed the music. She used to sit you on her lap and let you pound on the keys and you were quite young when the pounding turned into little tunes that made sense. You could play by ear very early on, but she insisted that you learn properly."

"I think I can remember that, but it's all so--so faded now. Sometimes, I have to look at a picture of her to know what she looked like."

He held her chin in his hand. "All you have to do is look in a mirror, and you'll see her looking back at you."

"You're only saying that because you love me. She was so much more beautiful than I could ever hope to be."

"Wait until you're a little older. She grew more beautiful with every day, and you're going to do the same thing."

She kissed him on the cheek. "I have to go now and see my in-laws, but we'll be back after dinner, and then we can have a long talk."

"I can hardly wait. I want you to tell me all about Europe. I haven't been there since my own honeymoon. Is it still as grand as I remember it?"

"Even more so. I'll tell you everything tonight."

"Give my regards to Harriet."

"I will."

Jessica and Zachary visited his parents, had a lovely dinner with them, and then spent the rest of the evening with Jessica's father. They went to bed in Jessica's old room, and it was comforting to sink down into the fluffy mattress and lay her head on the pillow that was so familiar to her. She slept soundly for the first time since she'd left home.

When she awoke in the morning, Zachary was already up and dressed. He leaned over her and kissed her cheek. "I have some business matters at the office I'd like to see to. You don't need me for anything here, do you?"

"Not at all. I'm going to spend the day up in the attic going through mother's things to see what I want to take with me."

He shuddered. "Thank you for sparing me that. I'll be back this afternoon. Have fun."

As she was brought up to do by her mother, Jessica said short silent prayers all of the time, mentioning things as she thought of them so that evening fatigue and sometimes forgetfulness didn't make her leave anything out. It was her habit to give thanks to God in the morning for whatever joy He'd brought her, and to make her requests at night. This morning, she gave thanks that Zachary was on his way to the office. She hoped it meant he was taking her father's advice seriously.

After breakfast in the kitchen with her father, Caroline, Cook, and Tommy, she put on her shabbiest dress that she usually wore when working in the rose garden and tied a scarf around her hair to keep off the dust she knew she would find in the attic. She took a pad of paper and a pencil to make a list, and ventured up the creaky stairs. She hadn't gone up those steps since she was a child looking for adventure and finding none. Cobwebs hung from the rafters and, before she started her search for usable items, she took an old broom left standing by the staircase and used its badly curved bristles to sweep the cobwebs down so they wouldn't get in her face. She looked over the furniture first, making notes of the items she thought she could use, and was surprised at how many pieces there were, barely worn, that needed only a good cleaning to make them serviceable. She chuckled aloud. Perhaps her father could keep his dining table after all.

After choosing what furniture she wanted, she started opening the trunks and boxes. There was a wonderful assortment of household linens, sheets, towels, and tablecloths, many embroidered by her mother. It brought back memories of the two of them sitting close to one another on the sofa in the evenings, her mother coaching her on her stitches, and showing her how to loop and angle her needle to get the finest lines and the most delicate flowers. Her childhood work was in one of the trunks, and she smiled at how inept the sewing really was. It made her cry to realize that her mother must have kept every one of them.

After she lost her mother, Caroline had taken over the task of teaching Jessica. Every young gentlewoman was expected to excel at needlework and dressmaking, and Caroline was determined that she would raise Jessica to the standard her mother would have wanted had she lived.

The most touching treasure Jessica found were the boxes and trunks with her mother's clothes. All her beautiful nightgowns and lingerie was folded and stored. A tall armoire, stuffed with the expensive gowns her mother had worn, held a particular treasure. Jessica could remember her in the blue silk ball gown she'd bought for the Governor's Ball one year, and a green velvet gown she made herself for a Christmas party she hosted. Jessica held it up in front of her and looked at herself in the pedestal mirror in the corner. Her father was wrong. She would never be as beautiful as her mother, not if she lived a hundred years.

By the time she was satisfied that she'd seen everything in the attic, it was late afternoon. She'd worked straight through the day without lunch. Her stomach complained loudly, so she went downstairs to find something to tide her over until dinner. Caroline and Cook were in the kitchen, arguing over whether it was best to fold the linens with the outside edges tucked inside for a neater appearance on the shelf. Caroline wanted them inside. Cook said, "What difference does it make? No one else is going to see them but us."

Caroline answered, "The difference is that there's a right way to fold them and a wrong way to fold them."

Jessica stood outside the door for a moment and listened to them. She had to suppress a laugh. Caroline and Cook had been arguing in the kitchen for as long as she could remember. They never raised their voices, never came to blows, and when it was over, it was over. Jessica knew that any spats were simply to vent everyday frustrations and didn't mean any hard feelings would result. Cook's kingdom was the kitchen. Caroline's was the rest of the house. Any dispute would ultimately be settled by which side of the kitchen door took precedence.

Jessica pushed open the swinging door and entered the battleground. "I'm starving. Is there anything to fill a poor girl's stomach in here?"

An immediate truce was called. Nothing was more important than seeing to it that the daughter of the house had anything she wanted. Cook went to the icebox to fetch a dish of cold chicken, and Caroline took Jessica's hand and led her outside.

"Just look at yourself," she scolded happily. "You're filthy. Let's get out to the back porch and get rid of some of that grime."

On the porch, Jessica stood obediently still while Caroline took the scarf off Jessica's head and shook it. Dust billowed out in the air. Jessica's skirt had cobwebs and dust covering it almost up to her waist and dust had settled thickly on her shoulders. Caroline shook her head. "Stay here. I'll have to get a brush."

She went back in the house and came out with a garment brush, which she ran over Jessica from her shoulders to her hem. "There, that ought to do it for a while. You can get a bath and a nap before dinner."

They went back in the kitchen just as Cook was putting a thick sandwich on the table. Jessica ate it eagerly while the two women fussed over her, bringing her a glass of milk and chattering about how she shouldn't let herself go so long without eating. She told Caroline, "As soon as I'm through with lunch, I'm going to have Tommy take a message to some movers to arrange to get the furniture and things taken to my house."

Caroline blinked back tears. "I know you're only going to be two blocks away, but it won't be the same around here with you living somewhere else."

"I've been gone for nine months already."

"This was still where you lived. Now it won't be."

With this, Cook also started crying. "We knew it would happen someday, but time went by so fast, and now, you're all grown up and a married woman."

"Yes," Caroline said. "The only thing you can do to make it up to us for growing up, is promise us you're going to have to have a big family and bring them here all the time."

Jessica jumped up and threw her arms around Caroline. "I promise. I want to have as many babies as God will give me."

Chapter 5

Jessica fidgeted cheerfully around the delivery men as they brought the furniture from her father's house to her new home. She pointed to the place she'd selected for each piece, having them move some things several times before she was satisfied.

Finally, they came to the most important item, her mother's piano. One of them carried in the bench first and she led them happily to the corner of the room. She clapped her hands in front of her in joy and smiled broadly. The front door would never accommodate the ornate instrument, so she'd flung open the double doors that led to the side yard, and it took four men and an assortment of wheeled conveyances and heavily woven tapes to get the piano in the house.

She fluttered around them as they put it in place. When they finished, she led them to the door, signed a receipt, and took a handful of money from her pocket, which included not only their fee, but a generous tip, and shoved it in the mover's hands.

"Thank you so much."

Jessica closed the door behind them and rushed back to the piano. She pulled out the bench, sat down, and played a few bars of Mozart, her head cocked, listening to the notes. She frowned and ran her hand over the top of the keyboard, muttering, "I'm so sorry you had to be moved. I'll have to have Mr. Prescott come out to tune you as soon as possible."

Jessica stood and walked around the room, smoothing seat cushions and straightening chairs. She smiled a small, contented smile. "All I need now is a baby, or two, or maybe even three, if there's time."

The next few months slipped by. Zachary left for his office every morning, but seldom came home at a regular hour. Some evenings, most evenings, it was quite late before he showed up. It wasn't unusual for Jessica to already be in bed when he arrived. She usually left a plate with dinner on the kitchen table for him. Sometimes he ate, sometimes he didn't. As he climbed into the bed next to her, she could smell whiskey, and occasionally, a strange perfume on him. If she asked the next morning where he'd been, he would simply tell her, "I've been working late."

They seldom ate together, and she found herself at the kitchen table of her father's home more often than at her own.

When she met her friends for lunch or ladies' club, she overheard rumors that he wasn't working late. One day she pulled a friend, Mary Basset, aside and asked her directly, "What's the gossip about my husband?"

Mary flushed bright red. "You never heard me gossip, Jessica, and if at all possible, I don't listen to it either."

"That's why you're the one I asked. I'll believe anything you tell me, and I know you won't lie to me or downplay or exaggerate what you know. Tell me what you've heard."

Mary sighed. "I don't want to be the one to tell you."

"I have a right to know. Everywhere I go people are buzzing about my husband's behavior. I catch bits and pieces of it, but when I come in the room, everyone shuts up all of a sudden. If you love me, you'll tell me the truth."

Mary looked at her sadly. "All right, if you insist."

"I insist."

"And if you're sure you want to know. Sometimes, a wife doesn't want to know."

"I never was one to go around with my head in the sand. You know that."

"I know." Mary took a deep breath. "I've heard from more than one person that he's been gambling almost every night. He's in debt to every man in our circle, and they won't play with him anymore. He's been going to the Bowery to find a game."

Jessica was horrified. "The Bowery? That's a terrible neighborhood."

"Yes. If he loses to the men down there he may get hurt."

"What else?"

"Jessica, I really don't--"

"What else!"

"He's been seen out with more than one woman, and no one describes them as ladies."

"Thank you for being honest with me, Mary."

"I'd just as soon not have been the one to tell you."

"You're the only one I'd trust to hear it from."

Jessica cried and prayed all afternoon. *Have I been foolish to disregard Father's warning? I'd been so hopeful that marriage and a home would move Zachary to change his ways.* She decided to speak to him, to pour out her heart, to plead with him to make an effort to have a happy home.

She waited up for him that night, passing the time by playing the piano and then reading by the gaslight in the bedroom for hours, but it was in vain. There was no sign of him. She fell asleep long before he came home.

The next morning, she waited until he was ready to leave for his office. She held the door for him and, as he went out, strengthened her resolve. She told him, "I want you to be home by six this evening. I'm cooking a special dinner, and there's something very important we need to discuss."

His face lit up. "Are you expecting?"

"We'll talk tonight."

He kissed her on the cheek. "I'll be home promptly at six. I promise."

As he walked jauntily down the front steps Jessica couldn't help but reflect that, so far, his promises hadn't meant anything.

She cooked all afternoon. When her husband came home at five-thirty, the table in the dining room was set. She directed him to his seat at the head of the table and hurried to the kitchen. He watched her intently as she brought out a beautifully browned roast, then returned and came back with two bowls of vegetables. She sat down to his right hand. He didn't comment until the meal was well under way.

With a raised eyebrow, he asked her, "Is it the help's night off, Jessica?"

"No, well, yes, actually. I didn't hire any. There's no real need of a household staff. I'm perfectly capable of running the house myself."

"I didn't expect to marry a servant. I can't have you cleaning, cooking, and doing God knows what else. Suppose the neighbors saw you hanging wash out on the line? How would that reflect on me? My wife should be above such things. Has your father completely forsaken his promise to support this house?"

"No, he's paying the bills. It's only that his portfolio still hasn't recovered from the whole 'Black Friday' mess, and I don't see any reason to saddle him with unnecessary expenses. He has enough to contend with right now, and I don't think he needs to worry about us."

"He gave his word. I never expected him to go back on it. It shouldn't be that difficult for him to earn the money."

Jessica bristled and drew herself up. "He hasn't gone back on his word. If I asked, my father would support us in the manner he promised before he would buy his own groceries. He gladly pays every bill I send him. It's simply that I don't see any reason to put an extra burden on him. Once his business has recovered, I'll hire a staff that meets your expectations. I'm sorry that your dinner disappointed you."

"On the contrary, dinner was excellent. I take it you've been doing the cooking all along. You seem to be an outstanding chef. The roast, the potatoes, everything, was quite good. I'm surprised. Where did you learn how to do all this?"

"From Cook and Caroline. All my life, we had the same cook and housekeeper in our home that are still working for Father today. From the time I can remember, I tagged after them and helped them do their work. I suppose they felt sorry for me since I didn't have a mother.

I learned everything there was to know about running a household, from cleaning the oven to keeping the books."

"I see. Your father told me you had amazing talents, but I had no idea they were this diverse. I wouldn't give much credit to your household staff. More likely than not, they didn't give a fig about you, but simply took advantage of the free help".

"Not at all. I love them and I know they love me, especially Caroline. I still remember that, whenever I was ill as a child, Caroline would watch over me. She would sit in the rocking chair by my bed and sometimes hold me on her lap and rock me. I can remember feeling safe and warm with her arms around me and her crooning lullabies."

"I don't suppose your father has let his own staff go?"

"He had to let most of them go quite some time back. Now there's only Caroline, Cook, and Tommy."

"He should know how we're doing with no help at all. Have you told him why you didn't hire someone? If he's so intent on being frugal, he would fire his own staff, too."

"Oh, no, he would never do that. They're family to us."

"Are they now? They certainly aren't family to me. Tell me, my dear, when is your 'us' going to mean you and I, and not you and your father?"

"I haven't thought about it that way. When we have children, I suppose."

He smiled broadly. "Is that what you wanted to talk to me about? Are we expecting?"

"No. I wish we were, but, no."

"Well, we've been married almost a year now and we certainly aren't making much progress on that front, are we? I wanted you to give me a son as soon as possible."

Jessica was shocked and angered by his bitter words. She glared at him. "I seem to have disappointed you in a number of ways. I'm sorry. As for our living expenses, if it's so easy to earn money, why don't you try bringing home enough to hire some household help? I know all about how you lived before we were married, and I know that you've gone right back to your old ways. Your gambling losses would seem to be more than adequate to pay staff salaries."

"What would you know about my losses?"

"It may surprise you. The men you gamble with talk to their wives, they talk to their friends, and some of them are my friends, too. You know how the gossip mill in our circle works. There isn't anything secret in Manhattan society, good or bad."

"What I win or lose gambling is none of your business."

"Really? I never heard anything about you winning. I wonder, when we become our own 'us' will it be my business then?"

"Your father and his staff may have taught you how to run a house and cook, but they don't seem to have taught you anything about a wife's proper place. Don't ever ask me about my affairs again."

He threw down his napkin, jumped up from the table, and stormed out of the house. Jessica took a bite of her dessert and then put down her spoon. She sat there with a frown. She'd planned to have a rational discussion with Zachary, to plead with him to try harder to be a good husband. Now he was gone. D*id he go to find a poker game or another woman?* Through the window behind her, a few flakes of snow began to fall.

It was less than two months until Christmas, their first anniversary. Christmas brought joy to everyone. Perhaps by then, he would be more receptive to her wishes. Perhaps by then, she could tell him she was going to have a baby. She sat at the dining room table and let thoughts of a baby and family take her away from her worries.

It would be so wonderful. I'd make little gowns for him, or her. I really don't care. I'd furnish a nursery in one of the empty bedrooms, with white curtains on the windows and pretty wallpaper. She'd seen the cradle from her own childhood in her father's attic and wanted to bring that home for her child.

Abruptly, her daydreams were interrupted by the memory of their conversation. *What if I did conceive, and Zachary didn't change at all? Do I really want to bring a baby into a home where there could be no happiness?*

Chapter 6

Jessica and Caroline came in the front door of Jessica's house carrying boxes of Christmas ornaments. In the center of the living room stood a small, well-shaped fir. One by one, they took the ornaments out of the boxes, unwrapped them carefully, and hung them on the tree.

Jessica stood back from time to time to survey their work. "I think maybe it was a good idea for me to borrow only the small ones. The others would have been too much for a tree this short."

Caroline smiled. "It will be beautiful. Your father said we wouldn't be putting up a tree this year for the first time since I've been at the house. Trees are so terribly expensive. We're all doing the best we can."

"He may have decided not to waste money on a tree, but I'm coming over in the morning and I'm going to decorate the house anyway. There are candles and ribbons and other things we can use that he already has up in the attic, and we won't have to spend a dime on them. Hard times or not, I can't let Christmas go without notice. It's the most special day of the year. It will cheer up everyone to have the houses all pretty."

Caroline handed her one of the blown glass ornaments. "It's hard for your father to deal with, not having enough money to do anything he wants. For so many years he never thought about how much it took to run the house, and now we think about every penny we spend."

"Father told me he had to put the three of you on half wages. He was hoping that wouldn't be necessary, but he didn't know what else to do. He can't let you go the way he did the others. You're all family to us. It's such a huge house. I'm hoping he can manage with only a housekeeper, a cook, and a groundskeeper. It won't be too bad in the winter when there isn't that much to do outside except to keep the snow off the walk. Have you heard from any of the people he had to dismiss? Do you think there's any hope of them keeping other employment, even with excellent references?"

"I haven't heard. Everyone's hurting, it seems. So many of my friends have lost their positions, and so they lost their homes. Not everyone has your father's heart. I'm not going to complain about half-wages. I wouldn't complain if I didn't get any wages at all, and neither would Cook or Tommy. We're happy to have a roof over our heads and something to eat. We're all getting older. Who would hire us, even if times were better? We'll manage. We're doing the best we can to hold down expenses. It is a big house, so we've shut down the rooms that aren't being used and that saves on heating and so forth. We've been able to cut back quite a bit. Before the stock market mess, even the help that didn't live in the house ate their meals there, so there's a big savings on groceries right there. There's no need to heat up the dining room or the living room either, for that matter. Now that we don't have guests anymore, your father's been taking all his meals in the kitchen with us. On the nights he comes over here for dinner with you, Cook doesn't even prepare a fresh meal, only warms up the leftovers."

Jessica bit her lip. "I can't get him to come here more than once a week. Zachary always—uh--works late—on Wednesdays, so Father has dinner with me to keep me company. He never did enjoy my husband, so it works out well. I'm quite happy to have Father all to myself."

Caroline looked as if she wanted to comment, she opened her mouth to speak, but seemed to think better of it. She closed her mouth, pursed her lips, and kept her thoughts to herself.

Jessica hung another glass bulb on the tree, "I know this must be the smallest tree in Manhattan, but think that I'll still have to get a step-stool to get the angel on top. I probably should have put that on first. I have a surprise for you. Wait until you see what I did with Mother's green velvet ball gown. I'm going to wear it on Christmas day."

"Your father will be tickled pink to see you in it. Whatever gave you the idea?"

"It's been so long since I had a new dress, I couldn't stand it anymore. Fabric is so expensive these days, not to mention buttons and everything else. When I went up in the attic that day, I remembered when I was a child, how I used to go up there and dress up in Mother's things. I thought, Why not? So I had some of the trunks brought here, and I've made myself several new outfits. Father kept every single thing she wore, all her gloves and hats and her lingerie, and her things were so beautiful. Her undies were all pressed and folded like brand new in a store. Of course, some of the fashions have changed so much I could never use things like the hoop skirts, but I picked out the boning from them and put them away. Someday I'll make myself new nighties from that beautiful silk fabric."

"Good for you. There wasn't any damage from moths?"

"Not a bit. The wardrobes and the trunks were all lined with cedar, and all the fabrics were as good as new."

"I remember now. Your father was in such a bad way when your mother passed we thought he was going to lose his mind. He wouldn't let us get rid of anything, even her stationery."

"You know, I think we should have Christmas dinner at Father's house instead of here. I'll bring everything we need the day before, and then I'll come over early Christmas morning and help cook. It will be great fun. I'll find a really big ham. The leftovers will last longer than a goose or a turkey would, and we'll have sweet potatoes, and pies, and candy, like the old days."

"That's going to cost a lot of money."

"I have a little nest egg I've been saving for exactly such an occasion."

Jessica sat in front of her dressing table where a pretty jewelry box stood to one side. She pulled it in front of her and opened it. It had two trays that lifted out. One had rings, the other held earrings. The box was quite well stocked with tasteful pieces. Jessica looked through them. She had laid out a piece of linen on the table in front of her and, one at a time, she took out an item and laid it on the cloth. Then she began picking them up one by one, and placing them back in the box. She held up a pair of emerald earrings and looked wistfully at them. They were her mother's. She could never part with them. She put them away and picked up a ring. That was also her mother's. She examined the cameo her father gave her on her sixteenth birthday, and the brooch she wore at her wedding.

She finally selected a heavy gold necklace chain, set it aside, replaced the trays, and closed the box. She picked the chain back up, hefted the feel of it in her palm. *Yes, you ought to bring enough to pay for a nice Christmas dinner.*

Jessica folded the chain in a handkerchief, and walked to the jewelry district. Standing hesitantly in front of a pawn shop on a Manhattan street, she took a deep breath, steeled herself, and walked in the door.

A clerk wearing a green visor and half-glasses looked up at her from his post behind the counter. "Good afternoon, young lady. How may I help you?"

Jessica walked to the counter, opened her handbag, and took out the gold chain. She handed it to him for his inspection. He took it from her without speaking, held it up and turned it around in front of his face. He looked at the markings on the clasp closely, then reached under the counter and brought out a small scale. He placed the chain on the scale and watched as the needle moved back and forth over the figures. When the dial settled, he told her, "That's fourteen troy ounces. That will bring you—uh—twenty dollars."

Jessica stuck out her chin. "But I remember my father saying that gold was bringing in twenty dollars an ounce."

The clerk snorted. "That was last September. President Grant has released a lot of gold since then, and it has depressed the price of the entire market. Twenty dollars is the best I can do. Take it or leave it. Of course, if you come into some money, you can always buy it back."

Sadly, she nodded her head.

The clerk picked up a green, cloth-bound ledger and flipped it open. "I'll need your name and address for my records."

She gave him the information, which he recorded in his book. He gave her a claim ticket and counted out the money to her. She folded it and tucked it in her purse. As she left the shop, a feeling of remorse and guilt washed over her. The chain had been a gift from her father on her eighteenth birthday. She determined that if things did improve, and she came into some money, or if her prayers were answered, and Zachary would suddenly start applying himself and bring home his pay for a change, the first thing she would do would be to redeem the chain.

On Christmas Day, Jessica sat at her dressing table. She was wearing the green velvet dress she made from her mother's gown and going through her jewelry box. She'd intended to wear her mother's emerald earrings, but couldn't find them. She frowned. *Did I drop them the last time I looked at them?*

She looked under the table, and then went to the bed, lifted up the skirt and looked under it. She bit her lip anxiously. *Whatever have I done with Mother's emeralds? I'll just have to wear something else.*

Jessica's father's house was festooned with Christmas ribbons. She and Caroline spent the afternoon a few days earlier winding them down the banister and tying them across the fireplace mantle. The ornaments that normally would have hung on a tree were stacked in

42

pyramids on dishes. The big table in the dining room was set for three. Jessica and her father were sitting on the sofa looking through a scrapbook. Caroline was straightening the silverware on the table. The big grandfather's clock struck eight. Jessica was beginning to grow impatient. She jumped up from the sofa and strode over to the front window. She pushed the curtains aside and looked out.

"There's no sign of Zachary, and I'm not waiting one minute longer. Caroline, let's serve dinner for the five of us in the kitchen. We'll have a grand time, the way we did before I married. If he shows up, he can eat in here all alone."

She and Caroline gathered up two of the place settings and carried them to the kitchen.

It had always been one of Jessica's favorite rooms in the house, warm, efficient, and homey. Pots and pans hung from a ceiling rack. A long wooden counter lined one wall. A large, plain wooden table was in the center of the room. It was covered in a white cloth and had been set with simple dinnerware for three people. Caroline and Jessica added the place settings they brought from the dining room. Jessica looked at the table for a moment and said, "Wait a minute."

She rushed back out the door and re-appeared a moment later carrying the centerpiece from the dining room. She put it in the middle of the table. With the addition of the two place settings from the dining room, it was set with two fancy places, and three plain ones.

Jessica held up one palm. "This will never do. Caroline, take everything off the table. We'll start over. This is Christmas, and we're really going to celebrate."

They switched things around until table was re-set with five place settings of the finest linens, dishes, and silverware. Jessica lit the candles. Tommy, the aging groundskeeper, sat at one side, Jessica's father sat at the head of the table. Cook, a plump, round-faced, smiling woman, was still at the stove, stirring a pot. Caroline and Jessica looked over their work.

Jessica opened her arms wide. "I'm starving. Let's get this food on the table and have a fine Christmas dinner."

The women scurried around the stove and table placing the food. There was a huge ham, already partially sliced, candied yams, mashed potatoes, several vegetables, and fresh-out-of-the-oven bread rolls. The women sat down at their places. They all smiled at one another and joined hands.

William McCarthy bowed his head and prayed, "Lord, we thank Thee for this bounty and for the hands that have prepared it. We thank Thee for the fellowship of our family and friends here this evening. We thank Thee for our many blessings and ask that You keep us ever mindful that no matter how many worldly goods we may have lost, we have Thy blessings and Thy salvation. Please watch over us and keep us safe in the coming year. In Jesus's name, Amen."

This was followed by a chorus of amens, and they eagerly started passing the dishes around, laughing and chattering.

A half-hour later, they were finishing their meal. Everyone was smiling and happy. Jessica leaned back in her chair. "Oh, my goodness. I think I'm going to pop. That apple pie was absolutely wonderful. Cook, you have outdone yourself. I can't believe you got all this done in only one day."

Cook grinned. "I got it done with the help of you and Caroline."

They were eyeing the dessert with the thought of a second portion when the sound of the doorknocker at the front of the house echoed loudly.

Jessica rolled her eyes. "My goodness. I wonder who that can be."

Caroline started to rise, but Jessica held up her hand. "Stay where you are Caroline. I'll get this one myself." She rose and left the kitchen. As she opened the front door, she found her husband leaning against the door frame. His overcoat was coated with snow. He reeled a little and braced his shoulder against the door frame.

"Sorry I'm late. I was un-unavoid-unavoidably detained. I hope I haven't missed dinner."

She had seen him drunk before, but never this drunk. "We were almost finished eating, but there are lots of leftovers." She waved him toward the dining room. "I'll get you a plate."

He walked carefully into the dining room and looked at the single place setting, "I thought you said you were finishing your dinner?"

"We were. Father and I ate in the kitchen."

"In the kitchen? Do you mean to tell me that you ate with the servants?"

"Yes, of course. We've done that a lot over the years since Mother died. Father always gave the help who didn't live in the house all the holidays off, and we would have our meal with Caroline, Tommy, and Cook. It's much nicer that way. The only time we ever used the dining room was when we had guests."

"I can't believe this. Do other people know about this?"

"I don't know. I don't think it ever came up in conversation before."

"I knew your family was unusual, but this is disgusting."

"Why? Because we'd rather spend our Christmas dinner with hard working people we can respect and care for, instead of out drinking with God knows who and doing God knows what?"

"You may disapprove of the company I keep, but not one of them would sit down to table with the help."

"I'm sure they wouldn't, but they don't know what they're missing."

"I'm surprised that the servants would make you feel welcome. They're every bit as much aware of the class distinctions as we are."

"Things are different at my father's home."

"Apparently so. Get your wrap. I'm taking you home."

"You go on home without me. I think I'll stay here. I have to help clear the table and do the dishes."

Belk crinkled up his nose in distaste. "Suit yourself. If you want to act like a scullery maid, go ahead."

He wheeled around and tried to make a dignified retreat but staggered a little and had to brace his hand against the wall to recover his balance. A sad Jessica watched him go. She went back to the kitchen.

Her father and Caroline were still sitting at the table. Jessica came through the door, smiling brightly. She sat at the table and picked up her napkin. "Caroline, I think I could eat one more, tiny sliver of that pie. What do you say?"

"I may have to have one myself."

Jessica's father grinned at her. "Was there any more of that chocolate cake?"

Jessica squeezed her father's hand. "Daddy, I've eaten so much that I don't even want to go home. May I spend the night here?"

He blinked back a tear. "That would be so lovely. Are you sure Zachary won't mind?"

"I'm afraid he's had one too many drinks of Christmas rum. If he even makes it home, he'll probably go right to bed and pass out. He won't even notice I'm not there until tomorrow.

Embarrassed by the frank conversation, Tommy stood. "If you'll all excuse me, I think I'll get to bed early. The way it's snowing, I'll need to be out shoveling the walk at first light."

Jessica smiled at him. "Good night Tommy."

Her father added, "See you in the morning. If I'm up, I may give you a hand with that shoveling."

Caroline placed the pieces of pie and cake on the table. "What about you, Cook? Are you going to have any more dessert?"

Cook waved a hand at her. "I couldn't eat another bite. I'll get started on these dishes."

Jessica's father put one of his hands on hers. "Was Zachary all that far into his cups?"

Jessica shook her head. "Quite far. I thought for a minute he was going to fall down."

"Jess, does he treat you all right?"

"He treats me well enough. He mostly ignores me, which is a blessing, since I don't care much for his company anyway."

"You told me right from the start that you didn't love him. I guess I hoped he'd find a way to win you over, but that would require a different kind of man entirely. I should have never let you marry him."

"At the time, there wasn't anything you could have done that would have stopped me. I'll be all right Father. I knew what I was getting into. I'm quite satisfied with my life. I have my music work at the church. I do love Zachary's mother, exactly as you said I would. She and I have lunch together at least once a week. I see a lot of my friends, and taking care of the house keeps me busy. I love my home so much. I love cooking. I've even begun to invent some of my own recipes, and the thought entered my head that I could write a cookbook. I may be able to get it published in some periodical like *Peterson's Ladies' Magazine* or *Godey's*. Oh, and I took home some of Mother's dresses, and I've been re-working them into things for myself. It's great fun. I get a brand new outfit at no cost at all, and when I'm wearing one, it makes me feel as if she's sending me a hug."

He looked at her closely. "Of course. I thought that green velvet you're wearing looked familiar. You made that from one of your mother's ball gowns, didn't you?"

"Yes. It had miles and miles of fabric in the skirt alone, and the skirts of dresses these days are much less full. I made this and still have enough fabric left over to do something else."

"You should have worn her green emeralds with it. I remember how beautiful she was in that gown."

"I intended to wear them, but I couldn't find them, so I settled for the pearls. I was looking at the emeralds only the other day. I must have misplaced them somewhere in the bedroom. Don't worry. I'm sure they'll turn up."

At the sink, Caroline and Cook exchanged a worried look, but neither commented.

McCarthy patted Jessica's hand. "Are you sure you're all right with him?"

"I'm sure. He's not all that bad, as husbands go. You should hear some of the stories my friends tell me. Did you know that there are even some husbands who strike their wives?"

"It's hard to believe, isn't it? Zachary may not hit you, but I had hoped for much more than that."

"As they say, I have made my bed. I'm all right, Father, really. I've decided to spend the night here, and when we get up in the morning, Cook will make us a big breakfast with some of this ham and her special biscuits, like in the old days. Won't that be wonderful?

He grinned at her. "It will indeed. You're going to find that the older you get, the more you long for the old days. You could stay here permanently if you wanted. You know that, don't you?"

"I know, Father, but I'm only going to stay for the morning. I want Zachary to wake up and find me gone. Maybe it will give him a reason to think about his behavior."

"Then why go home at all?"

"Because it's my home, not his, but it's more than the house. I still haven't given up on having a child. That's what I want more than anything."

"If you ever change your mind, remember that you will always have somewhere to go."

Jessica kissed him on the cheek. "I will, Father. Please don't worry about me so much. I'll be fine. Now, why don't you go on sit in front of that lovely fire in the living room and let us women finish cleaning up this kitchen. Otherwise, we'll put you to work scrubbing pans."

He held up his hands in surrender, "I'm on my way."

When Jessica woke the next morning she opened her eyes to a familiar room. She'd taken comfort from sleeping in the front bedroom where she'd grown up, and that she knew would always be hers. She shivered when she threw back the covers and got out of bed. The room was quite cold. She dressed hurriedly, trotted downstairs, and wrapped a shawl she found on the hat rack that stood by the front door around her shoulders. She looked out the window. The snow was about four inches deep, and the elderly Tommy was shoveling the walk, lifting only a little at a time. He paused, breathing hard. His breath showed white in the air. William McCarthy came out the front door and called to him, "Tommy! Let it go. It's too much. I'll get the Simpson boy to finish it up."

Tommy looked up from his work and shook his head. "I can do it, sir. It simply takes me longer than it used to."

"Nonsense. There's no use in either one of us killing ourselves over it. Now come on in here and rest up a bit. Later on, you can bring in some more firewood. We don't want to let the fires go out." He shivered dramatically.

Tommy nodded. "Yes, sir."

McCarthy went back inside and closed the door.

In the kitchen, Caroline sat at the table polishing the silverware, and Cook was mixing the biscuits in a big bowl. Jessica came in, poured herself a cup of tea, and sat at the table.

"I borrowed one of your shawls, Caroline. All of mine and Mother's are at my house. I'm afraid the fire in my bedroom went out. It's freezing upstairs."

"Even with the stove on, it's not so hot in here. I heard your father tell Tommy to bring in some firewood, but that was quite some time ago. He must be still trying to get that sidewalk cleared."

Cook took a coat off the rack that stood by the back door and put it on. "Well, I have to have the proper heat in the oven if I'm going to make the biscuits right. I'll go get enough wood for the stove right now."

She was only gone a moment when she ran back to the kitchen door and shrieked, "Jessica! Jessica!"

Jessica and Caroline both came running out of the kitchen door onto the back porch. Jessica asked, "What is it Cook?"

Cook pointed to a body lying at the side of the house. "It's Tommy."

Jessica and Caroline rushed down the stairs and in the direction Cook was pointing. Jessica knelt down beside the body and held her cheek close to Tommy's face. She looked up. "He isn't breathing. I think he's gone. Cook, please go call Father."

At the cemetery, piles of snow had been shoveled and more snow was falling. William McCarthy, Jessica, Caroline, and Cook were standing graveside. Pastor Fox held his open Bible in one hand and raised the other hand toward heaven. He didn't actually read from the Bible, but recited from memory, *"For God so loved the world that He gave his only begotten Son, that whosoever believeth in him shall not perish, but have everlasting life."*

The minister then turned to face the others and quoted, *"Therefore, if any man be in Christ, he is a new creature: old things are passed away: behold, all things are become new. For we must all appear before the judgment seat of Christ: that everyone may receive the things done in his body, according to that he hath done, whether it be good or bad."* He added, "Brother Thomas made his confession of faith many years ago and lived a life showing that his confession was genuine. Therefore, we may say in confidence that he is absent from this body and present with the Lord. Amen."

Jessica and her father walked to the minister and shook his hand. McCarthy was speechless with grief. He and Tommy had known one another since they were boys. Jessica smiled weakly at the minister and said, "Thank you so much. It was a very comforting service."

"It's a sad day for all of us, Jessica. Tommy was a man with true humility."

"He was. We'll miss him terribly."

Once they were back in the kitchen of the McCarthy mansion, Jessica's father told them that he needed to talk to everyone. Jessica and Caroline sat at the table with him, and Cook poured coffee. When she finished, she sat at the other end.

Jessica's father looked thinner and gaunter than ever. His forehead was deeply creased as he began the speech he'd prepared. "I don't need to tell you how much we're all going to miss Tommy, not only for his friendship but for the work he did for us. I've talked to the Simpson boy, and he will see to it that the snow is shoveled and that we have proper firewood and the fires are tended. Tommy has only been gone a few days, and I've only now begun to realize how much he was doing around here. He was acting as groundskeeper, driving me back and forth to the office, tending the horses, and keeping the fireplaces going. I could go on and on. Some of the work, I never even noticed until he wasn't here to do it. Not to mention, he did all of that with him over sixty years old. There's no way I can afford to hire another man full time to take up the slack. To that end, I've decided to try to cut back on some more of the maintenance around here. I talked to Simon Thomas at the firm, and he's going to buy the horses and the carriage. It's not only too expensive for us to keep them up, it's too much labor. There's a lot more involved in caring for horses than throwing them some hay once in a while."

Jessica leaned toward him. "But how will you get to the office?"

"It's too far to walk. I'll take the trolley, like thousands of others do."

"Father, you never ride the trolley."

"Not for many years, but I'm no stranger to it, my dear. I'll be fine."

"Are things getting any better, Father?"

"I've had some minor investments bringing in larger returns than they were a year ago. These things take time, Jess. It's only that it seems to be taking longer now than it ever has before. Then again, this was a bigger fall from the top. The old bear of Wall Street really did a job on us last September. Sooner or later, it will even out. It always does."

Jessica leaned her head on his shoulder, "I pray so, Father, for all our sakes."

"There are hundreds of thousands praying the same thing."

They'd made it through a year without going hungry. Now, winter had returned and it snowed heavily. Jessica came down the stairs of her home dressed for the day, except for a pretty pair of red silk house slippers peeking out from under her dress as she descended. She was in an exceptionally good mood, and humming a tune. She stopped at the bottom of the stairs to re-arrange a bouquet of red and white flowers. She smiled at them, and said aloud, "The very first amaryllis from my very own garden."

A loud pounding startled her. She went quickly to the door and opened it. The young man her father had hired to help with the chores was standing there, out of breath.

Jessica was surprised to see him. She opened the door for him, but he didn't come in, simply stood there, trying to catch his breath.

"Edgar Simpson, whatever—," she began.

"It's your father, Mrs. Belk. He's taken sick. Miss Caroline said for you to come right away."

Jessica grabbed a wrap from a stand near the door and rushed out, slamming the door behind her. She ran the two blocks through the snow-covered walk. The Simpson boy, already winded, stopped trying to stay with her.

When she reached her father's house, Jessica ran up the front steps, flung open the door, and rushed in.

Breathing hard, she called loudly, "Caroline? Where are you?"

Caroline's voice came from upstairs, "We're up here, Jessica."

Jessica ran up the stairs and to her father's bedroom. He was lying on the bed, and Caroline was holding a damp cloth on his forehead.

Jessica gasped, "What happened?"

"He didn't come down to breakfast this morning. He mentioned last night that he wanted to get to the office early today, so I came in to wake him and found him like this. He's breathing regularly, but I can't wake him."

"Have you sent for Dr. Mercer?"

"I had the Simpson boy go there first, before he came to fetch you."

Jessica heard the front door open and close, and she ran back out to the landing and looked down. Edgar Simpson had come in.

"Is the doctor on his way, Edgar?"

"Yes, Ma'am. He said he'd be here first thing. It ought to be any minute now."

"You bring him right up here as soon as he arrives."

"Yes, Ma'am."

Jessica went back to the bedroom. She sat gently beside her father and took his hand in hers.

"Father, it's Jess. Please try to wake up."

There was no response. She leaned forward and whispered in his ear, "Daddy? Please, please wake up."

To Jessica, it seemed like an eternity, but it was only a few minutes later there came the sound of the doorknocker pounding. Jessica jumped up and ran back to the landing. She looked over the railing. Edgar had opened the door for the doctor. He stood there with his bag.

Jessica ran down the stairs and grabbed his arm. "Dr. Mercer! Thank God you've come. It's Father. We can't get him to wake up."

A tall, lean man with a permanent look of concern on his face, spectacles, and ring of white hair around his head, the doctor had been treating the McCarthy family for three decades. He'd delivered Jessica into the world and eased Amanda out of it. He was well past the age where he could run up a long flight of stairs.

Jessica ran ahead of him back to her father's bedroom. Dr. Mercer followed her up the stairs and Jessica came rushing back out of the room and ushered him in. Caroline stepped back next to the wall as he sat beside McCarthy and checked his pupils, listened to his heart, and so forth. Finally, he said, "His heart and lungs sound fine, but there are other signs that make me believe he's had a stroke."

Jessica wrung her hands. "What can we do for him?"

The doctor stood and looked at her with sympathy. "I'm afraid there's not much we can do. A few patients recover somewhat after a while. Until he comes to, there's no way of knowing how much damage has been done. It could go either way. Sometimes people wake up with only a slight impediment. Sometimes there's complete paralysis on one side, and--sometimes, they don't ever wake up. We'll simply have to wait and see if he comes out of it. It could be a matter of hours or even minutes, or it might be a matter of weeks. There's no way of knowing."

Jessica sank to her knees by the side of the bed and grasped her father's hand. The doctor packed his instruments back in his bag and snapped it shut. He patted Jessica on the shoulder, "If there's any change at all, please send for me at once. If I don't hear from you, I'll stop by in the morning."

Jessica nodded. He shook his head, and left the room. Without taking her eyes off McCarthy's face, Jessica said, "Caroline, would you please send Edgar to Zachary's office. Have him tell Zachary what happened, and that I'll be staying here until—until—I'll be staying here for a while. He can come by when he gets the message. Perhaps, by then, Father will have recovered."

Caroline was gone for a few minutes before she returned. She stood next to Jessica and smoothed the strands of hair that had come loose and fallen over her face. "Your feet are wet. We can't have you catching pneumonia. There are still some of your mother's things in the attic. I'll run up and see if I can fetch you some dry shoes."

The kneeling Jessica stuck one foot out from under the side of her skirt and looked down at it. Almost hysterical, she cried, "Oh, I've ruined mother's silk slippers. They'll never be the same. Look at what I've done. I'm terrible to be so thoughtless. Mother must have loved these slippers. Father said that she embroidered them herself."

She began sobbing. Caroline said, "Slip them off. I'll do what I can to save them, but you have to take care of yourself. You must pull yourself together for your father's sake. You'll do him no good at all if you get sick, too."

Jessica nodded her head, sniffled loudly, and calmed herself. "You're right. He's going to need me. I'll be fine. You go find me some dry shoes."

It was well after dark. Caroline sat in the corner of McCarthy's bedroom, knitting by the light of a kerosene lamp, and Jessica was sat by the bed, a closed book on her lap. She had her head resting on her crossed arms and was dozing when the sound of the front door opening woke her. They could hear someone running up the steps.

"That must be Zachary," Jessica said.

Edgar came into the room, pulling off his hat.

"Is Mr. Belk on his way here, Edgar?"

"No, Ma'am. He wasn't at the office. I gave the message to the secretary, and he said he would tell Mr. Belk as soon as he returned."

Jessica sighed. "Did he say where Mr. Belk had gone?

"No, Ma'am, he didn't."

"Thank you, Edgar."

"Yes, Ma'am."

Several hours later, Caroline had gone to the kitchen, and Jessica was still sat by her father's bedside. She heard the front door open and close, and footsteps on the stairs. Her husband came in the room. Jessica glanced at him out of the corner of her eye, but didn't greet him in any way. She was very calm.

"I came as soon as I heard," he said. "How is he?"

"The same. He hasn't so much as twitched since Caroline found him this morning."

"What did the doctor say?"

"He said he couldn't tell us very much. He thinks it was a stroke, and that Father may recover completely, or he may die."

"How long will it be until you know?"

"It could be any minute, it could be weeks."

"Are you coming home to prepare dinner? I haven't eaten yet."

She glared at him. "I'm sure Caroline and Cook will be happy to find you something to eat."

"I have no intention of eating in the kitchen with the help."

"Of course not. Ask Caroline to put a setting in the dining room for you."

"Do you intend to spend the night here?"

"Yes. I'll stay here until I know what's going to happen, one way or the other. The doctor said he'd come back to look at Father again in the morning."

"That's ridiculous. You said it could be months. He obviously doesn't even know you're here. You may as well be home and sleeping in your own bed. Who's going to take care of our house?"

She looked at him with her face twisted in such a venomous expression that he took a step back. "I'm sure the house can do without me for a day or two. It's too early to make decisions of any kind. Hopefully, father will wake up in the morning and be his old self. We'll see what Dr. Mercer has to say when he gets here."

Belk spun around and left the room without speaking. Jessica listened to see if he went out the front door, or if he went to the kitchen. When she didn't hear the door close, she assumed he'd gone to the kitchen to ask for a dinner.

His stomach must have gotten the better of him.

For a week, the doctor came early every morning and examined McCarthy again. Jessica and Caroline stood by, Caroline twisting one corner of her apron and Jessica wringing her hands and biting her lip.

The doctor put away his stethoscope. "I'm afraid there's been no change at all. I don't think you can realistically expect any recovery."

Jessica held back the tears as she walked downstairs with the doctor. "Dr. Mercer, I've been thinking about this a great deal. I'm sure you're aware of our financial situation. It's very expensive to run two households. It would be much easier for all of us if I moved him to my house, which is much smaller, and we closed this one down. Do you think it would do him any harm?"

The doctor scratched his chin and thought it over. "No, I don't think it would do him any harm at all. You can get an ambulance to take him there tomorrow. It would probably be easier for everyone involved if he were with you."

Jessica tried to manage a small smile of gratitude. "Thank you, Doctor."

That evening, Jessica was still sitting by the bed, a shawl around her shoulders, her hands clasped in her lap, her face etched with grief, when Zachary walked in the room.

He had a sour expression on his face and looked down at her in disgust. "There was no dinner again when I got home, so I thought I'd track you down. I see you're still here. Has there been any change?"

"No, and Dr. Mercer says there likely won't be any change either."

"It's been a week. This is ridiculous, you sitting here day in and day out. How much longer are you going to keep this up?"

"Until tomorrow. By the time you decide to come home from your office, I'll be home and dinner will be waiting for you."

"Now you've come to your senses. There's no reason Caroline can't care for your father until—as long as necessary."

"Oh, Caroline will be at our house, and so will Cook."

"Whatever are you talking about?"

"It may take a long time for Father to—to die. There's no point in trying to run two households, and it simply makes sense for us to close up the larger house and do everything from our place. We have plenty of room. There are two bedrooms in the servant's quarters. You should be quite satisfied with that. You can tell your friends that you have finally found a household staff. I'm sure they'll be suitably impressed."

"Have you talked to them? They're in agreement to this plan of yours?"

"I haven't spoken to Caroline and Cook yet. I intended to do it in the morning. I'm quite sure they'll agree."

Belk thought it over for a moment then nodded his head in agreement. "I find this to be a satisfactory solution."

"Yes, I thought you would."

"I must insist on one thing."

"What's that?"

"There will be no more of this liaison downward, no eating in the kitchen with the servants."

"Of course. Whenever you're home, which isn't often, after all, our meals will be served in the dining room. Where I choose to eat when you're gone will be none of your affair."

"Suit yourself."

The next morning, Jessica sat in her father's usual seat at the head of the kitchen table. Caroline sat to her right, and Cook next to her.

Jessica took a deep breath and began, "Dr. Mercer has given me permission to move Father to my house until—for the time being. It will cost us less upkeep, especially since it's already cold, and the cost of simply keeping the fireplaces going in a house this size is outrageous. I would appreciate it if you could see your way clear to come with me. I'm sorry to have to ask you both to move and to leave the home you've known for so long, but I'm going to need you more than ever."

Cook reached in the pocket of her apron and took out a letter. She held it up. "Uh, Jessica, I have something I'd like to show you. I wrote to my sister and told her how things were here. We may officially only be servants, but we know what's going on. I'm sure you're aware that in every house, downstairs knows what's going on upstairs."

"Yes, of course. The walls have ears, as they say."

Cook went on, "So, knowing the situation, I wrote to my sister Nora. She mentioned some time ago that she was retiring from service. Her own employer has had some hard times of his own and, like your father, was reluctant to let go of help that had been with him for so long. Nora and I have both accumulated a tidy sum over the years, thanks in large part to the generosity of your father and her Mr. Breckenridge, and we thought it might be a good time to buy a little place of our own and retire. To tell the truth, my back isn't in very good condition, and lifting pots and pans and standing on my feet all day is taking its toll on me. I know you have no trouble finding your way around a kitchen, and neither does Caroline. I'm sure the two of you can manage without me."

Jessica's mouth fell open. "Cook! You wouldn't be making this up simply to make me feel better about the situation?"

"No, dear, not at all. Here, read the letter for yourself."

Jessica took the paper, unfolded it, and began to read, "Dear Delia," She looked up from the letter. "Oh, my goodness. Here you've been all my life, and I realize I never heard your first name. You've always been, 'Cook.'"

She went back to the letter, "Dear Delia, I have spoken to Mrs. Breckenridge, and she seemed quite relieved that she will have one less servant on her payroll. I have my eye on a little house down in Soho that would be exactly what we need. Whenever you're ready to begin this next chapter of our lives, let me know. Yours, Agatha.' Well, Cook, or should I call you Delia? If you're still living in Manhattan, you can't be a stranger to us. You'll come to visit every now and then."

"Of course I will, as long as I'm able. It would make me very happy."

The three women all clasped hands and smiled, but the smiles were forced.

When Zachary finally came home that evening, the clock in Jessica's bedroom read that it was past midnight. Jessica sat in the big chair that looked out the window, a throw across her knees and a book lying open on her lap. He tossed his coat across the bed. "You're up late. I take it that your father and the servants have all moved in."

"Yes, they have, but only Caroline will be living in the house. Cook has decided to retire and move in with her sister."

"You're usually of the early-to-rise group. Were you waiting up for me?"

"Yes, I was. There was some estate business that I thought we should discuss, and I didn't want it to wait until tomorrow. I'd like to get an early start on carrying out my plans."

"Your plans? If you've already made your plans, why wait up to discuss them with me? Your father made it quite clear before we were married that none of what happens to his estate when he dies has anything to do with me."

"No, it doesn't. Think of it as a courtesy on my part. You are my husband, after all."

He sat on the bed facing her. "I'm waiting anxiously to hear what sort of scheme you have in mind now."

"Dr. Mercer says it's only a matter of a week or a few days now. Father is losing weight rapidly. I have no idea of the state of Father's holdings, so I'm going to his office tomorrow to see exactly where we stand. His secretary has been taking care of things since the stroke, but I can't wait any longer."

"The secretary! I should have seen to this as soon as your father became ill. Who knows what Downing has been up to all this time? He's probably cleaned out anything that was left."

"It's only been a week, and Joshua Downing has been at Father's firm for years. Father trusted him. I'm sure everything is in order."

"What do you think you can do while the old man— while your father is still alive? Won't you have to wait until the estate is settled?"

Jessica picked up a pack of papers from the table and held them out to him. He scanned them quickly.

Jessica explained. "These were in the bedside table in Father's room. I found them when I was packing the things I thought we might need here."

"These documents give you full power to do anything you want with his business or the house."

"Yes, and that brings us to my plan. Whatever situation I find at the firm tomorrow, I've decided to put father's house on the market right away. Even with no one living there, it will be a drain of my resources I can hardly afford."

Jessica now had her husband's full attention. "How much do you think you'll get for it?"

"I talked to an agent this afternoon. He seems confident that it will bring a hundred thousand."

"Only a hundred thousand? I would think it would bring more than that. It was built with all the finest materials. It has to be ten thousand feet of living space, and at least five acres of land right off the park."

"Under normal circumstances, I would ask for much more, but given the continued state of the economy, the sheer size of the house makes it affordable to very few people. The agent says that if he can't interest a private party, he thinks we may be able to sell it to the city for use as a museum or some such thing."

"If you do sell it, what do you plan to do with the money?"

"I have no reason to believe that I'll find good news at the firm tomorrow. After the agent has been paid, I expect that the remaining funds from the sale will support us for a very long time, possibly for the rest of our lives if we live conservatively, if you stop spending money as if there were no tomorrow, and if you stop gambling away every penny you make and start bringing some of it home for a change. We could eventually be quite wealthy if we wanted."

"How would you arrange that?"

"It isn't up to me, it's up to you."

"How so?"

"Father was never one to talk business at home but, even as a child, I picked up enough to know that the stock market is ninety percent perception and only ten percent work. You're quite handsome. I'm sure you're very aware of that. You're also quite charming when the spirit moves you. You have an excellent education, even if you didn't really apply yourself when you went to university. All of these things impress people looking to invest their money. You would make for a very successful broker if you would only put forth a continued effort."

She raised an eyebrow. "So, these are your options, live frugally, but comfortably, for the rest of our lives, or live very well by working hard and making yourself a success in your own right. Or you continue as you have been, in which case, you can pack your things and move out tonight. I'm sure your mother will be kind enough to take you back in. I know your parents are struggling to get by the same as we are, but I'm sure she would be too tender-hearted to turn her back on you.

He was stunned by her speech. He considered for a moment. "Let's say we continue our lives together for the time being. It isn't too late for us."

Jessica couldn't fight back a small spark of hope. She looked up at him. "I knew when we married that you didn't really love me, but I hoped that, over time, you would develop affection for me. Maybe it would be better if we had another chance, but you must change your habits. We will stay together, as you wish, but I won't change my mind. Father tolerated you for my sake, but I will not support a lazy profligate."

He grimaced. "You are too kind, my dear."

"Yes, I am."

The next morning, Caroline was in the kitchen stirring a pot of something at the stove. There were two places set at the table, with a small pitcher and a sugar bowl in the center. Jessica came in, dressed to go out. "Good morning, Caroline."

"Good morning, Jessica. How are you this morning?

"I'm fine. I've given Father his bath and changed his bedding. I told him I was going to the office today to take care of his business."

"I talk to him, too. We probably shouldn't tell anyone else that, though. They'd think we were potty."

"I asked about it. Dr. Mercer said that he didn't know if anyone with Father's condition could hear what was said to him or not, but that it certainly couldn't do any harm. Besides, it makes me feel better."

"Me too. I've cooked up some oatmeal for us."

"I'll wait until I get home to eat."

"You'll do no such thing. How can you expect to make business decisions on an empty stomach? This may not be ham and eggs, but it's good for you all the same. You know very well that Mr. McCarthy never left home without a good breakfast in his stomach, even after things went wrong."

Jessica sighed and sat at the table. Caroline spooned up a bowl of the oatmeal and placed it in front of her. Jessica put some brown sugar and milk on it and took a bite.

"M-m-m. This is so good. It warms the tummy right away. You're right about working on an empty stomach, and this could turn out to be a very long day. I hope the weather stays nice for a while. I wonder if it will snow. You could almost smell it in the air yesterday."

"It's that time of year."

"I can't believe Christmas is only a few days away. It's been the last thing on my mind. If I get finished at the firm early enough, I'll have to stop on the way home and find a gift for Mother Belk. She's such a dear."

"I'll cook up a nice fat hen for dinner."

"That sounds wonderful."

William McCarthy's secretary was at his desk when Jessica arrived. He jumped to his feet, "Good morning, Mrs. Belk. It's nice to see you again. What can I do for you today?"

"Good morning, Joshua. First off, I want to thank you for keeping things going while Father is ill. I haven't had an opportunity to speak with you, but it's time for us to have a frank discussion."

Downing swallowed hard. "Yes, Ma'am."

Jessica pointed to the inner room. "Let's go to Father's office."

She walked through the door to the inner office, and Downing followed her. She sat at her father's big desk and was slightly dwarfed by it.

"I've moved Father to my own home for the time being, but it looks as if it's only a matter of a few days before he slips away from me." She had to pause and clear her throat before she could continue. "I need to know everything about the condition of the firm so I can decide what to do with it."

"I'm afraid that there isn't any good news to be found. The assets never recovered from the crash. We're barely covering the expense of keeping up the office."

"Let's take a look at the books. I'm sure there are decisions to be made."

A few hours later, Jessica still sat in her father's chair, and Downing in front of her. Jessica sighed deeply, closed the ledger she had been reading, rested her chin on her palm, and looked up at him. "It's even worse than I feared. I don't know how or why Father kept this from me for so long."

Downing shrugged. "He's been eating into his personal savings to support the firm and his family ever since the crash. He was always optimistic about an eventual recovery. So am I. I'm confident things will turn around. I simply don't know how long it will take."

"I'm afraid I can't wait for any recovery. I'm putting Father's home on the market today, but there's no telling how long it will take to sell it. I'll have to liquidate all his holdings as soon as possible or I won't even be able to pay my account at the butcher's next month, much less maintain this office. Mr. Downing, do you have any prospects at all of other employment?"

"To tell the truth, your decision to close the office doesn't come as a surprise to me. I would never have left you in the lurch, but I have been making some discreet inquiries as to the future. I haven't received any offers yet, but if you would be so kind as to write me a reference, I would appreciate it."

"Of course. I'll also talk to some of Father's associates. I'm sure many of them are quite aware of the quality of your work."

"Thank you."

"Well, let's get about the business of closing down the firm it took my Father a lifetime to build, and may James Fisk and Jay Gold and the other greedy charlatans who caused this thing come to realize what they've done to the whole country."

"How soon do you think you'll be closing?"

"As soon as possible. We have to sell the assets that are left first. Of course, you will receive some sort of severance package once that's done. I'd like to get it taken care of before the end of the year."

"I'm so sorry to see all this happen."

"As am I, Mr. Downing. As am I."

Chapter 7

After two weeks, Jessica hadn't received a single offer on her father's house, and she was out of money. She was already being extended credit at the butcher's and the grocer's, but knew that would end soon if she couldn't make a payment. More than the bills, she had to find a way to feed four people. She sat at her dressing table, looking through her jewelry box. She took out a pearl necklace and looked at it sadly. She held it up against her cheek to feel the cool smoothness of the stones. *You ought to bring enough to feed us for a few weeks*. She wrapped the necklace in a cloth and put it in her purse.

Jessica stood on the street outside the pawn shop where she sold her gold chain. She paused again outside the door, then pushed it open and entered.

The pawnbroker looked up from behind the counter. Even with the recession, he didn't get a lot of upper class women in his shop, so he remembered her. "Good afternoon, Ma'am. Nice to see you again. What can I do for you?

"There are two things this afternoon."

She took the strand of pearls from her bag and unwrapped it. She spread the cloth on the glass counter and gently placed the pearls on it.

"How much would you be able to give me for these?"

The pawnbroker picked up the pearls and examined them closely. He ran his fingers over them, and looked up at her. "Well, there's not a big market for these nowadays."

"That's the same thing you said to me the last time I was in here."

He pursed his lips. "Maybe so, but it's just as much the truth now as it was then. I'll give you twenty dollars for them."

"Those pearls are perfectly matched and there's not a scratch on any one of them."

"Twenty dollars."

Jessica nodded. The pawnbroker looked under the counter, took out some bills and counted them out on the glass top. Jessica picked them up, folded them, and put them into her bag.

He brought out his ledger. "I'll need your name and address again."

"Mrs. Zachary Belk, 6233 Central Park West."

He wrote the information in his ledger, and then looked up at her. "You said there were two things today. What else can I do for you?"

"I need something for my mother-in-law for Christmas, maybe-oh-two or three dollars?"

He walked a short distance down to another counter and pointed to the contents. "How about a pretty pair of earrings? I have everything in here from fifty cents to a hundred dollars."

Jessica went to the case and peered inside. She gasped, "Those emeralds, where did you get them?"

"They've been here for a while. I can make you a very good deal on them, but they're more than two or three dollars."

"I asked, where did you get them?"

"As I said, they've been here for some time, so I can give you a break. I'll let you have them for fifty dollars. As I told you, there isn't a big market for fine jewels these days."

"They're stolen. They were my mother's." Her voice began to grow loud. "Where did you get them?"

The pawnbroker waggled a finger under her nose. "Listen, Ma'am. I don't deal in stolen goods. I keep very good records, and I have only the carriage trade for my clientele."

Jessica had to restrain herself from reaching across the counter and grabbing him by the front of his shirt. Instead she glared at him and almost yelled, "I-said-where-did-you-get-them?"

He took the earrings out of the case and looked at the tag, then flipped through his ledger. When he found the entry he wanted, he smirked and pointed it out with his finger, "They were brought in last December by a--" He paused, and looked at her pointedly, "Mr. Zachary Belk. He probably needed the cash to buy you something nice for Christmas."

Jessica couldn't speak for a moment. She swallowed hard. "I see. I'm sorry to be a problem. Thank you very much."

She turned to go, and he called after her as she rushed out of the shop, "What about that something nice for your mother-in-law for Christmas?"

When Jessica reached her home, she rushed to her bedroom and opened the jewelry box. Her mother had jewelry for the many parties and balls her parents had attended, but those days were over. Jessica seldom wore anything other than the small diamond studs her father had given her one Christmas. She spread a towel on the table and laid out the collection. She tried to remember each piece her mother had left her, but it had been so long, she wasn't sure.

The emeralds were tied to sentimental memories of Christmas, and were the ones that meant the most to her. Nothing else that stood out in her mind was missing, but she knew that didn't mean other pieces weren't gone. In a sudden panic, she thought about her father's things. After closing his house, she'd brought his small jewelry box home with her and put it in the bottom drawer of her chest. William McCarthy kept only a basic assortment, an expensive watch he wore on a heavy gold chain, a diamond stick pin, cuff links, and a gold ring.

Jessica cried when she found that the only items still in the box were the watch and chain. She took both boxes to the attic and locked them in one of the steamer trunks she'd taken on her honeymoon and then took the key and put it inside a shoe she seldom wore. It was a horrible mess, feeling that she had to hide things from her own husband. She cried for a while longer and then went downstairs.

Caroline was dusting the furniture. "I heard you come in. I—Jess, you've been crying. What's happened?"

"He's pawned my mother's emeralds and some of father's jewelry, too. I've hidden away the rest of it so he can't sell anything else that doesn't belong to him."

Caroline's eyes flashed angrily, and she pressed her lips together in a tight line. She didn't ask who Jessica meant.

There was no chance that Jessica would get any sleep that night. The clock on the table said two o'clock. Jessica sat at the little table by her bedroom window when she heard the front door slam downstairs and the sound of someone coming slowly up the steps. Belk was drunkenly half-singing, half-humming a tune. He came in the room and stopped abruptly when he saw Jessica.

His lip curled. "Well, I see the little woman is waiting up again. Were you so enchanted with your love for me that you couldn't retire until I was lying next to you?"

"Hardly. I wanted to talk to you."

"And what would you like to discuss so late at night, or should I say, so early in the morning?"

"We were running out of cash and I took a necklace of mine to a pawnshop to see what I could get for it."

"Did you, now?" He was suddenly more sober than a moment earlier. "Was it worth much?"

"He gave me twenty dollars for it. If I'm frugal, that will buy food for us for the rest of the month."

"So you thought you'd wait up for me to give me that good news?"

"No. I waited up to tell you that I've changed my mind."

"Changed your mind about what?"

"When we had our last discussion we talked about options. There was the first, where we stayed together and things improved, or the second, where you got out of my house. I've decided that you no longer have a choice in the matter. I want you to get out."

"I'm quite comfortable here. I have no intention of getting out."

"I said I wanted you out of here. While I was at the pawnbroker's I discovered that not only am I married to a lazy, good-for-nothing, adulterous, drunken gambler, I am also married to a thief. My mother's emerald earrings, which you stole from me, were at the shop. He told me you pawned them almost a year ago. When I was a little girl she would tell me that someday they'd be mine, and now you've gone and sold them without even asking me."

He sneered at her and said sarcastically, "How can you say I stole them? What about our wedding vows? Isn't everything I own yours, and everything you own mine? What about two souls joined as one and all that?"

"You have no right to be invoking our marriage vows. You tossed them away almost from the first day we were married. Legality is another matter. I know my rights. They belonged to me. You knew I would never have parted with those earrings."

"I am sick and tired of your superior attitude. May I remind you that my family has been at the top of New York society since the Revolution, and you are barely two generations removed from a plow? My grandfather was an ambassador. George Washington was a guest in our house. Your grandfather was a common farmer and your father scraped his way up the ladder one filthy rung at a time. I'm quite sure that's why you enjoy your gardening so much. The dirt feels right at home on your hands."

"Any dirt I get on my hands is considerably cleaner that what you have on yours. You're no better than a common thief, and neither is your father. I know all about his shady business dealings. Look what it's got him. He hasn't a penny left to his name."

He strode to her chair, grabbed her by the arm, and jerked her to her feet. His face was scarlet. "My father has dined with governors of states and princes of Europe. You aren't fit to speak his name, you low, common urchin."

She grimaced in pain and tried to pull free from him. He grabbed her other arm and shook her. "I'll teach you to show your betters a little respect."

He flung her on the bed, knocking the breath out of her, and started taking off his jacket.

Later, Belk lay on his stomach, snoring loudly. Jessica slid quietly away from him and pulled on her gown. The robe she wore the night before was on the floor, a large tear visible in the sleeve. She picked it up and put it on. She walked quietly to her bathroom and turned on the water in the tub. When she took off her robe and turned to face the mirror, she saw that both her arms had large bruises where he'd grabbed her. A tear ran down her cheek.

There was a knock on her bedroom door. Jessica turned off the water, pulled her robe back on, and went to the door, opening it only a crack. Caroline was standing there. "It's your father, Jess. He must have passed sometime during the night. It's finally over."

Jessica nodded. "I'll be right there." She went to her father's room. A small, decorated Christmas tree stood the table next to the bed. Caroline was straightening the covers, her face was wet with tears. Jessica patted Caroline on the back. "Would you please tell Edgar to fetch Dr. Mercer?"

Caroline nodded and left the room. Jessica sat by the bed and put her hand over her father's. "Goodbye, Daddy. Kiss Mommy for me."

She began crying quietly. She felt the dual emotions many people experience in her situation, grief and guilt. She loved her father more than any person on earth, and knew that she would never recover from his loss. At the same time, watching him waste away over the last few weeks had torn her apart. The relief she felt now that his suffering was over was the source of her guilt.

Later that afternoon, when the arrangements had been made and Jessica had time to think of personal things, she took all Belk's clothing and toiletries out of her room and moved them down the hall. When he came home she was in the kitchen with Caroline, but she was listening for him. As soon as she heard him open the door, she went to meet him.

"I've moved your things into the spare bedroom. I'll be locking my door from now on."

He pursed his lips and nodded. "As you wish, my Dear. It's a shame, though, that you never warmed to married life. You have no idea how much you've been missing all this time."

Jessica had no intention of discussing it further. She turned her back on him and went to the kitchen.

The gathering at the cemetery was impressive. Every member of the Mariner's church, all of McCarthy's business associates, neighbors, and friends had come to pay their respects. Jessica stood with Belk on her left and Caroline on her right. Belk's parents stood to his other side, their heads bowed. Pastor Fox was ending his message with a prayer. "We thank thee, Oh, God, for our brother's confession of faith in our Lord Jesus Christ and for our assurance that he now sits at thy right hand. In the name of Jesus, Amen."

There were murmured, "Amens," from the audience. As people left the gravesite, they began filing by Jessica to say goodbye. One of her father's business associates shook her hand and said, "He was a real friend, and this world is a poorer place without him, Jessica."

"Thank you, Mr. Argyle."

Another stopped as he walked by. "He was the most honest businessman I ever knew."

"Thank you, Mr. Hughes."

One of the women from her church hugged her. "I am so sorry, Jessica. I know how hard these last few weeks have been. It's really a mercy that at least it didn't happen on Christmas day."

"Yes. Thank you for coming."

Belk's mother and father were the last to leave. They walked up to Jessica and Belk. Harriet Belk kissed her son on the cheek, and then placed herself between him and Jessica, her back to Belk. He ignored them and began talking to his father.

Jessica hugged her mother-in-law. "Thank you for coming Mother Belk."

Mrs. Belk took Jessica's arm and steered her away from the men. "I'm so sorry, Jessica."

She leaned forward, hugged Jessica, and said softly, "Please come over and have tea as soon as you're up to it. There are things I need to discuss with you."

"I will."

Mrs. Belk's tone became more urgent. "Jessica, it's very important. I need to speak with you privately as soon as possible."

Jessica was puzzled by Mrs. Belk's apparent distress. Being in deep mourning, society wouldn't require Jessica to make social calls for a while, even to her in-laws, but something in her mother-in-law's voice was alarming. "I will. I'll come for tea tomorrow."

"Thank you. I'm sorry to have to press you at such a time, but it really can't wait. Four o'clock will be good."

Mrs. Belk went back to her husband's side, and Jessica went to thank the minister. "Thank you, Pastor Fox. It was a lovely service."

"I'll miss your father, Jessica. He lived his faith as much as any man I've ever known."

"Yes, he did. He often said that if he didn't believe he would someday see Mother again, he couldn't have survived after he lost her."

"When you think of them from now on, you can think of them together."

Tears sprang to Jessica's eyes. It was the most comforting thing anyone had said to her. She pressed her lips together and was unable to speak, but simply nodded her head. She turned to leave, and Belk, who had been standing to the side, took her elbow.

The next day, Jessica made good on her promise to visit her mother-in-law. She went up the steps to the Belk's house promptly at four. The Belk family had been wealthy for generations. The mansion was similar in elegance to the McCarthy estate, but beginning to look somewhat shabby. As Jessica approached the front door, she noticed peeling paint. She used the brass doorknocker, which was tarnished. The McCarthy home hadn't been kept in pristine condition since the crash, but it was obvious that the Belk home had been neglected for much longer. Mother Belk answered the door herself. She kissed Jessica on the cheek.

"Please come in out of the cold, Jess. I'm so glad you came."

Mrs. Belk led Jessica inside. "Have a seat, Jess. I have the tea almost ready. I'll get it."

"Let me help you."

"Oh, no. It's already brewed, and all I have to do is get the tray." She went to the kitchen. Jessica sat waiting on the sofa for several minutes, her hands folded in her lap. She noticed faded rectangles on the walls of the living room where there used to be paintings, and several pieces of furniture were gone, including the piano.

Mrs. Belk entered, carrying a tray with a teapot, cups, etc. She put the tray on the table, sat, and began pouring. "I'm sorry to keep you waiting, Jessica."

"I would have been happy to help you, Mother Belk."

"That's quite all right. It takes me a little longer than it would the maid, but I'm beginning to be quite proficient at taking care of things without help. Has Zachary told you that we had to let all our servants go?"

"No, he doesn't discuss that sort of thing with me."

Mrs. Belk poured a cup of tea and offered it to Jessica. Without looking up, she asked, "What sort of things does he discuss, Jess?"

Jessica looked at her a moment, took a sip of tea, and raised an eyebrow. "He enjoys telling me how inferior I am."

Mrs. Belk laughed and shook her head. "As if he had any room to talk. I've had the same treatment from his father for the last thirty-five years. They think that simply because their family is old society it gives them some sort of standing above the rest of us. My own father was much like yours, a self-made man. Of course, he never reached the level of success that Mr. McCarthy achieved, but he made enough money to make me attractive to my husband."

"That sounds familiar. Is that why he married you, for your father's money?"

"No, his family was doing very well at the time. I believe he was genuinely fond of me. I was quite attractive, if I do say so myself. He never took care of his inheritance, and it dwindled rapidly, but we never had any real money problems until '69. We'd been struggling for a few years, but the whole Black Friday thing pushed us over the edge, ruined us, you know, much as it did your father."

"It was terrible."

"I must admit, my husband wasn't an innocent bystander to the crash as your father and so many others were. He was among the most avid of the speculators that caused the stock market to collapse. We're quite penniless today. I'm serving my own tea, cleaning my own house, even doing my own laundry. My husband has lost every cent he had, and I will soon have gone through all the money my father left me trying to keep up this mausoleum of a house. My husband refuses to sell, even though our taxes have fallen behind so far they've sent us an eviction notice."

"Oh,no! I'm so sorry."

"This house has been in his family since the Revolution, and now we're going to lose it. He took out a mortgage on it when the market crashed and hasn't been able to make a payment since. I imagine the bank that holds the note will fight it out with the tax bureau for custody. It's a wonder they haven't sent us packing sooner, but these legalities take a great deal of time. Mr. Belk feels it would be beneath him to live in more affordable housing. What he intends to do when this is eventually sold out from under us, I don't know."

She took a sip of her tea. "Sometimes I fear he's losing his senses. My sister and her husband are well enough off that I would be welcome in their home, but not Thomas. They have a lovely home and, Stanley, her husband, is a respectable, hard-working man. Zachary's father alienated them years ago with his ideas of proper society. I'm afraid we've reached the end of the road. We've been living on credit for months, and our debtors are now reluctant to extend us more."

Jessica frowned. "I see. Is that why you wanted to talk to me, to ask for money?"

"Not at all. I'm aware that the situation in your own household is almost as dire as our own. No, I wanted to warn you."

"Warn me?"

"Yes. I'm sure you are aware that one of Zachary's favorite pastimes is gambling."

"I'm very much aware of that. He even stole some of my mother's jewelry to finance his habit."

Mrs. Belk closed her eyes and shuddered. "I'm so sorry, my dear."

"I found out when I took my pearls to the pawnbroker so I could buy groceries. I'd missed my mother's emerald earrings a while back and thought I had misplaced them. There they were in the pawnbroker's display case. The pawnbroker told me that Zachary brought them in."

"I'm so sorry, Jess. This is so humiliating. I didn't raise him to do such things, but I'm afraid he never was one to listen to anything I tried to teach him. The apple, as they say, did not fall far from his father's side of the tree."

"If you didn't want to ask me for money, what is it that you need to tell me?"

"Please understand. I love my son, disappointment though he may be. When you have children, you will know how it is. You love them no matter what. I'm very much concerned for his safety."

"His safety?"

"Yes. I'm not supposed to know this, but I overheard him asking his father for money, when, of course, there was none to be had. He's been losing money to people who have extended him credit, evidently a great deal of credit. They are the sort of people who don't take well to not being paid. Zachary sounded terrified."

"And you think they may actually kill him?"

"I don't think they'll go that far. There's no profit in murdering someone who owes you money, but they certainly wouldn't stop at doing him harm, possibly a great deal of harm."

"How much money does he owe them?"

"I'm not sure exactly how much it is, but I heard him tell his father that if he doesn't get his hands on five thousand in the next few days so he can make a payment on the balance, he'll be in big trouble."

"Five thousand dollars, and that's only a payment? It may as well be five million."

"Yes."

"Well, there's nothing I can do to help him."

"I know, my dear. I can't help but feel that he deserves whatever they decide to do to him, but that's not all. I am afraid that among the things I overheard was that they may also see fit to do you some sort of harm. He told his father that they had threatened you as well."

"Me? What good would it do for them to harm me?"

"Only that there may be some sort of inheritance for Zachary if you died, and if not, it would serve as a motivation to Zachary and others like him to pay their debts on time."

"I see. I don't know what I can do about it. I simply don't have any money to pay them."

"I know you closed your father's office and sold what assets were left. You weren't able to realize anything out of his holdings?"

"Hardly. I made almost enough to pay off father's debts, but there wasn't any left to handle my own. I'm afraid the only thing left from the whole estate is the house. If we don't get an offer on it in the next few days, I won't have enough money to pay the taxes that come due next month."

"I don't know what to tell you, Jess. I felt I had to warn you. Be careful when you're out."

"I will, Mother Belk. Let's hope I can sell father's house soon. It would make the difference."

Jessica put down her cup and saucer, rose, and picked up her bag. Mrs. Belk walked her to the door. "I'm sorry that this couldn't have been a happier visit, dear. These days, the only brightness in my life is when I have time with you."

"I know exactly what you mean. I gave up my church work while I was taking care of Father, and I've given up having lunch with my friends because it's too expensive to go to a restaurant and, if they have me to their homes, I can't afford to reciprocate. You and Caroline are the only real contact I have with other women. Tell you what, I'll stop by for tea tomorrow and we won't discuss anything sad, even if all we have to talk about is the weather."

"That sounds lovely. I'll look forward to it."

They kissed one another's cheeks and Jessica left. As she went down the steps, Jessica looked nervously from right to left. It was barely a quarter mile from her home to theirs. Before things went so terribly wrong, Jessica would have had her father's carriage drive her to the Belk estate and return to take her home. There was no money for carriages now. She walked the distance as quickly as she could without drawing attention to herself. She noticed every man on both sides of the sidewalk, and looked for a sign of a firearm tucked under his coat. When she reached her own front door, she ran up the steps, darted inside quickly, and bolted it shut after her. Her legs went weak, and she sank to her knees, sobbing aloud, "Oh, Zachary what have you done to us?"

Caroline came out of the kitchen, "Jessica, what on earth?" Caroline rushed to her and lifted her to her feet.

Caroline wrapped her arms around Jessica and patted her on the back. "Now, now, Baby. What is it?"

"Oh, Caroline,--" Jessica started, and the whole story came tumbling out. By the time she'd finished telling Caroline the mess Zachary made, Caroline's face was twisted with rage. "If they don't kill him, I may do it myself."

Chapter 8

Jessica walked through the living room toward the staircase, carrying a stack of folded linens. Her foot was on the bottom step when there came a knock at the door. She put the linens next to her handbag on the small table in the foyer and opened the door. A young man stood there. When he saw her, he jerked his cap off of his head and held it in front of him.

"Yes?" Jessica said.

"Mrs. Belk?

"Yes?"

"I have a message for you from your estate agent." He held out an envelope.

Jessica took it. "Thank you. Just a moment please."

She went to her bag, returned to the door, and handed him a coin.

"Thank you, Ma'am," he said, slapping his cap back on his head.

She closed the door and nervously ripped open the envelope. She scanned the letter inside, clasped it to her breast, took a deep breath, and looked upward. "Thank you, Lord." For the next hour, she prayed and thought over carefully what she should do with her future. Before it was time to set the table for dinner, she'd made up her mind.

That evening, Jessica and Caroline were having dinner at the big table in the kitchen. They heard the sound of the front door opening and closing, and Belk calling out, "Jessica?"

Jessica rolled her eyes and gave Caroline a disgusted look. "Excuse me, Caroline. It sounds as if I'm being summoned by Mr. Belk."

Caroline nodded. Jessica went to the living room where Belk was standing by the front door. He had Jessica's gloves in his hand and held them out to her. "I understand you were at my parents' home today. You forgot these."

She took them from him. "Thank you."

He huffed out a breath, as if he could smell something unpleasant. "My mother, who evidently has taken to listening to private conversations from the other side of doors, tells me that she has informed you of my situation."

"Yes. Pitiful, isn't it?"

"She also tells me that you haven't come up with any sort of a solution."

"What sort of solution could I possibly have? There wasn't any money left over from the settlement of Father's business. There were no cash assets from the estate, and it certainly isn't as though I could dig into a nest egg I had accumulated from money you brought home during our two years of marriage."

Belk's shoulders sagged. "Of course. I had somehow hoped you would have an idea that might get me out of this."

"I do."

"You do? But I thought you said--"

Jessica went to her bag and took out the letter from her agent. She handed it to Belk. He read it quickly and brightened right up. "This is wonderful news. An offer on the house! How much will we get from the sale?"

"I have no idea how much *I'll* get from the sale. I talked to my attorney. According to New York law, any property I brought into the marriage or anything I inherit is mine exclusively. It is my house, you see. The message didn't get here until it was too late for me to see the agent today. I'm going to his office first thing in the morning."

"You don't have to remind me that it's your house. Whether you said it aloud or not, I've been reminded of that every day of our lives together, and your father made it quite clear to me on the day I asked for your hand."

He took her hands in his and began talking in a coaxing tone of voice. "My mother gave me a proper dressing-down today, and she's right. I don't deserve you. I'm sorry I haven't been a good husband, Jessica. I want to do better by you. I'm hoping we can make a new start."

"A new start? Are you sure that your contrition isn't motivated by the prospect of fresh cash?"

"I'm going to try to make amends, starting now. I'll stay home from work tomorrow, and go to the agent's office with you."

"Stay home from work? That's amusing. How long has it been since you even made any attempt at work? You go tomorrow wherever you usually go, and do whatever it is that you usually do during the day, but for goodness sake, try to stay away from the games. I'll take care of this, the same way I've taken care of any business that had to be done since the day we married."

Belk's face tightened and he stepped away from her. "Suit yourself. I'm sure you can handle it."

"I'm accustomed to handling things."

"You know, my dear, some husbands would cuff you soundly for being so impertinent."

"Some husbands wouldn't have gotten themselves into this sort of trouble. Some husbands really work during the day, and some husbands would support their families."

"But I don't have a family, do I? After two years there are no children and no prospects of any. All I have is a skinny, spiteful wife, and a rude servant who somehow thinks it's proper to act as if she were my mother-in-law."

"Try to remember that your skinny wife has fed and housed you from the day we were married, while you squandered every penny you got your hands on and even stole my mother's and father's jewelry to feed your gambling habit, and that our rude servant has been working without wages for over a year."

Belk bowed cavalierly. "I am duly chastised, but hopeful of a brighter future. Things are looking up."

"We'll see."

With the relentless burden of paying her bills weighing on her, Jessica couldn't help but feel excited as she sat in front of the agent's desk. The stress seemed to lift as she signed her name on the papers he placed in front of her. For the first time in months, she would be out from under the constant pressure to find enough money to feed her family.

The agent took the papers from her one at a time as she added her signature. He clicked his tongue as she handed him the last one. "I know it isn't what we would have liked to get for the house, Mrs. Belk, but I'm sure you know how it is. In a market like this, people are very much aware of a buyer's advantage."

"Yes. I appreciate that. There's nothing I can do. I have to accept the offer."

"Actually, we're getting more than I expected. If I hadn't offered the house for several thousand more than I thought it would bring, we would probably have been offered even less."

"I know. It's only that, if I built it today, it would cost twice as much as it's selling for. My mother loved it so, and my father was so proud of it. I remember when I was very small, and Mother would entertain. As all children do, I would sneak out of bed and watch from the landing. The finest people in New York were guests in our home. The ladies were so beautiful in their gowns, and the men so handsome in their tuxedoes." She sighed, "Oh, well. No use being sentimental. Business is business."

"Correct. Business is business."

"How soon can we expect to settle on the agreement?"

"There's the mountain of paperwork to be filled out and filed. I'd say about a month to six weeks."

"I'd hoped it would be sooner than that."

He shrugged. "I'm sorry, but these things have to go through the usual procedures."

When Jessica returned home, she went directly to her bedroom. She no longer left her jewelry box sitting on her dressing table. She took the key to the attic, unlocked the trunk, and took out her jewelry box.

She sat on a piece of luggage and began going through the few items still in it. It was almost empty. What was left didn't appear valuable. She looked at her father's gold watch and the heavy chain. She lifted it out and held it in front of her. She remembered sitting on his lap when she was little, taking it out of his vest pocket and holding it up to her ear to hear the ticking. She looked at it sadly for a moment before she unhooked the chain. She placed the watch back in the box, coiled the heavy chain in the palm of one hand, and made a weighing motion. "Well, Father," she said aloud, "I believe that I would let us all starve before I would part with your watch, but I think the chain will feed us for the next six weeks."

She went downstairs and slipped the chain in her handbag. As she turned toward the door, Zachary came in.

Her face tightened with resentment. "You're home early today."

"What did he say? How much was the offer?"

"Ninety thousand."

"Ninety? I thought you said it would bring a hundred thousand?"

"Well, the only offer I have received is ninety thousand."

"I knew I should have gone with you. They always take advantage of a woman. They know you don't have the backbone to drive a good bargain."

"What would you have done, try to drive up the price and risk losing the whole deal? I'm not in a position to haggle, thanks largely to you."

"How long will it be before we get the money?"

"It will take four to six weeks to complete the paperwork."

"Four to six weeks? I can't wait that long! You can't wait that long."

"Well, that's how long it takes. Tell your hooligans that the house is sold, and they'll have their five thousand dollars in all good time."

Belk ran his hands through his perfectly groomed auburn hair and mussed it. "You don't understand. The five thousand was only a payment. They're going to want the whole sum."

"My Lord, Zachary, how much do you owe these people?"

Belk sank on the bed, dropped his head in his hands, and mumbled. "Twenty-five thousand."

Jessica gasped. "Twenty-five thousand? That's a fortune. Are you insane? Some men work very hard all year for less than a thousand dollars, and you're telling me that you've gambled away twenty-five thousand?"

"You don't know how it is. I never intended for this to happen. For years, I won as much or more than I lost. It's fantastic when you win, and it makes you feel—I don't know—euphoric, so you bet more the next time, and the time after that, and then, when you lose, you're betting even more, trying to win back what you lost in the first place. The amounts stop being real to you after a while. You always think you're going to win that one big hand that will make you break even. I was always lucky until I married you. I could even say that this is all your fault."

Jessica couldn't hide the disgust on her face. It wasn't the first time she had to resist the impulse to slap him. The only thing that held her back was the fear he would return the slap. "My fault? I can't believe you would say such a thing, even in jest, and it's obvious to me that you aren't jesting. If it weren't for how much it would grieve your mother, who for some reason still loves you, I'd leave town when I get the money for father's house and let them go ahead and kill you."

She knew she had the upper hand. "I can't stand to look at you, Zachary Belk. Go talk to these hooligans of yours, and see if you can put them off a while longer. I have to think this over."

He rubbed his hand over his face, started to say something, changed his mind, and left the room. Jessica didn't move until she heard the front door close downstairs. She had some serious things to consider.

It was after ten o'clock, the evening before she would sign the final papers to sell her father's home. Jessica hadn't gone to bed, but sat in her living room, still wearing her daytime dress. She was leaning back in the big easy chair beside the fireplace, deep in thought when Belk came in the front door. He came to where she sat and took the chair next to her. He looked at her warily. "Haven't gone to bed yet? You're up late."

"Yes, but then again, you're home earlier than usual, and this time you aren't reeking of some tart's perfume. I've been thinking all afternoon. Thinking about what I want for my life, and I thought you might like to hear my decision, so I waited up for you."

"You usually post your vigil in the bedroom."

"After what you did the last time, I thought it better to have our talk down here. Caroline is still in the kitchen."

He sneered. "I suppose you think she will protect you?"

"If I asked her to, she'd kill you in a minute."

"I'm sure she would, if she were capable of it. Perhaps I'll begin locking my bedroom door."

"That won't be necessary."

"Don't tell me that you've warmed to my embrace and decided to let me back into your room?"

"You have to admit, I was never cold to you, not until you forced me against my will."

"Yes, you always did your duty. So, what are you thinking? I'm sure you didn't sit there in front of the fireplace all evening waiting to discuss our intimacies."

"No, I didn't, not at all. I've come to a decision about the future. I'm signing the final papers on Father's house tomorrow. I'm to be there at ten o'clock in the morning, and the agent said it would take about an hour to go over all the papers. I want you to meet me at my attorney's office at eleven-thirty. You know where it is. I'm going to give you twenty-five thousand dollars, not one penny more. In exchange for that amount, you will get every last thing you own out of this house before I have to leave in the morning, and you will disappear from my life. I've already talked to an attorney, and it will be possible for me to get a divorce."

"Divorce? You would have to charge me with adultery."

"I'm sure you're guilty of it. You've been coming home stinking of someone else's perfume almost daily since the day we were married. You aren't claiming innocence, are you?"

"Whatever you say, as long as I get the money."

"The attorney has prepared the divorce papers already, and all I need is your consent so he can expedite the matter. You sign the papers, and I'll give you the check. I want you and your things out of my house. It will come as no surprise to your mother when you turn up at her doorstep."

"It wouldn't be a surprise, but I can hardly go home to Mother, since she isn't there."

"Isn't there?"

"No. Mother has gone to live with her sister. We've been evicted. The bank foreclosed on the house, and it's all shuttered and locked up."

"Where on earth is your father?"

"He's been sleeping on the sofa at his office, and it's only a matter of time before they kick us out of there as well. He hasn't paid the rent for months. What he does when they put him out is anyone's guess."

"I'm sorry, especially for your mother. She's a wonderful woman, and she deserved better, but then, so did I. Perhaps one of your so-called friends will take you in until you can find a job and get a suitable flat somewhere, or maybe you can make a pallet on the floor of your father's office. I really don't care."

He sighed deeply. "It may not be as dire as all that. The mortgage on our home did not include the furnishings, most of which are still inside the house. I may be able to get the bank to release them to me. If I can sell them, we should be able to get enough to live on for a while. Father's been selling off the art work and the better pieces of furniture to pay the bills for quite some time, but what's left should take care of me and my father for months. Our home was furnished with the best of everything."

"I hope your mother took the best of it with her when she left."

"You're too kind, my dear."

"That's right. I'm kinder than you deserve."

He managed a regretful look. "I think we had both better retire for the night. We have to be up early tomorrow."

The next morning, Jessica watched as Zachary carried his clothes out of the house without speaking. She didn't ask him where he was going, and he didn't offer to tell her. As he carried out the last piece of luggage, he turned in the doorway and gave her a little salute. "I hope we'll meet again under more favorable circumstances, my Dear."

"Leave your key. Once you've signed the divorce papers, I hope I never lay eyes on you again as long as I live."

Belk took the front door key out of his vest pocket and laid it on the table. He hung his head, went out, and closed the door. As soon as he was gone, Jessica ran up the steps to the bedroom he'd slept in to make sure he hadn't left anything behind. She breathed a sigh of relief. He was gone out of her house and, in a few hours he would be out of her life.

Chapter 9

Jessica arrived at the estate agent's office promptly. A stack of papers sat on the desk in front of her. She signed the last one and pushed it across the desk toward the agent. He handed her a check, and she read the amount printed on it out loud, "Eighty two thousand three hundred and forty dollars."

"I wish it were more Mrs. Belk, but of course, the back taxes had to be paid before the sale could be completed, and there's my commission and the costs of the paperwork."

"I understand. Thank you very much, Mr. Perkins."

"Not that it's any of my business, but do you have an investment plan?"

Jessica laughed. She folded the check and put it in a large manila envelope that fastened with a string. She pushed back her chair and stood. "I do indeed. I'm going pay off all of my debts, and give my husband twenty-five thousand dollars to get out of my life and never come back. Oh, and one more thing. If it isn't too late, I'm going to buy myself a pair of emerald earrings. Whatever is left will be deposited in the bank. I have an idea of how to make a small income and, combined with what's left of this, I should be able to keep my head above water financially for a very long time. That's a good plan, isn't it?"

He smiled at her. "It certainly is. I hope you enjoy yourself."

She grinned back at him, "I'm sure I will, especially the part where I divest myself of my husband."

She left the agent's office and headed for the second part of her day's business. Once her funds were deposited at her bank, she headed for her attorney's office. Belk waited for her outside. He took out his watch, looked at it, and put it back in his vest pocket. His face broke out in a wide smile when Jessica arrived carrying the manila envelope.

"Good afternoon, dear. You're right on time."

"Yes, aren't I always? My attorney is waiting for us. Let's get this settled, shall we?"

Belk tipped his hat and made a big show of opening the door to the building and letting Jessica go in first. He looked very happy.

The attorney's secretary showed them to his office and announced them. "Mr. and Mrs. Belk, sir."

The attorney stood to greet them. "Thank you, Arthur. Good morning, Mrs. Belk, Mr. Belk. Please come in and sit down. This will only take a few minutes."

Jessica took a seat but, instead of sitting, Belk stood behind her chair. The attorney looked irritated by this, but didn't comment. He opened a folder that had been sitting on his desk, took out some papers, and handed them toward Belk. "These are the preliminary filings. All I need is your signature on the bottom line of each one."

Belk picked them up and looked at them. "Give me a moment to read them, please. One of the things my father taught me was never to sign something I hadn't read."

Jessica said, "It's too bad he didn't include teaching you not to write promissory notes to thugs."

The attorney assured him, "It's quite uncomplicated. You agree that you do not contest the divorce, and that you will make no further claim on any properties held by Mrs. Belk."

Belk took the pen out of the ink stand, signed several papers angrily, and then shoved the pen back in the holder. "There. Where's my money?"

Jessica took a check out of her envelope and handed it to him. He looked it over, folded it, put it in his pocket, and tipped his hat, "I wish I could say it's been a pleasure, but I can't."

He wheeled around and stomped out. Jessica looked at her attorney and smiled broadly. "Thank you very much, Mr. Entwhistle."

He frowned. "It will take a year before the divorce is final, Mrs. Belk. You will not be free to remarry until then."

Jessica couldn't suppress a hoot. "Remarry? You have no idea how amusing that is."

Jessica made several stops on her way home. The first one was the pawnbroker. When she put her hand on the door to push it open she said a prayer that the emeralds hadn't sold and, there they were, in the case where she'd seen them before. It seemed to her they'd been waiting for her.

She stopped at a variety store and bought some tortoise-shell combs for Caroline and then went to the shop where they made the kind of signs you hang in a window. After that, she stopped at Edgar's house and asked if he could come with her to carry some packages. Always ready to earn a dime or so, he was happy to accompany her to the butcher's and the grocer's. After paying them what she owed, she bought more food and paid for it in cash.

Caroline was in the kitchen when Jessica and Edgar came in carrying grocery bags. They piled them on the table, and Jessica grabbed Caroline in a hug. "We're celebrating, Caroline. The bills and the taxes are all paid and, even better than that, Mr. Zachary Belk will be out of my life forever. I bought us a nice piece of beef to roast and some fancy trimmings for a party. The rest of the money is safely in the bank."

Caroline grinned at her. "Thank God. It's so good to see you with a smile on your face. It's been a long, long time."

"Yes, it has. Too long, but I intend to smile a lot in the future."

Caroline couldn't let go of her worry so quickly. "Jess, will we have enough money to last very long?"

"Not forever, if I don't do something else, but I also purchased this."

She reached in one of the bags and pulled out a sign. She held it up by the two little chains attached to the top. It read, "Piano Lessons."

Jessica swung it back and forth. "I intend to hang this in the front window. I already talked to two of my friends who have told me for a long time that they wish I would teach their children to play piano, and I will begin with them as soon as possible. I would have already started teaching them long ago but, of course, Mr. Belk felt it was beneath us, even when we were completely broke. If we live carefully, and I can get a dozen or so students, we should be able to have some financial breathing room. At least this house is paid for, and Father bought this particular home because of the big lot. I can always sell the other half if it becomes necessary."

Caroline began unpacking the groceries. "You've had quite a day. You must be exhausted. Why don't you go upstairs and rest a while? I'll get the roast in the oven."

Jessica kissed her on the cheek. "That sounds like a fine idea. I didn't realize it until now, but I am a little tired."

"You go ahead. I can manage. I'll call you when it's ready."

Jessica smiled at Edgar. "Would you like to stay for dinner?"

He grinned from ear to ear. "Yes, Ma'am. I sure would. It's been a long time since we had roast beef at our house."

"Run and tell your mother where you'll be. Caroline, let's make it a real party. Put on your best dress, and call me early enough for me to get dressed up a little. I want you to use Mother's bone china and stemware and the good silver. Set three places in the dining room. We're not going to eat in the kitchen tonight."

"In the dining room? What about Mr. Belk?"

"He won't be here for dinner, not ever again. He moved out all his things before I left this morning, and he won't be back. He may be hungry tonight, though I don't expect he'll come here for dinner. If he did, I wouldn't turn him away. It wouldn't be the Christian thing to do. Not that anyone would ever be unaware enough to mistake him for an angel. If he shows up, make him a plate and he can eat in the kitchen."

As a grinning Caroline pulled the roast out of a bag and began un-wrapping it, Jessica waltzed out of the room.

By the time she'd reached the top of the stairs, she realized she really was completely exhausted. She took off her dress, put on a robe, and lay down. She'd hardly put her head on the pillow before she fell into a deep sleep with a pleasant dream, the first she had enjoyed in a very long time.

Awake and much refreshed, Jessica came down the stairs a few hours later wearing the green velvet gown and her mother's earrings. She stopped at the bottom of the stairs and twirled around. Caroline beamed at her. "Oh, Jess. You look lovely."

The big table in the dining room was set for three with a lace tablecloth and the fine china. Edgar, wearing his church clothes, came in from the kitchen carrying a dish which he set on the table next to the other bowls of vegetables. Caroline wore a nice dress that was fairly new. She lit some candles.

Jessica said, "It's been too long since I had an occasion to get dressed up. Oh, I'm so happy you found some candles. I can't remember the last time we had candles. I'm so tired of the kerosene lamps. I even miss the gaslight, but we simply didn't have money to pay the bill anymore."

"I'm afraid the candles are quite old. I hope they aren't too dried out. I've been hiding them in the back of the pantry. I was sure we would be celebrating something someday. Everything's on the table except the roast. You sit down, and I'll go get it so it can make a grand entrance."

Caroline went to the kitchen and, for the first time in her life, Jessica sat at the head of the table in the dining room. She reflected that she was taking over the role of head of the house one room at a time, first at the kitchen table, then when she locked Zachary out of her bedroom, and now in the dining room. It was an excellent feeling. She waved a hand at the chair to her left, "Have a seat, Edgar."

Edgar was more than happy to follow her instructions. "Yes, Ma'am."

He took the seat at Jessica's left side. Caroline reappeared carrying a silver tray with a beautifully browned roast. She placed it in front of Jessica. "I think it's perfect and all ready to be carved. Would you like to do the honors?"

Jessica looked at the roast and inhaled deeply. "Oh, this smells delightful. I can hardly wait."

She stood and picked up the carving instruments. "This will be the first time I ever carved a real roast, but I think I remember how Father used to do it. I hope it's nice and pink in the middle. What do you think, about a half inch thick?"

She made one cut through the meat, neat and clean. The slice of beef rolled away and the pink inner side was exposed. Jessica looked at it for a moment, swayed, and dropped the carving set onto the table. She wheeled around and vomited into a large potted plant sitting by the wall.

Chapter 10

Jessica lay on the sofa, still dressed in her green velvet gown. Caroline came in, carrying a glass of water and a saucer with some crackers. She put the saucer on the table and held out the glass to Jessica. "Sip some of this water, Jess."

Jessica sat up and took a few small sips. She swallowed, blinked several times, and took another drink of the water. "Good heavens. I don't know what came over me. I feel fine now."

"You were in such a hurry to get to the estate agent's office this morning that you barely ate any breakfast. Did you stop anywhere for lunch?"

"No, I had so many things I wanted to do-- settle the sale of the house, pay off Zachary, buy back Mother's earrings, pay my bills, and shop for dinner. I was running around all day. I wasn't even hungry until I came downstairs for dinner and then when I cut the roast my stomach just flipped upside down on me."

Caroline sat on the side of the sofa and put her palm on Jessica's forehead. "You don't have a fever. Jess, when was the last time you had your monthlies?"

"My monthlies?" She thought for a moment, frowning. "I guess it was before we got the offer on Father's house." Jessica looked puzzled at first, and then her face lit up with joy. Delighted, she grabbed Caroline's hand. "Do you think I'm--" She didn't even get the words out before her elated expression turned to one of horror.

"Oh, Caroline! I'll have no husband to help me, and I have no idea how much it costs for all of this. I can't possibly make enough money teaching piano to get me through a delivery and the lying-in time. What am I going to do?"

Caroline patted her hand. "Pray and think."

"Pray, of course, and think?"

"That's right. You can't do anything tonight, so take a day or two and pray and think about the problems and the answers. I'll pray and think about it, too. We'll come up with something, Jess. You have quite a bit of money left over from selling your father's house. We can live off of that for a long time, and by the time that's gone, God will have given us a solution."

"I counted on earning enough from piano lessons to make the money from the sale of father's house last for years. That isn't going to happen now."

Caroline picked up the saucer with the crackers and put it in front of Jessica. "One of the advantages of teaching piano is that you don't have to leave the house. You can teach right up until the baby comes. You got sick tonight because you went so long without eating and your stomach was full of acid. From now on, I want you to eat some crackers and sip on a glass of water every hour or so. It will keep your stomach from turning sour."

"How do you know these things?"

Caroline chuckled. "I've lived a long time and kept my ears open. I know all sorts of things. Some of them might surprise you. Now, I put the roast and the other food back in the oven to keep it warm. Edgar is still waiting in the kitchen, and I know that he would be very happy if you were to decide you felt like eating. He's been looking forward to that roast beef for a while now."

"I do feel better. I'll come and sit with you, but I don't know if I'll be able to eat anything."

"We'll see."

"What did you do with the palm tree?"

"Edgar and I rolled the pot out on the back porch. He can clean it up tomorrow."

"That doesn't seem fair, for him to have to clean up my mess."

"Let's think about that later. Right now, that roast is drying out. Come on in the dining room."

"I think I'll take off this dress first. If I do get sick again, I wouldn't want to get anything on it and ruin it."

After dinner, Jessica and Caroline came in the kitchen carrying the dishes from the dining room. Jessica shook her head. "I can't believe how much I ate. A little while ago that roast beef made my stomach turn completely inside out, but now I've eaten enough for three grown men."

Caroline chuckled. "You know what they say, you're eating for two, even if one of them is a teeny little thing."

An expression of wonder came to Jessica's face. "Two? I'm eating for two?"

She spread out her fingers and gently put her hand on her stomach. She looked down at it, awestruck. "Just imagine it, Caroline. I have another life growing here right inside me. I prayed for this every day from my wedding day, and even before that, and now it's finally happened.

Do you think it will be a little girl? I'd like so much for it to be a little girl."

"We'll see about that in around—oh—seven months. That will be September or so. You can spend that time thinking about names."

"Oh, I don't have to do that. I decided about names a long time ago. I promised Father the day I told him I was going to marry. I think it was the one thing that made him put aside his objections. If it's a boy, I'll name him William for Father, and if it's a girl, Amanda, for Mother."

"I like that. I like it very much."

Jessica grabbed Caroline in a hug. "A baby. I'm finally going to have a baby.

Chapter 11

The trees that showed through the windows were fully leaved, and a bouquet of summer flowers sat in a vase on each table. On the piano bench, a ten-year-old girl went through her lesson. When Jessica stood, her pregnancy was slightly showing. Everything about her had changed. Her hair was still pinned up, but she now wore it looser, with little curls framing her face, and she'd gained some weight, filling out the hollows in her cheeks. It became her. A typically radiant expectant mother, she was about five months along.

Jessica smiled at her pupil. "That's just fine, Pricilla. I want you to practice that piece for a half-hour every day, and start with your scales. I'm so proud of you, you're doing very well."

"Mommy says I'm very talented."

"Your Mommy is right."

There was a knock on the door. "That must be your mother, and she's right on time."

Jessica went to open the door. Pricilla's mother stood there. "Come right in, Martha. We were just finishing up."

"How did she do today?"

"She's doing wonderfully. She has a real gift for music."

Martha beamed, "I know. I think she gets that from me."

"Really? You never told me that you played."

"Oh, I don't play the piano. I studied violin when I was a girl. I was very good at it, too. I don't know why I didn't keep it up, but you know how these things are, you get married and you have a family and your husband and your children simply eat up all of your time." Martha clapped her hand over her mouth. "Oh, Jessica. I'm sorry. I didn't mean--"

"Don't give it a thought. I have never in my life been happier than I am right now. If my husband had been more like your Alfred, he'd still be around."

Martha leaned closer to Jessica and whispered in her ear, "Does Zachary know about the baby?"

"If he does, he didn't learn it from me. I haven't heard one word from him since he left, and that's fine as far as I'm concerned. I wouldn't care if I never saw him again."

"I haven't seen him at any of the social events all spring. It's as if he's dropped out of society altogether."

"I would hope he's too busy working to attend a party."

"I think you must be the bravest woman on earth. I would be terrified if I had to do what you're doing all by myself."

Jessica shrugged. "There were a lot of women who lost their husbands during the war exactly the way Caroline did, and they managed to get by alone. I can handle it. God is taking care of us, God and Mother's piano."

"I'm glad to hear you sounding so positive."

There was another knock on the door. Jessica told Martha, "That must be Thomas Mercer, Dr. Mercer's grandson. It's time for his lesson."

Jessica opened the door and a boy stood there with his books in his hands and a resentful look on his face.

Martha beckoned to her daughter. "Come along, Pricilla." She took some money out of her bag and slipped it in Jessica's hand.

Jessica put it in her pocket. "Thank you. I'll see you next week, Pricilla. Don't forget to practice your scales."

Pricilla gathered up her books and followed her mother out the door, giving little Thomas a flirtatious look as she passed. He crinkled up his nose in disgust. Thomas came in, and Jessica closed the door. "Did you find time to practice this week, Thomas?"

Thomas pouted out his lip, "Yes, I did. Mother wouldn't even let me go out to play baseball until I finished."

"Come along. Let's see how you did."

It was July, and Manhattan was stiflingly hot. When Jessica was young, she and her mother would join the rest of Manhattan society and spend the summer months in cottages in the Hamptons. The pregnancy was making her extra sensitive to the heat, and she missed those summers at the shore.

As Jessica walked down the street, little beads of perspiration trickled from under her bonnet. She thought about those childhood summers, and the only regret she had was that her father had never bought one of those cabins, but rented them. It wasn't that she would have gone even if she did own one now, but it would have been something else that might bring her income.

She stopped to look in the window of a ladies' shop, admiring an outfit she knew she could never afford and thinking that when she got her figure back she could copy the design and make herself one like it. She had two or maybe three months to go before the baby came and she was already tired of the few things she had to wear. She studied the dress, noticing how the lines of fashion had changed since the last time she bought anything. She reminded herself that it would be only a few more months now.

Jessica could hardly wait. She had several reasons to be in a hurry to meet her child. The smothering heat was only one of them. Ever the economist, she had used some of the excess bedding from her mother's linen closet and made herself only two outfits to accommodate her expanding body, wearing one while the other was in the laundry, day in and day out for months now. She was beyond bored with them. They were garments whose fabric she would never reuse. When she finished with them, she never wanted to see the cloth again.

She was mesmerized with the cut of the skirt on the dress she was studying when a reflection in the glass caught her attention. Zachary Belk was walking in her direction. She froze, hoping he would pass by and not notice her, but it wasn't to be. She could see that he'd recognized her, and then noticed her pregnancy. He stopped walking and his mouth dropped open. She remained intent on the window display until his voice behind her said, "Jessica!"

She could see Zachary in the glass, and hesitated before she turned to face him. She would have preferred to ignore him, but the good manners her mother had taught her overruled her first inclination. She took a polite tone. "Zachary. How are you?"

"More to the point, how are you? I'm astounded. You should have told me."

"The last time I saw you, I didn't know."

"You should have sent word."

"I assumed that someone in our circle of acquaintances would mention it to you."

"I'm afraid that since we parted I haven't been traveling in our usual circle of friends."

Assuming that he meant he had kept his old drinking buddies, she couldn't hide the feeling of disgust she felt. Her lips pursed. "I see."

"It isn't what you're thinking. I've been working rather long hours."

She almost laughed out loud. "Working? How novel. Working at what?"

"It was getting rather desperate for Father and me. I wasn't allowed to keep anything out of the house but father's clothing. We sold the office furniture before we closed the business and rented a small flat with the money. I was able to use some family connections to secure a position in a small brokerage house."

Jessica wondered if she should apologize for her previous tone. "I'm happy to hear it, Zachary. I hope you make the most of the opportunity. I've been wondering, how is Mother Belk? I haven't heard from her since she left town. I've been worried about her."

"As a matter of fact, I had a note from her the other day. She's quite content at her sister's house."

"I would like to have her address. I want to tell her the news. She and I often talked about grandchildren."

"I don't quite remember the address, but I'll see that you get it. She'll be delighted."

"Thank you. How is your father?"

"He's not doing all that well, I'm afraid."

"I'm sorry. Is he ill?"

"He isn't ill, but he's not been the same man since he closed the firm. The business wasn't all he lost, you know. He lost his company, his wife, his family home, and his reputation. That house was built by my great-grandfather, who fought with General Washington in the Revolution. After he was elected, President, Washington often stayed there when he visited New York. Losing that house was the final straw. Father fully expected to pass it down to me and to my son, and his son after him. He had visions of an American dynasty, maybe someday the Presidency. What happened was all too much for him. He seldom talks at all but, when he does, he says it was all his fault."

He shook his head. "When I leave for the office in the morning, he's sitting in a chair by the window, and when I come home in the evening, he's still sitting there in the same place, staring out into space. He barely speaks of anything else, and sometimes he goes for days without speaking at all. He sits in front of that window carving chess pieces out of scraps of wood he has me bring him from the lumber yard. He works on them for hours every day. They're piling up all over the place. Some days, he doesn't even get dressed."

"I am sorry. I hope he recovers. So the two of you are living together?"

"Yes, we have a small flat in Chelsea."

"He was always a robust man. I'm sure he'll be all right eventually."

"I hope so, but I'm afraid he may not, at least not for a very long time."

Jessica was growing fatigued. She needed to get back to the house and get a little nap before school was over and her first student showed up. Her energy didn't last long these days, especially if she went out in the heat. She didn't want to be in a position where she had to ask Belk for his help, "Well, I must be getting back to the house. I have students this afternoon."

"Students?"

"Yes. I've been teaching piano for a while now. I have a nice list of pupils. It helps me pay the bills."

"Jessica, I'd like to call on you. There are some matters we should discuss."

"I'd rather you didn't. We have no more business between us."

She turned to leave, but he caught her arm. "Please. I think you may be pleased to hear what I have to say."

She looked at him appraisingly for a moment, and then nodded her head. "Very well, if you'd like to come by this evening, my last student leaves at seven."

"I'll be there."

He made an attempt to kiss her on the cheek, but she drew back and turned her head. He stepped back. "Goodbye, Jessica. I'll see you at seven."

In the flat where the two Belk men lived, Zachary paced the floor. It was a very modest place, a small living room with shabby furniture in dull colors. One corner served as a kitchen, and a small table by the window was the dining area. There were two bedrooms so small they were barely large enough for a narrow bed and a table. Chess pieces sat on every surface. Arthur Belk sat in his chair by the window as his son paced in front of him, as he cut yet another piece of wood. There were wood chips on his clothes and piled up on the floor in front of him.

Zachary paused in front of his father. "I ran into Jessica today. She's going to have a baby. I could hardly believe it. It looks to me that it's due in two or three months. I'm going to have a son, Father, someone to carry on our line."

His father gazed at him, but didn't react. Belk continued his walking back and forth, talking more to himself than to his father. "After all this time, when she didn't conceive, I thought she couldn't and then, at the very last minute, it happened. You should see her, Father. She was always so thin and plain, but today she looked beautiful. She's put on some weight, not too much, and her face has filled out a little. Her hair is different too, and she looked absolutely radiant."

There was still no reaction from Mr. Belk, who was engrossed in his carving.

Zachary went on, "Oh, this baby is mine. I have no doubt at all on that score. You don't know Jessica the way I do, with her strict Baptist upbringing. No, there's no doubt at all. You'll see. When my son starts growing hair, those auburn waves will show you his true heritage. He'll be a Belk for sure."

He crossed the floor again. "I don't have much time before we leave New York. I have to find a way to make her come with us. I won't have my son growing up almost two thousand miles away from me. I must take advantage of this opportunity to win her back. She asked for Mother's address, and she said I could call on her."

He stopped pacing, took out his pocket watch and looked at it. "I have an hour. It's almost six. I have to go over there. I'll leave now, and I won't take a trolley. I'll walk so I'll have time to think up a solid line of reasoning to make her see that we have to be together."

Belk put on his hat and walked out the door. His father turned and stared out the window again.

In the living room of Jessica's house, Jessica and a little girl were at the piano when there was a knock at the door. Jessica closed the lesson book. "There's your mother, now, Mary."

Jessica stood and ushered her pupil to the front door. "That was very good. Don't forget to practice your piece and your scales every day."

She opened the door and Mary's mother was waiting. She could see Belk standing a short distance away, a few yards behind her. Mary's mother took the fee out of her bag and gave it to Jessica. She asked, "How did she do?"

Jessica smiled. "She did fine. She played her piece beautifully, but I do get the feeling that she didn't practice her scales enough. Her fingering could be a little sharper."

Mary's mother bristled. "That's exactly what she does. She likes the pretty parts, but doesn't like the work. This business of taking lessons was all her idea, and it's not one bit convenient. I have to disrupt my whole Saturday to bring her over here, and then either sit here and twiddle my thumbs while I wait or go shopping, and then come pick her up. I'm not going to pay for lessons if she's not going to apply herself."

"She's so talented. You must be so proud of her. It would be a shame for her to give it up. You'll do better this week, won't you, Mary?"

Mary looked sheepish. "Yes, Ma'am. Really I will, Mother."

Mary's mother took her daughter's hand. "Very well. We'll see you next week, Mrs. Belk."

Mary and her mother went down the steps. Jessica looked up to where Belk waited at the far edge of the walk. He came to the door, and she stepped back to allow him to enter.

He took off his hat. "I've brought Mother's address with me. I'm surprised she hasn't written you already. She always did love you like her own daughter."

Jessica closed the door. "I felt the same way about her. I miss our visits."

She led the way, and he followed her to the living room. He went to the sofa and sat on one side, expecting her to sit next to him. She took one of the two chairs across from him and sat stiffly on the edge of the seat. "You said you had something you needed to talk to me about?"

"Yes, first, let me give this to you before I forget. " He stood, walked to her chair, and took a folded paper from his jacket pocket. He handed it to her. Instead of returning to his seat, he sat in the chair closest to her and leaned toward her.

Jessica took the paper from him, "Thank you. I appreciate this. I'll write to her this evening."

Caroline came out of the kitchen. When she saw Belk, she stopped abruptly. "I'm sorry, Jess. I didn't realize you had company. I wanted to tell you that dinner is on the table."

"Thank you, Caroline. We'll only be a minute."

Belk had never before stood in Caroline's presence, but he did this time. "You should invite me to join you, Jessica. As I recall, Caroline is an excellent cook."

Jessica swallowed hard, cleared her throat, and managed to say, "Of course, I've forgotten my manners, but I've already set the table in the kitchen."

"You may be surprised to hear that it won't bother me at all to eat in the kitchen."

"Very well. I wouldn't want anyone to think I was rude. Caroline, would you please set another place at the table?"

Caroline made no effort to disguise her reluctance. "It's a good thing we're having a nice stew tonight, and there's plenty to go around. Yes, I'll set a plate for Mr. Belk. It will only take a minute."

Zachary smiled at her. "It's just as well that we have dinner together. What I came to talk about concerns you, too, Caroline."

Caroline answered stiffly. "Does it now? I can't imagine anything at all that you would want to discuss that involves me."

In the kitchen, the table was set for three. A plate of bread, butter, and salt and pepper, were already on the table. Caroline put down a large tureen. Belk took the seat at the end. It never occurred to him that perhaps he didn't have the right to sit at the head of the table. Jessica noticed, but without comment, she sat on his right. Caroline ladled out the stew into each of their plates and then sat on his left, her face stonily showing her resentment of his presence.

Belk bent over his plate and made a show of inhaling deeply. "Caroline, that smells delightful. I can't remember the last time I had anything like it. Believe it or not, I've been preparing my own meals for quite some time."

Caroline smirked. "I find that hard to imagine."

"It's easier to imagine than it is to eat."

That finally brought a small smile to Caroline's face. Belk took a bite and closed his eyes, savoring it. "Oh, this is heaven."

Caroline had always been proud of her cooking. "I'm afraid it's more potatoes and carrots than beef, but we did have a little meat left over from yesterday's dinner."

"It's wonderful. Caroline, you've outdone yourself."

Jessica was growing curious. "What was it you needed to discuss with me, Zachary?"

"Oh, let's eat first, and we can talk over coffee. I don't want to think about anything except how delicious this is."

"I do believe we can talk and eat at the same time."

"Very well, if you insist."

They all began eating. Belk had a few bites of his dinner before he paused long enough to speak. "I have some good news, at least, I think of it as good news."

Jessica's curiosity made her impatient. "You do? What news is that?"

"I've come into an unexpected opportunity, and I'll be taking the advice of Horace Greeley and going west. I've inherited a house and a parcel of land from a distant cousin. It's in a thriving little town in Kansas, and Father and I will be moving there in a week. I've made inquiries, and it seems that I should have no trouble finding a position."

Belk took another bite of the stew and waited for her response.

It was Caroline who spoke first. "Moving west? That is good news."

Jessica knew he wasn't finished with the story he wanted to tell. "I'm surprised you didn't simply sell the property. I can't imagine you living in Kansas. You're New York, born and bred. Whatever happened to bring this about?"

He looked at her with all the sincerity he could muster. "Let me start by saying, I'm a changed man, Jessica. Having you toss me out was the best thing that ever happened to me. I've stopped drinking anything stronger than a glass of wine, and even that only now and then, mostly because I can't afford it. I go to work every weekday—on time—and I do my best every minute I'm there. My gambling is a thing of the past. I have totally given up buying anything on credit. I haven't had a new suit in months, and I'm proud to say, I don't owe a cent to anyone, except of course, to you. I've learned to pay as I go, and it's a much more comfortable life than I had before."

"I'm happy to hear it."

"Still, I want to go where there are more opportunities. I'm looking forward to a new life in Kansas. I'm barely getting by at the brokerage house. Don't get me wrong, I appreciate that my friend was willing to put me on, but I'm hardly making a living there. The economy still isn't fully recovered from the crash. I've had to start all over at the bottom of the ladder. There are so many men ahead of me my chances for advancement any time soon are remote. I have every confidence that I can be a success out west."

Jessica wasn't convinced he was telling the whole truth. "I'm happy for you, Zachary. I hope you find what you're looking for there."

"So do I. It could be a whole new life, a wonderful life. There's only one thing I need to insure it."

"What would that be?"

"I want you to come with me."

Jessica didn't have to take time to think it over. "No."

"Let me tell you some of the many reasons why you must come. First of all, there's no way you could possibly be making enough money teaching children to play the piano to support this house. I know you still have money in the bank from the sale of your father's house, but I'm also quite sure you are eating into your savings every day. What will you do when that runs out? What will you do with this big house then, sell it? If you do, where will you live?"

"I'll never sell it. It's so much more than only a house. My father thought very carefully before he selected it, and it has his stamp on it. Besides, what would I do with it if I went to Kansas? A house left empty will deteriorate more quickly than one that's occupied."

"Lease it out. Talk to your agent. I'm sure he has a waiting list of people looking for just such a home."

She was still unresponsive to him. "You said many reasons. What else were you thinking?"

"I'm thinking of our son. He's going to need his father."

"Our son? Has it occurred to you that it may be a girl?"

He paused. "Actually, it hadn't, but in that event, all the more reason for her to be with me. Look at how much you cherished your father. I would hope that my daughter would feel the same way about me, and I would do whatever I needed to do to insure her devotion. Would you deny your daughter that relationship?"

This hit Jessica where she was the most vulnerable. Her father was still in her thoughts every single day, and she cherished his memory, "Is there anything else?"

He went on eagerly, "You're still my wife. When we took our vows, we said, as long as ye both shall live. I don't believe that didn't mean anything to you."

"You took vows too. You promised to honor, love, and cherish, and to forsake all others, and you didn't do very well at any of those."

"You're right, and I'm sorry, but I promise you that things would be different. I'm different. I remember something else you promised."

"What would that be?"

"When you read that Bible passage for wives, the one about going where I go and living where I live."

"That's from the book of Ruth. Yes, I remember it."

"Come with me, Jessica. We can still make a life together. We can still be a family."

"It's too late. We're already well on our way to being divorced."

"It takes a year before that's final. All we have to do to nullify the proceedings is to start living as husband and wife again."

Jessica smiled. "I've already paid the attorney, and I'm sure no attorney ever gave a refund. It seems like a terrible waste of money."

Belk was encouraged by her smile. He tried to lighten the text of the conversation. "Once I'm established in Kansas, I'll give you the refund."

During this exchange, Caroline listened warily. Her expression made it plain that she didn't like the idea of reconciliation between them, but she remained silent.

Jessica looked at him hesitantly, still unconvinced. "Is there anything else?"

"Yes, there is one more thing. I need you, Jessica. I love you. I didn't realize how much until I lost you. Please think it over. The attorney from Kansas assured me that the house there is quite livable, fully furnished, and there is ample room for your gardens. It sits on a ten acre plat on the outskirts of town. The place is growing rapidly, and even has a college and a cultural life. At least give me a chance. Give it one year. You can lease out this house for that amount of time, and if you aren't happy in Kansas, you can always return to New York."

"I don't know. This is all very sudden."

"Promise me you'll consider it."

"All right. I'll think about it, but I won't make any promises."

"That's all I want. I don't want to push you, so I won't even ask you again. If you decide to come with me, contact me here, at the office." He took a business card from his vest pocket and handed it to her. "Here's the address of the firm where I'm working for the next few weeks. I intend to stay at the job until the day before we get on the train. I'm in my office during all the usual business hours. If and when you want to talk to me, send me a message. I'll be waiting anxiously to hear from you."

Jessica looked at the card and then placed it face down on the table. "What's the name of this town in Kansas?"

Belk smiled mysteriously. "We'll let that be a surprise for you. You'll enjoy it."

"Not that I've decided to come with you, not at all, but is it one of those places out west with a name like Hog's Breath Junction? I wouldn't want to tell my friends they had to write me at Spider's Nest Crossing or some such thing."

Belk laughed loudly. "No, you'll like it, I promise you."

"I'll let you know my decision by the end of the week. Now, let's finish our dinner with some less serious conversation."

Belk smiled. "Of course. Have you noticed how hot it's been lately?"

Chapter 12

The next morning, Caroline stood at the stove stirring a pot of oatmeal. Jessica came in dressed for her day. The table was already set for breakfast for two. There was a kettle on the stove and a china teapot on the table with a curl of steam coming from the lip.

Jessica poured herself some tea and took a seat, "Good morning, Caroline. How are you this morning?"

Caroline didn't turn to look at her. "Old. That's how I am this morning."

Jessica wasn't accustomed to hearing that sort of reply from Caroline, who had a normally sunny nature. "Nonsense. You're one of the youngest people I know."

"Tell that to my left knee. It was popping so loud this morning when I first got up that it sounded like I was making popcorn."

Jessica took a sip of the tea and almost burned her tongue. "Oh, I do love tea when it's like this, almost hot enough to burn. How do you manage to always have it at exactly the right temperature when I get to the kitchen? It's like magic."

"I fill the kettle and put it on the stove as soon as I come in the kitchen and get the fire started. The pot and the cups go on the warmer up top. When I hear you leave your room, I put the tea leaves and the hot water in the pot and put it on the table. By the time you get here, it's brewed and ready."

"How do you hear me leave my room?"

"There's a floorboard right in front of your door that creaks when you step on it. It doesn't make all that loud a sound upstairs, but it's right over the kitchen, and I can hear it down here."

"How do you know I'm not going into the bathroom?"

"That's the first creak I hear, especially nowadays. Then you go back to your room to dress. The second creak means you're coming downstairs."

"You would have made a good police officer. It occurs to me that I never once in my life came downstairs in the morning that you weren't already in the kitchen making breakfast. When I was little I used to think you slept in the pantry."

Caroline finally smiled. "Almost. My room in your father's house was only a few feet down the hall, the same as it is in this house."

"You don't have to stay in that little room any more. Now that there's only the two of us, and no Zachary Belk to protest proprieties, you could have taken one of the larger rooms upstairs."

"I don't really want to move. My little room suits me fine. It's cozy. I'm quite satisfied there, and it gives me a—a perspective on things that I may not have if I slept upstairs."

Jessica waved one hand toward a chair. "Sit down with me, and let's both have some of that oatmeal."

Caroline had two bowls on the stove warmer. She ladled oatmeal into them and placed them on the table. She sat to Jessica's right. They spooned brown sugar on their oatmeal and poured milk from a small pitcher.

Caroline said. "I've been worrying about you all night. You really shouldn't even be thinking of travelling when you're this far along."

Jessica wasn't surprised that Caroline knew what she'd been thinking. Caroline seemed to know everything. "My stomach problems have passed months ago. I never felt better in my life."

"You're making a mistake you know, going to Kansas with him. He hasn't changed at all, and you can't trust him."

"What makes you think I've decided to go with him?"

"You decided that last night. He scored a point for himself by reminding you of your marriage vows, and as soon as he started talking about how much that baby would need its father and reminding you of how much you loved and needed your own father, I knew you would go."

"I'm not in love with him, if that's what you're thinking. There was a time I wanted to be, but that was long ago."

"I know that, but you're making a big mistake if you believe him when he says that he really loves you. That man never loved anyone but himself, and he never will."

"You're wrong about that. I don't believe he loves me, but I think he will love his baby, maybe not for the same reasons that other men love their children, why my father loved me, for example. He will love his child because it carries on his line, his precious heritage. The Belk men think they're special, above the rest of us. Zachary's mother told me he even treated her as if he were superior to her."

"Not from what I know of her. She was—is--a fine lady. She spent quite a lot of time with your mother, and I had the chance to get to know her. You probably don't remember this, but when your mother was sick, especially toward the end, Harriet Belk came for hours almost every day and sat with her. They talked, and if your mother was able to sit up, they played a game of some sort. The professional nurse that your father hired took care of her body, but Harriet Belk took care of her spirit. As far as I know, Zachary and his father aren't superior to anyone, family heritage or not."

"He'll want this child to have the best of everything, and even if he didn't work to support me when we were together, I really do believe he'll work to support this baby. Besides, a baby needs a father, every baby."

"Maybe you're more aware of his intentions than I gave you credit for, but I don't trust him. I don't believe he loves anything, even his own baby."

"I think you're wrong, I think he will love it, and I will not deny my child the love of a father, whatever the basis for that affection."

"So we're definitely going to go with him?"

"I didn't make up my mind for sure until this moment, but yes, I'm going with him. I'll send Edgar to his office with a message in the morning, and I'll go see the agent about leasing out the house this afternoon."

Caroline wasn't happy, and the frown lines on her forehead gave her away. "I'll start packing. We don't have much time. I'll start with the things I know for sure that you'll want to have with you. He said the house out there was furnished. I wonder if it had china and so forth."

"Let's assume it doesn't. We can leave the everyday china for possible tenants. I don't want to leave Mother's fine china here where someone might misuse it."

"I don't have all that much of my own to pack, but you may have to sacrifice some things you've been keeping. You can't take everything with you, such as most of what belonged to your mother and father that you've kept as mementoes and won't actually use."

"I have to take all the clothes and linens that belonged to Mother with us."

"You can't be overly sentimental, Jess."

"It isn't sentimentality. I've been using Mother's clothes to make things for myself, and I've been using some of the finer linens to make things for the baby. I'll donate Father's clothes to a charity, and there are quite a few pieces of furniture in the attic I can sell. I don't know why I've hung onto all this for so long. There was so much I brought over here from Father's house when we sold it. It was foolish, really."

"It belonged to him, and that made it hard to part with. The sentimental value was pulling at you."

"It suddenly seems like there's so much I hadn't even thought about. I don't know where to start."

"Start with the agent who will rent the house. I'm sure he can give you the names of businesses that will be happy to help you, people who buy used furniture and that sort of thing."

"I don't have much time."

"We'll manage."

"Oh! It now occurs to me that I didn't even ask you if you were willing to come with me."

"Why would you have to ask?"

Tears sprang to Jessica's eyes. She went to Caroline and hugged her. "I assumed you would want to be wherever I went. Father's gone, Tommy's gone, Cook's gone. You're the only one left from my childhood. It's pretty frightening, Caroline. I've lived in Manhattan my entire life, and in all that time, in only two houses. I went from my father's house to my own house. Now I'm moving halfway across the country to a place I've never even seen, to live among people I don't know. I feel as if I'm starting a whole new life. I don't think I could do it if you weren't with me."

"You'll be all right, Jess. We'll be all right. God will take care of us."

Jessica went to see the rental agent early that afternoon. He wasn't very encouraging.

"It may take some time to find a tenant for a house that large."

Jessica had hoped for better news. "Will it rent faster if I sell the furniture?"

"Please, leave the furniture. It will look better to a prospective tenant if it already has what they need. Should they want to use their own furniture, I can arrange to sell yours. I have an auction house I work with from time to time in estate sales and I can promise you they are totally trustworthy and can get the best possible price for you."

"There's one thing I'm leaving in the house that I can never sell, my Mother's piano. I would have to put it in storage or have it shipped to me before I sold it."

"We can make those arrangements for you if the time comes."

"Thank you. I don't have a forwarding address yet, but as soon as I do, I'll write you."

Jessica sighed as she left the agent's office. The only things left to do were to say goodbye to her friends, and her students, and to pack her things.

Jessica had a limited amount of energy, so she had Edgar come over, and he and Caroline did most of the work. By the time they had everything sorted and wrapped, it looked like a mountain that filled half the living room. Just when Caroline thought they were finished with everything except the clothes they needed for the trip, Jessica remembered one more thing. She went to the front window and took down the sign offering piano lessons. "Slip this in there someplace where it won't get broken. You never know. I may need it again."

PART TWO

Chapter 13

They'd left Manhattan, New York, on a Monday morning and had been on the train heading west for a week. The first day was interesting to Jessica. She and Caroline watched from their compartment window as the landscape changed from the city skyscrapers of New York to the rolling hills of Pennsylvania.

About an hour out of Manhattan, Jessica told Caroline, "It's amazing. I've been to Europe twice, and I now realize this is the first time I have ever traveled west of the Hudson River."

Caroline laughed. "This is a beautiful country, Jess. You're going to love it."

Jessica was surprised by Caroline's comment. *How would Caroline know what the rest of the country looked like?* She frowned and tilted her head curiously. "It occurs to me that I have been very self-centered. I know nothing about your life before I came into it. You never talked about your early days. You're quite the mystery. We're going to have a lot of time to talk in the next few days. Tell me all about yourself."

Caroline hesitated. "Oh, I don't know that I'm all that interesting."

"Of course you are. Until this baby is born, you're the most important person in my life. I used to ask you about it when I was younger, but I remember you telling me that I was too young to hear it, and you'd tell me when I was older. Now, I'm older. Tell me. Were you born in New York?"

"No, I was born in Connecticut." Caroline paused.

"Don't stop. What did your parents do?"

"My father was the minister of a Methodist church. My mother was a school teacher until she married."

"How did you get from there to here?" Jessica swept her hand in front of her to indicate the railroad car.

"It was a long distance, Jessica, and not always a happy one."

"Please tell me. You know every single thing about me from my first breath to right this minute. It's only fair that I know more about you."

"All right, if you insist."

"I insist."

Caroline looked out the window as if there were a tableau of her life visible from the train and began. "Ministers don't always stay put in one church. When I was born, Father was pastor of one of the New Haven Methodist Churches. When I was three, he moved to a church in Harrisburg. Pennsylvania. We stayed there for around five years. I loved it there. When he went to a church in Frankfort, Kentucky, it broke my heart. The older children get, the harder it is to move them away from their friends. It wasn't long after that my mother passed away."

Jessica gasped. "You were almost the same age I was when my mother died!"

"Yes. I tended to you from the day you were born. I loved you the way any woman would when she has a baby around, but when Mrs. McCarthy died, I felt that you needed me to try to make up for losing her because I knew how hard it was to lose your mother. I took care of you the way I would have taken care of my own babies if they'd lived."

Jessica was stunned. "Oh, Caroline! I knew you were married once, and that your husband died in the war, but I didn't know you had babies. I want to know all about that, but go back to when your mother died. What happened?"

"My father married again, almost right away. No one thought the worse of him for it because he had me and my two brothers, one older and one younger than I was, and he needed someone to raise us. My stepmother was a kind enough woman, but she started in right off having babies of her own, and delivered three of them in four years. By then, I was twelve, and was expected to do my share of the housework. She taught me how to clean and cook and do the laundry, and I helped take care of her babies. She gave me an education that has stood me in good stead, and those skills made me able to have my position in your father's house. My stepmother didn't mistreat us. She was kind enough, but she didn't really love me and my brothers. My father did the best he could, but dividing up your attention between a hundred or so church members, a wife, and six children takes up all the hours in a day."

Jessica nodded sympathetically. "That makes me realize how blessed I was to have my father all to myself. If he took an interest in another woman, nothing must have come of it."

"I'm not surprised. It would have been hard for anyone to live up to your mother's standard. She was beautiful, kind, and loving. Everything a Christian woman should be."

"She was perfect."

"No, not perfect, only better than most, much better."

"You're not going to get away from your own story now. Tell me some more."

"Where was I?"

"Taking care of your step-mother's babies."

"I didn't mean to make that sound like a burden. I loved them."

"How did you come to meet your husband?"

"Where most young women meet their husbands. His name was Jeremy Akins and he was a member of the church. We never really had a chance to court properly. I was barely sixteen, and he was eighteen when we started noticing one another. We sat together at church suppers and picnics.

"When the Mexican-American War started up, some of the young men went off to fight. My older brother signed up right away. Jeremy felt it was his duty to go, and before he signed up, he asked me to marry him. What would normally have been a courtship of two years with us sitting next to one another in services and him calling on me in my father's parlor turned into us having two days to get ready for a wedding. My father married us in the church after the Sunday morning service. Daddy didn't want to do it, but he said it seemed somehow unpatriotic to say no."

"Did you at least have time to get a new dress?"

"No, I just wore the best one I had. It was new from Christmas, so it was still in pretty good condition. I carried a bouquet of daisies from the front yard. I didn't care. It was all exciting and romantic, I guess. We were like children playing dress up. Everyone thought the boys were going to go off and win the war in a few weeks and be home before we could miss them much."

"The war lasted a long time. It must have been horrible for you."

"It was horrible for everyone. People forget sometimes how the families of soldiers sacrifice too. The day we married, I moved all my things to his parents' house and we had a week together before Jeremy went off to training camp. I didn't see him again for almost a year, and a lot had happened by then."

"What?"

"He'd been gone about two months when I knew I was going to have a baby. I was about six months along when I lost my little boy."

"What happened?"

"I was about to go out in the yard to hang up the wash. I had been doing it right along, like all the women did, and didn't think anything about it. I picked up the basket full of wet clothes, and that was when it happened. I'm not going to go into that part. It was hurtful both ways."

"Both ways?"

"Yes. It hurt something awful in my body, and it hurt something awful in my heart. He looked like a little doll. I named him Jeremy after his father, and we buried him in a little box in the church graveyard. Jeremy's father had a headstone made and put his name and the date on it. At the top was the verse from Luke 23:43, 'Today thou shall be with me in paradise.'"

"Oh, Caroline. I'm so sorry."

Caroline's eyes misted up. "You never get over losing a child. Maybe that's the reason I've been nagging you so much to rest and take it easy with your own. I've been afraid something bad would happen."

"But you never said a word about it before now."

"No, and I never would have if you hadn't pushed me into it. Maybe it's just as well you hear about it. I want you to take good care of yourself."

"You said before, babies, like you had more than one."

"I had a little girl the next year. Jeremy came home on leave about a year after we were married. He was only there for a week, but by the time he left, I was expecting again. This time, I was careful not to lift anything heavy or get too tired. I carried her all the way to the day she was born with no problem except the morning sickness, and I had a wonderful, healthy little girl."

Caroline's voice cracked. She closed her eyes for a moment, remembering, and then went on, "I called her Nola, after Jeremy's mother. She was a good baby. She hardly ever cried. She walked before she was a year old."

Caroline smiled at her memories. "She was bald headed for the longest time, but she was pretty all the same. Jeremy never did get to see her. He died in Mexico."

"How sad. What happened to her?"

"Nola was a little over a year old when the influenza went around that winter. She got sick. The fever was so hot it ate up her little body and she never got over it. She's buried next to her brother. Her headstone has the verse from Luke 18:16, 'Suffer little children to come unto me, and forbid them not: for of such is the kingdom of God.'"

Caroline wiped a tear off her cheek. "Father Akins died the next year, and Mother Akins a few months after him. They'd left the house to me, but I couldn't stay there without work, and there wasn't anything I knew how to do but of take care of a house and clean."

"What about your parents?"

"My father had moved on to another church in Manhattan. I wanted to be near some sort of family, so I sold the house and got on a train to New York. I went to an employment agency there. They sent me to your father's house, and here we are today. That's it, that's my life story."

"Caroline! That's astounding. I can't believe I never knew all this."

"It wasn't time for you to know it. Now, you do."

"Did you love him, Jeremy, I mean?"

"I did. I don't think it was like your mother and father loved each other, but if he had lived, I hope it would have grown into that. I loved him as much as a girl that young can understand love. I've never told anyone this, but for a long time after he died, I was angry with him."

"Angry?"

"Yes, because he volunteered to get killed and leave me alone. I always expected he would live through the war, and he would come home, and we'd have more babies and get old together."

Jessica blushed and leaned close to Caroline. "The other part of being married, you know--how did you feel about that?"

"It seemed like a curious thing to me, why Jeremy wanted so much to do that. I knew I had to go along with it if I wanted babies, but they didn't tell young girls much about that sort of thing back then. Later on, I would listen to some of the other women who worked at the house over the years, different maids and so forth, and they would talk about being with a man that way as if it were the most important thing in life. I suppose if you were with the right man, once you learned how it was all supposed to go, it would be all right."

Jessica fell silent, thinking about what Caroline said. She didn't think she would ever learn to enjoy being intimate with Zachary. She'd heard some of her married friends talk about it, and they didn't seem to mind it at all. She'd even heard them giggle and say they were buying some lingerie or perfume so their husband would be more attentive that way. The women she knew who enjoyed their husbands' attentions seemed to be so much happier in their marriages. She yearned for a bond like that. The Bible certainly gave it a blessing. She sighed. She couldn't help thinking that she would be like Caroline, and live her life without ever finding pleasure in the physical side of marriage.

Each morning during the trip, Zachary left his father with Jessica and Caroline and went to the smoking car with other men right after breakfast. The only time she saw him all day was for meals. She and Caroline were on their own for entertainment. Father Belk stayed with them, but he seldom spoke more than a word or two, preferring to stare out the window. Jessica sometimes wondered if he heard them talking and was only ignoring them, or if he was lost in a world that had nothing to do with them. Sometimes at night, when she was making her requests of God, she asked Him to restore her father-in-law's mental health.

The landscape was already beginning to bore them by the second day, so they passed the time knitting and talking about their hopes for the future. Jessica wondered what the land around Zachary's house would be like, and would it have the correct soil for a rose garden? Father Belk continued his silent, vacant stare. Zachary spent almost all of the day in the smoking car, and Jessica wondered what could be so interesting there. He had promised her he wouldn't gamble. She wanted to believe him. He never asked her for money, so maybe that was a sign all he was doing was talking to the other men.

Each night was another night of restless sleep. Jessica was beginning to become accustomed to the noise and the swaying of the railroad car, but she missed her big, soft bed at home. Their tiny compartment was sufficient, but that was all that could be said about it. Each day, she had less energy than the day before. The journey seemed it would never end. Jessica began to think of it in stages, the first part leaving New York, the next parts crossing each state. When the train chugged slowly across the big bridge over the Mississippi, she knew it was almost over.

All that was left were Missouri and Kansas. Zachary still wouldn't tell her the name of the town where they would be living. He kept saying he didn't want to spoil the surprise. She didn't know if it was on the east side of Kansas or the west, up north toward Nebraska, or south, toward Oklahoma. As she looked out the window at the muddy water of the river passing below her, she wondered if she had one more state to cross, or two.

They traveled slowly through seven states. Delays in Ohio added to the time it should have taken for them to reach their destination. Friday afternoon, Zachary told her to pack up her things because they were only hours from their destination. They were finishing what Jessica hoped would be their last lunch in the dining car. The now-empty dishes were on the table in front of them. Zachary sat in the seat next to her, Caroline was across the table, next to Father Belk, who had eaten, but was now once again staring blankly straight ahead.

Jessica looked out her window as the landscape passed by. It was made up of hayfields that had already been harvested, leaving stubble burned brown by the sun. She saw an occasional corn field, and a few scattered trees on rolling hills. The slopes on the outsides of the track were dotted with six-foot tall sunflowers, one of the few things that the intense Kansas sun cannot wither.

As her fatigue increased, Jessica was growing increasingly impatient. "We left Topeka two hours ago. You said it was only a few more minutes back then. When are we going to be in this mysterious town, and why you won't even tell me the name?

Zachary smiled at her. "It's going to be a surprise, and I think a happy one."

"I'm so tired of this train. I'm beginning to think I'll spend the rest of my life on it. The surprise will be if we ever actually arrive."

"I would tell you to go back to our compartment and lie down, but it really should be any minute now. I was told that our little town is quite lovely, and it sits in the middle of the last clump of hills and trees in the state of Kansas. After you leave the county going further west, it's all pretty much flat prairie land through the rest of the state."

Jessica leaned toward the window, tilting her head on the glass, and tried to see what was ahead. "I can see a hill up there now. Let's hope it's one of ours."

The train sped up, gathering power to climb the hill, and then descended into a valley. The landscape was quite lovely, and the grass had escaped the browning effect of the sun. The train slowed down gradually and pulled into the station. Jessica was on the wrong side of the car to see the name of the town on the sign above the depot door. Caroline let out a whoop and began laughing.

Jessica raised an eyebrow. "Caroline? What on earth has gotten into you?"

Caroline wiped a tear away from her eye and was still laughing. "You'll see in a minute Jess. You're going to love it!"

The train slowly stopped, and the conductor opened the doors. They all stood and filed out of the train car.

Belk stepped off first. He took Jessica's hand and helped her down. Caroline paused on the step behind her, waiting. Jessica looked up and saw the depot sign. She too began to laugh. "Manhattan, Kansas! What a wonderful surprise, Zachary."

"I thought you'd enjoy the irony of it. You haven't really left Manhattan at all."

Jessica looked around her. The depot was clean, the people well dressed. "What I can see of it looks lovely."

"I'll get a carriage and have the driver take you right down the main street on his way to the house so you can get a really good look at the town."

He escorted Jessica to a bench sitting in front of the depot. Caroline and Father Belk followed them and sat next to her.

Belk told her, "You sit here in the shade while I inquire about a carriage."

Jessica and Caroline had become so accustomed to Father Belk's silence they had formed the habit of talking to one another in front of him as if he weren't there. Jessica told Caroline, "I'm going in the station to see if I can find the facilities."

"Again? Didn't you visit the ladies' room on the train only a half-hour ago?"

"Yes, and now I need to go again."

After Jessica walked away, Caroline looked straight ahead, but began talking to Father Belk, or perhaps talking mostly to herself. "I will be so happy when we get to wherever this is that we're going. I told her the trip would be too much for her. Look at the circles under her eyes. I don't think he cares at all about her as long as he gets what he wants. I know he's your son. Maybe you don't see it, but I certainly do."

She turned to look directly at him. "I wish you would start living your life again. I understand what happened, and I know you're blaming yourself. Maybe it was all your fault, or maybe you can put some of the blame on the other men in your business who led you along the wrong path. Whatever it was, you need to put it behind you and start thinking about tomorrow. Isn't it enough that we're going to have the responsibility of a house and a baby without having you act like an invalid?"

For the first time since they'd left New York, the senior Belk looked in her eyes, and she could see life in him. She fell silent, and the two of them sat there quietly until Jessica returned.

Caroline smiled up at her, "Did you find what you needed?"

"Yes, thank heaven." She sat down next to Caroline. "I hope that once this baby arrives, I won't have to worry about taking care of my needs so frequently."

Caroline scratched her cheek. "Uh, maybe we shouldn't be discussing this in front of Mr. Belk."

Jessica knitted her eyebrows together. "Oh, of course."

Time seemed to drag before Belk finally returned to fetch them. "I'm sorry it took so long. There were quite a few people who came in on the train, and it was a while before I could find suitable transportation. It's waiting there."

He gestured toward the end of the building, where there were a large buggy waited. "There wasn't anything available that was large enough to bring all of us and our belongings. I'll arrange for a wagon for the luggage and crates. Father and I will ride in that. You and Caroline will go ahead of us in the buggy. I've given the driver the address of the house. It will take a while for us to load up all our goods, so we'll probably be an hour or so behind you."

"Maybe we should wait here and all of us go together."

"No, I know you're tired. I want you to get to your new home and lie down a bit. I understand there's quite a nice restaurant in town, and we'll all have dinner there tonight. We can go shopping for provisions in the morning if you feel up to it."

"All right, I am tired. It will be good to lie down in a real bed that isn't moving around like the one on the train. Caroline and I will go ahead."

"The driver's name is Everett Snipes. I've told him to take you down the main street and tell you a little of the town's history. I think you'll be quite impressed."

Chapter 14

Jessica rode next to the driver of a small buggy with Caroline on her other side. They traveled slowly down the main street of the town. She couldn't guess the age of Everett Snipes. His eyes were deeply creased, and a grizzled beard covered most of his face. He wore denim trousers and a plaid shirt with the sleeves rolled up to his elbows. The frayed sleeve of his aged underwear showed.

The street had several impressive two-story buildings made out of yellow stone, and they were interspersed with the typical wooden framed western buildings.

Jessica looked back and forth as the driver pointed out the buildings while they drove down the street. "Is this called Main Street, Mr. Everett?"

Everett shook his head. "No Ma'am, this here's Poyntz Avenue."

"So many of these buildings are made out of that yellow stone. What is it?"

"That there's limestone. They dig it up out of a quarry right close to here."

"How interesting. Many of the buildings in New York, in my Manhattan, are made of brownstone, but I have no idea where they find it."

Everett pointed to an impressive looking building. "That there's the new Manhattan House Hotel. Well, it's a few years old now, but it's almost new. That women's suffrage person, that Susan B. Anthony, she came to town in '67 and the hotel told her to find lodgings elsewhere."

"Susan B. Anthony was here? How exciting. What did she do when they wouldn't give her a room?"

"The Pillsburys put her up at their place. There was some would of rather seen her run out of town, but folks here are mostly what I've heard called progressive. Our postmistress is a woman, Mr. Pillsbury's daughter, Annie."

"I'm sure that someday Mrs. Anthony will be victorious, and women will win the vote."

Everett snorted. "Wouldn't surprise me. Some of our biggest businesses are run by women. Mrs. Wareham runs the millinery shop, and there are some others out doing things that don't include seeing after their households, like that Mrs. Purcell, starting up all of those clubs and asking that Carnegie man for money for a library."

"I'd like to be able to vote someday."

"Don't take this personal, Ma'am, maybe you will, but I don't know if'n I'll live to see it."

Jessica couldn't help smiling at him. "I'm hoping that you do."

"Things are changin', that's for sure. Before the war, there was about twelve hundred folks living here in the county. Now, there's upwards of five thousand, most of them abolitionists. That's all right with me. I never did hold with slavery. I'm glad the war turned out like it did, but it's a shame it had to be so hard won. All those young boys dead, and so many of them that did get through it alive were all torn up over it, inside and out. It was a terrible thing."

"Yes, it was. I suppose all wars are terrible, even if they are fought for a good cause."

They went on in an uncomfortable silence for a moment, and then the driver spoke up. "This town used to be named Boston."

"Boston? How did it come to be called Manhattan?"

"Funny how those things happen, isn't it? This was Boston, and a bunch of folks were on a boat heading up the Kaw River aiming to start up a settlement and name it Manhattan. Then they got hung up on a sandbar right here. The folks already living here invited them to stay, and they said they would if they changed the name of Boston to Manhattan, so they did."

Jessica looked around her. The buildings were becoming further apart. "We seem to be leaving town, Mr. Everett."

"Yep. Your place is almost clear on t'other side. It used to belong to the Andersens, but they're all gone now."

"Yes, they were relatives of my husband. He inherited it when his cousin passed away."

The driver looked startled at this bit of information but didn't comment. Jessica pointed to the line of sunflowers growing along the road. "There certainly are a lot of sunflowers here. I've never seen them grow so tall, and the little black-eyed Susans seem to do quite well, too."

Everett nodded, but had stopped his chattering and didn't speak for the next part of the trip. It was a while longer before the buggy stopped in front of a large, two-story house. It had a porch that wrapped all the way around, and was made from the same yellow stone Jessica had seen in so many of the buildings in town. The house itself looked in reasonably good shape, but the yard was badly overgrown, and the picket fence was falling apart. All along the front of the house, rose blossoms stuck their heads above the weeds. Across the road, an almost identical house stood. Its yard was perfectly groomed. At the side of that house, a line of clean laundry waved in the breeze.

Jessica looked from one side to the other. "Oh, dear. Our neighbor's house is so lovely. Look at ours. The yard is in very sad condition. I'll make that my first priority. I must say, at least the roses seem to be winning their battle for survival. I can hardly wait to clear out the front yard."

Everett got down from the buggy and helped Jessica and then Caroline. He took off his hat. "They got snakes where you come from Ma'am?"

Jessica looked at him, wide-eyed. "Only the little striped garden snakes, quite harmless."

"Well, we got our share of rattlers here, Ma'am. They don't much care for people. They'll run off from you if you give them a chance. Just don't stick your hand in a bush somewheres you can't see what's in it."

"Oh, my goodness."

"Don't get all skeered now. They won't bother you, if you don't bother them."

Caroline put her hand on Jessica's back and steered her toward the stairs. "Thank you, Mr. Everett."

Jessica stopped walking. "Oh, no! I forgot to ask Zachary for the key. We'll have to wait on the front porch until he gets here."

Everett grinned at her. "I wouldn't worry about that, Miz Belk. It's prob'ly open. No one locks their doors here."

"Really? How delightful."

She went up the flagstone walk, stepping around the weeds that had grown up in the cracks. At the top the six stairs, she had to stop and catch her breath.

"Are you all right, Jess?" Caroline asked.

"I'm fine. All I need is some rest."

Caroline tried the door. The knob came off in her hand and the door swung open. Jessica tried to look brave.

Everett, hat still in hand, asked her, "Is there anything else I can do for you Ma'am?

She smiled gratefully. "No, thank you, Mr. Everett. My husband will be along soon."

Everett nodded. "I'll be getting' back to town then. Awful nice to meet you folks. I hope you enjoy living here."

He went back down the path, took the horse's halter and led him into a U-turn on the narrow road, then climbed back onto the buggy and drove off. Jessica almost regretted allowing him to leave. *I wonder what's waiting for us inside.*

Jessica hesitated at the door. Caroline finally asked her, "Aren't you going to go inside?"

"I'm afraid of what I'll find there. Snakes? Spiders? Rats?" She shuddered.

"We have to do it sooner or later. I'll go first."

Caroline pushed open the door and went in. Jessica walked closely behind her. In the hazy light, she could see furniture covered with white sheets. Cobwebs hung in the corners. The draperies were pulled tightly shut, and the light was filtered and dim. Caroline said, "You're already overtired, Jess. Sit down somewhere for a minute. Let me get some light in here so we can see what we're dealing with."

Jessica carefully folded back the sheet that covered one of the big easy chairs. She sat down, and a big puff of white dust billowed up from the cushion. Caroline went to the windows one at a time and pulled back the draperies. Light came flooding into the room.

Caroline looked around. "It looks as if we're going to have our work cut out for us. I've never seen so much dust in my life. You wouldn't think so much could get in here, what with the doors and windows all shut up like they were."

Jessica ran her finger across the top of the chair-side table and looked at it. "This is the strangest dust I've ever seen. It's like the finest talcum powder. No wonder it filtered right through the sheeting and into the upholstery."

Caroline swiped some of the dust on her finger, too. "You're right. I've never seen dust so white. Not like our pitch-black, New York dust at all."

Jessica wiped her finger on her skirt. "Well, first things first. It seems like forever since we left the train station. I need to find the washroom."

She tried to get up from the chair, but her pregnancy made it difficult. She laughed. "I'm going to need some assistance here. I should know better than to sit back like that when I'm as big as a whale."

Caroline came over and held out her hands. "Here, Jess, take my hands."

Jessica wrapped her hands around Caroline's wrists and Caroline helped her to her feet. Jessica looked toward the hallway. "Now, let's see where that washroom is."

They went through every room of the lower floor of the house looking for a washroom. After they were sure they'd been everywhere, they stood in the kitchen and looked at one another.

Caroline said. "It doesn't seem as though we're going to have one in the house, Jess. The home seems to be missing our big city conveniences. The facilities must be out back. "

Jessica blinked rapidly. "I'm afraid of what else may be out there, too."

Caroline went on, "Well, it won't be the first time you had to use one of those things."

"No, but it's been a very long time. Normally, I would be able to handle it. I was thinking about what he said about rattlesnakes. If the front yard is all that overgrown, I can only imagine what the back yard is like."

"Oh, you're right. Let's go upstairs and look under the beds."

"Under the beds? Oh, I know what you're talking about. Chamber pots, I remember those."

They went slowly up the stairs, Caroline climbing behind Jessica, as if she might have to catch her. Jessica took one step at a time and held tightly to the rail. They finally reached the top of the stairs, where she paused and wiped the dust from the handrail on her skirt. She was breathing hard. She coughed and exhaled sharply to expel the dust she had breathed in from her lungs. "Zachary said we would go into town tomorrow and get provisions. That will have to include a lot of supplies to get this place clean enough to live in."

While Jessica caught her breath, Caroline went down the hall opening the doors. She stopped at one toward the front of the house. "This looks like it would be your bedroom here."

They went inside. Caroline opened the draperies and then, with some difficulty and popping joints, she got down on one knee and looked under the bed. She pulled out a chamber pot and held it up triumphantly, "Aha! Here we go. I'll leave you to it while I look for a bedroom for the others and myself."

Caroline went out, closing the door. Keeping her eye on the pot, Jessica started unbuttoning her jacket. She spoke out loud. "Hold on, Jess, hold on, we're almost there."

A few minutes later, Jessica had taken off her dress and was wearing only a loose camisole and pantaloons. The much appreciated chamber pot sat by the foot of the bed with a cloth covering it. She carefully pulled the top coverlet from the bed to keep the dust from falling on the sheets beneath, and draped it across the chair. The dust puffed up. There was a knock at the door. Jessica called out, "Come in."

Caroline opened the door. "All set Jess?"

Jessica yawned. "I'm fine, only really, really tired. I haven't had to use a chamber pot since I was a child, but I managed. Now, all I can think about is sleep. Don't wake me when Zachary gets here. I want to rest."

"I think that's exactly what you should do, sleep until you wake up all on your own. I've been looking around the upstairs. There are three bedrooms up here, and

Mr. Belk can sleep in one of the others, at least for tonight. There's no reason for you to be disturbed."

Jessica got in bed and pulled one of the sheets up over her. As her head sank into the pillow she closed her eyes and let out a relieved sigh. "O-o-o-h. It's so good to lie down in a bed that's perfectly still. Either this mattress is very, very good, or I'm very, very tired. After being shaken all over on that train for the last week, you have no idea how delicious that sounds."

Caroline picked up the chamber pot and walked softly out of the room. By the time she closed the door, Jessica was breathing regularly, sound asleep.

Chapter 15

Caroline heard the front door open and looked over the railing. Belk came in carrying a suitcase in one hand and a box of groceries in the other. His father entered next, went directly to the front window and stood looking out. The driver of the wagon, a burly young man in denim, came behind them, carrying a trunk. He put down his load in the living room and went back out. Caroline came down the stairs.

Belk looked up at her. "Is Jessica resting?"

"Yes. She went right to sleep almost the minute we got here. I promised her that we wouldn't wake her."

"When the wagon driver told me how far out of town we would be, I knew Jessica wouldn't want to go back for dinner, so I persuaded him to stop for some food."

Caroline looked at him pointedly. "Well, I'm not letting you wake her. If she's hungry, she'll let us know."

Belk grimaced. His face turned red, and he dropped the suitcase he was carrying and tossed the box of groceries on a chair. He strode across the room to where Caroline stood at the bottom stair and almost charged into her, stopping only far enough away that he wasn't touching her. "I'll have you remember that you are a servant in this house. Don't assume to tell me what I can and can't do with my own wife, or you will be looking elsewhere for employment."

Her hands were hanging down by her side but Caroline balled up both fists angrily. She took a deep breath, which gave her a moment to reconsider the answer she had intended to give. Finally, she hung her head and meekly replied, "Yes, sir."

Having won the skirmish, Belk nodded curtly in satisfaction. "Take Father upstairs and get him settled."

"Yes, sir," Caroline murmured.

She crossed the room and put her hand under Father Belk's elbow, guiding him toward the stairs. Zachary stormed out the front door. As Caroline passed the chair with the groceries, she took a few pieces of fruit from the box and put them in her pocket. Leading the old man, she went up the stairs, softly telling him, "I'll do whatever I need to do to protect my girl."

At the top of the steps, she led him to a room at the end of the hallway. "I think you'd like this room. It has a window that looks out at some pretty trees." She took one of the apples out of her pocket and put it on the table. "If you get hungry, this will tide you over until we can get something cooked. There ought to be a chamber pot under the bed, or you can go to the outhouse in the back yard if you want to risk wading through the overgrowth out there."

She left him to himself and headed back down for the kitchen, mumbling to herself, "Stairs, stairs, stairs. My knees aren't going to like that. I don't know, but if it's all right with Jessica, I think I'd rather have that little room downstairs for my bedroom than a big one up here. I know it will be all right with Mr. Belk. He can puff himself up and talk about it as the servant's quarters."

Just then, Belk came back in the front door carrying a box. She snapped her mouth shut and continued on her way to the kitchen without looking at him.

By late afternoon, the living room, dining room, and hallway were stacked with shipping crates and luggage. One of the trunks had been opened, and a few things taken out and placed on top. Caroline was in the kitchen. The whole house was covered in the fine, white dust. She went out the back door and took wood from a pile of kindling stacked there. She carried it to the kitchen and put it in the stove, went back to the hallway and took some crinkled up papers out of one of the packing boxes, and she placed those on top of the wood.

There was a kettle sitting on the stove, which was also covered in dust. She picked it up, found a few suitable pots from the pantry, and went back out to the porch. At the right end was a pump handle. She pumped it several times and dirty water spewed out of the faucet. She let the dirty water fall off the porch and kept pumping for a while until the water began running clear. Then she rinsed the kettle and pots both inside and out several times as she pumped, and when she was satisfied they were clean, she finally filled them with water, took them to the kitchen, and put them on the stove.

The pantry that was off to one side of the kitchen was a small room, lined with shelves that held assorted kitchen supplies, a stack of towels, dishes, and pots and pans, most of them looking as if they'd seen better days. She came back to the kitchen with several pieces of cloth and used one of them to wipe the dust from the stove, took another one back outside to the pump and wet it, then came back in and wiped down the stove another time. She looked in the pantry again and found a cylinder of long kitchen matches. She took one of the matches and told it, "Let's hope you still work." She struck it on the stovetop, and it burst into flame. "Thank heaven," Caroline said.

She held the match to the papers and wood and it started to burn. There was a well-worn broom leaning against one corner of the pantry. Caroline started the task of cleaning the entire kitchen. It took her a while, and when that was accomplished to her satisfaction, she started dinner. While the meal was cooking, she cleaned the dining room and set the table there for three. Thinking of their spat at the bottom of the stairs, and how Belk reminded her of her status in his eyes, she would eat in the kitchen without a qualm. She knew how Belk felt about eating with the servants. When dinner was ready, Belk was in the living room, unpacking his clothing from one of the trunks. Caroline went to call him to eat. "Dinner is ready, Mr. Belk."

"Go tell Father," was all he said. Caroline started up the stairs and he added, "If Jessica is still sleeping, don't disturb her. You can take her a plate when she wakes up."

Caroline didn't comment, but felt she had somehow won a small victory. The men ate in the dining room, and Caroline ate alone in the kitchen. She listened for bits of conversation, but throughout the entire meal, didn't hear Zachary speak one word to his father.

Once the dishes were cleaned, she found the trunk with the bed linens and spent the rest of the evening cleaning and making up the bedrooms so they would have somewhere to sleep. She started with Father Belk's room. He sat in the chair by the window and watched her work.

When she was finished, she told him, "I know you must be exhausted, the same way I am."

He nodded, and said, "Yes, I am."

Zachary Belk carried his things to the bedroom next to Jessica's in the front of the house. Caroline cleaned it, not with as much effort as she had put into Father Belk's room, and made up the bed. He went in and closed the door as soon as she was finished.

The downstairs room she'd chosen for herself wasn't much larger than the pantry, but it would hold the bed and chest from the smallest bedroom upstairs. She'd already made several trips up and down that day, and her knees were aching.

Her pride and the stubborn streak in her wouldn't let her ask Belk for help with the furniture. The next time she climbed the stairs, she took several lengths of rope up with her. To save her knees as many trips as she could, she slid the mattress down first and then took the bed apart, stacked the pieces, tied them together, and used a rope tied on each side of the frame to lower the parts onto the mattress.

The little chest had three drawers. She took each one of them out, stacked them at the top of the stairs, took a few steps down, lifted each drawer to the next level, and took another few steps down, repeating the process until the only thing she hadn't brought downstairs was the body of the chest itself. "I'll do that in the morning."

At the bottom, she carried the pieces one at a time to her room and re-assembled the bed. She stacked the drawers in a corner, put the linens on the mattress, and almost collapsed on it. She hadn't knelt for her bedtime prayers for a few years, and usually said them sitting on the side of her bed. This night, she lay prone with her joints aching and talked to God, reminding herself of Proverbs 16:18, *"Pride goeth before destruction, and a haughty spirit before a fall."*

Chapter 16

It was much later than usual by the time breakfast was ready the next morning. Caroline had the kitchen fairly well cleaned and scrubbed to her own exacting standards. She hadn't set places at either of the tables, but enough dishes to set four places were stacked in the kitchen. The tea kettle, a coffee pot, and a pot of oatmeal were heating on the stove when Belk came in. "Good morning Caroline. Did you sleep well?"

Caroline was wary, but always polite, "I'm afraid I did. It was well after sunup before I woke. I found some coffee in the supplies you brought home last night. It's ready, if you'd like some, and the oatmeal will be ready in a minute or two. We haven't any milk, but there's sugar."

"I'm famished. Father and Jessica are still sleeping, so I didn't disturb them.

He surprised Caroline by sitting at the kitchen table. Caroline realized he was waiting for her to serve him. She poured his coffee and placed a bowl of oatmeal in front of him. He sipped the coffee. "This is quite good, isn't it? I must admit, I worried about the quality of things available out here."

He picked up his spoon, put some sugar on his oatmeal and tasted it. After nodding his approval of the dish, he looked up at her. "Sit down, Caroline. We need to talk."

Caroline poured herself a cup of coffee and sat at the other end of the table. Belk pursed his lips. "I think we need to clarify our—our status. I know that Jessica thinks of you as a friend, even a second mother, as it were, and has been overly indulgent with you. I was quite tired yesterday and may have over-reacted at what I took as insubordination. If you took offense, I do apologize. However, I am the master of this house and insist that certain proprieties be observed. I have no intention of trying to change your relationship with Jessica. I'm quite sure it's too late for that. I am also aware that we need you in the house. Jessica is certainly in no condition to manage on her own. So, let me define our boundaries. I want you to help Jessica in any way you can and see after Father. You are an excellent cook, and I would like you to take full responsibility for the kitchen. It's only appropriate. I will not have my wife working as a scullery maid."

Caroline relaxed in her chair, sipped her coffee, and looked at Belk thoughtfully. If there were ever a time to be frank, this was it. "I've been doing a bit of thinking myself. I can look after Jessica and your father, and I can manage the cooking and kitchen work. I can even give you the respect you think you deserve, but I'm no longer a young woman. I'm too old to carry enough water for four people. I need someone to help me with the heavier work to be done, cleaning floors, the laundry, and so forth. I've been looking over the property. There's a little one-room cabin out back where I assume the former owners' help lived. When we thought we were going to have a home in the center of town, I assumed we would be walking to the stores and church and so forth, but now I see that would be impossible. We'll need two horses."

"Why two?"

"You're going to need a horse for yourself to ride to whatever work you find and a rig for us. I also suggest you get a cow and some chickens so we can have milk and eggs already here. If I can find seed in town I may be able to plant a late garden."

Belk looked surprised. "Well, you have been doing some thinking, haven't you? I don't think I've ever heard you speak more than five words at a time."

Caroline nodded. "I'm only being practical. I've written down a list for groceries and the like. I packed some things that would travel and brought them from home, salt and baking powder and so forth, but we need some meat and butter and other things that won't store for very long. She took a paper out of her apron pocket and handed it to him.

He glanced at it. "You're quite right. I should have asked the driver to fetch me this morning and drive me back into town, but I didn't think of it, so I have quite a hike set out for me today. I'll do my best to come back with as many of the things you've requested as possible."

They heard sounds from upstairs. Belk stood. "I believe Father is up. I'll see that he gets himself dressed."

Caroline also stood. "I'll look in on Jessica."

She tapped lightly on Jessica's door. When there was no answer, she peeked in. Jessica was still sleeping soundly. Her breathing was regular, but appeared shallow. Caroline looked down at her fondly, and then frowned. She sat on the side of the bed and leaned over to look closer. She whispered to her, "Jess, it's me, Caroline."

Jessica didn't stir. Caroline said in her regular voice, "Jess? You've been sleeping for over fourteen hours. I know I promised not to wake you, but I think you need to get up now."

Jessica fluttered her eyelids, opened her eyes, and looked at Caroline as if she were having trouble focusing, then closed them again. Caroline inhaled sharply, put one hand over her mouth and stood up. She rushed out of the room and came back a moment later with Belk. Caroline waited anxiously behind him while he sat down next to Jessica, picked up her hand and leaned down close to her face. "Jessica? Jessica?"

Again, she fluttered her eyes, then closed them. He ran his hand through his hair. "What should we do? I think we should get a doctor, but it will take me at least an hour to walk into town."

"There are neighbors right across the road. See if they would take you in to find a doctor."

He jumped up and ran out of the room. Caroline sat, picked up one of Jessica's hands, and held it in both of her own. She held it to her lips and kissed the back of it. "You'll be all right, baby. He's gone to fetch the doctor."

Belk ran down his front steps and trotted across the street. He went up the neighbors' steps and knocked loudly on the door. After a moment, a man in work clothes, fifty or so, appeared.

Belk explained, "I'm Zachary Belk. My family moved in the house across the road yesterday. My wife is only a few weeks away from giving birth, and there's something wrong with her. We can't wake her up. I don't have a horse yet, and I wondered if you would be so kind as to take me into town so I can find a doctor?

The man nodded sharply, and opened the door, standing aside for Belk to enter. Belk went in. They cut through the house, which was furnished simply but spotlessly clean. As they passed through the kitchen, the man said to his wife, a nice-looking, somewhat matronly woman with gray at her temples, "This here is our new neighbor, Mr. Belk. His wife is sick and she's expecting. I'm taking him into town to fetch the doctor."

The wife nodded at him and he led Belk out the back door.

Drying her hands on a towel as she went, she hurried across the street and knocked on the Belk's door. Caroline came out of Jessica's bedroom and looked down from the top of the stairs. In his hurry, Belk had left the front door open, and she could see the woman standing on the other side of the screen door. She called down, "Yes?"

"I'm Adele West, from across the road. I understand that Mrs. Belk is doing poorly and I thought I'd see if I could help."

"Thank you so much. Please come in. She's up here."

Adele opened the door and came in. She climbed the stairs quickly, and Caroline led her to Jessica's bedroom. She looked closely at Jessica's face. "What's her name?"

"Jessica. Jessica Belk, she's been sleeping since yesterday afternoon."

Adele West gently shook Jessica's shoulder, "Jessica, wake up. I'd like to meet you."

Again, Jessica's eyelids fluttered, but she didn't waken. Adele looked up at Caroline. "When is her baby expected?"

"In about two months. We're not exactly sure."

Adele pressed her palms against each side of Jessica's stomach. She said, "Her stomach is normal, not hard like it would be if she were in labor. That's a good sign."

She took the covers down and examined Jessica's clothes. "There's no sign of blood or water. That's a good thing, too. How long has she been like this?"

"She went to bed yesterday around six in the afternoon. When I tried to wake her this morning, all I could get was for her to open her eyes for only a bit, like she did right now. Then she went back to sleep."

Adele rearranged the bedding and took one of Jessica's hands in hers. She asked Caroline, "You came in on the train?"

"Yes, we came here from New York."

"That's what, a five or six day trip?"

"It was five days altogether. There was a problem with the rails somewhere in Ohio that held us up."

"Did you have a compartment or did she have to sit up in a car?"

"She had a compartment, so at least she did have a place to lie down and sleep."

"Before the trip, was she sleeping more than before she was in a family way?"

"A little, maybe."

"When I carried my first one, I slept better than twelve hours a day for the last two months, and there wasn't a thing wrong with me. I'm no doctor, but I have four children of my own, and I'm a trained midwife. I've helped deliver quite a few babies. My guess is that she was just plain exhausted. I wouldn't worry too much unless the doctor finds something I can't see. Your daughter will probably wake up when she's good and ready, and she'll be fine."

"I hope you're right."

"She looks a little pale. Does she eat much meat?

"Not really, not since carrying the baby. The sight of a beef roast or fried eggs turned her stomach for the first few months. It doesn't bother her anymore, but she hasn't eaten that much beef since that first time it made her sick."

"I think maybe her blood is a little thin. A piece of beef would do her good."

"When I get a chance to go into town and get the supplies I'll try to find something nice."

Adele patted Jessica's hand. "Let's let her be until her husband comes back with the doctor."

"I have a pot of coffee on the stove. Do you have time to sit and talk for a while?"

"I would love that. It's been pretty lonesome out here since Helen Andersen died, and her husband left town. The only chance I get to talk to another woman is at church or when we go to the store."

They went downstairs, and in the kitchen, Adele sat at the table while Caroline poured two cups of coffee. The sugar bowl was still on the table.

Caroline sat. "I'm sorry we don't have any milk or cream in the house yet."

Adele leaned toward her and smiled. "You only arrived yesterday. If there's anything I can give you, please don't be too shy to ask. Folks in Kansas take care of one another."

"Thank you. I may have to do that, but of course, if I did, I'd repay it as soon as I could."

"I know. Do you have any other children?"

"Jessica isn't my daughter, not my real daughter. Her mother died when she was only five. I raised her like she was my own. I was one of the servants in her father's house since I was only a young woman. I hear tell that there's no love stronger than that of a mother for a natural born child, but I don't see any way for a person to love someone more than I do her."

"She's lucky to have you. Do you get along with her husband all right?"

Caroline looked away for a moment. Finally, she said, "I'll do whatever I need to keep her happy."

"I understand. I'm finished with my morning chores. Let me help you with some of this cleaning."

"That would be a Godsend, Adele. I didn't know how I could get it all done by myself."

With the horse trotting quickly, a buggy with Belk sitting next to a doctor came driving up to the front of the house. The doctor pulled it to a stop, and Belk jumped down from his side and ran to the front gate. He waited impatiently for the doctor, an older man, to get down, find his bag from the buggy, and follow him.

"She's upstairs."

Once inside the house, Belk ran up the stairs toward the bedrooms. The doctor took the steps one at a time, pausing every third step or so.

In the kitchen, Caroline and Adele were still washing things from the pantry. They heard the screen door slam. Caroline said, "That must be Mr. Belk with the Doctor."

Caroline and Adele went to the living room in time to see the doctor climbing the stairs. He saw Adele and broke out in a grin. "Good morning, Adele. I'm happy to see you're here before me."

At the top of the stairs, Belk urged him on. "Please hurry, doctor."

"I'm hurrying as fast as I can. My knees aren't as young as yours."

The doctor finally reached the top of the stairs. Belk got behind him and almost pushed him into Jessica's room. Caroline and Adele arrived close behind, but waited in the hall and looked in the open door.

In the bedroom, the doctor placed his bag on the table beside the bed and opened it. "I don't know why you called me. Adele here is one of the best midwives in Riley County." He took his stethoscope from the bag and his watch from his vest pocket.

Belk began pacing and running his hands through his hair. "You've got to save this baby, doctor."

Frowning, the doctor glanced up at him and put his stethoscope to Jessica's chest. "I intend to do the best I can to save both of them."

"Of course, but you don't understand. This baby is very important."

The doctor was trying to listen to Jessica's heart. He waved a hand in Belk's direction. "Hush!"

He listened and looked at his watch for a while before putting it away. "I want you to help her sit up so I can listen to her heart and breathing from the back."

Belk rushed forward and lifted the sleeping Jessica into a sitting position. She moaned a little and muttered something they couldn't understand. The doctor placed his stethoscope against Jessica's back and listened some more.

Almost whining, Belk said, "What is it? Is she going to be all right? What about the baby? Is he all right?"

"I said, hush!"

Belk stopped talking. After a moment, the doctor sat back. "All right, you can put her back down now. Adele, stay here with me. Would you others please wait in the hall?

Belk turned to leave, but paused at the door. "Are you sure I shouldn't wait here?

"No. I need to examine her without distraction. Please wait outside, and close the door behind you."

Belk and Caroline waited in the hall. As was his habit when he was frustrated, Belk paced back and forth, walking the full distance of the corridor.

Finally, the door opened, and the doctor and Adele came out. Belk rushed to him. "Is she going to be all right?"

The doctor shrugged. "Well, I don't know what to tell you. Her heart is fine, her breathing is all right. She doesn't have a fever, isn't in labor, and her reflexes are normal. She responds to stimuli by opening her eyes, however briefly, and seems to be trying to say something, so she isn't in what I would call a genuine coma. She might awaken any minute, or she could go on like this for a while. Considering what you told me about the trip from New York on our drive out here, it's probably extreme exhaustion. The body has a way of shutting down to heal itself in cases like this. Her gums are quite pale, and I wouldn't be surprised if she weren't anemic on top of everything else. According to what you told me, the last few weeks have been very traumatic for her emotionally, giving up her home to the care of a stranger and the long train ride. She had all this taking place in late pregnancy. It was too much, simply too much."

Belk's face drained of color. "Is there a hospital in town? Maybe we should move her there."

The doctor shook his head. "Nearest hospital is in Topeka. As long as there's someone here to see after her properly, I believe she'll be better off if she stays right where she is."

"What about the baby? Is he all right?"

The doctor frowned at Belk. "The baby seems to be fine, right strong heartbeat."

"Thank God. This won't harm his development will it, her sleeping like this?

"I don't think so. You could try talking to her when you're in there, rub her stomach. It will keep the child stimulated."

He looked at Belk, then to Caroline. "Now, I need to talk to whoever would be taking care of her personal needs."

Caroline was the one who answered him. "That would be me."

"Very well, come with me."

The doctor and Caroline went back in the bedroom. Belk started to go with them, but the doctor closed the door before Belk could follow them in.

Standing behind him, Adele spoke up, "Why don't we go back downstairs and have some coffee while we wait?"

Belk gave a curt, angry nod, and the two of them went to the kitchen. Belk took a seat and waited to be served. He'd seen to his own needs when he and his father were living alone, but if there was a woman in the house, no matter how slight an acquaintance she may be, he expected her to take the servant's role. Adele smiled and poured the coffee. It was only a few minutes before Caroline and the doctor came down.

Caroline asked him, "Can I get you a cup of coffee, Doctor?"

The doctor nodded. "I need to get back to town as soon as I can, but if you would give me about a quarter of a cup, I could drink it down and be on my way. I think everything is well in hand with Mrs. Belk. It's a matter of wait and see."

Caroline poured him the coffee. "Would you like sugar in it?"

"No, don't have time." He turned up the cup and, true to his word, drank it all down at one time.

Belk stood. "Doctor, I'd like to ride back into town with you. We need a great many supplies, and I have no transportation other than the kindness of my neighbors."

"Certainly."

"Thank you. Caroline, I'll see how many of the things I can get crossed off your list."

Once Belk and the doctor were back in town, Belk asked the doctor to stop the buggy in front of the bank. If he was to buy anything that cost more than the few dollars he had in his pocket, he would need to see if their funds had arrived from New York. Mr. Wilkes, the bank president, assured him that everything was in order, and Belk withdrew three hundred dollars from the account. Mr. Wilkes was somewhat concerned at the large amount.

Belk explained, "We only arrived yesterday, and our place turned out to be a good distance from town. I have to find a horse, a wagon, a cow, and quite a few other supplies. My housekeeper gave me a list."

He took the paper from his vest pocket and showed it to the banker, who chuckled. "This is quite enough to start up housekeeping. It's a good thing we have women in our lives, or we wouldn't be able to get anything done."

Belk found nothing amusing in this. Through clenched teeth, he said, "I suppose that depends on the women, doesn't it?"

Belk left the bank and walked directly across the street to the saloon. At the bar, he said, "Give me drink of the best whiskey you have."

The bartender reached underneath and pulled out a bottle of Jack Daniel's. "This here's a pretty new brand but I think right highly of it. Comes out of Tennessee." He poured a glass for Belk, who sipped it and nodded.

"It will do. Thank you." He tossed a coin on the bar, turned around to survey the room, and leaned back against the bar. There were a few poker games going on, and he had to resist the urge to join them. *There will be plenty of time for that later*. For the time being, Jessica's condition was still foremost in his mind.

He thought he knew where to find the help he needed and went to the livery stable, where he found Everett, the driver he'd hired to drive Jessica and Caroline to the house. He greeted him. "Good morning. I'm Zachary Belk. You drove my wife out to our new home yesterday."

Everett looked at him for a moment, "Oh, yes. I 'member. How're you liking the house?"

"It's very nice, but there are a number of things we need and, being new to town, I have no idea of where to find anything. After you show me a good horse and a wagon, I thought perhaps, for a dollar, I could get you to show me around."

Everett. "I'd be right glad to, Mr. Belk. Judd Parsons is the owner here. He can fix you up with a fine animal."

Late that afternoon, Caroline sat in a straight-back chair by Jessica's bed. She'd bathed Jessica and dressed her in a lace-trimmed nightgown. Her hair had been pulled over her shoulder and Caroline leaned over, brushing it gently and talking to her. "So, Mr. Belk rode back into town with the doctor to get supplies. I gave him a pretty long list. He's been gone all day. I don't know how he's going to get back with all those things, but he said he would bring home as much as he could. Adele and I got you bathed and changed. She stayed here with me all morning, and the two of us cleaned your room first, and then went downstairs and cleaned the rest of the kitchen. We cleared a little pathway to the outhouse so we won't have to be afraid of stepping on a snake, and cleaned up the inside of it. You were right about the walk, it was overgrown something awful, but when we cut back the weeds, there was a pretty little limestone path. I'm not saying that this Mrs. Andersen who lived here before us was a bad housekeeper, but this white Kansas dust had settled on everything inside the house, and the weeds have taken the place over outside."

She put the brush on the table and relaxed a bit, holding Jessica's hand. "You're going to be fine. I'm sure of it. You'll get all rested up, and then you'll wake up, and you'll be fine. Of course, your room and most of the downstairs ones are nice and clean now, but I haven't gotten to deep-down cleaning the other upstairs rooms. I think what I'll try to do, is to get one room cleaned up every day. Mr. Belk said he would get me some other help, but heaven knows how long that's going to take. I suppose he should concentrate on finding a position first."

Jessica opened her eyes and made a small smile before her lids fluttered a little, and she drifted back off to sleep.

Chapter 17

It was dusk when a horse pulling a farm wagon came down the road. It had a bench seat in the front and a platform with wooden sides in the back. Belk was driving. The back of the wagon was loaded with supplies, including a bale of hay and a crate of chickens. A cow was tied to the back. A young woman sat next to Belk. He drove around the house to the back porch before he stopped. Caroline came out of the kitchen.

The first thing Belk said was, "How is Jessica?"

"She's the same. I looked in on her only a few minutes ago."

"This young lady is Mimi. You said you wanted some help, and I've brought you some."

"I'm pleased to meet you Mimi, very pleased."

Mimi was a pretty, dark haired girl wearing braids and a plain prairie dress. She looked Indian. The girl nodded, but didn't speak. There was no expression on her face. Belk got down from the wagon. He made no move to help her, and the girl climbed down unassisted. He walked to the horse's head and took hold of the halter. "I'll unload this hay first, and then we'll bring in the supplies."

Caroline nodded, and followed as he led the horse in the barn. Inside, Belk stopped the wagon. Mimi untied the cow and put her in a stall. Belk stood there looking at the harness a moment. "I never had to unhitch the harness before. We always had people to do that for us."

The girl stepped forward and easily began removing the harness.

"What is the horse's name?" Caroline asked.

"They called him Juniper."

"That's a strange name for a horse. Did they say why they call him that?"

"I haven't the foggiest idea, and I didn't ask."

Belk watched Mimi at work on the harness. "Well, I didn't know I had hired an expert at horses. Mimi, if you'll take care of the animals, Caroline and I will get the supplies to the kitchen."

He walked to the back of the wagon, set the crate of chickens to the ground, and tried to heft the bale of hay. He was much too weak. He grunted and stopped trying to pick it up. With great effort, he finally pulled it off the end of the wagon and let it drop.

He looked a little embarrassed when he told Mimi, "I'm evidently not well suited to lifting bales of hay, either. I guess we can simply cut the cording on it and use the pitchfork to put it in the proper place. We do have a pitchfork, don't we?"

Caroline nodded. "Yes. I saw one when I was in here this morning."

He picked up a box of groceries, walked out of the barn and toward the house. Mimi had the harness down. She led the horse into a stall and closed the gate, then picked up the harness, looked around until she saw a nail sticking out of a post, and hung it up, looping it so the ends weren't dragging on the ground. She looked at Caroline and waited.

Caroline smiled at her. "Good enough. Let's get these things into the house."

Mimi didn't move. She pointed to the horse, "Water."

"Water?"

"The cow and the horse need water."

"Oh, of course, water. There's a pump at the end of the porch."

Mimi again looked around until she found a pail, picked it up, and walked toward the house. Caroline went after her. "I'm afraid that none of us knows the least thing about taking care of animals, but I do know that, since we live so far from town, we needed a cow, and we're going to need the chickens, too. It's looks to me as if you have quite a bit of experience in that field. Am I right?"

"Yes."

"You're an Indian, aren't you?"

"Yes. I'm Kansa Tribe. Whites call us Kaw, after the river. We are part of the Sioux Nation, the Southwind People. There are not many of us left now. Soon, all of my people are being forced to move from here to a place called Oklahoma. Chief Allegawaho struggles to keep this from happening, but I know he cannot win. If I have a place to stay, and work to do, I will not have to go."

"Kansa, Kansas. I guess that means they named the state after you, your people, I mean."

"Yes."

"I'm very happy to have you here, and I hope it works out. There's a nice little cabin for you, so you'll have your own home. I'm afraid it's only one room, not very fancy, and probably badly in need of a cleaning."

"It will be all right. I am happy to be here, where I will have work to do, a place to sleep, and food to eat."

"Mimi's an unusual name for an Indian, isn't it?"

180

"My name is Kimimela. It means butterfly in the Sioux language, but it is too hard for whites to remember, so they call me Mimi."

"Kimimela. What a pretty name. I'll try to remember that."

"It doesn't matter. I have answered to Mimi as many times as I have to Kimimela."

"Well, Mimi, welcome to our home. I hope we all enjoy one another's company. You go ahead and take care of the animals, and when you get finished, come on in the house. Our neighbor was kind enough to lend us some things for dinner, and it's been ready for a while. I don't know how long it's been since you ate, but I feel like I'm starving."

"Thank you."

The table in the kitchen was roughly set for four. Father Belk sat on one side. Caroline stood at the stove. Belk came in, looked at the table, and wrinkled up his nose. "This arrangement will suffice for this evening, but as soon as you're finished unpacking and cleaning, my family will take our meals in the dining room. You and Mimi can eat in here."

Behind her back, Caroline clenched a fist that he could not see, then answered meekly, "Yes, sir. Everything's ready. I tried to get your father to eat earlier, but he wanted to wait for you."

"He spoke to you?"

"A little. When I told him that dinner was ready and said I would bring him a plate to his room if he wanted, he said, 'No, I'll wait for Zachary.' I think he was a little lonely, sitting alone up there all day. Mrs. West was kind enough to help me with the cleaning and lend us a few things we needed for tonight's meal. She was so sweet. She helped me clean all afternoon."

"Her husband has a great deal in common with Father. He seemed to be listening to everything I told him, but he never had more than one or two words to answer me."

"We're lucky to have the people like the Wests right across the road," Caroline said.

"Yes. Farmers. They'll be very suitable friends—for you and Mimi."

After breakfast the next morning, Caroline went to Jessica's room. Jessica lay there as she had the day before. She didn't stir when Caroline checked her linens, put on a fresh nightgown, washed her face, and brushed her hair. When she had done everything she could think of to make Jessica comfortable, Caroline pulled the chair up to her bed. She prayed for her and talked to her until it was time to go back downstairs and make lunch for the men.

As soon as she was finished with that, she came back upstairs and talked and prayed some more until it was time to prepare dinner. She didn't come back up that evening. Her knees told her they weren't up to a third trip.

The third day, she did the same thing, with a few tears added to the praying.

Adele helped Caroline carry the frame of the chest downstairs and put together her bedroom in the little room off the kitchen. It was sparsely furnished. She'd covered her bed with a well-worn, handmade quilt and put her Bible and a kerosene lamp on the table.

When the rest of the household had gone to bed, Caroline couldn't resist the impulse to look in on Jessica one more time. She put on her nightgown and a flannel robe and slippers, and climbed the long flight slowly. She sat by Jessica's side. After a long while, her eyelids began to droop. She got up to leave, but paused in the doorway. Putting the lamp back down on the table, she awkwardly got down on her knees, something she hadn't done in a long while. She leaned against the bed, propped her elbows on the quilt, and bowed her head. "Dear God, I won't ask You to wake Jess because I know You are letting her sleep so You can take care of her. Keep her angel watching over her, and please give me the strength to do what I have to do for her sake. In Jesus's name, amen."

She struggled to get to her feet, made the long trip down the stairs to her room, got into bed, sighed deeply, and turned off the lamp. She lay there in the dark for a while, and was still talking with God when she fell off to sleep.

The next morning, the table was set, and Caroline was at the stove turning over bacon that was frying next to several eggs in a big pan. Father Belk sat at the table, waiting for his breakfast. Through the window, Caroline could see Mimi cutting down the weeds in the back yard with a scythe. The edge of the door to the living room was pushed open, and Jessica's voice said, "Oh! That smells so good. I'm starving."

Caroline was frozen to the spot. She calmly put down her fork, and turned around. Tears began streaming down her cheeks. She rushed to Jessica and hugged her tightly. Her voice caught, "Oh, my baby. You're awake!"

"I'm awake and ready to eat a side of beef or whatever else you have on hand. I see that someone made the trip to town to get supplies. It must be after nine o'clock. How long have I been asleep?"

"Three days."

"Three days? What on earth--?"

"We were worried sick when you didn't wake up that first day. Mr. Belk went into town for the doctor and he said all we could do was wait."

"Wait? Wait for what?"

"Wait and see if you woke up. Oh, Jess, it was so much like when your father was sick that I was worried out of my mind, but you're awake now, and you're--"

"Hungry. I'm awake and hungry."

Caroline clapped her hands together. "Ha, ha! Now, that I can do something about."

Jessica sat next to Father Belk. He put his hand over hers and smiled at her. "Welcome back, Jessica," he said.

Caroline scooped two eggs and several strips of bacon from the pan onto a dish, opened the oven door, took out a pan of biscuits and added two of them to the plate, which she then placed in front of Jessica. Jessica took a bite of the bacon and talked with her mouth full. "Oh, this is so good. You'll have to forgive me if I make a pig of myself. Is the tea ready?"

"I haven't made any tea since you were asleep, but the kettle is hot. It seems that everyone else in the house drinks coffee. I kept it on the stove just in case."

While Jessica ate heartily, Caroline prepared Father Belk's plate, and he also began eating his breakfast with gusto. Caroline went to the pantry and returned with the china teapot and a tea canister.

Jessica looked up. Through the top of the Dutch door that leads to the back yard, she could see Kimimela working.

"Who's that girl working in the yard?"

"That's Mimi. She's a Kaw Indian. Mr. Belk hired her to help out. She's really quite wonderful. She hasn't been afraid to tackle anything. She even sees after the horse like an expert."

"Horse? We have a horse?"

"Yes, the first day you were sleeping Mr. Belk rode back to town with the doctor and brought home a very serviceable wagon, a horse, a cow, some chickens, the kitchen supplies, and Mimi."

"Zachary did all that in one day? How wonderful. He's really has begun showing some initiative. How did he pay for all that?"

"I didn't ask."

Jessica poured herself a cup of tea and then sipped it while she gazed out the window, watching Kimimela work.

Father Belk patted her hand. "I'm glad you're awake, Jessica. We were all worried about you."

"Thank you, Father Belk. It's good to be back, even if I didn't know I was gone so long."

Caroline went to the door and called out, "Mimi, breakfast is ready."

Caroline returned to the stove and prepared Kimimela's plate. As she put it on the table, Kimimela came in and made a sudden stop when she saw Jessica. Jessica smiled at her, "Good morning, Mimi. I'm Jessica Belk. I'm awake."

"Good morning, Mrs. Belk. I am happy to see you."

"Please, Jessica is fine."

On the sideboard, there was a washbasin, soap, and towel. Kimimela quickly washed her hands and sat at the table. Jessica asked Caroline, "Where's Zachary?"

"He's still upstairs. He's been sleeping in one of the other rooms so he wouldn't disturb you. Should I wake him?"

"No, let him sleep. Sit down and eat with us."

Caroline made one more breakfast plate and sat in the last chair at the foot of the table. Jessica asked Kimimela. "How much is Zachary paying you?"

"He isn't paying me anything. I have my own cabin and my meals."

"Nothing? That's not right. He has to pay you something."

"We didn't talk about it that first day. It's all right."

"No, it isn't. Once I get everything straightened out, I'll see to it that you get some sort of appropriate wage."

The door from the living room opened and Belk came in the kitchen. "Good morn--Jessica! Oh, thank heaven you're awake. How did you get down here?"

Jessica laughed. "The usual way."

"You should have called me to help you. You might have had a spell coming down the stairs and fallen. You could have harmed the baby."

"I'm fine, really."

Belk looked at the table and sneered. "Isn't this cozy? Caroline, please bring the Belk family's breakfasts to the dining room. We'll eat there. Come with me, Jessica, Father."

Jessica stuck her chin in the air. "I'm fine right here."

"Suit yourself," Belk said, with ice in his tone.

Jessica and Father Belk both went on eating and made no move to leave the room. Caroline didn't reply, but stood and got a plate for Belk. He exited to the other room, and Caroline followed him, carrying his breakfast.

In the dining room, Belk sat while Caroline went to the credenza to get the silverware. She gathered the utensils with one hand while holding his plate in the other. She quickly set up his meal at the head of the table, and he took a seat.

She asked him, "Would you like coffee or tea?"

He fumed. "I would like coffee, and salt, and pepper. And some sugar and cream. And some jam and butter." He smacked one palm on the table. "From now on, try to do things properly, and set this table for three. I won't make Jessica come in here this morning, but after this, she will be having her meals in here the way she should. Don't make me tell you again."

"Yes, Mr. Belk."

He looked back at the kitchen door. "Where's my father?" He jumped from his seat and went back in the kitchen. "Father, please come to the dining room."

Father Belk's plate was empty. He picked up his cup and followed Belk, but as he went out of the room, he looked back at Jessica with a twinkle in his eye.

Kimimela carried her plate to the wash basin. "I have to get back to work."

She took another drink of her coffee, and went out the back door. Jessica pointed toward Caroline's chair. "Caroline, now that they're all gone, sit down and tell me what's been going on here while I was asleep."

Caroline spent the next few minutes filling Jessica in on the events of the last few days. Jessica pushed back her chair. "Let's take a walk around the house so I can get a good look at it."

Caroline frowned. "Don't you think you should rest some more?"

"Now that I have a full stomach, I feel wonderful. I don't think I've ever been that hungry in my entire life." Jessica walked out the kitchen door onto the back porch. She called back inside to Caroline, "Mimi has done some wonderful work out here, Caroline. She's cleared the weeds for quite a distance around the house. Come walk around this place with me. I want to see what we have here."

Caroline came out carrying a shawl. "Put this on. The mornings are getting chilly."

Jessica wrapped the shawl around her shoulders, and Caroline held her by the elbow as they went down the stairs.

Jessica said, "Let's walk around the house first and see what sort of shape it's in."

The two women walked in a circle around the building. They stopped by the picket fence that bordered the front. Several of the slats had fallen off and lay on the ground. Jessica looked at the house across the road. "I wonder how long it will take to get our place looking as nice as that one."

"That's the Wests' house. Adele is wonderful. You're going to love her. I haven't met her husband yet, but if he's anything like her, they're going to be ideal neighbors. He drove Zachary to town the first day you didn't wake up."

Jessica pointed at a window. "We'll need a new screen on that window, and probably all the others, too. It looks to me as if the whole house needs painting."

Jessica reached over the picket fence and broke off one of the roses. She held it to her nose and sniffed the fragrance. "How lovely. I can hardly wait to get this front garden in order, but first I want to go into town and see if I can get some seeds or cuttings to make a late vegetable garden out back. I understand that it's a much milder climate here than we have in New York."

Caroline clucked her tongue. "I think you better leave the gardening to me and Mimi. It's too close to your time for you to be going into town or doing any gardening."

"But I feel fine."

"All the same, I won't let you take any chances by riding in a wagon over this road. It isn't all that well kept. Who knows what five miles of shaking around would do? You don't want to go into labor halfway to town, do you?"

Jessica sighed. "I guess you're right. OH! I wonder how long it will take to get the doctor here when it finally happens."

"I don't know, but we don't have to worry about it. Adele West is right across the road, and she's a trained midwife. The doctor said she's excellent. I've already talked to her about it, and she says that her first baby took a long time to come, so the doctor will probably have plenty of time to get here if you think you need him. If he doesn't make it, it should be all right anyway. She's had four of her own, and she's delivered dozens of others.

"That's comforting to know. I don't expect that I'll ever have another one, so I don't want anything to go wrong with this one."

"It isn't my place to ask, but you don't think that someday you and Mr. Belk will—you know?"

"That's up to him. He's been acting like an adult for the last two weeks, but that doesn't really make up for what he did before. He has to prove himself to me before I trust him again. I was a fool. Father tried to warn me about him, but I didn't listen. I was so hardheaded and so determined to marry him. I thought he would change. I thought I could handle him. I thought a lot of things. I had no idea of how completely a woman puts herself into a man's hands when she marries him."

"That's true. It's bad when you marry the wrong one."

"The way I did."

"I didn't say that."

"No, but we both know it's true."

"Let's pray that he'll take advantage of his second chance."

Jessica sighed. "I've been doing that all along, but yes, let's pray some more about that."

They had by then completely circled the house and come back around to the back door.

Jessica walked down the footpath away from the house. "Let's take a look at these other buildings."

They went in the barn. The horse stuck his head out of the stall and nickered at them. Jessica patted him on his head and scratched between his ears. "Oh, aren't you pretty? Is it a mare or a gelding?"

"I never asked."

"What's its name?"

"Juniper."

"Juniper? How funny." Jessica leaned over the stall door and looked at the animal.

"It's a gelding. I wonder if he's saddle broke. After the baby comes, I'll have to get myself a proper saddle so I can ride him into town. I always loved my rides in Central Park."

"This one came in pulling the wagon. I don't know if he's saddle trained, but we should have a saddle horse anyway. We'll be getting one soon."

"We will? Why do we need two horses?"

"I told Mr. Belk that, once he found a position and was riding into town every day, we would need a rig for us. I wouldn't want to be this far out of town and not have transportation."

"Of course not. This place isn't exactly what I imagined. I was expecting a nice house in town where we could walk to the stores and to church."

"I had the same idea, but living out here might have advantages. There's ten acres, twice as much as our house in New York, and we could have a really big garden, not only for flowers, but fruit and vegetables, too. Mimi's going to start clearing that next."

Jessica poked around the barn. "This is a nice barn. It looks very well built, but it's like the house. It could use some repairs and painting inside and out. What else is there?"

"Let's go see."

They walked around the grounds. As she spoke, Caroline pointed to the different buildings. "There's the outhouse, which has been thoroughly cleaned and is usable now without being afraid of spiders or snakes. Like all the buildings, it needs painting, but other than that, it's in good shape. There's Mimi's house, cabin, really. It has one room, but it's quite nice. There are a few sheds. One of them is a smokehouse. Over here to the other side of the barn is an orchard. I know you'll love that. I've already picked quite a bit of fruit and I'm going to start canning it. There're several kinds of trees ready to harvest, apples, peaches, pears, and cherries. We even have two walnut trees. The orchard is bordered by bushes with all kinds of berries. Everything has gone a little wild, but a good pruning this fall should get them in shape. When we go into town, we can get the jars for canning and have fruit all winter. I haven't done that since I was a girl, but I'm sure I can remember how to do it, and Adele said she would help. If we got our gardens planted and bought some more livestock, we could pretty much feed ourselves with what we have here. There's even enough room to grow hay and grain for the animals."

"More livestock, besides the horses and a cow?" Jessica laughed. "I can't imagine Zachary having anything to do with livestock."

Caroline hooted. "No, but Mimi is quite capable. She started right off taking care of the horse, and I asked her about the other things, a cow, more chickens, maybe even a few hogs, and she told me that she grew up taking care of stock."

"She's a real treasure, isn't she?"

"So far. She seems to have a really sweet nature, and to be a hard worker."

"Still in all, she's young and pretty, and some day some man is going to see that and take her away from us. We can't become too dependent on her."

"No, she'll leave us someday, that's for sure."

"I like that we have enough room for a really nice garden. If we can get a little land cleared, we can put out some vegetables that come to season quickly and get them in before the first frost. I wonder when that is?"

"I'll ask Adele. We're further south here than in New York, so we should still have maybe two months. I can't wait for you to meet her. You're going to love her."

Jessica suddenly stopped walking, took hold of Caroline's elbow, and leaned against her.

Caroline felt a panic rise up in her chest. "Are you all right?"

"I'm fine, only tired again, all of a sudden. I may be overdoing it for the first day. Let's go back inside."

Caroline wrapped an arm around Jessica's waist, and they went back in the house. As they came inside, there was a knock. They walked through the house to the living room. The main door was open, and Adele was standing on the porch, holding a box with the heads of plants sticking over the top. Jessica steadied herself by holding onto the back of a chair as Caroline went to the door.

Caroline told Adele, "You came at exactly the right time to meet Jessica. She's up and awake."

"I saw the two of you walking in the yard, so I had to come over to say hello, and welcome to the neighborhood."

Jessica smiled at her. "Thank you so much." She sat in the easy chair and slumped back.

Caroline looked worried. "Jess, I know you're tired. Shouldn't you go upstairs and rest?"

"I don't think I want to walk up a flight of stairs right now. I'm fine. I can rest here. I want to talk with our new friend. Please sit down for a while Adele. Caroline's been telling me about you. Would you like something to drink?"

Adele sat close to Jessica. She took Jessica's hand and held it. The look she gave her was more of an examination than a greeting. "No, thanks. I'm fine. All the signs are for a late winter, so I brought these over plants for you."

"Signs? What signs?" Jessica asked.

"The animals haven't even started growing their winter coats yet, and the trees are still putting out new fruit, things like that. If your girl can get some land cleared, she can put out these shoots right away. They're big enough to give you a considerable head start, and you can get some tomatoes and so forth. We don't get frost until around the end of October and sometimes even later than that."

"We were talking about that only a few minutes ago. You must have been reading my mind."

Caroline spoke up, "You know, that first day, when you were sleeping, Adele came over and looked at you before the doctor even got here, and she told us almost exactly the same thing he did."

"That's remarkable. Did you have medical training?"

"Not formally. Not in a hospital or anything like that. Before we moved out of town to this house, I helped a midwife deliver a lot of babies and then delivered some without any help but the Lord's, and of course, I had four of my own."

"That's wonderful. It makes me feel so much better to know you're right across the road if I need you."

"I'm so glad to have someone living here again. Helen Andersen was a wonderful neighbor and friend. It broke my heart that she died so young."

"Her husband was a distant cousin of my husband's. That's how we came to inherit the property when he died."

"Died? Jacob Andersen isn't dead."

"I don't understand. Zachary said--" Jessica leaned toward Adele. "Please tell me what you know about how Jacob Andersen came to leave this property."

"Jacob inherited this place from his father. It belonged to his grandfather before that. Helen came to live here after they married, about fifteen years ago. They never were blessed with children. After Helen died, he went a little crazy. If you ask me, he was carrying a load of guilt. He was never a very good husband. Helen did the best she could to keep the place up, but he was always too busy drinking and gambling with the trash in Junction City. He disappeared for almost a year, and when he came back to this area, he didn't come back to the house. Last I heard, he's living in a little rented shack in Junction City and working at a livery stable when he's sober enough. He told some people that he went to New York and got cheated out of the deed to the house in a poker game."

Jessica slumped back in her chair, dropped her head, and closed her eyes. "I should have known. I wanted so much for my baby to have a father that I was willing to believe anything he told me."

She looked up at Caroline, tears welling in her eyes. "He'll never change will he, Caroline?"

"It doesn't look like it, Jess. What are you going to do?"

"What can I do? I'm two thousand miles away from home. I'm almost ready to deliver this baby. Now I have the responsibility of Father Belk as well. When Zachary left this morning, he said he was going into town to talk to someone about a position. Let's hope he finds one."

Jessica lay on the bed, still dressed, when Belk came home. He sat on the bed next to her and put his palm on her stomach. "How is my son today?"

"The baby seems to be fine."

"How are you feeling?"

"I'm tired, Zachary."

"You probably tried to do too much. You shouldn't wear yourself out like that."

"I'm not tired from overdoing. I'm tired of you."

"Of me? What do you mean?"

"I found out today that you didn't inherit this house at all, that you won it by cheating the rightful owner in a poker game."

"I didn't cheat anyone. Many losers like to think they lost because they were cheated."

"That's hardly the point."

"Then what is the point?"

"The point is that you lied to me to get me to come out here."

"I had to lie to you. You were carrying my son, and I knew if I told you the truth you wouldn't come with me.

My son has to grow up with me, not only in the same city, but in the same house."

"Why? So you can teach him all the wonderful skills your own father passed down to you?"

"I know you won't believe this, but I realize how many times I've been responsible for my own troubles, and by association, your troubles. It isn't as if that's the way I meant it to be. I start out every day trying to do the right thing."

"Don't try to tell me you're comparing yourself to the Apostle Paul?"

"I don't understand."

"I didn't really think you would. In the Bible, Paul said he wanted to do good but failed every day."

"That's it exactly. I don't intend to make such a mess of things, but I always do. It never works out the way I expect."

"That's because you're never able to learn from your mistakes. You keep doing the same things over and over. I hoped you would change. I wanted so much for us to be a family that I kept giving you another chance, but when I heard how you got this property and realized what a terrible thing you'd done to me by luring me out here with such a lie, I gave up hope. I'm finished with you."

"So what do you expect now? I'm not leaving here, and you certainly can't leave."

"My house in New York isn't rented out yet. I can go back there."

"Not now, you can't. You're too far along in your pregnancy. You haven't even recovered from the journey out here. If you tried to make the trip back to New York in your condition, you could kill the baby."

Realizing the truth of his words, Jessica reacted almost as if he had slapped her.

"So, I'm trapped here, aren't I? At least until the baby comes, and I'm back on my feet."

"I'm afraid so."

He got down on one knee in front of her and took her hands in his. She jerked away from him and turned her face to look out the window.

He dropped his head and sighed. "Oh, Jessica, please try to understand. I don't want it to be this way. I'll try to do better. I really will. What do you want from me?"

"I want what I've always wanted. I want you to work and earn a living for us. I want you to stay sober. I want you to stop gambling away what money we do have. I want you to take care of your family. I don't care if you have to take a job at the livery stable cleaning out stalls."

Through clenched teeth, Belk said, "You surely can't expect me to do menial labor?"

"I expect you to do whatever you have to do to take care of your child. The money from selling Father's house isn't going to last forever. Coming out here wasn't cheap, and buying everything we need to get settled in this house will cost a small fortune. I can be very frugal, but if the agent in New York can't get someone to lease my place, in a few years we won't even have money to buy food."

"I was going into town in the morning to look for a saddle horse. I've already been to every one of the businesses. There aren't all that many, and none of them were interested in me, but tomorrow I'll go again and see if someone else will talk to me. I'll try, Jessica. I promise."

He went to her and leaned over to kiss her on the cheek. She turned her face away. He straightened up and looked at her as if he hated her. "So that's the way it's going to be?"

"I'm afraid so."

"Now that you've recovered from the trip, I was thinking of moving into your bedroom, but I suppose that's out of the question."

"We could hardly be having relations now."

"I was aware of that. I simply wanted to be closer to you."

"I can hardly stand to look at you, much less sleep next to you. No, if you really mean to get a job and act like an adult, if you prove yourself to me, then we'll see if I can ever have feelings for you again."

"I'll do my best, Jessica. I really will."

She nodded and looked away from him.

Chapter 18

The next morning, Zachary was up and dressed early. He didn't take time for breakfast, but rather plucked an apple from the barrel on the back porch and took a few bites from it before he and Mimi hitched up Juniper and drove off in the direction of town. He was determined to find some kind of position. *I won't work as a common laborer, but there's surely some sort of employment for a gentleman in this town.*

There was no stock broker in Manhattan for Belk to find a job in his usual line of work. There was no financial advisor firm and no insurance company. He started at the bank. He thought he may have an advantage since he'd already been there that first day he came to town. He dropped Juniper's reins over the hitching post, dusted off his suit, and went inside.

Mr. Wilkes sat at his large desk on the side wall. Belk walked over, stuck out his hand, and re-introduced himself. "I'm Zachary Belk."

Mr. Wilkes, the bank president, stood and shook his hand. "Yes, I remember you. What can I do for you today?"

"I'm seeking employment. I studied business at Columbia University, and I have an extensive background in stocks and financial matters. I believe I could be an asset to your firm."

Mr. Wilkes shook his head. "I'm sorry, but we don't have any openings at the present time. You may have better luck at one of the newspapers. See Mr. Davis at the *Mercury* or Mr. Kirk at the *Republic*. A man with your education isn't always easy to find out here."

Wilkes looked him up and down. Belk was well dressed, in what appeared to be expensive clothing. "If that fails, you should try Wareham Mercantile. Ask for William Wareham. You can tell him I sent you."

"Thank you, Mr. Wilkes."

A bit disheartened, Belk left Juniper standing where he was and went a short distance down the street to the *Manhattan Mercury* newspaper office. He had no better luck there, and there found none at the *Republic,* either. By the time he turned in the direction of Wareham Mercantile, he was thoroughly discouraged. At the store, he asked the first male employee he saw for William Wareham. The clerk went to an office on the side of the large show room and came back out followed by a smiling man in his thirties.

Belk shook his hand. "I'm Zachary Belk. I've only recently moved here, and Mr. Wilkes at the bank said I should talk to you regarding employment."

Wareham seemed impressed by Belk's attire. He nodded. "Come to my office, and we'll talk it over."

Belk followed Wareham to the office. Wareham took a seat behind the desk and then waved a hand at the wooden, straight backed chair that sat in front of it. "Have a seat, Mr. Belk."

Belk sat stiffly in the offered chair, feeling humiliated by the need to apply for a job that was clearly beneath him.

Wareham smiled at him. "Now, tell me a little about yourself."

Belk forced a smile. "I have a business degree from Columbia University and, until recently, I worked as a stockbroker and financial advisor in my father's firm in New York."

"Why did you leave there?"

"The crash of Black Friday hurt us more than it was possible for us to overcome."

Wareham nodded his head. "I understand. A lot of firms went under because of the crash. What brought you to our Manhattan?"

Belk didn't want to tell a lie that he may be caught in, so he chose his words carefully." I came into a piece of property here and decided to take my life in a whole new direction."

"I don't know if I have anything here that suits your background, Mr. Belk."

Belk tried to hide his distress. *If I don't find something at the Mercantile, I don't know where I can go after this. I certainly don't want to go home and tell Jessica I'm still without a job.*

"I wasn't all too keen on being a stockbroker anymore. I was hoping I might find something entirely different here."

"Well, in that case, I may be able to help you. Since I handle all the bookwork here, I don't have anything in the office. We are a rapidly growing city, Mr. Belk, and, therefore, have an increasing demand for a better line of men's furnishings. Would you consider a sales position in the men's clothing department?"

Belk's pride rose up in his gorge and, to force it down, he swallowed hard. "Yes, certainly I would."

"Very well. You can start Monday morning. Come in to the office at eight, and I'll show you the system here."

They covered a few details before Belk left. Wareham walked him to the front door, introducing him to the other employees as they went. Belk smiled, shook Wareham's hand, and left the big store feeling totally humiliated. *I'm the son of one of America's founding families, and now I must earn a meager living measuring other men's inseams.*

The only consolation he could find in the situation was that he could go home and tell Jessica he was employed. He would keep his ears open for other opportunities. Surely the job would help him to meet the wealthier men in town, men who might be able to provide him with a position more suited to his background. He didn't want his son to be raised thinking his father was a common clerk in a common store in a common town. Both he and his son deserved better than that.

He went to the saloon, where he looked for Everett, but couldn't find him. He asked the bartender, "I'm looking for Mr. Snipes. Do you know where I might find him?"

"If he's not drinking here, he's usually working at the livery stable."

"Thank you."

Belk went to the stable and found Everett with his pitchfork in hand, tossing hay into the manger. He called out, "Mr. Snipes."

Everett looked over his shoulder. "Mr. Belk. What can I do for you?"

"I need to purchase another horse and the appropriate tack."

"Sure, nuff. We got some here you can buy."

Everett led Belk to a small, fenced field out back where a half dozen animals grazed a few yards from the fence. "You look them over. I'll go get Judd, and you can talk a deal with him."

Belk gazed at the horses. *When I remember the fine saddle horse I had before the Crash, these beasts are a pitiful sight.* He chose the best looking animal, a black gelding with a blaze down his face and four white stockings, and decided it was the one he wanted.

Everett came back with Judd Parsons, who owned the livery stable. Belk had met him on the day they arrived in town, when bought Juniper and the wagon.

Parsons nodded. "How do, Mr. Belk. What can I do 'ya today?"

"I find myself in need of a saddle horse. I like that black gelding with the white stockings. How much do you want for him?"

"He's a right fine looking animal, if I do say so myself. I'd need two hundred for him. Everett, go fetch Thunder over here so's Mr. Belk can take a good look at him."

Everett picked up a lead hanging on the rail and slipped between the bars of the fence. Belk watched as Everett walked toward the group of horses. As he approached, they lifted their heads and looked at him. He talked to them as he drew near, a language Belk didn't recognize

I suppose I'm expected to bargain for him. He said to Judd, "That's a lot of money. You'll include the saddle and the other tack?"

Judd drew his fingers over his chin, pulling at an imaginary beard. "Well, I don't know about that. I s'pose it depends on how fancy a rig you have in mind. I got a half dozen saddles inside. You can look 'em over once't you decide on the horse."

In the field, Everett walked up to Thunder, took something from his vest pocket, and held out his hand. The horse stuck out his head and nibbled from Everett's palm, and Everett snapped the lead on the halter. He led Thunder to the gate and Judd opened it. Everett led the horse out far enough for Belk to walk around him to do his inspection. Belk had a small amount of knowledge of horseflesh. *I've seen this done, I can at least look as if I know what I'm doing.* Pretending to know more than he really did, he ran his hands over each of the animal's legs with no idea if they were sound or not, then looked at its teeth. He patted Thunder on the flanks and a cloud of dust rose up. He asked, "How old is this animal?"

Judd scrunched up his nose. "I'd say 'bout four years."

Belk raised an eyebrow. "Really?"

Judd scuffed the toe of his boot in the dirt. "Well, I didn't raise him, so I don't know for sure."

"I see." Belk turned to Everett. "You seem to know him quite well. How old is he, Mr. Snipes?"

Without looking at his employer, Everett said, "He's seven or eight, I reckon, but he's a fine piece of horseflesh, if I do say so myself. Only thing is—." He glanced at Judd, whose face turned red. Everett went on.

"He's a mite temperamental. If'n you took him, I'd say keep a cut-up apple in your pocket 'til he gets to know you. He'll do 'bout anything for a slice a' apple."

"Thank you for your honesty, Mr. Snipes. I'm quite sure I can handle him."

"I wouldn't let Mrs. Belk ride him. He'd be a bit too much for a lady."

"I doubt that Mrs. Belk will be up to riding for quite a while."

"Now, Mimi, she can handle any horse God put on this earth, so's if it came to it, she could ride him."

"Thank you for the information. We're quite satisfied with Juniper. I doubt Mimi would ever have occasion to ride my mount. In your opinion, is he sound?"

Everett scratched his stubble. "Yes, sir, I'd vouch for that. Now, he won't pull a wagon, like Juniper does. He's strictly a saddle horse."

"Fine." Belk turned to Judd. "Now, let's have a look at those saddles."

Belk chose a saddle and tack, and the bargain was struck. He told Everett, "You can saddle him up while I go to the bank and get the money, and, for God's sake, brush him down to get rid of that dust."

When Belk returned with the cash, the horse was clean and ready to go. Judd filled out the bill of sale, and Belk folded it and put it in his wallet. As Belk prepared to mount, Everett handed him a few pieces of sliced apple. "'Fore you get on, give him these, so's he'll think kindly of you."

Belk let the horse take the apple from his palm and wiped his hand with a pristine, white handkerchief.

Everett held the bridle and said, "He's going to buck you a bit at first, to test you out, but he ain't mean. Just hold on."

Belk sneered. "I'm quite sure I can handle him." He stuck his foot in the stirrup and heaved himself onto the horse's back. Thunder stiffened his legs and hopped around the yard. Belk grabbed the saddle horn, a device new to him, and held on until the animal settled down. Proud of having survived the initial confrontation with the horse, he turned and rode off with a wave of his hand. Thunder pranced and sometimes skittered sideways, but Belk kept control. By the time he reached the wagon and Juniper, he felt he had the animal well in hand. He tied him to the back of the wagon and drove home, a man with employment, such as it was.

Chapter 19

The next few months passed quickly, and soon it was late autumn. On the trees, the last few leaves were clinging to the ends of branches. One or two shriveled apples hung from the trees. There were still a few tomatoes reddening on the vines in the vegetable garden. Kimimela, wearing a blocky woolen coat over her dress, carried a large wicker basket filled with cabbage, a few small squash, and asparagus. She was leaning over to harvest the last of the little tomato crop. A few flakes of snow fluttered past her face and she looked at the sky, then bent over and started picking faster.

In the house, Father Belk sat at the kitchen table carving out a knight with great attention to detail. Caroline was standing at the other end of the table, holding a large bowl with her left hand while she cut butter into flour with a fork to make a piecrust. From upstairs, came Jessica's voice, "Caroline."

Frowning, Caroline stopped blending the pastry and listened. The voice came again, more urgent this time.

"Caroline! I need you. Please come upstairs."

Caroline dropped her fork, rushed out of the kitchen and into the living room. She paused at the bottom of the stairs and called up.

"Jess?"

"I'm in my bedroom, Caroline."

Caroline went up the stairs as quickly as her age allowed. She hurried to Jessica's bedroom. Jessica stood by the window, her eyes wide open and frightened. She looked at Jessica, and then down at her feet. Caroline followed her glance. Jessica was standing in a puddle of milky water.

"I was afraid to move. What should I do?"

"Your water has broken. That means it's time for the baby to come."

Caroline went to the window and called to Kimimela, "Mimi, come up here right now! The chilly wind blew a few dried leaves in the room. She closed the window and told Jessica, "Let's get you into a dry nightgown."

Kimimela came running up the stairs and stopped in the doorway. "What is it? Is it time?"

"Yes, the baby is coming. Run across the road and get Adele."

Kimimela ran out of the room and down the stairs. Caroline went to the chest, opened a drawer, and pulled out a plain white nightgown.

"There's no need in messing up one of your nice gowns. We'll use this one. It's almost worn out anyway. Now, let's get you changed."

By the time Kimimela came back with Adele, Jessica sat in bed. Caroline was rolling up the wet clothing to take downstairs. Adele went to the bedside and Kimimela waited by the door.

Adele sat on the bed next to Jessica and put her hand on Jessica's forehead. "Good morning. Mimi tells me the baby is coming. How far apart are your pains?"

"I'm not having any pains, but my water broke. Caroline said that meant it was time."

"She's probably right, and now it's only a matter of how much time. Is the water still coming, or has it stopped?"

"I don't feel it anymore. I think it stopped."

"Let's take a look."

Adele folded down the covers. She slipped her hand under Jessica's hips to feel for water, pulled it out, and then pressed both of her hands on Jessica's stomach, tilting her head as if to listen. After a moment she looked at Caroline. "She's not in labor yet."

Jessica asked, "How long is it going to be?"

"No telling. These things happen when they're good and ready. You could go into labor any minute, or it could be tomorrow or the next day."

"What do I do in the meantime?"

"Exactly what you're doing now, take it easy, rest, drink as much water as you want. We'll get everything ready for the delivery." She turned to Caroline, "We need a stack of clean towels and some soap. Does Mr. Belk have a Macintosh?"

Jessica asked, "He has one hanging on the peg by the kitchen door. Why do you want his raincoat?"

"I'm going to slip it under you. There's going to be a lot of water and some blood and we don't want to ruin the mattress."

"I hope it happens quickly," Jessica said. "I hate the thought of lying here in bed and waiting."

"You don't have to lie here and do nothing. Get up and move around if you want, but I don't want you going up and down stairs. You can read, or you can embroider.

We'll sit with you and we can talk. Keep yourself occupied, and the time will pass faster."

"Should we have Mimi go fetch the doctor?"

"Heavens no. He'd get all aggravated if we got him out here and you weren't even in labor. There's plenty of time for that. Most times, the first baby takes half a day or longer to get here, and that's not until you start having pains."

Jessica picked up a book from the bedside table and opened it. "I haven't finished this. Maybe by the time I'm done, things will start happening."

Adele sat in the chair by the window. Caroline sat at the foot of the bed, and Kimimela stood in the doorway. They were all staring at Jessica, who laughed at them. "Do you all plan to stay around here and stare at me until it's over? If it took a day or two as Adele says it might, your eyeballs will wear out."

The others laughed and Adele stood to leave.

Caroline told her, "I'll be right downstairs. If you need me, give a yell."

Adele said, "I'll be right across the road."

Mimi added, "I have work to do."

Adele said, "Mimi, before you go, fetch that raincoat, and I'll get everything ready."

Despite all their preparations, the day wore on and Jessica didn't go into labor. She had no appetite for dinner and stayed in her room all evening. As usual the next morning, Caroline was at the stove stirring a pot. Father Belk sat at the table polishing the silver.

Caroline talked as she worked. "Jess is sleeping late today. That's good. She needs to get a lot of rest."

Then she heard a thready voice call her, "Caroline."

Caroline cocked her head and listened. There it was again, louder and more urgent, "Caroline, please come upstairs."

Caroline put down her spoon. She hurried out of the kitchen, through the house to the stairs, and went up them as fast as her arthritis would allow. By the time she reached the bedroom, she was breathing hard. She rushed in the room. Jessica was lying on the bed with her back to the door, curled up on her side. Caroline leaned over her. "Are you all right, Jess? I thought I heard you calling me."

"I was calling. I think it's time for the baby to come."

Caroline rushed to the window and opened it. She shouted, "Mimi."

Mimi, dressed in her heavy coat and wearing a wool scarf wrapped around her head, was cutting a pumpkin from a vine. A small wagon next to her had a few pumpkins on it. Caroline leaned out of the upstairs bedroom window. Mimi looked up at her. "Jessica thinks the baby is coming. Run across the road and get Mrs. West."

Mimi put down the pumpkin and ran quickly toward the road. Caroline closed the window and shivered. "Mimi is getting Adele. She will know if it's time to get the doctor. Are you chilly? It's getting cold out there. Let me get another blanket for you. I wouldn't be surprised if we didn't get a big frost tonight."

She took a blanket off of a stand in the corner and spread it out over Jessica.

There was the sound of hurried footsteps on the stairs, and Adele came in the room. "Mimi tells me you may be ready to have your baby. Roll over on your back and let's take a look."

She pulled back the covers, checked the bedding, and pressed her hands against Jessica's stomach "When did the pains start?"

"A few hours ago, but they weren't really that bad until the last one."

"How long has it been since that?"

"About ten minutes."

"Where do you feel it the most?"

"In the small of my back."

With her hands still pressed against Jessica's stomach, Adele looked at the clock sitting on the table.

"Tell me when you get another one."

Almost immediately, Jessica started breathing in gasps and squinched up her face.

"Now, it's happening now."

Adele watched the clock. "Tell me when it lets up."

After a few minutes, Jessica nodded. "There, it's going away."

"Congratulations. It looks like we're going to have a baby today." Adele walked toward the door and tilted her head to Mimi and Caroline to follow her. They went out in the hallway. Adele said to Mimi, "This baby is coming fast. Go to Mr. Belk's business and tell him he should come home soon if he wants to be here when the baby arrives."

Mimi spun around and ran down the stairs. Adele went back into the bedroom.

Adele put the chair next to the bed and told Caroline, "I want you to get the towels and things I told you to gather up the other day and bring them up here.

Then put a few big pots of water on the stove. This baby isn't going to wait for any doctor."

"She isn't in any trouble is she?"

"Not that I can see. I never saw a firstborn coming so fast. Don't worry. Everything looks fine, and I've lots of experience."

Belk's horse came galloping down the road. Thunder skidded to a stop in front of the gate, and Belk jumped off, leaving the reins hanging. He ran in the house and up the stairs. He started to charge in the bedroom but stopped and listened, then knocked hesitantly on the door. Caroline, beaming from ear-to-ear, opened the door, "Mr. Belk. Come in and meet your baby."

"Is he all right? Is everything all right?"

"Everything is fine as can be. She had an easy time, and Adele knew just what to do."

Belk stepped inside the bedroom. Wearing a frilly nightgown, Jessica was lying in bed, holding the baby. A shock of curly auburn hair showed. Belk was in rapture. He walked to the bed in a trance, staring at the baby. He leaned over and hesitantly touched the blanket.

"He's beautiful, Jessica, simply beautiful. Caroline said you had an easy time."

Jessica smiled. "I don't know if I would describe it that way, but that's what Adele and Caroline tell me."

"I know you had your heart set on naming him after your father but I would really like to call him Zachary, Junior. You can name the next one William."

She laughed. "It may not be the right time to talk to me about another one."

"Can I hold him? Can I hold little Zachary?"

Jessica held out the baby. Belk reached for it as Jessica said, "Even though she has your hair, I think she'd like it much better if we called her Amanda, after my mother."

Belk froze. He took a step back and dropped his arms. A look of disgust twisted his face. "It's a girl?"

"Yes, a beautiful, perfect little girl. She hardly cried at all. The first time they put her in my arms, I would swear she smiled at me."

Belk turned and almost stomped out of the room.

Chapter 20

As the sound of the horse galloping away from the house reached them, Jessica's mouth dropped open. Caroline's face hardened with rage. "That man is the biggest fool I ever saw. Here God gives him a beautiful, healthy daughter, and he doesn't appreciate it one bit."

Tears sprang up in Jessica's eyes. "I knew he'd be disappointed it wasn't a boy, but I hoped he would love her after he saw her." She sobbed, "Oh, Caroline, why do I keep expecting the best of him when I've never seen anything but the worst?"

"I think you expect the best of everyone because that's the way your own heart is. It's the nature God gave you. Now, you look exhausted. You go on and get some rest. Amanda may be sleeping now, but she's going to want to nurse soon."

Caroline took the sleeping baby from Jessica's arms and put her in the cradle. She went back to the kitchen to start dinner.

From the window, she saw Kimimela come riding up and slide off Juniper's back. Caroline came out of the kitchen and walked beside her as she led the horse to the barn, unsaddled him and drew fresh water. Caroline said, "If the doctor's coming, it's a waste of time. The baby's already here, a little girl. Adele was wonderful, and everything is fine."

"I'm glad to hear it. There was a sign on the doctor's door saying he was out. I asked the sheriff when he'd be back, and he said the doctor has gone to a terrible farm accident."

Belk didn't come home until after midnight. He stayed in his room for a few hours, but in the morning, he saddled up his horse again. He needed two things, a drink and a poker game. He set out at an easy canter. In town, he kept going, steering the horse toward the southwest road that led to Junction City. He didn't want to spend his evening under the watchful eyes of people who might carry tales.

It took a while, but he finally saw the buildings of his destination rising in the distance. Junction City derived its name from the meeting point of the Smokey Hill and the Republican Rivers where they form into the Kansas River. Three railroads met there, keeping the town bustling. It was frequented by soldiers from Fort Riley looking for a little amusement, and Belk had heard it had a more relaxed atmosphere than Manhattan. There were two saloons along the main street, one a wood building with a piano player and tables for poker or faro, and one simply a tent with a wood platform resting on two barrels.

Belk tied his horse to the rail in front of the most prosperous one and went inside. He ordered a drink, watched the action at the various poker games, and asked the group that was the best-dressed if he could sit in. He'd barely been dealt his first hand when a woman walked behind his chair and ran her hand down his arm. "Buy a girl a drink?" she asked in a husky tone.

He turned to look up at the face of a pretty, blonde, young woman. "Sure, have a seat," he said.

"There aren't any more chairs. We could go sit at another table."

"I just got dealt my first hand. Here's a place to sit." He swung one knee out from the table and she settled herself on it and draped her arm across his shoulders. She made a signal to the bartender, who brought over a glass of whiskey-colored liquid that Belk knew very well was likely weak tea. He didn't care, and took a coin from his vest and flipped it to the bartender. The girl nuzzled his neck. "My name's Emmalou. You're new around here. What's your name?"

"That doesn't really matter, does it? Let me play a few hands first, and we can get better acquainted later."

"Anything you say, long as the drinks keep coming every once in a while. You wouldn't want me to lose my job, would you?"

"No, I wouldn't. Does your job include a trip upstairs later on in the evening?"

She drew back a little. "Nope, that'd be Mary or Lulu over there. I'm strictly a downstairs girl."

"I see. All right, downstairs it is, for now."

Belk played for a few hours, winning some and losing some. When he was slightly ahead, he dropped out. His experience had taught him it wasn't a good idea for a newcomer to win too much money, even in the finest drawing rooms of Manhattan, and certainly not in a seedy, wild-west saloon, where he didn't know who might take out the frustration of losing with a Colt .45.

Emmalou walked him to the door as he left. She wrapped an arm around his waist and pulled close to him.

She gazed at him with enchantment written on her face and said softly, "I was a downstairs girl up until tonight, but come on back again. You may be able to change my mind."

He grinned at her, pulled her outside of the saloon, pressed her tightly against him, and kissed her fervently before he shoved her away. "Think about that until the next time I see you, my angel-faced, downstairs-only, Emmalou."

He mounted his horse and touched his finger to his hat in a salute before he wheeled the animal around and cantered off toward home.

As he rode, Belk laughed with pleasure at the girl's starry eyed infatuation with him. Even when he and Jessica were first married, she'd never looked at him that way.

It was an enjoyable ride. He had several glasses of whiskey under his belt, and his selection of a horse, with Everett's advice, had been perfect. Thunder had a 'rocking chair' smoothness to his gait, and Belk relaxed back in the saddle as his body moved loosely to the horse's rhythm, leaving him free to mentally pursue a different plan for his life. He laughed aloud several times as he loped back to the house where Jessica and an unwanted daughter waited for him.

It was early morning before Belk arrived home. He dismounted a short distance away from the house and walked Thunder in the barn quietly. He unsaddled the horse and led him to the stall. There was still about an inch of water in his bucket and Belk made no effort to draw fresh water from the pump at the end of the back porch. Kimimela had told him that it was necessary that the animal have fresh water every time he went out, but Belk didn't want the noise to wake up anyone in the household. He opened the back door slowly and, once inside, crept up the stairs and to his bedroom. He undressed and slipped into bed, thinking he had gone unheard, and fell immediately into a deep sleep.

In her cabin, Kimimela heard the horse long before it reached the place where Belk dismounted. She lay in her bed listening while he put Thunder in his stall and went in the house. She listened for the whooshing of the water pump, and when she didn't hear it she angrily huffed out a breath of air. She got up, went to the barn, took the bucket to the pump, and filled it to the halfway mark.

In her room, Jessica had the hearing of the mother of a newborn baby. When she heard the back door close, she looked at the clock. The moonlight shining in the window told her it was after three in the morning. She rolled over and closed her eyes, thinking silent prayers until she drifted back to sleep.

In her bedroom off the pantry, Caroline woke with a start when she heard the back door open. She had no clock in her room, but her body rhythms told her it was closer to sunup than it was to sundown.

Father Belk was of an age when sleep frequently eluded him on any night, and this night he had waited anxiously for the sound of his son's safe return. When he heard the creak of Belk's foot on the top step, he was finally able to fall asleep.

During the next few months, he would often lie there awake, listening for that creak of the step.

Chapter 21

By the end of November, Jessica had regained her strength. She and Adele became quite close and one day they were sitting in kitchen chatting when Jessica told her, "I haven't been in town since I got here, Adele. This is the longest I've ever gone in my life without attending Sunday services. How far is it to the closest Baptist church?"

"Mine is only two miles from here. It's on the left side of the road, just before you get to the turn onto Poyntz Avenue. You can't miss it."

"Good. I'm really looking forward to it. I miss the services, especially the music."

Sunday morning, Zachary slept late. Jessica and Caroline were cooking breakfast when Jessica told Father Belk and Kimimela, "We're going to church this morning. Would the two of you like to go with us?"

Father Belk surprised them all by answering, "I was raised Methodist, and that's the church Harriet and I attended. I don't think I'll go with you this morning, but I might go another time."

Jessica's mouth dropped open. She hugged him and said, "That's the most words I've heard you speak at one time since we came here, Father Belk.

"I suppose it is. I didn't have much to say up until now."

"I hope you'll feel comfortable talking more. Amanda needs to have you tell her all about your family."

"After what we put you through, I wouldn't think you'd want her to hear about it."

"She should be proud of it, but keep it in the right place in her heart."

He thought this over. "I know what you're trying to say. We were too proud, too quick to let it make us—I don't know—haughty."

Jessica asked Kimimela, "Would you hitch up the wagon for us, Mimi? Maybe you'd like to go to church with us?"

Kimimela said, "I would like to go with you. I am curious about this Baptist Church."

Jessica dressed Amanda in her best little outfit, a dress made from one of her grandmother's pillowcases. Caroline put on her best dress. She hadn't worn it since the party Jessica gave in celebration of her divorce filing back on the day she first realized she was expecting a baby.

When Kimimela had the wagon ready, Jessica handed Amanda to Caroline. "It's high time I learned how to drive this thing." With Kimimela on the end of the bench, Jessica in the middle, and Caroline on the other end, they started off. Kimimela drove the wagon around the house and out onto the road. Once they were headed into town, she stopped Juniper. "Trade places with me," she said to Jessica

She stood, and Jessica slid over into her seat. Kimimela pointed to the foot brake. "When you want to stop, pull back on the reins. If you need to stop faster, push your foot on the brake here. She handed the reins to Jessica. "Give him a slap." Jessica did as she was told, and Juniper obediently started walking.

After a moment, Kimimela said, "If you need him to go faster, slap them again."

"A nice easy walk will be just fine for now."

By the time they pulled up in front of the church Jessica felt confident she could handle the wagon. It really wasn't all that different from the lightweight carriages she'd occasionally driven during their family summers on Long Island, only larger and less refined.

As she climbed down from the wagon, a gust of wind blew her bonnet off her head and the hair she'd pinned in a chignon at the back of her neck came tumbling loose. It whipped around her face, and she pushed it back so she could see. Caroline handed her the baby and climbed down.

The members were filing into the church, shaking hands with the pastor, who stood at the door. Jessica whispered to Caroline, "I must look a fright. When we get inside, I'll see if there's someplace I can put myself back together."

They took their place in the line of church members and, when it was their turn, Jessica held out her hand. "I'm Mrs. Jessica Belk, and this is Mrs. Caroline Akins. We've only recently moved here from New York."

The pastor was around thirty-five, not quite as tall as Zachary, with sandy blond hair and blue eyes. Jessica noticed how they crinkled at the corner when he smiled at her.

"Welcome to First Baptist, Mrs. Belk, Mrs. Akins. I'm Pastor Daniel Fields. We're happy to have you with us."

"Thank you. It's good to be here. I've missed being in church." Jessica was surprised by the handshake. His palm wasn't as soft and smooth as their pastor's in the city had been. It was as rough as a farmer's. She went in the church, and she and Caroline took a seat near the back of the building. There was an altar at the front with a podium. On one side was a piano. As soon as she saw it, Jessica couldn't turn her eyes off away. She sat there mesmerized, wanting to run up the aisle and let her fingers caress the keys.

It was only a few minutes before Pastor Fields closed the door and came to the front of the church. Jessica waited for the pianist to take her seat, but the pastor started the service alone. They sang several hymns acapella, he preached his sermon, they sang another hymn after the invitation, and with a closing prayer, they were dismissed.

Jessica held Caroline back from leaving until all the members were gone. The two of them were the last ones out of the building. When she stopped at the door, Jessica could hardly restrain herself. She shook hands with Pastor Fields again. Standing next to him was a young girl, around eight years old. She had pale blond hair and the same blue eyes.

"This is my daughter, Emily."

Jessica held out her hand and shook Emily's. "I'm very pleased to meet you, Emily."

Emily smiled up at her. "Thank you. I'm pleased to meet you, too." Emily looked down the path, where another girl stood. "Daddy, Annie is waiting for me. Can I go play?"

"You go ahead. We'll have dinner in about an hour." Emily ran down the path, and she and the other girl ran across the street and in the house.

Jessica looked back at the pastor, took a deep breath and blurted out, "I couldn't help but notice that you didn't have a pianist this morning. Is he or she on vacation?"

"No, my wife played the piano for us. She went to be with the Lord two years ago, and we haven't had anyone since then."

Jessica tried to control her enthusiasm. "I play, and there's nothing I would love better than to be able to play for services. Do you think I could do that?"

He scratched his earlobe. "Are you a baptized Christian?"

"Yes. I'm a—I mean, I was a member of the Mariner's Baptist Church in New York since I was saved at twelve years old. Mrs. Akins was a member, too. We came here this morning because we needed to find a new church home."

"We'll have you come forward to join us next Sunday, if you like, and you can begin playing for services the week after that. I'm sure our members will be very happy to have someone at the piano again."

"Wouldn't you like to have me play for you so you'll know I can do it well enough?"

"I don't think that will be necessary. I've been praying for someone to be sent to us. God was a little slow to answer me on that, but it seems He's found you."

She had to fight the impulse to rush up the aisle and attack the instrument with Mozart. "I'm afraid I'm a little rusty. I haven't played for several months. Could I come by one day this week and practice a little?"

"That would be fine. If I'm not here, the church will be unlocked. Just come on in and help yourself."

"Thank you so much. I can't tell you how much this means to me."

He smiled at her and his eyes crinkled up again. "It will mean a lot to all of us."

On Wednesday afternoon, Jessica had Kimimela show her how to hitch up the wagon, and she, Caroline, and Amanda drove to the church. When they arrived, Pastor Fields was on the roof, hammering down some shingles that had blown loose in Sunday's wind storm. He called down to them, "Go right in, Mrs. Belk. I'll come down and start up a fire for you to warm the place up."

"I hate to bother you," she said.

He was already halfway down the ladder. "It's no bother. I keep the stove ready. All I need to do is light the kindling."

Inside, he took a long match from a box sitting near the stove and struck it, holding the flame against the wood chips until it caught. "Play as long as you like. I'll be on the roof if you need me."

Jessica waited until he left before she opened the hymnal to the first song and began to play. Feeling her fingers glide across the keys was heavenly to her. She went from one hymn to the next.

The pastor's daughter, Emily, walked with her girlfriend Annie on the way home from school. A few hundred feet away from the church, the sound of the piano reached her ears. She stopped abruptly, and Annie went on a few steps ahead of her, then turned around to see where she'd gone. Emily stood there, frozen, while the notes of *Amazing Grace* drifted through the air. The song ended, and Emily, suddenly awake, dropped her books on the road and ran the rest of the way to the church

She hurried in the building and stopped in the doorway, watching while Jessica turned the page and started the next song. Drawn by the music, Emily walked slowly down the aisle and to the piano. She pressed one hand against the side of it and closed her eyes. Jessica stopped playing. "Hello, Emily. Your father said I could practice for a while. I'm going to start playing for services here."

"Please, play some more."

"All right. Why don't you sit down there with Caroline?"

Emily took a seat in the pew next to Caroline, and Jessica played for another half-hour. She closed the hymnal and picked up some sheet music she'd brought with her. She ran through a Chopin nocturne a few times, slowly at first, with a few mistakes, and then perfectly. When she'd finished, she folded up the music sheets and stood. "I think we'd better be heading home and start dinner," she told Caroline.

"Do you have to?" Emily pleaded.

"I'm afraid so. I'll be back Sunday, and maybe I can play some more then."

"That last thing you played. It was beautiful. I've never heard anything like it."

"It was written by a Polish man named Chopin."

"I love it. Can you play it again Sunday?

"All right. I'll stay after the service and play it for you."

At home, Jessica's life was in turmoil. Zachary quit his job at the Mercantile, declaring to Jessica that it was beneath him. He slept away half the day and stayed out late every night. Jessica seldom saw him, which suited her fine. She felt that the less time she had to spend with him, the better.

The winter went on. It was growing colder, and the last of the vegetables they'd planted when they arrived were gone. The pantry shelves were lined with Mason jars full of produce from the garden. With no money coming in, Jessica and Caroline did what they could to live frugally. At the same time, she was grateful for the meat and eggs from the chickens and the milk from the cow.

Jessica found joy in baby Amanda and the rest of her family. Father Belk totally regained his desire to live, and did what he could to help around the house and the grounds. Kimimela was able to teach him how to milk the cow, a feat achieved with much laughing and whooping, and one overturned bucket.

Most of all, Jessica found solace at her church. She couldn't wait until Sundays to play the piano, so she began timing her Wednesday trips into town for supplies to end at the same time Emily arrived home from school. Caroline would sit in a pew holding Amanda, sometimes dozing and, since she would have Sundays to play hymns, Jessica would play the classical music that she loved. Emily would run home to sit and listen to her, begrudging the time when she had to leave. Jessica and Emily were developing a bond deepened by their love of music.

The week before Christmas, Jessica brought in the sheet music for piano for Handel's Messiah. As she spread out the sheets across the music rack, she told Emily, "This is written by an Englishman named Handel."

"An Englishman?"

"That's right."

"And the other one was Polish?"

"Yes, Chopin."

"And the Nutcracker, the one you played last week, he was Russian?"

"Yes."

Emily looked at her dreamily. "So, all over the world, there are people making up music?"

"Yes, Emily. All over the world."

Chapter 22

On Christmas Eve, a bright moon shone through Jessica's bedroom window, lighting the whole room. The wind outside whipped the dry snow up in frothy clouds. The door opened quietly and Belk walked in, past the bed where Jessica appeared to be sleeping, and went over to the cradle. He looked down at the baby, now three months old, grimaced, and shook his head. He turned, walked up to the bed, and placed an envelope on the table next to her. He left, and closed the door with only a hushed click of the latch.

In the hallway, he picked up his satchel and walked quietly down the stairs and to the living room. A large Christmas tree stood by the front door. There were only a few wrapped gifts under the tree. He picked up a small box that had his name on the tag and stuffed it in his bag before he went out the front door. His horse was saddled and waiting at the front gate. He hooked the satchel over the saddle horn, mounted and rode down the road to where a wagon waited a short distance away.

Emmalou sat in the driver's seat. The several pieces of luggage in the back of the wagon contained everything she owned in the world. Belk dismounted and tied Thunder to the back of the buggy. Emmalou slid over to make room for Belk as he got in the driver's seat. He picked up the reins and smacked the horse. As the wagon pulled away, Emmalou linked her arm in his, and grinned at him. "Merry Christmas," she said.

He returned her smile. "Merry Christmas to you."

By the time Jessica came into the kitchen carrying Amanda the next morning, Caroline, Kimimela, and Father Belk were already gathered around the kitchen table. Jessica put Amanda in her grandfather's arms, poured herself a cup of tea, and sat at the head of the table. She took the letter Zachary left on her pillow from her pocket and held it in front of her.

"I have something I want to read to all of you," she said. She unfolded the letter and began, "Dear Jessica, I'm sorry to say that once more I have been a disappointment to you. I'm quite sure that you will be better off without me in your life, and will get along very well once I am gone. I have heard that there are great opportunities for a man such as myself in California and have decided to seek my fortune there. I wish nothing but the best for you."

She handed the letter to Father Belk and he re-read it silently. Caroline looked stunned, but not surprised. Jessica took a long drink of her tea, and looked from one to another of her family members.

"He was right. I will be better off without him. He hasn't been bringing home any money since the day we got here. All he gave us was worry and grief. I've been thinking it over, and we must make a plan of sorts. We'll find a way to get by."

Caroline asked, "What are you going to do?"

"I'll be going into town Wednesday. I need to go to the bank to withdraw some money for feed and supplies."

On Wednesday, with Kimimela watching, Jessica hitched up the buggy. She drove into town and stopped the wagon in front of the bank. Caroline, carrying Amanda, took a seat on a bench by the front door, and Jessica stepped up to the counter. She handed her little passbook to the teller.

"I'd like to make a withdrawal, please."

The teller looked at the book and frowned.

"You're Mrs. Belk?"

"Yes."

"Would you excuse me for a moment, please?"

"All right."

The teller went to an office and spoke to the man at the desk. After a moment, he came back to Jessica. He didn't go back around the counter, but instead stopped next to Jessica. "Our president, Mr. Wilkes, would like a word with you please."

At first, Jessica was puzzled by the request, but then her stomach knotted up. She had a feeling that she wouldn't like the conversation with the bank president. "All right."

The teller led her to the office, and Mr. Wilkes stood to meet her. He waved her toward the chair that sat in front of his desk. "Please have a seat."

Jessica sat. The teller left the office and closed the door. Mr. Wilkes ran his hand over his balding head and frowned. "Lowell tells me that you claim to be Mrs. Zachary Belk."

"Claim to be? Of course I'm Mrs. Belk."

"Is there anyone in town who can vouch for you?"

"You have my passbook. Why do I need someone to vouch for me?"

"I'm afraid that this is a rather uncomfortable situation, Ma'am."

"Please stop beating around the bush. Tell me what the problem is."

"The problem, I'm sorry to say, is that the other Mrs. Belk has been a regular customer. She and Mr. Belk have been in here several times over the last few months."

Jessica gasped. "I assure you, there is no other Mrs. Belk except my husband's mother in Connecticut. How old was this woman?"

"She was around twenty or so."

"Then I don't think it was my mother-in-law. I am the only Mrs. Belk authorized to take money out of this account."

"I'm sorry, but I need some other proof that you are who you say you are before I can discuss this further. The other Mrs. Belk had legal papers to show me. Is there anyone in town who could identify you?"

"There are my neighbors, but they've gone over to Abilene to visit one of their children for Christmas. I don't know anyone else—oh," she held up a finger, "the man who picked us up at the train station and drove us out to the house. His name was Everett. He should remember me. He was very nice. He was quite a talker."

"There's an Everett Snipes who drives folks from time to time."

"I don't remember his last name."

"I know where he spends his time. I'll see if I can get him in here.

Mr. Wilkes went back out to the teller, said a few words to him, and the teller left.

Jessica sat awkwardly in front of the desk, waiting. It was around fifteen minutes before the teller came in the front door of the bank with Everett by the elbow. He led him over to the office, escorted him inside, and left. Everett took off his hat and peered at Jessica. "How do, Ma'am. You sure are looking better than the last time I saw you."

Jessica breathed a sigh of relief. "I'm so glad you remember me."

Mr. Wilkes asked, "Everett, can you tell me where you've met this lady before?"

Everett scratched his beard. "It was--uh--early last fall. I took her and her family from the train station out to the Andersen place."

Wilkes nodded. "And you can verify that she is Mrs. Zachary Belk?"

"Sure can. Her husband was the one who hired me, and me and him seen one 'nother every once't in a while since then, mostly in Junction City."

"Mr. Belk was in here frequently with a young blonde woman. I don't think she lived in Manhattan. Do you know who she was?"

Everett's face turned red. He scuffed one foot on the floor. "Uh, well, I'm sorry, Ma'am."

Wilkes was growing impatient. "It's a legal matter, Everett."

Everett grimaced. "I seen him with Emmalou Tinsdale at Harvey's place in Junction City from time to time. They seemed to know one 'nother right well."

"Thank you, Everett. You can go now."

Jessica stood and offered her hand to Everett. He blinked in surprise, wiped his own hand on his trousers, and then shook Jessica's hand gently. She smiled at him. "Thank you, Mr. Snipes. I appreciate it."

The banker waited until Everett had left the office. "Well, Mrs. Belk. I'll fetch our records and we'll see if we can discover exactly what has been going on here."

He went to a file cabinet, took out a ledger, flipped through some of the pages until he found the one he wanted, and scanned it.

"Here's how it's recorded. Your bank in New York wired an original deposit of five thousand to us on September fourteenth. Here are the papers opening the account. Is that your signature?"

He handed her some papers over the desk. She looked at them.

"Yes, that's my signature. I wasn't up to making the trip into town, so Zachary brought the forms out to me and I signed them."

"It was a joint account."

"Yes. We needed supplies, horses, livestock, and a great many things for the house."

"I see. Since then, he has had other funds wired from New York and made quite a few withdrawals. Your current balance is three hundred, forty two dollars, and twenty three cents."

Jessica's mouth dropped open, and she slumped back in the chair.

"Three hundred dollars? But my passbook says I have over three thousand dollars."

"I remember that Mr. Belk came in one time and said that he'd forgotten his passbook at home, so we gave him a duplicate. That must be the one he's been using."

"I suppose he took my legal papers to use here. I don't know what I'm going to do. I have four mouths to feed, not to mention the livestock. There will be taxes to pay. I can't get by for long on three hundred dollars."

"I'm sorry, Mrs. Belk. If I were you, I'd wire my New York banker right away and make sure that any funds you have left there were safeguarded."

"He may have been on a joint account here in Kansas, but he certainly had no authorization to take money out of my New York funds. Can I have him arrested for this?"

Wilkes shrugged. "Not your husband. In Kansas, everything belongs to him. They may arrest the woman for impersonating you."

"That wouldn't do anything to get my money back. If she's with him now, she'll get her punishment sooner rather than later."

"I'm sorry, Mrs. Belk. May I suggest you transfer what's left of your money here into an account that no one but yourself can access?"

"Yes. I'll do that."

He said, "I'm familiar with the Andersen place. If you plant a good size garden next spring, and can make this money last until next fall, what with the fruit trees and vegetables you grow, you can feed your family."

"Mrs. West gave us some vegetable shoots when we first arrived, and we've been very blessed with the things they put out before the frost killed them off."

"Next year, you can grow even more. Now, let's get that new account opened."

"Of course, and then I'll send a wire to my New York bank right away."

Jessica filled out the forms transferring what was left of her money to a new account and kept twenty dollars in cash to buy her supplies. As soon as she left the bank, she gave no word of explanation to Caroline, but went directly to the telegraph office and sent a wire to her New York bank.

That accomplished, she went by the feed store for hay, oats, and chicken feed, and stopped at the general store for flour and a few other things. Then it was time for her last errand of the day.

With Jessica driving the wagon, it pulled up in front of the church and stopped. Caroline held Amanda on her lap. Pastor Fields was wielding a big pair of clippers as he trimmed the little orchard that stood between the church and the parsonage. Jessica called out, "Good afternoon, Brother Fields."

Fields stopped his work and looked up. He broke out in a wide smile. "Good afternoon, Mrs. Belk."

Jessica climbed down from the seat and took the baby from Caroline. "I've come to practice the piano for a while."

The minister nodded at her. "The door is open. Go right ahead. Stay as long as you like."

Amanda started fussing. Jessica rocked her a little and told Caroline in a soft voice, "I'll feed her first, and maybe she'll take a nice nap while I play."

Caroline frowned at her. "Are you sure you're up to it after the news you got from the bank?"

"I think playing will make me feel a great deal better. I've been looking forward to it since Sunday. Besides, it will help me feel better." Caroline took a seat in the back pew.

The minister turned his attention back to his work, shaping the trees into an umbrella that would make it easier to reach the fruit when it came in next summer. The two women went inside the church. Jessica took Amanda to the ladies' room for a while and when she came out, handed the sleeping baby to Caroline.

"That ought to hold her for a while."

She walked to the piano and ran her fingers across the keys, making a soft arpeggio. She sat down on the bench and picked up the hymnal, closing her eyes and opening the book. It fell to page 110 and she began playing, "Pass Me Not O Gentle Savior." When she finished, she turned to Caroline and smiled. Caroline had laid the baby on the pew next to her and both of them were sleeping soundly.

Jessica turned the page and played another hymn, and another, and another. After a while, she stopped and began sobbing, her face in her hands.

From next to her, the voice of Pastor Fields said, "Mrs. Belk?"

Startled, Jessica looked up. Her face flushed, and she wiped away her tears. "Oh, I'm sorry."

"I'm going to be your pastor, Mrs. Belk. Tell me what's bothering you, and we'll pray about it."

Jessica took a deep breath, held it, and let it out slowly. "I do need someone to pray with me. Let me sum it up for you. My husband has stolen almost every cent I had and run off to California. I have reason to believe he's with another woman. I have four mouths to feed, not counting Amanda and the livestock. I have no job, and with a little baby to see to, no prospect of getting one. Mr. Wilkes from the bank tells me that if I can make it through until next harvest, my place will produce enough food to take care of us. Let me tell you, I am very good at cultivating roses, but I have no idea at all how to plant and raise corn or anything else that will feed my family. I have no idea what we can do to survive."

"I understand you've hired a young Indian woman to help out. I'm quite sure she knows everything she needs to know to raise food."

"Mimi? Yes. She's been holding us together since we arrived. After my husband dragged us out here, he found didn't care much for the rustic life. Mimi taught me how to harness the horse to the wagon and how to drive it. I don't know what we would do without her, but she's very pretty. What will happen when some young man comes along and marries her? He'll take her away, and we'll be left to fend for ourselves."

"Maybe so. You should learn as much from her as you can before that happens. Now, let's talk to the Lord." He knelt on one knee in front of her and took one of her hands in his. He closed his eyes, bowed his head, and began, "Dear Lord,--"

A voice blasted from the back of the church "Brother Fields!" There stood Mrs. Charlotte Vickers, middle-aged, stout, with a pinched mouth and her face tightened into an ugly frown. One disapproving eyebrow lifted almost up into her hairline.

Fields stopped praying and looked up at her.
"Sister Vickers. I see you're back from visiting your sister in St. Louis. This is Sister Belk. We were talking with the Lord."

"I'm so sorry to interrupt you, but do you think it's really proper for the two of you to be in here alone?"

Caroline straightened up and said, "They weren't alone."

Mrs. Vickers turned quickly and saw Caroline. "Oh, excuse me, then. I'm sorry. I was only thinking of what sort of gossip might go around if –well, you know."

Fields got to his feet. "Thank you, Sister Vickers. I know you're always looking out for the welfare of our church and our members."

Mrs. Vickers chin shot up in the air, "Members? I don't recall her becoming a member."

"She joined us while you were away. She's going to be our new pianist."

"Really? How fortunate for us."

Fields smiled at Jessica. "Mrs. Belk, Mrs. Vickers is our star vocalist." He turned to Mrs. Vickers. "Was there something you needed today?"

"Needed? Oh, no. I only wanted to ask about the solo I wanted to sing this Sunday. I thought I'd find out what the topic of your sermon was going to be so the song would fit in with it."

"I hadn't decided yet, but you've given me an excellent idea. I think I'll preach on James, chapter three, verses five and six."

"James, three, five and six? What subject is that?"

"One that every preacher should touch on from time to time."

"Well. I'll look it up when I get home, and then I'll decide what to sing. I don't want to disturb you any further."

Jessica smiled. "Mrs. Vickers, I'd be more than happy to play for your song. There's nothing more beautiful than a voice with the right accompaniment. If you'd like, we can practice a while right now. Please stay, that is, if you don't mind me playing for you."

Mrs. Vickers considered this. "I would like to have an accompanist again. It's much more demanding to perform acapella, but I've always preferred to have an instrument to sing with. I've been working with no more help than a pitch pipe for such a long time. I haven't chosen a song yet."

Fields put in, "One of my favorite songs is, *The Old Rugged Cross.*"

Jessica put her palms together. "Oh, that would be so lovely."

Mrs. Vickers pursed her lips. "Well, if you think so."

The pastor nodded. "I'll be getting back to that orchard." He went out of the door, and Mrs. Vickers stepped up next to the piano. Jessica flipped through the song book in front of her and played the introduction. In a highly vibrato voice, Mrs. Vickers began.

"On a hill far away, --"

Down the road, Emily and her friend Annie were skipping home from school. When she came close enough to hear the piano and the singing, Emily paused briefly in the doorway, and entranced as always, went up the aisle. She stopped next to Mrs. Vickers, who was finishing the song. Ignoring the older woman, she watched Jessica.

Mrs. Vickers had her head thrown back and her eyes closed. She was just trumpeting out the last words, "--And exchange it someday for a crown."

Jessica applauded her. "You have a wonderful voice, Mrs. Vickers."

Mrs. Vickers smiled demurely. "Thank you. That was very nice, Mrs. Belk. You play very well."

"Thank you, Mrs. Vickers. Please call me Jessica."

"All right, Jessica. I'll see you Sunday morning. Good bye."

"Good bye."

Mrs. Vickers walked up the aisle, and Jessica smiled at Emily. "Hello, Emily."

Emily grasped Jessica's hand. "Please play some more."

"All right. What would you like to hear?"

"Anything. No, play something I can sing to."

Jessica played another tune, and Emily stood close to her with her left palm pressed against the side of the piano to feel the vibrations and sang as loudly as she could. As she finished the hymn, Jessica looked at Emily and saw tears running down her cheeks.

"Please don't stop," the girl pleaded.

"All right. What would you like to hear?"

"The one that German man wrote, about the moonlight."

"You mean *The Moonlight Sonata* by Beethoven?"

"Yes. That one. I love it."

Jessica started the first notes of the melancholy work, and Emily closed her eyes and pressed both hands against the piano, letting the vibrations travel up her arms and all the way into her heart.

Mrs. Vickers stopped at the general store on her way home. It was owned by a couple from the church, Mr. and Mrs. Hailey. Another woman from the church, Lucinda

Webb, was just wrapping up her shopping. "Good morning, Lucinda," Mrs. Vickers said.

"Good morning, Charlotte. How are you today?"

"I am simply wonderful. I just came from the church. We had to practice my solo for Sunday morning."

Lucinda Webb blinked, "We? Is someone singing with you?"

"Oh, no. My voice is much too distinctive for me to sing in a duet. No, Mrs. Belk, our new pianist is going to accompany me. She plays sufficiently well."

"Mrs. Belk? Oh, yes. She joined the church a few weeks ago. She and her family moved into the Andersen place out west of town. I must say, after the way they came into that property, I was surprised that she even showed her face in a place of worship, but you can't necessarily blame her. I wouldn't want to hold it against her when she could be entirely innocent of the whole thing. It could be all her husband's doing. Lord knows, when my George was alive, he did things that mortified me from time to time."

Mrs. Vickers lifted her chin and smiled. "Yes, I remember that. He liked to have a drink now and then, didn't he?"

"That's all water under the dam now, my dear."

"Yes, and isn't that how he died? He got drunk and fell into the water at Pillsbury Crossing?"

Mrs. Webb's face turned crimson. "Let's not discuss that any more, if you please."

"Still, it's so strange for a man to drown in two feet of water."

Mrs. Webb's face turned crimson. "As I recall, your own husband was known for having a drink or two."

Mrs. Vickers almost charged the other woman. "Can we please change the subject?"

"Certainly. I'll see you Sunday, Charlotte."

Her lips pressed tightly together, Mrs. Vickers watched Lucinda Webb leave the store. Then she whirled around and stepped up to the counter. She barked out the words as she ordered the things on her shopping list. A silent Mr. Hailey fetched the items quickly and added up the total. Mrs. Vickers paid for her purchases, gathered them up, and walked briskly out the door.

After a hurried walk down the street to her home, she dropped the bag on the kitchen table and went into the parlor. She untied her bonnet and put it on the mantle under the painting of her deceased husband that hung over the fireplace. She picked up the Bible lying there and carried it over to the window for some sunshine to help her fading vision. Blowing off some of the dust that had accumulated on the cover, she opened it and turned through the pages until she found the lines she wanted.

She read aloud, "James, three, verses five and six. "Even so the tongue is a little member, and boasteth great things. Behold, how great a matter a little fire kindleth! And the tongue is a fire, a world of iniquity: so is the tongue among our members, that it defileth the whole body, and setteth on fire the course of nature: and it is set on fire of hell."

She closed her Bible and pursed her lips. Speaking to the picture of her husband as she often did, she said, "That's exactly what I was trying to tell him. I'm glad he listened to me. It's a very good subject for a sermon. There's nothing worse than a gossip.

Chapter 23

As her family sat down to dinner, Jessica stood at the end of the table, took a deep breath, and announced, "Once we're finished eating, there's something we all need to talk about."

Caroline nodded and resisted the temptation to ask for the subject matter right then. They ate their meal as always, but once the dinner dishes were cleared, they all remained sitting at the kitchen table. Jessica held Amanda on her lap. Caroline and Kimimela sat with their hands folded, waiting for Jessica to tell them what it was she needed to say. Father Belk absent-mindedly carved out a knight.

Jessica plunged right in. "I've been to the bank. Zachary and the tart he ran off with have forged my name to documents and stolen almost every penny I had from the sale of Father's house. I've arranged things now so he can't steal another cent from me, but I'm afraid that it's too late to do us much good. If we're very careful with our pennies, we can make it through until the next harvest. I feel as if I'm right back where I started before we sold Father's house. If we're very, very careful with the money we have left, we can live off the crops and the livestock for food indefinitely. We have enough land to grow our own hay as well as the vegetables, but I need cash for seed, taxes, and who knows what else?"

Caroline's brow creased. "I wish we had been able to bring your Mother's piano with us. You could give lessons again."

Jessica nodded. "Leaving that piano was one of the hardest things I've ever had to do, but I don't see how I could teach out here. Even if we had the piano, who would come all this way out of town to study? Let's pray that the estate agent is able to rent out my house in New York before we go completely broke."

Caroline's face lit up. "Jess! Brother Fields said you could come in and play any time you wanted. Maybe you could give lessons at the church."

Jessica considered this, tapping the fingertips of one hand on her chin. "Oh, Caroline! Do you think it would be possible? It gets dark too early for me to do it during the week, and I would never ask to do it on the Sabbath. It would have to be Saturdays."

She started to get excited. "I could put an ad in the newspaper. If I can get one student, the word would spread. I probably won't be able to get a lot of students in such a small town, but every little bit will help us. If only there were something else I could do."

Caroline said, "You're one of the best seamstresses I ever saw. Maybe you could get work at the dress shop or the milliner's."

Jessica frowned. "How can I do that when I'm nursing a baby and can't be away from her for more than a few hours?"

Caroline thought. "Maybe they would let you bring work home with you. I'm not too bad with a needle myself, even with the arthritis. I can do the easy things. At least I'd be pulling my own weight. We could get a bolt of pretty white linen, and I could hem handkerchiefs, or sew some nice aprons and things like pillowcases, and you could embroider them or trim them with lace and see if you could sell them at the general store."

Jessica shook her head. "You're already cooking, doing the laundry, cleaning, and helping with Amanda. That's more than pulling your own weight."

Father Belk looked up from the chess piece he was whittling. "I wish I could do something to help out. Anything. I feel utterly useless. I should go upstairs and put a bullet in my head so at least you won't have to feed me." He held the chess piece up to his temple as if it were a gun.

Jessica jumped up from the table. "Don't you dare talk like that!" She pointed to the carving in his hand. "You aren't useless at all. Look at how beautiful that knight is. I bet someone would love to buy a hand-carved chess set. You must have dozens of them put away by now. If we could market some of those, and I can teach piano, and Caroline and I can sew, we should be able to keep our heads above water. Remember when I said I would make my way without Zachary? Well, we will, all of us. We can do it. I've been praying for God to help us, and all the time He's already given us everything we need."

Through all this, Kimimela had watched silently from the other end of the table. She stood and went to the door. "I should go someplace else. I cannot help. I cannot make money. I am only another mouth to feed."

Jessica's mouth dropped open in surprise. "Oh, Mimi. We need you. We could never make it without you."

Mimi dropped her head. "I cannot teach or sew fancy linens or carve beautiful things. There's nothing I can do to bring money to the house. What good am I?"

"You're the one who makes all this work, Mimi. If you left us, who would take care of the animals and help us with the fields? I don't know enough about raising vegetables to feed anyone. Even if I did know, if I had to do all that without you, when would I have time to do anything else? This family must stick together."

Kimimela went to the door and paused with her hand on the knob. "Family? I am not family."

Jessica gasped. "Of course you are.

Kimimela looked at her through tears. "My people have all been sent to Oklahoma, and if I leave here, they will send me there, too. If you are sure I will not add to your burden, I will stay."

Jessica smiled. "Please stay. We need you."

Kimimela nodded, went out, and shut the door.

Wednesday afternoon, Jessica fed Amanda before she left the house and told Caroline, "I don't know how long I'll be gone. If she gets hungry, give her some cow's milk."

She drove the wagon to the front of the church, climbed down, and went inside. Pastor Fields was smoothing out the putty after replacing a window pane. He looked up at her and grinned. "Some of the boys were playing ball in the road and they hit a ball a little further than they expected. How are you today, Mrs. Belk?"

A bit nervous, Jessica smiled tightly in return. "I'm fine, much better than yesterday, thank you. I hope this won't be imposing in any way, and please feel free to tell me if that is the case. I wanted to ask you if I could use the church on Saturdays to teach piano lessons. I don't have an instrument at home and, even if I did, it would be too far for my students to come."

"I think that would be very nice. I know that Emily will be thrilled to be your first student, and I'll pass the word around. How much do you charge?"

A wave of relief flooded over Jessica. *Maybe we'll be able to survive after all.* "I get twenty-five cents for an hour lesson, but I would never charge for Emily."

Fields shook his head. "I insist on paying you. We wouldn't want Mrs. V—uh--any of our members to get the wrong idea, would we?"

"Thank you so much. I can't tell you how much this will help us. If you're sure she wants to study with me, I can start Emily this afternoon."

"I can't think of anything she would like better, but I won't tell her. We'll let it be a surprise."

"I have some errands to run. I'll see you tomorrow. Thank you again."

Jessica rushed out of the church and climbed back in the wagon. She slapped the reins on Juniper's back, trotted him into town, and parked the wagon in front of the Wareham Millinery Company. The air was cold and crisp, and a light snow blew down the street, but Jessica had anticipated the weather and dressed warmly. She climbed down from the wagon, went around to the back, and took down a wicker basket. She folded back a cloth to reveal a hat she'd made out of the scraps of her mother's green velvet gown, a few feathers, and bits of lace. It rested on some finely embroidered linens. She took a deep breath and entered the shop.

Inside the store, an attractive woman was standing behind a counter. She smiled at Jessica. "Good morning. How may I help you?"

"Are you Mrs. Wareham?"

"Yes, I am, but please, call me Sarah."

Buoyed by her good news about the piano lessons, Jessica smiled brightly, marshaled her courage, and spoke up. "I'm Jessica Belk. I'm looking for work. I have a young baby, so I can't work away from home, but if you would consider allowing me to take my work home with me? I believe you'd be very satisfied with what I can do." She pulled the hat she made out of the basket and held it up.

Sarah took it from her and examined the workmanship. "This is lovely. As a matter of fact, I could use some help. The town is growing by leaps and bounds, and business has been very good. It's difficult for me to find the time to make hats here, and some of my clientele don't like mass-produced items. If I provide you with the materials and a drawing of what I want, do you think you could make it up to my design?"

Jessica's heart was pounding in her chest. "I'm sure I could."

Sarah nodded. "Good. Not that you can't design some of your own as well, but I would want to approve them before you made them up. You could sketch out your ideas and show them to me first."

"I'd be very happy to do that."

At that moment, the bell at the top of the door jingled, and a well-dressed woman entered. Sarah smiled at her. "Good morning, Lavinia. How are you today?"

"I'm fine, thank you so much." She stopped and stared at the hat in Sarah's hands. "That's a lovely hat you have there. I don't remember it being here a few days ago. Is it new?"

"Yes. It's a one-of-a-kind design. This is Jessica Belk, and she made it especially for us. She will be designing an entire line for me. Jessica, this is Lavinia Wilkes. Her husband owns the bank."

"So nice to meet you, Jessica."

"I'm very happy to meet you, Mrs. Wilkes. I've met your husband. He was quite kind to me."

"That's always nice to hear. Please call me Lavinia. Now, let me get a better look at that hat. I think it will go very nicely with an outfit I was planning on buying, and I think it will look even better with this dress than the hat I'm wearing."

She pulled the pins out of her hat, put it on the counter, then took the one Jessica had made out of Sarah's hands and placed it on her head. She turned her head this way and that, admiring herself in the oval mirror that stood on a pedestal on the counter.

"I love it! How much is it, dear?"

Jessica didn't know what to say, but Sarah, ever the savvy businesswoman, didn't hesitate. "Being an exclusive design, it's a little more than the ones where you see yourself coming and going. I'm going to have to ask for two dollars."

Lavinia blinked. "Well! That will use up my hat allowance for a while, but I have to have it. I'll wear it out."

Sarah smiled widely. "It does look lovely on you. I'll just put your other one in a box."

"I don't want to carry it around. Have your boy run it by the house for me."

"I will, Lavinia. Thank you so much."

Mrs. Wilkes turned her attention back to Jessica. "As for you, Jessica, you're quite wonderful. I insist on getting first chance to look at everything you make. Is that acceptable, Sarah?"

"That will be fine. I'll hold everything she brings in at the back of the store until you've seen it."

With a wave of her hand and the air of a grand lady, Lavinia Wilkes swept out of the store. Jessica blinked several times and realized she'd been holding her breath. She huffed out the air. "She forgot to pay for it."

Sarah chuckled. "She never pays. I send a bill to her husband once a month. She's my best customer. She must have more hats than any woman in either Manhattan, the one here in Kansas or the one in New York. I do believe that you and I are going to do a lot of business together, Jessica. I'll set up an account with you in my ledger and pay you at the end of the month. You get half of the retail price of anything I sell that you make from your own materials and twenty five percent of anything you make using my materials. Is that acceptable?"

"Acceptable? It's wonderful. Thank you so much, Sarah."

Jessica picked up her basket. Sarah noticed the neatly folded linen lying in it and reached out to touch the embroidery. "This is beautiful. Is this your work too?"

"Thank you. Yes, it is. I'm going to take it to the Mercantile store and see if they might be interested in carrying some of it."

"When you get there, ask for my son, William Wareham. Tell him I sent you."

"I will. Thank you so much."

"We ladies must stick together."

"I'll see you next week."

Jessica left the shop as if she were floating. She already had one piano student, and was now commissioned to make ladies' hats at the nicest store in town. She was having a wonderful day.

Leaving the wagon hitched where it was, Jessica carried her basket down Poyntz Avenue to the Wareham Mercantile. It was much grander than the general store where she bought her kitchen supplies, with glass-topped counters full of merchandise and carved-leg tables displaying linens and clothing. Jessica looked around and spotted a clerk standing behind one of the counters. Encouraged by her success at the Millinery Shop, she walked right up to the woman and smiled at her. "I would like to speak to Mr. William Wareham, please."

"Certainly," the woman said. "Just a moment." She walked across the room to an office door and returned shortly, followed by a young man. He nodded and smiled at Jessica. "I'm William Wareham. What can I do for you?"

"I'm Mrs. Jessica Belk. Mrs. Wareham from the millinery shop said to tell you she sent me. I have some needlework here that I hoped you might consider carrying."

He frowned. "Belk?" Are you related to Zachary Belk?"

Knowing how gossip traveled, Jessica took a deep breath. She decided to meet the matter head-on. "Yes.

He's my husband, but he's deserted our family, and I find it necessary to earn a living by myself."

He tilted his head and smiled at her. "What can I do for you?"

She took the stack of three linens out of the basket and laid them out on the counter for him to inspect, but he didn't seem interested. His attention was focused on the chess pieces they'd been covering in the bottom of her basket. He picked up a knight and held it up to examine it.

"These are very nice pieces. Are they also in your line?"

"Yes. My father-in-law makes them. I didn't bring one of the boards with me, but he does those also."

"How many sets does he have completed?"

"He has a whole drawer full of them, but I'm not sure how many complete sets."

"Bring me three sets to start. We'll see how they do. I have a supplier who comes in here every few months. He services stores all over the northwest corner of the state. He isn't carrying anything like this right now, but he may be interested in adding these to his line. As for the linens, let's take a look."

He unfolded one of the cloths and looked it over. "Yes, these are quite nice. Leave these here, and bring me more when you come back. Did my mother explain our bookkeeping procedures for paying our suppliers?"

"Yes, she did. That will be fine. I brought the embroidered things with me, but we also do plain work, napkins, aprons, and so forth."

"Good. I'll look forward to seeing them."

"Thank you." Jessica glanced at the clock on the wall. It was almost three, and she had to stop at the

Manhattan Mercury to place her ad before she went to the church. She smiled at William Wareham. "Thank you so much. I'll bring you what I have next week. Goodbye."

As Jessica drove, her stomach rumbled, and she wished she'd had the foresight to think about carrying something for lunch. It would be a while before she could eat. The thought of stopping at the restaurant in the hotel occurred to her, but she dismissed it immediately. Restaurants weren't anywhere on her list of affordable items. She stopped the wagon in front of the general store, went in, and bought an apple. It would have to do. She munched it and continued her drive, grateful that Juniper was well behaved and could be handled with one hand on the reins.

She began planning out her schedule. The days were short this time of year. She was already rising before dawn and retiring after dark. After sunset, the family made do with as few lamps as possible. She wondered if the cost of kerosene for the lamps would override her profits if she stayed up and used enough of them to give her light to sew. She had to be sure she had enough light that her work didn't suffer. Anything she brought to the store for Mr. Wareham to sell would have to be top quality.

That afternoon, Emily came home from school at precisely three o'clock. She went to the parsonage and put her schoolbooks on the table. It didn't surprise her that her father wasn't in the house. She ran out the door and to the church where he was sweeping the floor. "Hi, Daddy. I'm home. Do I have any chores today?"

"I have a surprise for you."

Emily's face broke out in a grin. Surprises were few and far between in her young life. "What is it?"

"Mrs. Belk is going to be here in a few minutes."

"She comes every Wednesday. That's not a surprise."

"It is today. She's going to give you your first piano lesson, that is, if you want to learn how to play."

Emily shrieked and ran to him, flinging her arms around his waist. "Oh, Daddy! Really? Am I really going to get to play like Mommy did?"

He chuckled. "It will take some time and a lot of work on your part to get to play as well as your mother did, but yes, starting today."

"In a few minutes? She'll be here in a few minutes?"

"That's right."

Emily released her grip on her father, ran down the aisle, and out the front door. She stopped at the end of the path to the church and looked up and down the road. Her father hadn't said if Jessica would be coming from home or from town. In a moment, Emily caught sight of the wagon and ran as fast as she could to meet it. Jessica pulled the horse to a stop and Emily scurried up to the seat next to her. She was out of breath and gasped, "Daddy said you were coming to give me a piano lesson."

"That's right. If you want one, that is. I wouldn't want to force you to play the piano against your will."

Emily flung her arms around Jessica's waist and held her tightly. "Force me? Who wouldn't want to play the piano?"

"All right. Let's get started."

Emily proved to be an eager pupil. She listened intently to every word Jessica told her and soaked up the instruction like a thirsty sponge. Before the first lesson was over, Emily could read and play well enough to pick out a little tune. It turned out to be a much longer lesson than usual, but Emily was reluctant to let Jessica leave.

"I have to go now, Emily. If I don't, it will be after dark before I get home."

Emily sighed, brushing the tips of her fingers across the piano keys. "All right. You won't come back until next week?"

"The usual thing is to have a lesson once a week, but there is something you could do for me."

Emily's eyes shone with eagerness. "What? I'd do anything for you."

"I put an ad in the *Manhattan Mercury* asking for students, but if you could let your friends at school know about it, maybe some of them would be interested. I'll give you an extra free lesson for every new student you can find for me. How about that?"

"I'll get you so many girls that you'll have to be here every day."

"My place is a long drive from here. I'd like to see them all on Saturdays so I don't have to make so many trips into town." Jessica thought for a moment. "I'll tell you what. If there's more students than I can handle on Saturdays, I'll come in Wednesday afternoon and then I can just stay for the prayer meeting that evening. I'll bring Mrs. Akins with me so I don't have to drive home alone after dark."

"Oh, that will be wonderful. You'll have Amanda with you. I can play with her while you teach the other children."

"I'm sure she will love that. She took to you right away. Now," Jessica said, standing, "I've given you one finger exercise and one tune to play in your book. I want you to practice your lesson every day for as long as you like, but don't skip any days. I mean, you can skip Sunday if you want-- if it seems like work, but if you want to do it, I'm sure the Lord won't mind. I'll come back Saturday morning for your next lesson. That's only three days, but I have a feeling you'll be ready."

"I will. I'll practice and practice."

As Jessica walked out of the church, she could hear Emily enthusiastically attacking the piano. She couldn't help but chuckle and wondered how Pastor Fields would feel about the little simplified, six note, Mozart piece by the end of the next three days. She found him on his knees, pulling weeds by the path.

He stood and brushed off his hands. "You wouldn't think there'd still be weeds growing this late in the year, but it's been a warm winter. I have to keep after them until we get a hard freeze."

"I'm looking forward to next spring so we can get our garden in."

"How did Emily do with her lesson?"

"She's remarkable, really. She wants it more than any student I've ever had, and she has a natural ability."

"She didn't get it from me. I believe I told you her mother played."

"Yes, you did. Maybe talent is inherited. My mother was a wonderful pianist. I'd like very much for Amanda to play when she's old enough. Well, I better get going, or I'll miss dinner."

She put her things under the seat and climbed up in the wagon. Fields unhitched the horse. As he handed her the reins, his hand brushed hers, and she blushed. Both of them pretended it hadn't happened. He walked the horse around and onto the road facing the right direction.

She gave a short wave. "Bye, now. I'll be back Saturday morning."

"I know Emily will be waiting for you."

A few yards down the road, Jessica looked back over her shoulder to see the pastor still standing where she'd left him, looking at her as she drove away.

On the drive home, Jessica was sure that Juniper had to be every bit as hungry as she was. She didn't want to hurry him, so it was well past sunset when Jessica finally arrived back at her house.

Kimimela ran to meet her as she pulled in the back yard. After she climbed down from the wagon, Kimimela led the horse in the barn to bed it down for the night.

Jessica fairly bounced up the steps and into the kitchen. Caroline, holding Amanda on her knee, sat at the table. The aroma of dinner filled the air. Jessica's breasts were aching and beginning to leak, so the first thing she did was feed Amanda. "Oh, Caroline! That all smells so delicious. I'm starving. All I had to eat for lunch was an apple."

Caroline stood and went to the stove. "If I'd known you were going to be gone so long I would have packed you a lunch. We've been waiting dinner for you. We were starting to get worried. I never expected you to be gone so long. What on earth have you been up to?"

"It's been a wonderful day! Brother Fields said I could use the church to give lessons and he'd make Emily my first student. I gave her first lesson, and she wouldn't let me go. Isn't it wonderful? I already have my first piano student, and Mrs. Wareham already sold the hat I took to show her, and her son, who runs the Mercantile, took my linens and wants to sell Father Belk's chess sets. We're going to be all right, Caroline."

By the time Jessica fed the baby, Caroline had dinner on the table. There was a platter of fried chicken, mashed potatoes, gravy, green beans, and fluffy cornbread. Caroline called out the door, "Mimi, soup's on. You let that horse wait for his brushing until after we eat."

Father Belk came downstairs from his room. When Jessica told him the Mercantile wanted three of his chess sets, he almost cried.

Kimimela came in the kitchen. She washed her hands quickly and sat at the table. They all joined hands and bowed their heads. Jessica's prayer was short and simple. The sound of her stomach growling almost drowned her out as she said, "Lord, Thank You for your bounty, and thank You for our new hope. In Jesus's name, amen." The amens were echoed by the rest of the family, and they happily filled their plates and passed the dishes around the table.

Chapter 24

A few weeks later, winter had set in to stay for a while. Juniper stood at the post in front of the church with a big blanket covering him, all the way from his tail up to his head. Trees were completely without leaves, the grass a dreary shade of gray, and snow was blew outside the church window.

Jessica sat on the end of the piano bench teaching a pupil, a young girl about Emily's age. Emily stood to one side, her hands down to her sides, holding her music book in one hand and twitching the fingers of the other hand in unison with the pupil. When the girl finally labored to the end of the piece, Jessica stood and said, "That was very nice, Samantha. I'll see you the same time next week. Don't forget to practice your fingering exercise."

Samantha crinkled up her nose. "I hate that. It's so boring."

"I know, but your exercises are the foundation of your work. It's like building a house. If you don't get the foundation right, the rest of it won't be right."

"All right. I'll do it, but I still won't like it." Samantha took her music and trotted out of the church. Jessica looked at Emily. "All right, Emily, your turn. I always save the best for last."

Grinning from ear to ear, Emily hurried to the seat and opened her book on the music stand. Jessica sat next to her. "Let's hear how you did this week."

Emily started playing a simple beginner's arrangement of a Mozart etude and played it quite well. Jessica looked up to see that, at the back of the church, Pastor Fields had stepped inside to hear his daughter play. He wiped a tear from his cheek.

With the days growing shorter and shorter, the Belk family spent what they could of the daylight hours working on their crafts. Kimimela took care of all the outside work. It was minimal in the dormant season. Caroline cooked, and she and Jessica cleaned, but as soon as the chores were finished, both of them turned to their needlework.

When her store of fabrics was depleted, Jessica brought home a bolt of creamy white linen that Mr. Wareham gave her for the wholesale price. She cut it into large squares and rectangles, and Caroline hemmed the pieces into pillowcases, napkins, table runners, and men's' and ladies' handkerchiefs. The napkins and handkerchiefs were pressed and folded, ready for Jessica to deliver.

For the finer items, Jessica sat by whichever window gave her the best light and embroidered pretty patterns of flowers and ivies. Once the word got around that she did such lovely work, she began getting custom orders for monogrammed items.

Lavinia Wilkes wanted a fancy tablecloth and twelve matching napkins, all with a large W and yellow roses. Mrs. Hendricks fancied a lace-trimmed nightgown with clusters of rosebuds around the collar, cuffs, and hem.

Jessica made two hats a week, one of her own design, and one of Sarah's. Mrs. Wareham couldn't keep them in the shop. Father Belk took to tramping through the woods looking for suitable pieces of wood to carve and delighted in finding wood of different hues and textures. On Saturdays, Caroline and Amanda went with Jessica, and they left early to get to the church to teach her pupils.

Emily would always be her last student of the day. Jessica scheduled her that way so she could work with her until the girl was satisfied, or until Jessica knew that any more time spent on a lesson would be too much.

Pastor Fields was always at the church ahead of her and had the Ben Franklin stove that stood in the corner glowing by the time she arrived. Jessica and the preacher spent the time before Jessica's first pupil arrived talking. Jessica, with Emily leaning her head on her arm and holding her hand, sat on one side of the aisle, and Fields on the other. Caroline brought her knitting and sat in the back pew where the light from one of the windows gave her an advantage, and Amanda usually slept on the pew next to her.

Jessica and Fields chatted about the weather, the piano, the price of flour, and whatever else came to mind. On Saturday mornings, Jessica found herself rushing around the house to get ready earlier and earlier.

Jessica had as many pupils as she could handle in the time allotted to her. There were demands for every piece of needlework she could deliver. She soon knew they were going to survive financially. With each dollar she earned, she began to worry a trifle less than before.

Adele's husband, Henry West, slaughtered two hogs and brought the sides to Kimimela, who wrapped them in cloth and hung them in the smoke house. She gathered bits of wood from the apple trees to make the fire.

The chickens provided fresh eggs every day, and once a week, a meal. Kimimela kept a careful count of the poultry, leaving enough eggs to hatch so the flock increased a little at a time. The cow gave them all the milk they needed.

Everett visited Kimimela from time to time and brought her a bow and quiver of arrows. After that, Kimimela often came out of the woods carrying or dragging an animal she had shot, raccoons, game birds, rabbits, and once, even a deer. She cured the hides and saved them.

By eating the fruit and vegetables Caroline had canned in the fall, cutting down the amount of meat in their meals, and relying on beans for protein, they were able to pass the winter without using any of the money in the bank. If there were no unforeseen expenses, Jessica would even be able to add a small amount to her nest egg.

When spring finally came, and the ground was thawed enough for planting, Kimimela cleared the old gardens and then expanded them into larger plots. This year, there would be an acre of corn and one of hay. Caroline had saved seeds from the summer before, and started the corn, tomatoes, squash, and peppers on trays layered with the rich brown dirt from the compost pile. Trays of seedlings lined one wall of the barn waiting for the final frost to pass. One afternoon, Jessica left Amanda in the care of her grandfather, wrapped a woolen shawl around her shoulders, and she and Caroline walked all the way around the property. The rich smell of the freshly turned earth drifted up to them. "Do you think it's warm enough to start with the house painting?" Jessica asked Caroline.

"I haven't the foggiest idea. It's so different out here from New York. You should ask Adele or Henry, or maybe ask the pastor Saturday.

"I will. I was thinking that it's an awful lot of work and I should see about hiring someone to help."

"Hiring someone? Are we doing that well financially that we can hire another person?"

Jessica couldn't resist sounding a little smug when she answered, "We are. I thought that, if it works out, we could even keep him around to help with the planting. It's one thing to put out a garden of tomatoes with a shovel and a hoe, but if we're going to grow an acre of corn and one of hay, we need a proper plow."

"Do you think Juniper will be willing to pull it?"

"I've been riding all my life, and he's the sweetest natured horse I ever knew. I would think he'd do anything we asked him. He's such a gentle soul. He never kicks when we hitch him up to the wagon."

Caroline tilted her head and squinted at Jessica. "I can see the wheels turning in that head of yours. What else are you planning?"

"We'll paint and repair everything, and then we'll plant every inch of ground that will take a seed. What we can't eat or can, we'll carry into town and sell to the general store."

"You're becoming quite the entrepreneur, aren't you?"

Jessica laughed. "I guess I am. It's amazing how much my life has changed, isn't it? I was born into money, and until father's firm went bankrupt, I never gave it a thought, literally, never gave it a thought. I wasn't the least bit interested in the price of my 'Grand Tour' through

Europe, or my gowns. I had no idea how much money it took to run a house. All my life there were servants. The bills were paid without me even being aware of them, and there was food on the table. In some ways, Zachary did me a favor. I thank God every night for all that He's given us. I thank Him for Amanda, for you, Father Belk, Mimi, and this house, and Adele and Henry right across the street. We're all healthy and pulling our own weight. It's a wonderful feeling, Caroline, knowing we can take care of ourselves. Well, with God's help, we can take care of ourselves."

A blessed and bountiful summer passed into another fall. Soon, there was a Christmas tree in the corner with a handmade gift from each member of the family to each other member. Amanda was now a year and three months old, toddling around with a little wooden horse lovingly carved by her grandfather in one hand and a fistful of the discarded gift-wrap ribbons in the other. Father Belk was pulling on a new sweater Caroline knitted for him. Caroline was modeling a new robe that was a gift from Jessica. Kimimela sat on the sofa, running her fingertips over the soft cotton fabric of a dress Jessica had made for her.

The most impressive gift was the one Jessica received from Kimimela, who was experiencing her first Christian holiday. It was a stack of butter-soft pieces of fur and leather Mimi had cured from her hunting successes and from the hides of the hogs they had slaughtered that fall. Jessica had never worked with fur or leather before, but with Kimimela's help, she could learn.

The worst of the cold weather was still ahead of them, and Jessica planned to make something warm for each member of the family, and to use the scraps for ladies' hats.

When the last gift had been opened and appreciated, Jessica stood to make an announcement. "I've been saving the best present for last. I got a letter from our rental agent in New York, and he's finally found a tenant for my house there. They've signed a one year lease at one hundred dollars a month."

Caroline couldn't hold back the tears. She wrapped her arms around Jessica. "Oh, Jess. That's wonderful."

Jessica had a few tears of her own. "We can finally stop scrimping and saving and relax a little. The first thing I'm going to do is paint the whole house inside and out. We'll do Mimi's cabin and the barn and especially have someone build us a whole new outhouse."

The celebration was suddenly cut off by a loud knocking. Jessica went to answer it. "That must be Adele and Henry come to wish us a Merry Christmas."

When she opened the door, she was surprised to see Everett standing there, his shoulders hunched against the cold.

"Mr. Snipes, please come in out of the cold. How nice to see you again. Would you like some coffee?"

He shivered. "I surely would, Miz Belk. I don't ever remember it being so cold on a Christmas Day."

"Please sit down. I'll be right back."

Caroline stood. "I'll get it for him."

While Caroline went to the kitchen to get the coffee, Everett looked around uncomfortably. He sat on a straight-backed chair in the corner. Jessica pointed to one of the large, upholstered chairs. "You'd be much more comfortable over here."

Everett's face reddened. "Thank you, Ma'am, but my clothes ain't all that clean. They probably smell right strong of horse sweat. I'm fine right here. I won't be staying long."

Caroline returned from the kitchen carrying a cup and saucer and a plate of cookies. She handed him the cup and saucer, put the cookies down on a table next to him and smiled warmly.

"Would you like cream and sugar with your coffee?"

He managed a weak smile in return. "Oh, no thank you, Ma'am. I like it plain."

He juggled the cup and saucer carefully, then took the cup and placed the saucer on the table next to the cookies. Instead of using the handle of the cup, he wrapped his hand around it and looked at Jessica apologetically. "I run off without my gloves. It feels right good to hold a warm cup. I never was too good with these fancy dishes. I wouldn't want to break one of them."

Jessica sat on the chair closest to him. "I want to thank you again for your assistance that day at the bank."

Everett blushed and ducked his head. "Oh, it wasn't nothin.' Only saying what I knowed."

"All the same, you were a great deal of help to me."

Everett took a slurp of the coffee and looked at Jessica sheepishly. "I feel real bad about the reason I come out here today, Miz Belk."

"I'm happy to see you again, and you can be sure that you are always welcome in our home, but I am rather curious as to the cause of your visit."

"Well, I run into Mr. Wilkes from the bank and I wuz telling him about your Mr. Belk, 'bout what I heard, and he reckoned that since everyone else knows 'bout it but you, you not having been in town since last Sunday, that someone ought to have the common decency to come out here and let you know what's happened."

Jessica glanced at Father Belk, took a deep breath and sat up straight. "I take it you have news of my husband?"

Everett's face turned an even darker shade of red. "Yes, Ma'am. I'm right sorry to be the one to tell you." He paused and twisted his face into a grimace. "Emmalou Tinsdale come home from California last week, and she says that her and Mr. Belk were in San Francisco, and he was in a card game when one of the other fellas 'cused him of cheatin.' A fight broke out, and Mr. Belk was kilt. She said she did her best to save him, but it didn't do no good. I believe her, too, cuz she got cut something awful right on her face. She used to be a right pretty girl, but those days are behind her forever now. I wish I could give you more information about what happened out there, but that's all I know right now."

Stunned, Jessica could only nod. Father Belk shrank down in his seat and dropped his head as a shudder of grief ran through him. Kimimela sat stone-faced. Jessica stood and walked toward the door.

"Thank you for coming to tell us, Everett."

Everett stood. "I'm right sorry, Miz Belk, but that ain't all I got to tell."

Jessica steeled herself to receive the rest of the news. From the almost fearful expression on Everett's face, she expected it to be even worse. "What else, Everett?"

"Emmalou didn't come home alone, Miz Belk. She has a baby with her. A little boy, and his hair is the color of new bricks."

Behind her, Jessica could hear a gasp escape from Father Belk. "I see. Thank you, Everett."

Everett took a last, long drink of the coffee and put down the cup. Jessica went to the door to see him out, but he didn't move. He looked at her sheepishly and took a deep breath. "Uh, those cookies sure do look good. Would it be all right if I took them with me?"

Jessica put her hand on his shoulder. "It was so kind of you to come all the way out here to see us. We have a whole kitchen full of cookies. Let me wrap some up for you."

Everett exhaled loudly. "That would be right nice of you, Ma'am. Living alone in that hayloft over the liv'ry, I don't get treats like that every day."

Caroline waved at Jessica to stay where she was. "I'll get it."

Caroline went to the kitchen. Everett stood in front of his chair awkwardly waiting. Amanda tottered over to him and looked up. He smiled down at her.

Jessica introduced her. "That's my daughter, Amanda."

He smiled at the baby and held out his hand. Amanda wrapped her fingers around his thumb. "I can tell that. She sure has her daddy's hair."

Caroline returned and handed Everett a package tied with a red ribbon.

"We owe you a big debt of gratitude for bringing us Mimi. I don't know what we'd do without her. Thank you again."

"Yes, Ma'am." She shuffled his feet. "Like I said, I'm sorry to bring you bad news. I guess I'll be seeing you in town, then."

Jessica closed the door, and Caroline said, "The gossip mill will have a party with this news. Mrs. Vickers is going to love it."

Jessica stuck out her chin. "Let her gossip all she wants. No one in this house is guilty."

Father Belk sighed. "So, Zachary finally got his son, and now he'll never know either one of his children. Ironic, isn't it? I guess I'll grieve for him. Whatever he was, it was my fault. Let's hope his boy turns out better than he did."

Jessica sat next to her father-in-law and patted his shoulder. "You can't blame yourself for Zachary's faults. He was a grown man."

"Even so, I didn't set the best example for him. Do you think I'll ever get to meet my grandson? You wouldn't mind, would you? I don't want you and I ever to have any bad feelings between us."

"It's only natural for you to want to know your own flesh and blood. The next time I go to Manhattan, I'll see what I can find out. It shouldn't be too difficult to do. This is still a small town, Father Belk. I imagine your grandson's mother will be living in Junction City, but I'm sure something can be arranged."

Chapter 25

By the next Sunday, everyone in Manhattan, Kansas knew about the red-headed baby boy Emmalou brought back from California. There was a light dusting of snow on the ground outside the church. Pastor Fields stood at the door greeting the members. The sound of the piano playing drifted out the open door. Mrs. Vickers stood at the end of the walk talking to a small knot of women.

"Now she's a real widow. It's a sight better than being a grass widow. At least she can hold her head up, being that she's a woman whose husband is really dead and not just run away with some other woman."

Mrs. Hale agreed. "As much as I hate to say it, she's better off without that sort of man in her life. That husband of hers certainly didn't appreciate her. She seems like such a nice person."

Mrs. Vickers arched an eyebrow. "Far be it for me to judge someone, especially now that he's dead and gone, but he was a regular scoundrel."

Mrs. Hale smiled. "We'll have to take her under our wing, won't we? We'll just ignore the gossip. Whatever her husband did, it certainly wasn't her fault. She lives as good a life as any of us. She's even supporting his father, and I don't know if I myself would be that charitable, even if it were my Christian duty. She works very hard to get along. Giving her our friendship is the Christian thing to do, isn't it?"

Mrs. Vickers nodded. "Uh, yes, of course. We'll take her under our wing."

Mrs. Hale added, "And we'll ignore the gossip."

Mrs. Vickers pursed her lips before she added, "Oh, of course we will. You know that I never listen to gossip."

Mail was seldom delivered to Jessica's name at the post office, so she hadn't formed the habit of asking for it all that often. One day in March, when she arrived at the church to give her Saturday lessons, the pastor and Emily were there waiting for her as usual.

Fields said, "Good morning Mrs. Belk. How are you today?"

"I'm fine. How are you?"

"Doing well, with the Lord's blessing."

"And how are you, Emily?"

"I'm fine." Emily grinned at her. "I didn't get the breakfast dishes done yet, so I can't stay, but as soon as I finish my chores, I'll come back."

"All right, Emily."

Jessica sat in the pew on the right side of the aisle to wait for her first pupil, and Daniel Fields sat in the one on the left, as they had been doing for a while. Amanda had been weaned a few months earlier, and she and Caroline preferred to stay home while Jessica taught. Jessica started the conversation. "Emily seems to be so good to do her chores. I've never heard you have to remind her."

"Yes, she's very good, but I'm afraid I can't take any credit for it. Her mother taught her that. When she was only two years old, Jennie had her helping to make her bed in the morning. It didn't matter if it wasn't smooth and straight. The idea was that she did it every day, as soon as she got up. Then, on each birthday after that, she was assigned more tasks." He chuckled.

"Jennie had a way of telling her what she could do next as if it were one of her birthday presents, and she loved it. When she was three, she could help set and clear the table. When she was four, she learned how to fold the linens. That's the way it went. When Jennie went to be with the Lord, Emily naturally took over doing more and more. I still do the cooking and laundry, but she's the one who does most of the cleaning and keeps the house looking nice."

"That's a big burden for such a young girl."

"Yes, it is, but she took it on herself, and she doesn't seem to mind. I never asked her to do any of it."

There was an awkward moment of silence and then he snapped his fingers. "I don't want to forget to tell you, Annie Young has a letter for your father-in-law."

"I'm stopping by the millinery before I go home. I'll pick it up then." Jessica liked Annie Pillsbury Young, the postmistress, and enjoyed chatting with her when she made her trip in to collect her scarce mail. Father Belk hadn't had a letter from anyone since they arrived. The news made Jessica uneasy.

They talked about the weather for a few minutes, and then Samantha arrived for her lesson. Fields stood and smiled at her. She couldn't help but notice again how the corners of his blue eyes crinkled when he smiled.

"I guess I better get to work," he said. "I need to cut some firewood. I'll see you at the service in the morning."

"Good bye, then."

As soon as Jessica finished Emily's lesson, always her last of the day, she went to pick up the letter. As usual, Annie was behind the counter at the post office. She asked, "How are you doing, Jess?"

"We're doing so well, Annie. The Lord is really being kind to us. I understand that you have a letter for Father Belk."

"Yes, just a second now." Annie leafed through a stack of letters and handed one to Jessica. She read the name of the sender. It was from someone in New York, a name she didn't recognize. A cold chill ran down Jessica's spine.

"Thank you, Annie. I wish I could stay for a while, and we could chat, but if I don't get on the road home, I won't get there before dark."

"You go ahead, Jess. I'll see you next time."

All the way home, Jessica felt apprehensive about the letter. From time to time during the long drive, she reached in the pocket of her coat and ran her fingers over the envelope, as if she could read the message inside with her fingertips.

It was a warm day for late March, and Kimimela was already hoeing in the garden when Jessica drove the wagon around the house and climbed down. Caroline was taking clothes from the line and putting them in a basket. As she worked, she handed each clothes pin to Amanda, who ran to put it in the bucket. Jessica led the horse in the barn, and Kimimela came in to take off the harness.

"You can go back to the garden, Mimi. I think I've learned how to handle the harness. Goodness knows I've watched you do it enough times."

"That's all right, Jessica. I'll see to this."

Jessica took the box of millinery supplies off the back of the wagon as Caroline came out of the kitchen to greet her. "How did it go today?"

"It was very nice. Every one of my students showed up on time. Mrs. Wareham has four hats for me to make, and Mr. Wareham has ordered more pillowcases, as many as we can make."

"That's all good news, but it doesn't match the look on your face. You're worried. What's happened?"

"Nothing, really, only this."

She took the letter out of her pocket and held it up for Caroline to read the front of it.

Caroline took a sharp breath. "A letter for Mister Belk, the first one after all this time? Oh, Jess, it has to be bad news."

"That's what I was afraid of. Let's take it to him.

Caroline followed Jessica in the house. "He wasn't in the kitchen when I came out. He must be upstairs in his room."

Jessica went up the stairs and knocked on the door of Father Belk's bedroom. He opened the door. His vest and pants were speckled with wood chips. He had a piece of wood in one hand and a knife in the other. He smiled broadly when he saw her. "You're home early. Good. I know Mr. Wareham has been waiting for some more of these sets. You can tell him I have another one almost done, one with a fancy board. I—what is it, Jess?"

Jessica took a breath. "I have something for you."

She handed him the letter. He took it and stared at it for a moment, then frowned at her. "This is from Agatha, my wife's sister."

"I'll let you read it in private."

"No, don't go. Please."

She nodded, and they went in the room. There was a bed on one side, a table, lamp, and a chair on the other. His finished work was spread out on the table, and there were wood chips on the floor. He sat on the bed and she on the chair. His hands trembled as he stared at the envelope for a moment, then tore it open. He took out the letter, unfolded it and started to read aloud.

"Dear Arthur, I'm sorry to write you that our dear Harriet ---"

His voice caught. He read the rest of the letter to himself, then dropped his head and handed it to Jessica. He was sobbing. As Jessica read, tears began to run down her face too.

He struggled to catch a breath. "What a mess I've made of my life. I never caused her anything but grief, and she was the finest woman who ever lived."

Jessica nodded as she read. "That's what my father said about her, too, and he was right. She was so kind to me, and I loved her so much."

She sat next to him and put her arm around his shoulder as they both wept.

Chapter 26

By late May, there were spring flowers blooming along the path to the church. The trees were full of blossoms, and red-wing blackbirds and bluebirds, wove nests in the branches. The service was over, and the church members filed out. Pastor Fields was saying good bye to the last few people. Caroline held Amanda's hand. Jessica, with Emily close to her, came out last. Jessica carried some music sheets.

Pastor Fields shook Caroline and Amanda's hands and then smiled at Jessica. He took her hand in both of his and held it something he'd never done before. "Thank you, Sister Belk. I can't tell you how much your playing helps the service. Not to mention how much you've done for Emily."

"I love playing, and I love Emily."

She wrapped her free arm around Emily's shoulder, and the girl leaned into her, smiling happily.

He blushed a little. "Will you be coming to the May Day picnic Wednesday?"

"Oh, yes. Father Belk even said he'd come with us. He's not attended services, but when I told him about it, he said he always loved a picnic."

As they talked, he kept his grip on her hand, and she made no attempt to pull it away.

At the end of the walk, Mrs. Vickers stood in a cluster of women. She and Mrs. Hawkins noticed the scene being played out at the church door, and they exchanged a knowing smile. Mrs. Hawkins tilted her head at Jessica, and the women all looked in her direction. With one exception, they all smiled approvingly.

"I wondered how long it was going to take for him to think about courting her," Mrs. Hawkins said.

Mrs. Vickers raised an eyebrow. "Do you think it's really proper? Her husband hasn't even been dead four months."

"Maybe not, but he's been gone for almost two years. I think she deserves some extra leeway for that. God knows, Emily needs a mother. Look at them. Wouldn't they make a lovely family?"

Mrs. Vickers pursed her lips and frowned. "Maybe you're right, but I'd hate to see them rush into anything. You know how people gossip."

Mrs. Hawkins gave Mrs. Vickers a long look and bit her tongue.

Jessica was aware the other women watched her and the preacher. She slipped her hand out of his. "I think we better be going."

"I'll walk with you to the wagon."

Caroline and Amanda went ahead of them. Jessica, Emily, and Fields took their time walking down the path.

Fields helped Caroline into the wagon first, and then held Jessica's hand again, as if he intended to help her up, but she made no move to go. He didn't rush her, but stood with her hand in his.

"I'm looking forward to the picnic. I'll get to meet Mr. Belk at last. You know, Mrs. Belk, not many women would take in their husband's father the way you did. Especially considering-- considering everything that happened."

"He was never anything but kind to me. I could never turn my back on him."

Jessica gave Emily a hug. "How are you doing with your new lesson, Emily?"

"I love it. It's so much fun."

Field's face beamed with pride. "She practices for hours. I never have to remind her. If I can't find her, I know where she'll be, in there pounding away at the piano. I can hear her improving every day."

"As her teacher, I'm glad to hear it. She really is my best student. Some of them act as if I were torturing them."

Fields helped her in the wagon. Their eyes met for a long minute.

Jessica picked up the reins. "We'll see you Wednesday, then."

"Yes, Wednesday."

On Tuesday, Jessica and Caroline cooked all afternoon for the Mayday picnic. Wednesday morning, they loaded everything in the wagon. At the church, tables and chairs had been set up under the flowering fruit trees. On the other side of the church, children played games. Buggies were lined up along the road. Jessica and her family drove up with Father Belk at the reins this time. Fields was talking to some of the men, and Emily playing a circle game with some of the other girls. When they spotted the wagon, both of them stopped what they were doing to go meet it.

Fields held up his hand to help Caroline down. "Good morning."

Jessica made the introductions. "Father Belk, this is Brother Daniel Fields, our pastor. Pastor Fields, this is my father-in-law, Thomas Belk."

Fields stuck out his hand. "I'm pleased to meet you at last, Mr. Belk."

"Thank you. I'm happy to be here."

Fields took Jessica's hand to help her down from the wagon and again, held it longer than necessary. Their eyes met, and they both smiled and blushed. Caroline and Father Belk exchanged a knowing look.

Emily took Amanda's hand and led her off toward the other children. "Come on over here with me, Amanda. I'll show you Vernon Hughes new puppy."

Fields finally released Jessica's hand and lifted one of the baskets out of the back of the wagon. He stuck his head low over the top of it and inhaled. "I don't know what you have in these baskets, but they sure do smell good."

Jessica handed one of the other baskets to Father Belk. "I'm afraid that Caroline gets most of the credit for that. She's one of the best cooks in the country. She made her special buttermilk fried chicken and walnut apple pie."

Caroline hooted. "Jessica knows her way around the kitchen every bit as well as I do. I did most of the cooking for today because she was sewing up until the last minute before we left."

As they took the baskets off the wagon and carried them toward the tables, Mrs. Vickers stood next to Mrs. Brooks and two other women. "I do believe that our pastor is paying a great deal of attention to someone who was so recently widowed."

Mrs. Brooks looked sideways at Mrs. Vickers. "Yes, as we discussed only the other day, recently officially widowed, but he's been gone a very long time, so it isn't as if he died at home a few weeks ago."

Mrs. Vickers sniffed. "I think he may be hurrying this along."

Mrs. Brooks nodded. "Jeanette Hawkins and I were talking about it only yesterday. She told me how happy you were about it. If their friendship were to develop into something important, Emily would have a new mother to raise her, and our church would have a new first lady. Isn't it wonderful?"

Having no more success at stirring up Mrs. Brooks on Wednesday than she had with Mrs. Hawkins on Sunday, Mrs. Vickers dropped the subject. She stuck her nose in the air. The other two women smiled at Mrs. Brooks and nodded their heads.

Once the children were corralled, and everyone seated at the tables, dinner began. After asking the blessing, Pastor Fields and Emily sat with Jessica's family. The grounds were filled with the sounds of fellowship and a good meal. After desserts were served, a middle-aged couple, Joyce and Walter Thom, walked over to them.

They had already met Jessica and Caroline at Sunday services, so Fields introduced them to Father Belk. Walter shook his hand.

"Pleased to meet you, Mr. Belk. I hope we get to see more of you." He turned to the pastor. "Brother Fields, my brother and his wife are coming to visit from Kansas City tomorrow. They have to go home Saturday, and I'd like you to meet them before they leave. Would you and Emily be able to come to dinner tomorrow evening?"

Fields nodded. "Thank you. We'd love that. What time should we be there?"

"Julie likes to have dinner on the table by six, so around five-thirty, and we can talk awhile."

"That would be fine. We'll see you then."

Mr. & Mrs. Thom smiled warmly at Jessica and walked away.

In listening to the conversation, Jessica saw an opportunity. "Do you often have dinner at member's homes?"

"From time to time, usually when there's some sort of occasion like this one, kinfolk visiting."

Caroline chimed in immediately. "We should have you out to our place. How about one day next week?"

Grateful that Caroline was the one who made the invitation, Jessica blushed and looked down at her lap.

Fields grinned. "We would love that."

Caroline went on. "Now that I think about it, why wait until next week? If Friday would be all right for you and Emily, come then. We eat around six ourselves, but be as early as you can. Jess can show you around our place. It's still a little ragged here and there, but we're fixing it up as we go. Maybe you can offer her some advice on what she needs to do."

Fields's eyes met Jessica's. "It will be our pleasure. Friday it is."

Jessica fluttered around the house for the next two days and couldn't keep her mind on her work. She cleaned the already pristine living room and dining room until they sparkled. On Friday, Caroline shooed her out of the kitchen repeatedly. "Go work on your sewing. You've already missed two days this week. I'll take care of dinner."

Over and over, Jessica would sit down to sew only to find herself gazing dreamily out the window at the ruby-throated hummingbirds sipping nectar from the redbud tree that bloomed outside her bedroom. It was around four o'clock when she heard a buggy drive up to the house. She ran to the mirror, pinched her cheeks, and bit her lips to redden them.

She waited in her bedroom until she heard the knock at the front door and then walked leisurely downstairs to open it. Fields and Emily were standing there, Emily holding a fistful of lilacs that Jessica recognized as having come from the bushes that grew along the sides of the parsonage.

Emily proudly held them out to Jessica. "These are for you. Thank you for inviting us."

"Oh, thank you, Emily. They're beautiful." Jessica buried her nose in the blossoms. "Don't they smell wonderful? I think lilacs are the best smelling flower God created. You know what? Adele from across the road mixes up a potion that she uses to make cuttings sprout roots. I think that if I can get some of that from her, I can start my very own shrubs from these. Wouldn't that be wonderful?"

"Yes, Ma'am."

Caroline came out of the kitchen. "I thought I heard you out here. Emily, how about you come help me tend to Amanda while Jessica shows your father around the grounds?"

"Sure. Can I help with the cooking? Daddy says I'm not old enough, but I think I am."

"I wouldn't want to disagree with your father, but I stood Jessica up on a chair and let her start cooking when she was a lot younger than you are now."

Emily scowled at her father. "See, Daddy? I told you to stop treating me like a child."

He chuckled. "I see indeed. Very well, Caroline, teach her whatever you want. I'm sure it will be wonderful."

Emily trotted off to the kitchen with Caroline, and Jessica waved a hand at the front door. "Let me show you around my kingdom." She led him outside and started at the rose garden in the front of the porch. Some of the blossoms were six inches wide.

"They're thriving now, but you should have seen it when we arrived. The weeds and sunflowers had almost completely taken over the space. I was too far along with Amanda to get to it for a while, but Mimi cleared the weeds from around the roses and then gave them a good pruning. That first spring, she spread out a thick dose of compost, and they just soaked it up and started blooming. It was almost a miracle. She certainly has a way with her when it comes to plants and animals. I really have to give her credit for the corn and the hay and the vegetable gardens, too."

Jessica led him from the front rose garden and wound her way around one side of the house, talking all the way.

He said, "You're certainly proud of the place, aren't you?"

"I am. I hated it for a while, because of the way Zachary came into it, and because of the way he tricked me to bring me out here, but I'm happier now that I've been in a long time. It's as if my life started over again the day he left. I don't hate him, or I guess I should say I don't hate his memory. He was pitiful, really. He had so much to be grateful for, and he wasted all of it. I'm sorry for him. I'm sorry for the way he lived, and for the way he died, but he gave me Amanda, and he brought me here. It seems like God's blessing started pouring out on this place from that day until now."

"I don't know the whole story of your marriage, but I know enough to appreciate how you've had to struggle. You deserve every good thing you have now. Lord knows, you worked hard enough for it."

"Not only me, all of us. It's funny, isn't it? I was born wealthy, and I never earned one cent in my whole life until the day I gave my first piano lesson. That was after the first time Zachary and I separated."

"Why did you take him back?"

"I was expecting, and he convinced me that my baby needed a father. That was when he was sure I would have a boy. He left when Amanda was born. Oh, well, it was his loss."

Jessica shrugged and went on. "He did me a favor by leaving. It gave me my own life back. We're not scraping for every penny now, but my aim is to be as self-sufficient as possible. We have enough acreage to grow a good size garden and even enough corn and hay for the livestock. The barn is huge, and there's a smokehouse, henhouse, Mimi's cabin, the silo, and a pole barn. Caroline bought jars and puts up a lot of the produce so it lasts all year."

"Jennie used to can the fruit from the trees around the church."

"I hired a teenager, Brian Otts from down the road to help with the painting and some of the repairs around here. Father Belk does as much as he can reach from the ground, but I couldn't let him get up on a ladder. Brian is getting the top half of the taller buildings. We have a nice size creek running across the back of the property, and there's even a pretty little waterfall about a foot high. Let's walk down this way so you can see it."

They walked down the path that wound through the orchard and come out to a gurgling stream. They stopped and silently watched the water tumble over the falls. He reached down and found a stone, which he tossed in the water. Jessica laughed.

"What's funny?" he asked.

"You, throwing that rock. Father Belk did the same thing, and so did Brian the first time he came down here. Is that something all men do, throw rocks into the water?"

He shrugged. "I guess so."

It had all been very proper between them. Jessica hoped he would take her hand, but he hadn't touched her. She waited for him to say something that would move the relationship forward, but he hadn't said it. She was right about the changes in her since Zachary left. It was time for her to make a move.

She pointed downstream and was about to say something when she let her foot slip on a rock, and she almost fell in the water. He caught her, and held her tightly to him. She held her breath, closed her eyes, and leaned into him. After a moment, he took one hand and tilted back her head so he could see her face. They gazed at one another. He kissed her forehead, then her cheek. She didn't move. He took a deep breath and said, "I think we better go up to the house and see if Caroline needs some help in the kitchen."

She put her head on his chest. "I don't want to go up to the house. I don't want ever to move from this spot."

"We have to go sooner or later, or they'll come looking for us."

"I suppose you're right."

Reluctantly, she stepped away from him. He took her hand in his and held it all the way back to the house.

"I wouldn't want you to slip again," he told her with a grin. *I wonder if he knows I slipped on purpose.*

Caroline had prepared a lovely meal, and everyone enjoyed the food and the company, but Jessica didn't really keep her mind on dinner. When the meal was over, Father Belk showed Fields how to carve a piece of wood while the four females cleared the table. Caroline and Jessica carried away the plates with leftovers and stowed away the food. Emily carried the dishes, and Amanda, who demanded she be allowed to help, was given the non-breakable items like the silverware. When the chores were completed, they sat in the living room and the adults talked politics and life while the girls went to Amanda's room to play with her dolls.

When it was time for them to leave, everyone gathered on the front porch. The men shook hands and Father Belk surprised them all. "I'll see you in church next Sunday, Pastor."

"See you then. Goodbye, Caroline. Goodbye, Amanda."

The little girls hugged one another. Jessica walked to the buggy holding Emily's hand. Once they were in the buggy, Fields looked down into Jessica's eyes for a long moment and said, "I'll see you Saturday morning."

She noticed again how his eyes crinkled when he smiled and it ran a little thrill through her heart. "Goodbye, Pastor Fields."

He chuckled. "I think when we're away from the church it would be all right for you to call me Daniel."

She blushed and gave a short nod. "Goodbye, Daniel."

He slapped the reins on the horses back and, this time, it was Jessica's turn to watch as he drove away.

That evening, Jessica sat at the vanity in her bedroom brushing her hair when there was a knock at the door. "Come in," Jessica called.

Caroline entered, carrying some linens. She put them in the bottom drawer of the chest and said over her shoulder. "I think Pastor Fields enjoyed his visit today."

Jessica smiled at her reflection in the mirror as she went on brushing. "I enjoyed it myself."

"I thought you did. When you came back from the creek both of you were blushing."

Caroline sat on the bed and leaned toward Jessica, who turned to face her. They were suddenly two conspirators. Jessica put down the brush and whispered to Caroline, "He kissed me, sort of, I mean, it wasn't on my lips, just on my forehead and cheek, but it was a kiss all the same."

"Of course he did. I knew he would the first chance he had."

"Caroline, it was as if I had never been touched by a man before, not once in my whole life. I pretended I was going to fall into the creek, and he caught me. When he put his arms around me, I knew my heart must be beating so loudly he had to hear it, and when he started kissing me, I thought I might faint. Remember the time we talked about how some women enjoy—you know?"

"I remember."

Jessica closed her eyes as she remembered. "I think I'm beginning to understand. When he caught me, he held onto me way longer than he needed to. First he kissed my forehead, and then he kissed my cheek."

"Well! You had quite a day."

"Yes, the most wonderful day of my life. I don't think I've ever been this happy. I can hardly wait to see what happens next."

Chapter 27

Expecting a wonderful day, Jessica eagerly looked forward to seeing Daniel on Saturday, but the day turned out to be quite ordinary. At the church, she found Mrs. Vickers talking with Daniel and Emily nowhere in sight. Mrs. Vickers waved at her.

"Good morning, Jessica," Mrs. Vickers said. "I know you don't start your lessons for another half-hour. I can't make it for Wednesday evening rehearsals the way we usually do, and I thought if you came early, we could take the time to practice my solo for the Sunday service."

"That would be fine, Mrs. Vickers."

Daniel waved at them. "Good morning, Mrs. Belk. I have some work to do, so I'll leave you ladies to your music." He went out the side door.

Jessica played for Mrs. Vickers until her first pupil arrived, and she stayed busy all day. She'd made it a habit to take a half-hour break for lunch, and Emily joined her and then stayed to watch the rest of her pupils until it was her turn to take her own lesson. It thrilled Jessica to see how quickly Emily was learning, and how devoted she was to the work. She never complained about the exercises or the time spent practicing. When they reviewed her last lesson, Jessica said, "I have something special for you today, Emily."

Emily's face lit up. "You do? What is it?"

Jessica pulled a few sheets of paper out of her books. "I wrote up a special arrangement of 'Blessed

Assurance." I think if you practice it this week, by next Sunday you'll be ready to play it in front of the congregation."

"Really? Do you really think I can do it?"

"I'm sure you can. The way I wrote this up, it's actually much easier than some of the work you're already doing. You're the best student I ever had."

"Do I have that much talent?"

"You have a great deal of talent, but you have something that's every bit as important and maybe even more. You love it, and you work really hard at it."

Jessica and Emily worked on the piece until it was quite late. Jessica said, "I have to go now, Emily, but you practice this week."

Emily's answer was fervent. "I will! I really, really will. Thank you so much. I can't believe I'm going to play in front of the congregation."

The next day, Jessica's whole family attended the services. When they entered the church, Mrs. Vickers made a point of welcoming Father Belk. She asked him several pointed questions. "I understand that you're Jessica's father-in-law?"

He smiled at her. "Yes. I have that good fortune."

"And her family consists of her daughter, you, Mrs. Akins, and an Indian girl?"

"Yes, and a horse, a cow, and other livestock."

"But Mrs. Akins isn't really related to any of you?"

"Not related technically, but she raised Jessica after her mother died, and Jess thinks of her as her mother."

"I see." Mrs. Vickers walked away abruptly.

At the end of the service, when the members were filing out, Jessica caught Mrs. Vickers and beckoned to her. Piqued by curiosity, Mrs. Vickers rushed right over. Jessica drew her aside, and Mrs. Vickers leaned in to hear what Jessica had to say. "I'd like to ask a favor of you, Mrs. Vickers."

For all her faults, Mrs. Vickers was always happy when she could be a help to someone, ---providing she felt that someone was worthy. Jessica had earned that position by playing for her solos and not playing so loudly that the piano drew attention away from her voice.

"Of course, my dear. What can I do for you?"

"Emily is doing very well with her lessons. You know how she adored her mother--"

"Oh, yes. Jennie Fields was a wonderful woman."

"Yes, I'm sure she had to be to raise such a wonderful child. Well, I've been told that Jennie was amazingly talented on the piano."

"She was. She played better than anyone I've ever heard. Not that you aren't gifted too. I mean--."

"I understand. I think that Emily must have inherited her mother's gifts, because she's making wonderful progress in her lessons. I believe she's ready to play for the services, but I'm afraid her nerves might get the better of her. If you could come by here next Saturday at four in the afternoon and listen to her, it would be a great help. That way, her first audience would be only you and her father. I think it would make it easier for her on Sunday morning."

"What a splendid idea! Of course I'll come. I can hardly wait to hear her."

"Thank you so much. I'll see you then."

Mrs. Vickers drew herself up importantly and left, pausing to shake the pastor's hand as she went out.

As usual, Jessica's family was the last to leave. Fields and Emily waited by the door to say goodbye.

He held Jessica's hand longer than necessary and told her, "I wanted to thank you again for the wonderful dinner last week."

"I'm happy you liked it."

Standing next to them, Caroline said, "I put a nice, big bird in the oven before we left. It should be ready by the time we get home. You and Emily could come out again today."

Emily was thrilled. "Can we go, Daddy? I want to go."

Daniel never took his eyes off of Jessica's as he said, "We'd like that very much. We'll be there as soon as I hitch up the buggy."

As they rode home, Jessica leaned into Caroline's shoulder. "I suppose that chicken is big enough to feed seven people?"

"Oh, yes. I actually put two of them in, just in case someone else should be there for dinner."

Fields happily went to hitch his horse to the buggy. He backed out of the barn, and Emily, perhaps even more eager than he, climbed up in the seat immediately and watched him. He was putting the harness on the horse and adjusting it when Emily said, "Hurry up, Daddy. We don't want to be late."

"I'm hurrying. I'm hurrying. I don't want to be late, either."

In a matter of minutes, they were headed for Jessica's place. They were hardly on the road when Emily said, "It seems like it takes forever to get there, and once you're there, it seems like you have to go home right away."

He wrapped one arm around her shoulders. "You really like Mrs. Belk, don't you, Emily?"

"I love her."

"I'm happy to hear that. I've been thinking about her a lot lately."

"I know. Your face gets all mushy when you're around her."

"You know you're the most important thing in my life, don't you?"

"Yes, I do, but some day I'm going to get married and maybe move away. If I married a missionary or something, I could wind up in South America or somewhere, and you'd be all alone. You should be thinking about asking Mrs. Belk to marry you so that won't happen."

Daniel laughed. "I was hoping you wouldn't get married for a few more years. You should at least wait until you're twelve."

"Oh, Daddy. Don't be silly. I mean when I'm old, like eighteen."

"How would you feel about it if I married Mrs. Belk later on this year?"

"I don't know why you have to wait. You should marry her right away."

"Her husband hasn't been dead very long. There are some people who wouldn't think it was seemly for her to remarry so soon."

"I know who you mean. You're talking about Mrs. Vickers. Why do you care what she thinks?"

"Don't say negative things about anyone. It isn't what Jesus would want us to do. I'm sure Mrs. Vickers means well and is only thinking about the good of the congregation. Whenever Mrs. Belk was ready, we'd have the ceremony."

"I would love that."

"She wouldn't be replacing your mother. No one could ever do that."

"I know that. She would have her own place, though."

"You're more grown up than I realized."

"Yes, I'm not a child anymore."

"What about Amanda? Do you think you would mind having her live with us?"

"Would you still like me best?"

"Emily, I will never love anyone more than I love you, not even Jessica, and I love her something awful."

"Then I think it would be fine for Amanda to live with us. She could be my little sister. I could teach her all the things I know, like how to braid her hair and how to tie her bows. This is exciting. You could have a Christmas wedding. Would that be enough time to keep Mrs. Vickers from gossiping about it?"

"What did I just say? Mrs. Vickers doesn't gossip. She's only concerned that everyone's behavior is up to her standards."

"All right, we'll put it that way. Would a Christmas wedding be up to her standards?"

"I hope so, but I don't want to get ahead of myself. I haven't even asked Mrs. Belk yet if she'll have me. She may turn me down."

"I don't think so. When she's around you, her face gets all mushy, too. Christmas is a long way away, but I think you ought to ask her today. She's very pretty, you know. Someone else might come along and snap her up. I saw Eugene Lamont staring at her this morning."

"Eugene Lamont? He must be fifty years old."

"Maybe so, but he's not ugly, and he earns an awful lot of money from those horses he raises. That might be very attractive to someone who's had to work as hard as Mrs. Belk."

"Maybe you're right. He must be rich. I heard him say that men come from all over Kansas and Missouri to buy his horses."

"We, he looks at her mushy all the time and goes out of his way to talk to her, so you better stop wasting time. There aren't all that many unmarried women around here. If you lost out on getting Mrs. Belk, and she marries Mr. Lamont, who knows how long it might be before someone else I like comes along?"

It had never occurred to Daniel that he might have competition for Jessica's hand. Emily was right, eligible women in this part of the country were scarce. For a long time he hadn't even thought about remarrying. He was finished grieving now. Daniel nodded, set a determined jaw, and slapped the reins on the horses back.

Caroline had prepared another lovely meal. In the dining room, they were all around the table while everyone ooh-ed and ah-ed over the dessert.

Daniel shook his head. "That was delicious, Caroline. You certainly know how to cook. I didn't think anything could beat that apple pie you brought to the picnic, but this peach cobbler is even better."

Caroline beamed at the praise. "Those are our own peaches. I canned them from our crop last fall."

Jessica stood. "She puts a few pieces of clove in each jar. That's what gives them that lovely flavor. Now, you men sit and have some more coffee. Caroline and I will get these dishes out of the way, and we can all sit on the porch for a while. There's a lovely spring breeze that we should enjoy while we can. It won't be long before it gets hot again."

Emily jumped up. "I want to help with the dishes and so does Amanda. Right Amanda?"

The little girl nodded her head vigorously. "Yes, me too. I want to help too."

Emily said, "I heard Caroline say your sow had a litter last night. You two should take a walk and you can show Daddy the new piglets."

Jessica's face reddened. Caroline smiled and winked at Emily.

Caroline picked up the plate with the last of the chicken. "That's right. Emily, Amanda, and I can handle the dishes. You two go out and look at the livestock."

Father Belk chimed in. "I'll just sit here and have another helping of that cobbler. There's such a little bit left in the dish it seems a shame to make you go to all the trouble of saving it."

Caroline chuckled. She picked up the coffee pot and poured him another cup. "You may as well have something to wash it down with."

As soon as they were out of sight of the house, Daniel took Jessica's hand. They made a stop at the barn so he could admire the litter of little pigs. They leaned over the rail of the pen and he tried to count them.

"How many did she have? The way they're all piled up in there it's hard to tell where one ends and the next one begins."

"It's hard to believe, but she has seventeen piglets."

He whistled low. "Is that some sort of record?"

"I don't know. Adele said it was the biggest litter she ever heard of. Her boar is their daddy."

"I was about to ask where she was bred, you not having a boar here."

"Adele and I have a mutually beneficial agreement. She does everything under the sun for me. She even delivered Amanda. Once in a while, she lets me sew her a pretty apron."

"I know your work is beautiful, but that sounds a little one-sided."

"That's what I keep telling her. I'm blessed to have her for a neighbor. From the first day, she was a help to us."

"Good friends are a gift from God, for sure."

"These piglets ought to be a good size by October. With a litter this big, we'll have meat to last all winter and won't have to eat so many beans this year. I thought I'd keep one or two of the females and use them for breeding next year. Mrs. Otts, our handyman Brian's mother, has a litter, and she said she would trade me one of her males for one of my females so they could breed right."

He took her hand again and they strolled out of the barn and down the pathway. When they reached the spot by the creek where they stood before, he stopped and turned to face her. He took both her hands in his. "This is the place where we stopped the last time."

"Yes, it is. Aren't you going to throw a stone in the stream?"

"I almost have to, don't I?" He bent over, picked up a stone, and tossed it into the stream. "Now that I have that out of the way,--."

"I don't think you had your heart in it that time."

"I have other things on my mind."

"Do you? What might that be?"

"Emily is very fond of you, you know."

"I'm fond of her."

"She thinks she would enjoy having a little sister."

"Does she?" Jessica waited for him to go on. He cleared his throat, scuffed the side of his shoe on the ground, and squinted in the glare of sunlight sparkling off the water. Jessica waited, and waited. Finally, he cleared his throat again. She waited until she couldn't stand it anymore. "For a man who earns his living preaching you seem to be having some trouble saying what you have on your mind."

"Well, Emily--"

"Yes, Emily--?"

"She thinks we should have a Christmas wedding."

"I see. What do you think?"

"I wish it could be today, but it's been such a short time since your husband died, it would be scandalous, even though he's been gone over a year."

"Over a year and a half."

"Right, but he wasn't officially, uh, deceased, until last Christmas when Emmalou came home with the news.

You understand, as a minister, I have to observe certain traditions."

"I can think of one tradition you've forgotten all about."

"What's that?"

"You haven't actually proposed to me."

"Then I'll do it up proper. I've been thinking it over for a while." He dropped to one knee, cleared his throat yet another time, and began. "Mrs. Jessica Belk, I think I fell in love with you the first time you walked up to my church. Your bonnet had fallen off, and the pins came out of your hair so it blew in the wind. The sun was behind you and it made a halo around your face. I was struck with the notion that God had sent an angel to me. Since that time, I've learned to respect you for your integrity and work ethic, and I've come to love you for your sweetness and your kindness. I can't imagine spending the rest of my life if you aren't a part of it. Will you marry me, Jessica?"

Jessica didn't hesitate. "I have given this some thought myself. Yes, Daniel, I will, and I wish we didn't have to wait, but I know you're right. I love the idea of having the ceremony on Christmas Day. You know what I'm going to do?"

"What?"

"As I said, I've already given it some thought. I've been reworking Mother's clothes for the last three years for me and Amanda, and I'm tired of it. I'm going to buy a bolt of fabric that has never been used before and make Amanda and myself a brand new dress for the occasion. I want to start my new life in a new gown."

"Would a bolt be enough to make something for Emily?"

"It certainly will. What fun the three of us will have."

He held onto the branch of a tree to pull himself up off his knee and took her in his arms. "Do you think it would be proper conduct for me to kiss my betrothed?"

She threw back her head and laughed, "I certainly hope so, because I've been waiting for it for a very long time." He wrapped his arms around her and drew her to him. She tilted up her chin and closed her eyes, waiting for the kiss she had only been dreaming about for a long while. He kissed her forehead first, the way he had the other time. Then he kissed her cheek, her earlobe and her neck. She didn't move or open her eyes the whole time. By the time his lips touched hers, her heart was pounding. The first kiss was soft and lingering. He drew back a little, then kissed her again, with a little less restraint. Jessica thought she was going to faint in her effort to remain a lady.

He stepped back and held her out at arm's length. In a husky voice, he said, "It's going to be a long wait for Christmas this year. Let's go tell the others."

Chapter 28

Jessica thought a great deal about her wedding. The first thing she did was buy fabric for the dresses. It would be a winter wedding, so she chose cotton velveteen, much less expensive than the silk velvet her mother had worn. There was a pale ivory for herself, pink for Amanda and Emily, and burgundy for Caroline. She had to order a whole card of ivory lace that would be used to trim all four of the dresses. She made her own dress first. When it was finished, she hung it on the coat rack in the corner of her bedroom and placed a pair of lambskin dancing slippers her mother had worn under the dress. It was the last thing she looked at every night before she fell asleep. She told Daniel it gave her sweet dreams.

They began to be seen together in public, but always accompanied by the children. "Let me show you some of the best things about Manhattan."

He took Jessica and the girls in his buggy to Pillsbury Crossing, a shallow place in Deep Creek not far from her house. It was in a beautiful, wooded area.

Jessica whooped when he drove his buggy right out into the water. They sat for a while and watched the girl's playing in the froth at the bottom of the little waterfall. "The pioneers came this way to cross the creek here." Daniel explained. "It's only a foot deep now, but you can't take it for granted. If there's a lot of rain, it sometimes it gets quite high."

Jessica loved the spot. "I can't believe how beautiful it is here. Promise me that we'll come here often. I'll pack a picnic basket, and we can stay all afternoon."

"I promise."

Another time, he took his buggy off the road and they climbed to the crest of one of the taller hills in the area. He drove up alongside a row of deep ruts in the prairie grass and stopped the wagon. "See the ruts there," he asked, pointing to them.

"Yes. It looks as if a lot of wagons have come here."

"This is part of the Oregon Trail. The Easterners who settle the whole northwest region of this country pass through here and their wagons make these ruts."

"You'd have thought that the rain would have washed away all trace of them."

"They used this trail for several decades, thousands of them. The ruts are so compressed now, they're petrified."

"It might be fun to say we drove on the Oregon Trail. Can we go in them?"

"We could, but it would be easier to get the buggy down in them than it would to get it out again. There's no telling how far we would have to go before we found a place that would be safe to drive out without breaking one of the wheels."

"I see." They sat silently for a while, each thinking their own thoughts. The land there was beginning to stretch out into the flat prairie of western Kansas. It had very few trees, and the wind tugged at Jessica's bonnet. She thought about those pioneer women who'd come west just as she had, but without a house to come to, or a town to go get their supplies from, or even a church to give them spiritual support. Suddenly what she had felt was her own hardship seemed foolish to her.

Amanda broke the spell by saying, "Mama, I want to go home. I'm tired of this place."

With her wedding dress completely done, Caroline's dress was next. Caroline hadn't had a new dress in years, and some of the ones she wore under her ever-present apron were threadbare. Jessica wanted it to be extra special so, even though Caroline was a good sized woman, she didn't skimp on the fabric or the trim. Every stitch was sewn with love and appreciation.

In October, she cut a dozen of the white roses and as many of the pink that were still thriving in the front yard and hung them upside down to dry. When they were ready, she trimmed the stems and tied the white ones with ivory ribbon and a leftover bit of lace from her dress. They would make a lovely bouquet for her to carry down the aisle. The pink ones were shaped into little bunches for Caroline and the girls to pin to their dresses.

The girls grew like the wildflowers over the summer, and Jessica didn't want them to outgrow their dresses before they even had a chance to wear them, so she waited until November to cut their fabric. Even then, she made them a little large, just in case they grew even more in the month ahead.

Jessica took two heavy sheets of paper and drew out the lines of music staffs so she could write out the song that Emily would play for the ceremony. The girl was overjoyed to know that she would be providing the music, but as talented and hard-working as Emily was, she still needed pieces that would be easy for her to play.

In December Jessica made hats for herself and Caroline, and bonnets for the girls. Over the months while all this was taking place, Jessica never let up on the sewing work she did for Mr. and Mrs. Wareham's shops. Her one self- indulgence was spending extra money for lamp oil so she could work later at night.

On the morning of Christmas Eve, Kimimela and Father Belk came back from a trek in the little woods down by the creek dragging a young Ponderosa pine. They placed it in front of the living room window and the whole family helped decorate it. When Amanda went to bed, Jessica put the gifts under the tree. She and Caroline spent the last few hours of the day in the kitchen, baking cakes and cookies for the wedding dinner. It was a bit past her usual bedtime before she finally climbed the stairs to her room.

There was something else Jessica had sewn for the occasion, and she took it out of the drawer and held it up in front of herself to see in the mirror. It was a white nightgown made of the softest linen, trimmed with lace, and embroidered with tiny white roses. After admiring her reflection, she folded it up, wrapped it in the tissue paper, and put it back in the drawer. She drifted off to sleep thinking about the next day and dreaming about living with a man who really loved her.

Jessica was sleeping soundly. There was snow falling outside the window. A little Christmas tree sat on the table by her bed. Her wedding gown was hanging on the coat rack in the corner. The calendar on her table said December 24.

In her cabin, Kimimela also slept. She had a new dress of her own for the wedding. Suddenly, her eyes popped open and she sat up in bed. She could hear the muffled sound of a horse walking slowly through the snow. She knew instinctively that it was well after midnight. She frowned and tilted her head to listen. The sound of the hoof beats stopped in front of the house and then she heard a soft thud. Kimimela jumped from the bed, pulled on her boots, wrapped a blanket around her, and hurried out of the cabin.

She came running around the side of the house. In front of the walk, a black horse stood with his reins hanging down and holding his right forefoot in the air. The crumpled body of a man lay on its side next to the horse. Kimimela stooped down and rolled him over on his back. A small cry escaped her. She jumped up and ran in the house, leaving the door open. She bolted up the stairs two at a time and pounded on Jessica's door. "Miss Jessica! Miss Jessica!" she hollered.

In a moment, Jessica opened her door. "Mimi? What on earth? Is it Father Belk?"

"No, it is him, Mr. Zachary."

"Mr. Zachary? What do you mean?"

"He is here, out front. He is lying on the ground."

Jessica pulled on her robe and she and Kimimela ran down the stairs and out the door. They bent over Belk's body. Jessica slid her hand inside his coat, and pressed it against his chest. "He's still breathing. We have to get him in the house. He'll be too heavy for us. Run get Mr. West."

Kimimela jumped up and ran across the road. She pounded on the door of the Wests' house. Henry West answered.

Mimi pointed to the body lying in the road. "Please help us. It's Mr. Zachary, and we must get him inside."

West took his coat off of a coat rack near the door and pulled it on as he followed Kimimela down the walk. He picked up Belk by the shoulders.

"Get his feet."

Kimimela grabbed Belk by the feet. Jessica ran ahead and held the door open. "Please put him on the sofa."

Kimimela and West carried Belk to the sofa and stretched him out. Jessica helped West take off Belk's coat and shoes. She took a blanket off the back of the sofa and covered him.

Henry West asked, "Is there anything else I can do for you tonight?"

"No. I'm so sorry to disturb you. Thank you so much for helping us. I'm not going to try to get him upstairs tonight."

"I'll be going, then."

"Again, I'm so sorry to have to bother you in the middle of the night like this, but we could never have managed by ourselves. Thank you."

"That's all right, Jessica."

He left and closed the door. Jessica put her palm on Belk's forehead. She could smell whiskey on his clothing. She told Mimi, "He doesn't seem to have a fever, and he's breathing regularly. I think we should let him stay here until he wakes up."

Jessica and Kimimela stood for a moment looking at Belk's sleeping body and then Kimimela went to the door. "I'll go see to the horse."

She led the limping animal to the barn, picked up the foot it had been favoring, and looked at it. She took the hoof pick from the shelf and ran it around the inside of his hoof, flicking out a rock the size of a walnut. *Zachary Belk is more of a fool than I thought he was to have ridden a horse that was limping and never even dismounted to check on him.* She took a glob of greasy substance out of a tin and smeared some of it on the inside of the hoof.

Jessica stood in the living room, looking down at Belk with tears streaming down her face. "God forgive me. I was actually relieved you were dead. I was so happy, so very happy, and now you've ruined everything."

She turned to find that Caroline, hearing the ruckus, had come out of her room and was looking at her with sympathy. She put her arm around Jessica's shoulders. "Are you all right?"

"No." Jessica gripped the rail and plodded back upstairs. When she reached the top, Father Belk stood with tears running down his face. Jessica shrugged. "I'm going to have to go ask God for forgiveness for the thoughts I have. As for your son, I don't think there's anything seriously wrong with him. He's reeking of whiskey. Let him be for now. He can explain it all in the morning."

There was no more sleep to be had for any of them that night, but they all went back to their rooms. Jessica lay in her bed looking at the wedding dress in the corner. It had brought her such joy to select the fabric, cut it out, stitch it together, and embroider it. It was joy she'd expected to last for the rest of her life, joy that was now vanished.

She lay awake as long as she could tolerate it, but got out of bed when the sun began to glow over the horizon. Jessica looked at herself in the mirror to see that her eyes were puffy from crying. *It doesn't matter what I look like now.*

She dressed, put on her coat, and went out to look for Kimimela. She found her in the barn, milking the cow. "As soon as you're finished here, would you take Juniper and go tell Daniel what's happened. I'll see to the chickens and the other livestock."

Kimimela looked up at her and didn't say anything, but gave a curt nod. A few minutes later, she brought the bucket of milk in the kitchen where Caroline had coffee brewing. Jessica sat at the table with her hands folded in front of her. The sideboard was lined with colorful Christmas cookies, and pies and cakes they'd made for the wedding party. Kimimela put the bucket on the countertop. "I'll go see Mr. Daniel now."

Jessica simply nodded, and Kimimela left.

The sun was well up by the time Kimimela came cantering up to the front of the parsonage. The doors of the church and parsonage had Christmas wreaths on them. She dismounted, ran up the lane, and knocked. Pastor Fields opened the door.

"Mimi? What is it? Is Jessica all right?"

"No. She sent me to tell you that Mr. Belk came back last night."

"Mr. Belk? Do you mean Zachary?"

"Yes. Mr. Zachary."

The color drained out of Daniel's face. "Tell her I understand."

"I'm sorry, Mr. Daniel. I'm sorry for you and Miss Jessica and all of us. This is a terrible thing." She ran back to her horse, mounted, and rode back in the direction of the house.

Chapter 29

By ten o'clock Christmas morning, the cow had been milked, the chickens, horses, and hogs fed, breakfast prepared, but barely eaten, and the kitchen cleaned. Dreams had been destroyed, hearts broken, and Zachary Belk was still sleeping on the living room sofa. Amanda, now two years and three months old, stood in front of him, staring at him. She reached out one finger and touched his hair, the hair exactly like her own. He opened his eyes. At first, he was disoriented, then he focused on his daughter. "You must be Amanda. Good morning. I'm your father."

Her eyes grew wide, but the normally talkative child didn't say anything in reply. She stared at him curiously. He swung his feet to the floor and sat up. Still groggy, he rested with his elbows on his knees and looked around the room. It was decorated for Christmas. There was a big tree with gifts under it in one corner.

He spoke to the child again. "It looks as if your mother has done some renovations. I wonder where she got the money. Where is everyone?"

Still, Amanda didn't answer, just stared at him. He stood, wobbled a little, and then went toward the kitchen.

Caroline was at the stove, Father Belk sat at the table with a mug of coffee. Jessica was setting the table for lunch. Belk entered with Amanda following behind, still watching him.

He had a weeks' worth of beard, his eyes were bleary, and his voice hoarse when he said, "Merry Christmas, everyone."

No one answered. Belk picked up a mug, went to the stove, and poured himself some coffee. He sat at the table next to his father. Jessica picked up Amanda and put her in her high chair.

Belk took a long drink of the coffee and looked around the room at each of them. "I thought at least that my own father would be happy to see me home."

Father Belk kept his eyes on the table and said, "As your father, I'm glad you aren't dead. I can't say I'm happy to see you come back here."

Belk was surprised to hear his father speaking. "It seems you have quite recovered the ability to communicate since I left. Where else would I go? This is my family, my home."

Jessica shot him a resentful look. "We were told last spring you had died in a knife fight in San Francisco."

"Really? Well, they got the message partly right. I did come close to dying, but the ministrations of an excellent doctor pulled me through. Who was the bearer of this inaccurate message?"

"The girl you ran away with came home with the story."

"Did she now? I wondered what happened to her. When I regained consciousness several days after the fight, she was gone. I would have been here sooner, but it was quite some time before I could travel. I needed to heal, and I had to have a bit of luck at the tables to get enough money for the trip home."

"You aren't welcome here. I want you out of the house, and I don't care where you go. Maybe your young lady will take you in. I plan to file for divorce as soon as I can find an attorney."

"File for divorce if you must. I can't contest it, since everyone in town is probably quite aware of my infidelity, but I'll not be getting out of my own house. I own this place. My name is the only one on the deed. You can stay here and take up your marital duties, or you and your— your entourage, can find accommodations elsewhere. If you haven't sold the house in New York, get on a train and go back there. You never liked it here anyway."

"I'd rather starve to death than take up any marital duties with you. I have no intention of going back to New York. I'll look for a suitable place to live tomorrow. I've made some friends in this town. I'm sure I can find one who would advise me."

"Suit yourself. Father and I will manage without you."

Father Belk spoke up. "I'd be going anywhere Jess went, that is, if she'll have me, and if I know anything about Mimi, she'll go with us."

Jessica went to Father Belk and stood behind his chair with her hand on his shoulder, presenting a united front.

Belk smirked at them. "So that's how it is? I see. Very well, do as you please. I shall get along quite well by myself."

They avoided Belk as much as possible all day, which he spent mostly sleeping in his old room. That night, Jessica was in her bedroom brushing her hair when

Belk tried to open the locked door. He turned the knob, then rattled it loudly. He knocked on the door.

"Go sleep in your own room," Jessica called out. He kicked the door open. The sound of the splintering doorframe was like a shotgun blast. Jessica jumped from her seat and backed into a corner.

"This is my house," Belk shouted, "and I'll sleep where I please."

He leered at Jessica as she quickly pulled a robe around her. "I see that childbirth didn't do anything to harm your figure. You're lovelier than ever. You really should re-think your decision to forego your marital responsibilities."

Without comment, Jessica pushed past him and went out of the room. Caroline and Father Belk had both come out of their rooms to see what the noise had been about. Jessica threw her hands out to indicate her frustration, and went into Amanda's room. The child was sleeping soundly. Jessica closed and locked the door. She squeezed herself onto the edge of the bed, hoping that even Belk wouldn't kick in his daughter's door.

The next morning, Jessica was up early. The door to her own bedroom was open, and she peeked around the door to see if Belk was sleeping in her bed. There was no sign of him. She dressed hurriedly in case he should reappear.

She thought it would be best to ask advice from Mrs. Wareham as to renting a house in town. When she went in the millinery shop, Mrs. Wareham was showing a hat to a pretty blond, who stood in profile to Jessica. She could only see the right side of the girl's face, but could tell that she was quite attractive. She didn't recognize her from

Manhattan. When Mrs. Wareham looked up and saw Jessica, her eyes opened wide with surprise. "Good morning, Jessica. I wasn't expecting to see you until after the first of the year."

The blonde stiffened, and walked to the other side of the room, looking at hats. Jessica walked closer to Mrs. Wareham to keep her conversation private. "I didn't come to pick up any work. I wanted to ask you if you knew of any houses for rent in town. I can't afford anything expensive, but it should have four bedrooms."

Mrs. Wareham paused to think. "The Peterson place has been empty for several months. They've been in Topeka. Mrs. Peterson's mother is ill, and I don't know how long it will be before they come home. I don't know if they'd be interested in renting. You could check with Mr. Wilkes at the bank. He'd be the one handling it. Is this for someone we know?"

"I may as well tell you, since everyone will know it soon enough. My husband came home Christmas Day. I came right here from the attorney's office where I filed for a divorce. Since the house is in his name, and he refuses to leave, I must find another place to live."

The blond dropped the hat she was looking at on the floor. When she turned to face them, Jessica could see that the left side of her face had a ghastly, jagged scar running from her hairline, across one eye, and down her cheek to her jawbone. "He's alive?" She blurted out. "I thought I killed that piece of trash in San Francisco. Well, you tell him that he better stay out of my way, because if I ever see him again, I'll finish the job, and no jury in the world would convict me."

Jessica gasped. "You must be Emmalou."

"That's right."

"You stabbed him? I heard that he was caught cheating in a card game, and one of the men killed him."

"That's the story I put out when I come home because I was too ashamed of telling the truth, but it was me that stabbed him. He was going to take my baby and give it to some rich folks to raise. Said I wouldn't be a fit mother for him, but to tell the truth, I think they was going to pay him. I wasn't about to let him get away with that. I told him I'd kill him first. I got in a good lick at him with a butcher knife, but he took it away from me and come after me to kill me. Look what he did to my face before he fell out from the bleedin'. I thought sure he was dead, so I took my baby and left."

"That's terrible. I can't blame you. I'd do the same thing to save my Amanda."

"My baby is the best thing that ever happened to me. I'd fight a grizzly bear for him if I had to. I'd like to apologize to you for what I did, running away with your husband like that. He told me a whole pack of lies about you and made me think I was rescuing him from a terrible life. It wasn't long before I found out the truth about him, and since I been back here, people have been telling me the truth about you, too. I did you awful wrong, Mrs. Belk, and I'd take it right kindly if you could find it in yourself to forgive me."

Jessica reached out and put her hand on Emmalou's arm. "There was a time when Zachary had me fooled too, Emmalou. Of course I forgive you."

"I thank you for that. It will help me sleep easier nights knowing you understand. You really are the Christian lady everyone said you were."

318

"Good luck to you, Emmalou. If you're ever in town with your son, I'd appreciate it if you looked me up and let him meet his sister. Mrs. Wareham will always know where to find me."

Emmalou blinked back a tear. "That's right kind of you. I'd be happy to do that, but why aren't you staying at the house and running him out of it? I heard how you worked so hard to fix it all up."

"The house belongs to him, and he said I could stay and be his wife, or I could get out, so I'm getting out."

"I'm sorry to hear that, but I can't say as I blame you either. Ain't no house worth living in with him. I feel awful bad about all of this. It's my fault. I wish there was something could do to make it right."

"It isn't your fault, Emmalou. He would have left me when my money ran out anyway, and probably have sold the house out from under me in the bargain. I've learned how to take care of myself since then. I'll be fine."

"This world would be a better place sure enough if he had died back in California. I can't say as I wouldn't try to kill him again if I got a chance. I don't care if he is my baby's father. He better stay away from me and mine."

Jessica felt nothing but pity for the girl. "I'm so sorry this has happened to you."

Emmalou's bitterness spilled out of her as she went on. "Not none of it was your fault, Miz. Belk. When I met him I was a beautiful, carefree young woman. I had plenty of beaus, too. I got courted by more than a few of the young men in Junction City. Then he came along with his good looks, free-spending ways, and charm, and tol' me that by running away with him, I was saving him from an hateful, ugly woman who was making his life miserable.

He can lie with the best of them, can't he? Look at you. You're one of the prettiest women in these parts, and I can tell from what I learned here today and from what everyone I met since I got back who knows you says, you got a good, Christian, forgiving heart."

"Thank you, Emmalou. Promise me that someday you'll bring your baby out to meet his grandfather?"

"His grandfather? Does his grandfather live in Manhattan?"

"Yes. Father Belk lives with me."

"That good for nothing Zachary Belk went off and left you and left his own father behind, and you didn't throw him out of the house?"

"No. Father Belk stayed with me."

"Why did you keep him?"

"I could never turn him out. I love him like my own father. He'll be moving with me to the new house."

"God love you, Mrs. Belk. You're a better woman than I would ever be. All right, I promise I'll come see you and bring the baby with me as soon as you get to living in a different house than living with a toad like Zachary Belk."

After she left the millinery shop, Jessica went to the bank and explained her situation to Mr. Wilkes. He tugged at an earlobe. "I'm so sorry to hear all of this Jessica. The Peterson's didn't expect to be gone this long, and they never said anything to me about renting out their place, but I'll send a wire to them in Topeka. I should hear back in a day or so. Meanwhile, I'll ask around and see if there's anything else in case they say no. I'll get in touch with you."

"Thank you, Mr. Wilkes."

He sighed. "Life sure can throw some funny things at you, can't it?"

"It sure can, Mr. Wilkes."

As the day wore on, Emmalou Tinsdale became more and more angry. She stewed over the situation all afternoon. When it was time for her to go to work that night, she dressed in a short, low-cut taffeta dress. Her arrangement with her friend, Estelle, was that she would pay all of the rent on the cabin, and Estelle could live there rent free in exchange for caring for the baby while Emmalou was working. She had to be the saloon by eight o'clock, but Estelle hadn't come home. The baby was sleeping peacefully in the dresser drawer she used for his bed. As the minutes ticked off the clock, she paced back and forth waiting for Estelle.

At eight-thirty, she wrapped a blanket around the baby and took him over to another friend's house. "Jolene, Estelle ain't come home yet, and if I don't get to work, George will fire me. I can't make a living anywheres else in this town. Would you watch the baby for me tonight?"

Jolene reached out and took the baby from her arms. "Course I will. He's no trouble at all. He probably won't even wake up 'fore you get back."

"Thank you so much, Jolene. I don't know what I'm going to do with that Estelle. She's got me between a rock and a hard place."

"You go on, Emmalou. I'll see to him."

Emmalou rushed down the street, entered the Dirty Dog Saloon, and hung her wrap on a hook by the door. The bartender looked up. "You're late."

"I'm sorry, Sam. Estelle didn't come home, and I had to take the baby over to Jolene's house. I couldn't leave him alone."

"Why not? He'd probably sleep all night."

"He usually does, but I don't want him to wake up and not have someone with him. I spent enough nights alone when I was little, and there's nothing worse than waking up and not having anyone come to see about you."

"Yeah, yeah. See if you can get one of those boys over there to buy you a beer."

Emmalou strolled around the room, stopping to talk to a man here and there. She looked around and found the person she wanted to see. Jacob Andersen had been home from New York for several months, saying how he would kill the man who had cheated him out of his family home if he ever saw him again. Emmalou had a feeling that it wasn't idle boasting.

Jacob was playing poker with three other men. They all wore soiled work clothes. She went to his table and leaned over his back, wrapping her arms around his neck. "Hey, Jacob. You'd never believe what I found out today."

He shrugged away from her. "Get off my back, Emmalou. That face of yours would scare a buffalo."

Emmalou was used to the barbs. She heard them almost every day. The other men guffawed, but she ignored them. "Buy me a beer and I'll tell you all about Zachary Belk."

He threw his cards on the table and jumped up to face her.

"Belk? What do you know about him? I heard he was dead, got caught cheating some man in California and finally got what was coming to him. What did you hear?"

"Buy me a beer. A girl has to earn a livin'."

Jacob waved at the bartender, who'd been waiting for the order. Emmalou leaned up close to Jacob. "Let's go sit where we can talk in private."

Jacob scooped up his money from the table. "I'll be back in a few hands, boys."

Emmalou led him to an empty table in the corner. The bartender brought her drink and set it down in front of her. Jacob dug in his vest pocket and tossed some coins on the table.

"Bring me another one too, Fred."

"About time. You been nursing that last one for over an hour."

The bartender raked the coins into his hand and walked away. Emmalou leaned in close to Jacob. "I was in Mrs. Wareham's millinery over in Manhattan today, and who should walk in but Mrs. Zachary Belk. Turns out she's a right fine lady, Jacob. She told Mrs. Wareham that he come back on Christmas Day. She came in town to get a divorce and to find a place to live because he was throwing her and her baby and his own father out of the house.

"That's the lowest man what ever was. He cheats my house away from me, he ruins your life and leaves you with a baby, and now he's throwing his own wife and child out on the street. He doesn't deserve to live. I've got a good mind to take him out of his misery."

Emmalou twisted her damaged mouth into a smile. "That's exactly what I was thinkin'. You'll get your chance. From what I hear, he won't be welcome in any establishment in Manhattan. If I know him, sooner or later, he'll show up here looking for a game."

Jessica and Caroline sat at the kitchen table while Caroline made a list on a tablet. Belk swaggered in and went to get a cup of coffee. Jessica ignored him and told Caroline. "I talked to Mr. Wilkes at the bank today and we can move into the Peterson place as soon as he gets a confirmation from them. It should be one day next week. If we--"

Belk interrupted her. "Are you sure you want to go? Would it be such a bad thing to stay here and be my wife?"

"I can't even imagine it."

"It would be quite lonely without anyone here."

"Oh, you won't get bored. There's a lot to do. The cow needs milking at five in the morning, after that you turn the horses out to pasture, then you have to feed the chickens. After breakfast you slop the hogs, then--"

"How droll. If Mimi goes with you, I'll simply hire someone to take her place. I'm the grandson of a Senator from New York. Surely you don't think I would dirty my hands with farm chores?"

"Hardly. You seem to dirty your hands with anything but honest work."

"This is beginning to bore me. I believe I'll seek some amusement elsewhere. My horse has a stone bruise and is lame. He needs some time to heal. I'll have to take yours. What stupid name do you call him? Oh, yes, Juniper. Don't wait up for me."

He strode from the room. Jessica sadly shook her head. "It's somewhat incredible. He never changes, and he never learns. At least if he gambles today, he's gambling on his own money and not mine."

A few minutes later, they heard the horse trotting around the house toward the front.

As he went through the living room, Belk saw Jessica's little handbag sitting on the table by the door. He picked it up, took what cash he found there, and stuck it in his pocket before tossing the bag to the floor.

Belk was a great many things, but stupid wasn't one of them. He knew very well that there would be no welcome for him in Manhattan. It was a long ride to Junction City, but if he wanted a game, and he wanted it the way an alcoholic wants a drink, he would have to go to there.

Belk also knew that poker games often prove unsafe for a man who wasn't averse to shoving the occasional ace up his sleeve. Before he left, he slid his little Derringer into the waistband of his trousers and pulled his vest down over it. He spurred the horse into an easy lope and headed out of town.

At the Dirty Dog, Emmalou sat with a man at a corner table when Belk pushed open the door and sauntered inside. She saw him immediately and slid down in her chair, moving her body so that she could watch him over her companion's shoulder and duck out of sight if he looked her way. He looked around the room, but his attention stopped at one of the tables where men were playing cards. It had one open seat. He went to the bar and tossed a coin on the counter.

"Give me a bottle."

The bartender handed him a bottle and a shot glass. He picked them up and strolled up to the table. "Anyone mind if I sit in?"

He looked a little haggard, but his clothing appeared prosperous. They all nodded permission and one of the men took his foot and shoved the empty chair away from the table. Belk sat down and tossed a coin in the pot.

His back was to Emmalou, and she pushed back her chair quietly and slipped out the back door without going to get her wrap. She hurried down the street and turned at a corner, then went down to a wood shack at the edge of town. By the time she got there, she was shivering in the December night. She pounded on the door with the side of her fist. In a minute, Jacob Andersen opened the door. She stood there shaking as much from excitement as the cold and hugging herself. She grinned at him. "I told you he'd show up sooner or later."

"I'm glad it was sooner. If I had to wait very long, I swear, I'd have gone to Manhattan to find him and kill him. When did he get here?"

"He showed up a few minutes ago."

"Let's go, before he takes off for someplace else."

"He ain't going nowheres. He bought a whole bottle of whiskey."

"You're right. He won't be going anywhere soon. Let's give him a chance to get some 'a that whiskey in his gullet.

"Let me in, for heaven's sake. I'm freezing out here."

He opened the door. She went in the shack and stood in front of the wood-burning stove to warm herself. "The way I figure it is, we got time to make up a plan."

Later, Emmalou pulled one of the moth-eaten blankets from Jacob's bed around her shoulders and they set out on their mission. She and Jacob stood outside the Dirty Dog, peering in the window.

Emmalou pulled at Jacob's sleeve. "He's getting up. Look, here he comes."

They ducked around the side of the saloon.

Having won a few hands and finished his bottle, Belk was ready for the long ride home. He came out of the swinging saloon doors, staggering a little. He went to the hitching post and untied his horse, put the reins around the horse's neck, and managed to get one foot in a stirrup before Jacob and Emmalou came out of hiding. Belk saw them over the horse's back.

Jacob had his gun in his hand and was aiming it right at Belk's head. He called out, "It's time you got what was coming to you, Belk."

Belk looked at Jacob contemptuously as he hauled himself onto the horse. "Who are you?"

"You don't even know who I am? I'm the man what's about to kill you, and I want you to know who did it. I'm Jacob Andersen. You stole my house from me."

Belk slid his right hand under his vest and gripped the handle of the Derringer. He doubted Andersen had the guts to shoot him, but he would be ready.

"You lost it fair and square. If you don't know how to play poker, you should stay out of the game."

The gun in Jacob's right hand was shaking so hard he had to brace it with his left. "I'll show you."

Belk pointed his own gun at Jacob. Jacob fired first.

The bullet blasted through Belk's thigh. Belk aimed his gun at Jacob's chest but, spooked by the gunfire, Juniper stepped backward just as Belk fired.

The bullet hit Emmalou in the side of her neck, spinning her body around and throwing it to the ground. Blood spurted out of the wound in a pulsing arc. Belk heard the last words that gurgled out of her, "My baby."

Belk fired again, hitting Jacob in the shoulder. Juniper whirled around in a circle as Belk tried to control him.

Terrified, Juniper bolted and ran frantically down the street, seeking the security of his stall at home. With only one foot in the stirrup, the drunken Belk couldn't keep his seat. He swayed a few times as he grasped frantically to find the saddle horn. As the horse raced around the corner, Belk was unable to correct himself and went flying off the left side. His foot slid through the stirrup all the way up to his ankle, and his body flailed up and down with every step the even more terrified horse took as he headed for home, dragging the thrashing Belk behind him. The wound on Belk's thigh pumped out a gruesome trail of blood as he went.

At the sound of gunfire, the few remaining patrons of the saloon rushed out into the street to find a lifeless Emmalou lying in the dirt, and a bleeding Jacob kneeling beside her.

"He done this," Jacob shouted. "Zachary Belk. I shoulda killed him when I had the chance."

The sheriff had joined the crowd. "Who did it, Jacob?"

"Like I said, Zachary Belk. Me and Emmalou was just going into the Dirty Dog when he come out. He was so drunk, he couldn't hardly get on his horse. I yelled at him that he was a robber and a cheat, and he took one of those fancy little guns and shot Emmalou. I pulled my piece and got off a shot at him, and then he fired again and got me."

The sheriff looked for the bartender and found him at the front of the crowd. "Sam, how many shots did you hear?"

Sam thought for a moment and answered, "Three. One louder than the others."

"Which came first?"

"One that didn't make so much racket came first, then the loudest one, and then another just like the first."

"That holds up your story, Jacob. You get on over to Doc's and get that shoulder seen to."

Chapter 30

The morning sun crested over the horizon. Frost in the air made Kimimela's breath puff out in visible clouds. She'd already milked the cow and was feeding the chickens in the backyard. The sound of hoof beats caught her attention, and she turned her head to listen. Juniper came walking around the house to the barn. He stopped in front of her and, exhausted, hung his head.

Cursing Belk in her native tongue, Kimimela grabbed the reins. She saw a streak of blood on the horse's side, more on his leg, and on his tack. She walked him to the water pump and ran to fetch the bucket from his stall. She drew water for him, and he plunged his nose into the bucket, drinking deeply.

When Kimimela loosened the girth and pulled off the saddle, it left a wide smear of thickening blood on her hands. She cleaned the saddle, wiped it down, and put it in the barn to dry, then washed Juniper, dried him, put the horse into a stall, and looked him over closely. She brought him more fresh water, and tossed some hay in the trough.

Kimimela stopped at the water pump to rinse off her hands again and then went up to the back door. Caroline was already in the kitchen. Kimimela said, "The horse has come home without Mr. Belk."

Caroline shook her head. "The fool was probably too drunk to ride and fell off somewhere. He'll find his way home, sorry to say."

"There was blood on the saddle, a lot of blood, and blood on the horse. I put him in his stall."

Caroline's shoulders sagged. She stopped her cooking. "It seems that, with that man, it always goes from bad to worse. I don't want to wake Jessica and Father Belk and tell them this when we don't really know anything. What should we do?"

"Wait. We will hear soon, one way or another."

Caroline nodded. "I suppose that's best, no use getting everyone upset when we don't know how it's going to come out in the end."

"Juniper was very tired. I have some herbs that I will feed him to give him more strength."

Father Belk was the first one to come downstairs, but Caroline waited to. A few minutes later, Jessica and Amanda made their appearance.

Caroline said, "Sit down. We have to talk."

Jessica put Amanda in her high chair and sat next to Father Belk. The two adults looked fearfully at Caroline, and before Caroline started speaking, Jessica reached out and put her hand over Father Belk's.

Caroline sighed. "Mimi came in earlier and told me that Juniper came home alone, and that there was a lot of blood on his saddle. She's out there now, looking after him."

Father Belk closed his eyes and his head drooped. "I think we can all figure out that this is going to be bad, one way or another. What on earth could he have gotten himself into now?"

Jessica said, "I don't know if I should wait here or go to town and see if anyone knows what's happened."

Caroline started dishing out their oatmeal. "Either way, we're going to need to keep going. Let's go ahead and have some breakfast."

Her outside chores taken care of, Kimimela came to join them for the meal. The only sound was the clinking of spoons on the bowls of oatmeal. Sensing that there was some sort of stress occurring, even Amanda ate quietly, with none of the running chatter she usually brought to the table.

There was no news until that afternoon. They had just finished lunch when there was a knock at the front door.

The color drained from Jessica's face. Caroline stood. "I'll get it."

Caroline came out of the kitchen wiping her hands on her apron and went to the door. It was Everett, hat in hand.

"Good morning, Miss Caroline, Ma'am. Is Mrs. Belk at home?

"Yes, please come in. I'll get her."

She turned toward the kitchen but Jessica and Father Belk had already followed her.

Jessica forced a polite smile. "Please come in, Everett. May I get you some coffee?"

"Thank you, Ma'am."

"Have you eaten? We have plenty of stew left."

"Thank you Ma'am. I ain't et since last night."

They went to the kitchen, and Caroline dished up the stew they'd had for lunch. Everett dug in right away and didn't start talking. Jessica braced herself. "I believe you have some news for me."

Everett filled his mouth. Father Belk was growing impatient. "What is it you've come to tell us?"

Everett twisted up the side of his mouth and squinted as if he feared being struck. "It seems like I never come out here to tell you something you're going to want to hear. I hate to have bring this kind of news to you, but they found Mr. Belk's body laying right on the middle of the road outside Junction City. It looks like he musta fallen off his horse, got his foot caught in the stirrup, and he got drug for quite a ways. He had a bullet hole in his leg, and they can't tell did he die from being drug, or did he bleed to death."

Jessica had been holding her breath. She exhaled loudly. "We were afraid of something like that. The horse came home several hours ago."

Everett shoveled another spoonful of food into his mouth. When he swallowed, he said, "You can come claim the body anytime you want. Mr. Simms, the barber, he serves as our undertaker. He has Mr. Belk in the back of the shop."

When Everett finished his meal and stood to leave, Jessica held the door for him. "Thank you for coming all the way out here, Everett."

"That's not all I come to tell you."

"What else is there?"

"Emmalou Tinsdale, she's the girl he run away with--"

Jessica was surprised Emmalou's name came up. "Yes, I met her at Mrs. Wareham's shop only the other day."

"Well, someone shot and kilt her last night. Jacob Andersen said it was Mr. Belk what done it, and he— Jacob, was the one what shot Mr. Belk in the leg. Jacob has a bullet in his shoulder, too. I talked to Mr. Simms, and he told me that they were taking the baby up to the county orphanage tomorrow."

"Where is he now?" Father Belk asked.

"Mrs. Simms, here in Manhattan, took him in for the time bein'. There wasn't nowheres in Junction City for him, and no one there to claim him. Emmalou didn't have no fambly. The sheriff from there brought him up here with him in the wagon when he brought Mr. Belk. I thought him being your grandson and all, even if he is a— well, you know. You might want to take him in. He's an awful purty baby, if I do say so."

Father Belk spoke up immediately. "Of course, we'll be in town right away to bring him home."

Everett paused in the doorway. "I'll tell the sheriff you're coming to git him so's no one else will take him for adopting fore you can git there." He tugged at an earlobe. "I feel right bad about it that every time you see me these days I'm bringing bad news."

Jessica managed a weak smile. "We appreciate it that you're willing to make the trip all the way out here. Thank you."

"If'n it's all the same to you, I'll go on out the back door so's I kin say hello to Mimi."

"Of course." She saw him out and closed the door.

Father Belk looked apologetically at Jessica. "I know I spoke right up about taking in the baby, and maybe I should have talked it over with you first. I hope it's all right with you to bring him here, Jessica."

Momentarily stunned by the prospect of raising her husband's child with another woman, Jessica blinked a few times. Father Belk looked so pitiful, so pleadingly at her, she couldn't resist. She said a silent prayer that God would grant her the grace to welcome this baby into her heart and her home. It was only a moment before she was able to wrap her arms around her father-in-law and hug him. "Of course it's all right. He's family. We'll all go together right away to bring him home. I'll get Mimi to hitch up the wagon."

When Jessica went to the yard, Everett was still talking to Kimimela. She told the girl, "We're going into town, and we need you to hitch up the wagon. If Everett hasn't told you the news, Mr. Belk is dead."

"I understand."

"We will be giving the undertaker directions for a funeral this morning, but that isn't all. It seems Zachary has murdered the young woman he ran away with and left her child an orphan. We're going to get the child and bring him home."

Always the stoic, even Kimimela gasped at this news. "Mr. Belk murdered her? Why? Why would he do such a thing?"

"Probably no one will ever know. The sheriff seems convinced that he did it."

"I'll have to hitch up Juniper. Mr. Belk's horse is still favoring his sore foot."

"My poor horse must be exhausted from last night. Are you sure it won't hurt him?"

"He has had a night's rest. Let him walk at the speed he chooses."

Everett helped Kimimela hitch up the wagon. By the time Jessica and Caroline cleaned the breakfast dishes, Kimimela brought the wagon to the back door. They all wrapped themselves in their winter wear, and Jessica brought an extra blanket for the baby. "I think I'll sit back here with Amanda. Father Belk, would you mind driving today?"

"Not at all."

He climbed up to the bench and took the reins. "Come on, Caroline. Sit up here with me." Caroline got up next to him.

Kimimela held Juniper's halter until everyone was on board and then stepped back to let them leave. Jessica said, "Come with us, Mimi. We're adding to our family, and you're part of it."

Without comment, Kimimela climbed in the back of the wagon with Jessica and Amanda. Father Belk snapped the reins, and Juniper once more began the long trek into town.

On the drive down Poyntz Avenue, Jessica could see people on the sidewalk stop and look at them. It was still a small town and, by now, everyone in it would know what happened. Mostly too polite to be obvious, they would take note and then avert their eyes, as if they were afraid to gaze too long on the disasters the Belk family carried with them.

They stopped first at the barbershop to talk to Mr. Simms about the funeral. Jessica said, "I can't afford anything much, Mr. Simms. I'd like for it to be as simple as possible, especially under the circumstances. Could you arrange for one of the ministers to say a few words over him at the cemetery tomorrow morning around eleven?"

"You don't want me to get Pastor Fields?"

"I—no. I think someone else should do it. As long as he has a Christian burial."

"I'll see to everything, Jessica."

"Thank you. I understand your wife was kind enough to take care of Emmalou's baby. We're going by your house to get him and bring him home."

"She'll be sorry to give him up. She's already become attached to him."

When they stopped at the Simm's home, Jessica and Father Belk got down to fetch the baby. Kimimela stayed with Amanda in the back of the wagon.

Jessica knocked on the door. Mrs. Simms was holding the baby in her arms. She smiled at Jessica. "Tommy Meade already ran ahead to tell me you were coming, Jessica. God will bless you for this."

Jessica was amazed at the baby's resemblance to Amanda when she was four months old. His hair was a fuzzy blanket of auburn curls, his eyes were the same emerald green, and his chubby cheeks had the same dimples.

Father Belk reached out his arms, and Mrs. Simms placed the baby in them. He cradled the little head under his chin and rocked him back and forth. "We'll take care of you, little boy. Your grandpa has you now."

Mrs. Simms had tears in her eyes. She reached down and picked up a canvas bag. "The sheriff brought these things for him from Emmalou's cabin."

Jessica took the bag. "Thank you. Uh, Mrs. Simms, did the sheriff say what his name is?"

"I asked him, and he didn't have any idea. You might be able to find out if you went down to Junction City and looked up his mother's friends."

"Thank you."

They walked back to the wagon. Father Belk went around to the back. "I can't let go of him, Jess. You're going to have to drive home."

Amanda was quite taken with her little brother. She sat close to her grandfather all the way home and stared at the newcomer. Kimimela sat on his other side and gazed at the child with a wistful look.

"He looks like a big doll," Caroline said. "Where will he sleep?" All the bedrooms are already taken."

"Wif me, Mommy." Amanda almost shouted. "Can we make a bed in my room?"

It had occurred to Jessica on the way home that there might be a jealousy problem, and she was relieved to hear Amanda ask to share her room. "Sometimes babies cry a lot. He might wake you up at night."

Amanda considered this. "I'll come get you. You can take him to your room if he cries."

There were still plenty of apples in the fruit cellar from the autumn harvest. When they finally reached the house, Jessica told Kimimela, "I want you to cut up some apples for Juniper. He's done more in the last two days than any horse ought to be asked to do, and he didn't complain one time. He deserves a treat, and give some to Thunder, too. God knows what he's been through since last we saw him."

Jessica went to the attic where she'd stowed away Amanda's baby things and hauled down the rocking cradle and the boxes of clothes Amanda had outgrown. She had no idea why she'd kept them. At the time, she never intended to have another child. That was before she'd fallen in love with Daniel and started dreaming about another baby.

Everyone else was downstairs with the baby, and Jessica unpacked the clothes alone. She sorted out the ones that were too frilly for a boy, even a baby boy, and sorted what was left into sizes, keeping aside the things she thought could be used immediately.

In Amanda's bedroom, she moved some of Amanda's things to the top drawers of the chest and put the baby's things in the bottom. *That will have to do for the time being. Later on, I'll find him a chest of his own.*

As she ran her fingers over the soft white linen of the baby gowns she'd made from her mother's lingerie, she couldn't hold back the tears.

It would have been wonderful if God had blessed her and Daniel with another child. She wiped her face and set up the cradle in one corner of Amanda's bedroom.

She remembered the canvas bag Mrs. Simms gave her and went downstairs to fetch it. When she began unpacking it, she couldn't help crying again. The little garments inside were clean and pressed. The baby didn't have a large or expensive wardrobe, but Emmalou had seen to it that what he had was well cared for. She remembered what Emmalou had told her about Zachary wanting to sell the baby to rich people. She would have killed him too, if he had tried to take Amanda away from her. It was a conversation she would never repeat to anyone. Zachary had been disappointment enough to his father. He and his grandchildren need never know just how black Zachary's heart had really been.

The next morning, Jessica's entire family arrived at the ceremony for the burial. As they stood around the graveside, one of the local ministers stepped up to the grave and said, "I didn't know Zachary Belk, but I do know that, if he were able to talk to you today. He would want me to tell you this one thing, above all." He opened his Bible and read John 5:24, *He that heareth my word and believeth on Him that sent me, hath everlasting life, and shall not come into condemnation: but is passed from death unto life.*"

The minister said a prayer of dismissal. When the brief ceremony was over, Jessica thanked him and offered him an envelope with some money in it. He waved his palm in front of him. "That's not necessary, Mrs. Belk. I know what you have suffered. It was a privilege to be of some service to you."

As they rode home in the wagon, each of them sat in silence, thinking over the events of the last few days. A sense of hopelessness came over Jessica. She surrendered herself to despair.

Chapter 31

The next morning, there was a knock at the front door. Jessica came out of the kitchen and opened it. It was Daniel, and she gasped when she saw him. When the reality of Zachary's return had overwhelmed her, she thought she would have to change churches and try to never see Daniel again. The pain would be too much to bear. Now here he was, and her heart leapt at the sight of him. She had to hold herself back to keep from flinging her body into his arms.

He held his hat in his hands. "Jess, can I come in?"

"Yes, by all means."

"I see that you still have your Christmas tree up."

"Yes. I suppose it's inappropriate now. I didn't even think about it. I never take my tree down until after the New Year."

Still stunned by his visit, she didn't offer him anything to drink or invite him to sit down. He took her hand. "I don't care what any of the town gossips say, Jess. I'll resign my ministry if I must. I love you, and I want to marry you as soon as possible."

"I couldn't want anything more, but everyone will be scandalized if we don't wait for some proper amount of time to pass. We really shouldn't even be seen together for a while."

"He's been gone almost three years already. We've waited half a year for our wedding simply to satisfy some meaningless traditions. I have an idea on how we can get the gossips to keep their mouths shut, maybe even give us their approval."

"If you can do that, you'll be the first one in history. No, I can't do it, Daniel. We'd have to leave town."

"If I can get Mrs. Vickers and her friends on our side, will you marry me?"

"There's no way on earth she would be on our side."

"She has a tender side to her. She loves to help people. You might say it's her greatest weakness. Say yes, and we'll be married in a few days. We wanted a Christmas wedding, and the tree is still up in the church too. The minister from the Methodist-Episcopal is a friend of mine. He can perform the ceremony for us."

"If you can get Mrs. Vickers on our side, you can do anything."

"Does that mean yes?"

Jessica felt suddenly stronger. "Yes. I'm sick of Zachary Belk controlling me and ruining my life. He doesn't deserve another minute of it. The sooner we can get married, the better. I think Sunday, immediately after the regular service, would be perfect.

He brought her hand to his lips, turned it over, and kissed her palm. "I'll take care of everything. Give my regards to the rest of the family. I have to hurry if I'm going to get this done."

Daniel Fields had thought it over very carefully before he even went to see Jessica. He and Emily had been distraught since Kimimela delivered the news on Christmas morning. It ruined what he'd expected to be one of the happiest days of his life.

He went directly from Jessica's house to Mrs. Vickers home. When Mrs. Vickers answered his knock, her eyebrows shot up in surprise.

"Pastor Fields. I heard what happened. I'm so sorry. That Mr. Belk has been nothing but trouble to poor Jessica. He treats her terribly, he runs off with another woman and has a baby with her, then he shows up again in time to ruin your wedding, and now he's gotten himself killed in Junction City."

Daniel began his well-rehearsed speech. "I needed some advice from a woman, and since you're about the wisest woman I know, it seemed natural for me to ask you."

Mrs. Vickers appeared delighted. She smiled at him and made a sweeping motion with her arm, inviting him inside. "Well, please come in and sit down so we can talk. That's very nice of you to say. I was getting ready to have some tea. Have a seat. I'll be back in a few minutes."

"Why don't we sit in the kitchen? It's so much cozier."

"If you like. That would be nice. My husband and I used to sit in the kitchen for our tea."

The water was already boiling and, while Mrs. Vickers put out the cups and saucers, Daniel sat on a chair at the kitchen table. When the tea was ready, Mrs. Vickers put out a plate of cookies and sat across from him. "What's this problem you needed my advice to solve?"

"As you know, Jessica and I were to be married Christmas Day, and then it turned out that her husband wasn't dead, as everyone was told, so we had to call everything off."

"Yes, so sad. I know that you and Jessica were quite disappointed, but so was I. She'd asked me to sing for her."

"Yes, and Emily was going to play the piano for us. Such a shame. But now, he is really dead, and there's no doubt about that."

"Certainly not this time."

"When I proposed to Jessica last spring we waited to have the wedding out of respect for the tradition of a widow waiting a year."

"Yes, that would have been the proper thing to do, not that Mr. Belk deserved any respect, but traditions do."

"Exactly, and a pastor of a church has to be extra circumspect in these sort of things."

"He certainly does. He sets an example for his whole flock."

"Yes. As you know, during that wait, we were very careful to be above reproach. Now all of these horrible things have happened, and I really don't want to wait another year. I love Jessica, and Emily loves her. My little girl is growing up without a mother. If Jessica agrees, I want to go ahead with the wedding as soon as possible. You're a woman of great importance as a leader in our church and our community. I know that you would be on our side. You could explain our position. Jessica tells me you were going to sing '*Blest Be the Tie.*' How perfect that is for a wedding. It would be a shame if we didn't get to hear it. Do you think that if we went ahead and got married, we would offend any others?"

Mrs. Vickers swelled up, enjoying her new-found authority. "Don't you worry about a thing, Pastor Fields. If anyone dares to criticize, I'll remind them that you were willing to observe tradition, but circumstances interfered.

I agree with you completely. Normally, we think of the one year waiting period as something we do out of respect, but you're right. I don't see where Mr. Belk deserved respect of any kind, not at all. Anyone who starts gossip will have me to answer to."

"Thank you, Mrs. Vickers. It's such a relief to have someone in the congregation who understands."

He took a bite from one of the cookies. "Oh, this is delicious. Did you make these yourself?"

"Certainly. It's an old family recipe."

"You'll have to share it with Jessica."

"Oh, I'm sorry. I never share my recipes."

"I understand. Then I want you to promise to make some for church parties from now on."

"I'll be happy to. As a matter of fact, I'll bring some to have after the wedding."

"I know Jessica will appreciate that."

While they finished their tea, they chatted about less important topics, and Daniel had another cookie. When Mrs. Vickers walked him to the door she assured him, "Don't you worry about it. I'll take care of everything."

On New Year's Day, Father Belk escorted Jessica as she walked down the aisle. Emily played the piano, almost perfectly, the simple piece that Jessica had written out for her weeks ago, making it as easy as possible for her to play. For two whole days before the wedding, Emily practiced it for hours and got through it without any mistakes. Mrs. Vickers outdid herself in her rendition of *"Blest Be the Tie."*

Father Belk turned Jessica's hand over to Daniel. After too much delay, Jessica and Daniel were finally standing together at the altar. The Christmas tree, slightly balding, still stood on one side. In the first pew, Caroline sat between Amanda and Father Belk, and Kimimela, on the end, held Emmalou's baby. Mrs. Vickers, wreathed in an approving smile, finished her song and took a seat in the second row.

The church was filled with smiling members, all of whom had received a visit from Mrs. Vickers, who urged their understanding and support.

Daniel's friend, Reverend Joshua Hopkins, from the Methodist-Episcopal church, was officiating. "I now pronounce you husband and wife. You may kiss your bride."

Daniel kissed Jessica briefly, and they exchanged happy looks before they turned to face the congregation. Emily played the second piece that she'd been rehearsing as they walked down the aisle together, "*Thanks To God.*" The lyrics spoke of overcoming life's obstacles through the love of the Lord. It seemed even more appropriate now than it had the day Jessica selected it.

As the members and friends filed out of the church, Jessica, her family, and Reverend Hopkins were all standing at the door with Daniel and Emily to shake their hands. Mrs. Vickers was the last to leave. "It was a beautiful ceremony, Brother Fields, and Jessica, you made a beautiful bride."

Jessica blushed. "Thank you, Mrs. Vickers. Your song was truly inspired. I don't think I've ever heard it performed so well."

Daniel leaned over and said in Mrs. Vickers's ear, "It wouldn't have been possible without your help."

Mrs. Vickers preened. "I know."

She moved down the line and stopped in front of Father Belk, who was holding the baby in his arms. "Now, here's that new grandson of yours. It was so kind of you to take him in. What is his name?"

"We call him Ike."

"Ike? How—interesting. Is that a family name?"

"It isn't the name we'll put in the family Bible. That will be Matthew Isaac Belk. Matthew, which means, 'God's Gift,' because we all feel he was a gift from God, and Isaac, which means, 'laughter,' because we hope he will have a lifetime of laughter. We started calling him 'Matt,' first, and then, 'Ike,' and we all liked the sound of Ike, so it just stuck."

"I'm assuming that Jessica and Amanda will be moving into the parsonage. Will he be living with you or with her?"

Caroline said, "He'll be staying with his grandfather and me."

Mrs. Vickers eyebrows shot up. "You two aren't related, are you?"

"Not really."

Mrs. Vickers' nose went up in the air, and she peered at them through the bottom of her bi-focal lenses. "Do you think it's proper for you to live together, unrelated, in the same house, once Jessica has moved out?

Father Belk frowned. "I wouldn't want to do anything that might reflect badly on Jessica. Do you think people might think less of us, even at our age?"

Mrs. Vickers shrugged. "Well, you know how people are. There are some who might gossip."

Father Belk pursed his lips. "We wouldn't want that." He handed the baby to Kimimela and turned to

Caroline. "I'm a little old for this, and I certainly can't get down on one knee to ask but, Caroline, would you consider being my wife?"

Caroline, Jessica, and everyone within earshot were stunned.

Caroline looked at him for a long moment. Her face broke out in a wide grin, and she said, "All right."

Father Belk told Daniel, "We want to be proper. Would you perform the ceremony right now?"

Daniel laughed. "I'd be honored to. I can do the ceremony, if that's what Caroline wants. Some ladies would want to wait and get a new dress."

"This is a new dress. Jessica made it especially for a wedding, and it'll do just fine."

It was Jessica's turn to laugh. "And it's extra special to me and Caroline, because it's made out of material that was never used before for anything else."

Caroline said, "We can have the ceremony right now, can't we? I think that's an excellent idea."

Their friends were still standing around talking, waiting to go to the parsonage for the reception. Daniel raised his voice to make an announcement. "If you all would return to the sanctuary, we're going to have another wedding today."

The people exchanged curious looks, but went back inside and sat down. Caroline and the family were still standing at the door when Caroline whispered in Emily's ear, "Would you play for me the same song you played for Jessica?" Emily's answer was to turn around without speaking and run back up the aisle, where she jumped on the piano bench so fast she almost slid off the other end.

She propped up the music sheets that Jessica had written out for her and began playing.

Daniel and Father Belk were the first ones down the aisle. Daniel took his customary place in front of the altar with Father Belk to the left side. At the door, Jessica said to Caroline, "Wait, you have to have flowers." She handed Caroline the bouquet of dried roses tied with white ribbons she carried for her own wedding. Jessica, acting as bridesmaid, went down the aisle first, and Caroline came last, her face glowing like any bride, even one into her sixties, one who had been widowed for over forty years.

Daniel didn't want Caroline and Thomas Belk to be short-changed because of the suddenness of the whole thing, so he opened his Bible and performed the entire ceremony for them. When it was over, and he pronounced them husband and wife, Father Belk gave Caroline a quick kiss on the lips, and both of them blushed like youngsters. Except for perhaps a brush of the hands when at the table, it was the first time they had ever touched one another.

Several of the women brought covered dishes, and Caroline had done some cooking of her own for the little reception at the parsonage. Mrs. Vickers brought a large plate of her secret recipe cookies and was pleased that, when the party was over and it was time to retrieve her dish, it was empty. Even the crumbs were gone. Everyone enjoyed the meal and the fellowship. When the members began to drift out, once again, Daniel and Jessica assembled at the door to shake hands with their friends. Jessica leaned toward Mrs. Vickers and said softly, "You're a genius. Who knows how long this would have taken without you? You know how men are."

Mrs. Vickers smiled smugly, her lips pressed together. She nodded her head. "Exactly. I always say, there's a great deal of good to be found in observing the proprieties."

Like a queen at the head of a procession, Mrs. Vickers walked past the lingering church members, toward her home.

Daniel shook Father Belk's hand. "So you've named the little man Ike. Is that a family name?"

"No. It was a compromise. Mimi named him something in the Kansa language that I couldn't pronounce. We looked up the names in the Bible and what all they meant and chose Isaac partly because it sounded a little like the name she chose, and I could pronounce it.

Daniel asked Kimimela, who had been holding the baby almost the entire time, "What did you name him, Mimi?"

"I call him Akecheta. In my language it means 'Fighter,' because he will have to fight for everything in this life."

Jessica said, "We'll have to do everything we can to make that fight as easy as possible."

Daniel nodded. "I think before we go to dinner, I should finally take that Christmas tree out of the church before it turns into kindling."

Jessica said, "Go ahead, and we should get rid of the one at the house, too. I'm finally ready to give it up. My Christmas may have been delayed, but I do believe I have had the loveliest Christmas of my life."

Jessica stood with Daniel's arm around her waist and they watched the newlywed Belk's drive away with

Kimimela sitting in the back of the wagon holding little Matthew Isaac Akecheta Belk.

They smiled at one another. He kissed her on the forehead, wrapped one arm around her waist, and held her to him.

"Merry Christmas, Mrs. Fields."

"Merry Christmas to you, Mr. Fields."

"Me, too!" said Emily and Amanda in chorus, pushing between them and wrapping their arms around their waists.

THE END

Acknowledgements

I lived on Vattier Street in Manhattan, Kansas for two of the happiest years of my life, but that was long ago, so I needed to refresh my memory. A special thanks goes out to Lowell Jack for the information provided by his wonderful book, "A History of Manhattan, Kansas, Riley County and Ft. Riley."

Thanks are also due to the friends and family who helped, Sandy Novarro, Shelby MacFarlane, and my muse, Melanie Mabry.

Thanks also to my friends Barbara Winters and Mary Millard, for proofreading.

Other Books by Donna Mabry

The Alexandra Merritt Mysteries:
The Last Two Aces in Las Vegas
The Las Vegas Desert Flower
The Las Vegas Special
Rough Ride in Vegas
M.I.A. Las Vegas
The Las Vegas Sophisticate

Stand Alone Thrillers:
The Right Society
The Other Hand
Deadly Ambition

The Manhattan Stories:
Jessica
Pillsbury Crossing
The Cabin
Kimimela
D'Arcy Curran

Comedy:
Conversations with Skip

Biography:
Maude

www.donnafoleymabry.com